THE END OF THE WORLD

Stories of the Apocalypse

EDITED BY
MARTIN H. GREENBERG

Skyhorse Publishing
A Herman Graf Book

Skyhorse Publishing books may be purchased in bulk at special discounts for sales promotion, corporate gifts, fund-raising, or educational purposes. Special editions can also be created to specifications.
For details, contact the Special Sales Department,
Skyhorse Publishing, 555 Eighth Avenue, Suite 903, New York, NY 10018
or info@skyhorsepublishing.com.

www.skyhorsepublishing.com

10 9 8 7 6 5 4 3 2 1

Library of Congress Cataloging-in-Publication Data

The end of the world : stories of the apocalypse/edited by
Martin H. Greenberg.
p. cm.
ISBN 978-1-60239-967-9 (alk. paper)
1. End of the world–Fiction. 2. Science fiction, American.
3. Science fiction, English. I. Greenberg, Martin Harry.
PS648.S3E56 2010
823'.087608372–dc22
2010006101

Printed in Canada

Contents

COPYRIGHTS

Dancing Through the Apocalypse

Robert Silverberg

Humankind seems to take a certain grisly delight in stories about the end of the world, since the market in apocalyptic prophecy has been a bullish one for thousands or, more likely, millions of years. Even the most primitive of protohuman creatures, back there in the Africa of Ardipithecus and her descendants, must have come eventually to the realization that each of us must die; and from there to the concept that the world itself must perish in the fullness of time was probably not an enormous intellectual leap for those hairy bipedal creatures of long ago. Around their prehistoric campfires our remote hominid ancestors surely would have told each other tales of how the great fire in the sky would become even greater one day and consume the universe, or, once our less distant forebears had moved along out of the African plains to chillier Europe, how the glaciers of the north would someday move implacably down to crush them all. Even an eclipse of the sun was likely to stir brief apocalyptic excitement.

I suppose there is a kind of strange comfort in thoughts such as: "If I must die, how good that all of you must die also!" But the chief value of apocalyptic visions, I think, lies elsewhere than in that sort of we-will-all-go-together-when-we-go spitefulness, for as we examine the great apocalyptic myths we see that not only death but resurrection is usually involved in the story—a bit of eschatological comfort, of philosophical reassurance that existence, though finite and relatively brief for each individual, is not totally pointless. Yes, the tale would run, we have done evil things and the gods are angry and the world is going to perish, in a moment, in the twinkling of an eye, but then will come a reprieve, a second creation, a rebirth of life, a better world than the one that has just been purged.

What sort of end-of-the-world stories our primordial preliterate ancestors told is something we will never know, but the oldest such tale that has come down to us, which is found in the 5,000-year-old Sumerian epic of Gilgamesh, King of Uruk, is an account of a great deluge that drowns the whole Earth, save only one man, Ziusudra by name, who manages to save his family and set things going again. Very probably the deluge story had its origins in memories of some great flood that devastated Sumer and its Mesopotamian neighbors in prehistoric times, but that is only speculation. What is certain is that the theme can be found again in many later versions: the Babylonian version gives the intrepid survivor the name of Utnapishtim, the Hebrews called him Noah, to the ancient Greeks he was Deucalion, and in the Vedic texts of India he is Manu. The details differ, but the essence is always the same: the gods, displeased with the world, resolve to destroy it, but then bring mankind forth for a second try.

Floods are not the only apocalypses that religious texts offer us. The Norse myths give us a terrible frost, and in the Fimbulwinter, all living things die except a man and a woman who survive by hiding in a tree. The myths follow the usual redemptionist course and repeople the world, but then comes an even greater cataclysm, Ragnarok, the doom of the gods themselves, in which the stars fall, the Earth sinks into the sea, and fire consumes everything—only to be followed by yet another rebirth and an era of peace and plenty. And the Christian tradition provides the spectacular final book of the Bible, the Revelation of St. John the Divine, in which the wrath of God is visited upon the Earth in a host of ways (fire, plague, hail, drought, earthquakes, flood, and much more), leading to the final judgment and the redemption of the righteous. The Aztecs, too, had myths of the destruction of the world by fire—several times over, in fact—and so did the Mayas. Even as I write this, much popular excitement is being stirred by an alleged Mayan prediction that the next apocalypse is due in 2012, which has engendered at least three books and a movie so far.

Since apocalyptic visions are nearly universal in the religious literature of the world, and apparently always have been, it is not surprising that they should figure largely in the fantasies of imaginative storytellers. Even before the term "science fiction" had been coined, stories of universal or near-universal extinction brought about not by the anger of the deities but by the innate hazards of existence were being written and achieving wide popularity. Nineteenth-century writers were particularly fond of them. Thus we find such books as Jean-Baptiste de Grainville's *The Last Man, or Omegarus and Syderia* (1806) and Mary Shelley's *The Last Man* (1826), which was written under the shadow of a worldwide epidemic of cholera that raged from 1818 to 1822. Edgar Allan Poe sent a comet into the Earth in "The Conversation of Eros and Charmion" (1839). The French astronomer Camille Flammarion's astonishing novel of 1893, *La Fin du Monde*, or *Omega* in its English translation, brought the world to the edge of doom—but only to the edge—as another giant comet crosses our path. H. G. Wells told a similar story of near-destruction, almost surely inspired by Flammarion's, in "The Star" (1897). In his classic novel *The Time Machine* (1895), Wells had already taken his time traveler to the end of life on Earth and beyond ("All the sounds of man, the bleating of sheep, the cries of birds, the hum of insects, the stir that makes the background of our lives—all that was over").

Another who must certainly have read Flammarion is his compatriot Jules Verne, who very likely drew on the latter sections of *Omega* for his novella, "The Eternal Adam" (1905). Here Verne espouses a cyclical view of the world: Earth is destroyed by a calamitous earthquake and flood, but the continent of Atlantis wondrously emerges from the depths to provide a new home for the human race, which after thousands of years of toil rebuilds civilization; and we are given a glimpse, finally, of a venerable scholar of the far future looking back through the archives of humanity, "bloodied by the innumerable hardships suffered by those who had gone before him," and coming, "slowly, reluctantly, to an intimate conviction of the eternal return of all things."

The eternal return! It is the theme of so much of this apocalyptic literature. That phrase of Verne's links his story to the core of Flammarion's own belief that our own little epoch is "an imperceptible wave on the immense ocean of the ages" and that mankind's destiny is, as we see in his closing pages, to be born again and again into universe after universe, each to pass on in its turn and be replaced, for time goes on forever and there can be neither end nor beginning.

Rebirth after catastrophe is to be found, also, in M. P. Shiel's magnificent novel *The Purple Cloud* (1901), in which we are overwhelmed by a mass of poisonous gas, leaving only one man—Adam is his name, of course—as the ostensible survivor, until he finds his Eve and life begins anew. No such renewal is offered in Frank Lillie Pollock's terminally apocalyptic short story "Finis" (1906), though, which postulates a gigantic central star in the galaxy whose light has been heading toward us for an immense span of time and now finally arrives, so that "there, in crimson and orange, flamed the last dawn that human eyes would ever see."

There is ever so much more. Few readers turn to apocalyptic tales these days for reassurance that once the sins of mankind have been properly punished, a glorious new age will open; but, even so, the little *frisson* that a good end-of-the-world story supplies is irresistible to writers, and the bibliography of apocalyptic fantasy is an immense one. Garrett P. Serviss's *The Second Deluge* (1912) drowns us within a watery nebula. G. Peyton Wertenbaker's "The Coming of the Ice" (1926) brings the glaciers back with a thoroughness that makes the Norse Fimbulwinter seem like a light snowstorm. (I had a go at the same theme myself in my 1964 novel, *Time of the Great Freeze*, but, unlike Wertenbaker, I opted for a thaw at the end.) Philip Wylie and Edwin Balmer's *When Worlds Collide* (1933) tells us of an awkward astrophysical event with very unpleasant consequences for our planet. Edmond Hamilton's "In the World's Dusk" (1936) affords a moody vision of the end of days, millions of years hence, when one lone man survives and "a white salt desert now covered the whole of Earth. A cruel glaring plain that stretched eye-achingly to the horizons. . . ." Robert A. Heinlein's story "The Year of the Jackpot" (1952) puts the end much closer—1962, in fact—when bad things begin to happen in droves all around the world, floods and typhoons and earthquakes and volcanic eruptions worthy of the Book of Revelation, culminating in a lethal solar catastrophe. J. T. McIntosh's *One in Three Hundred* (1954) also has the sun going nova, at novel length. And, of course, the arrival of atomic weapons in 1945 set loose such a proliferation of nuclear-holocaust stories that it would take many pages to list them all.

Modern-day writers continue to find literary rewards in dancing through the apocalypse. Twenty such jolly visions of ultimate disaster are presented here: Fredric Brown's sardonic, unforgettable "Knock"; Lucius Shepard's bleak and all-too-realistic "Salvador"; Poul Anderson's Wellsian "Flight to Forever"; Michael Swanwick's eloquent, ferocious "The Feast of St. Janis"; Edward Bryant's neatly understated "Jody After the War"; Lester del Rey's sly "Kindness"; and more than a dozen more.

The possible variations on the theme are endless. In a poem written nearly a century ago, Robert Frost speculated on whether the world will end in fire or in ice. Though he asserted that he himself held with "those who favor fire," he added that "for destruction ice is also great" and would suffice to do the task.

Fire or ice, one or the other—who knows? The final word on finality is yet to be written. But what is certain is that we will go on speculating about it . . . right until the end.

The Hum

Rick Hautala

"Can you hear that?"

"Hear what?"

"That . . ."

Dave Marshall rolled over in bed and struggled to come awake. He blinked, trying to focus his eyes in the darkness as he listened intently.

"I don't hear anything, sweetie," he said as he slid his hand up the length of his wife's thigh, feeling the roundness of her hip and wondering for a moment if she was interested in a little midnight tumble. He felt himself stirring.

"Don't tell me you can't hear that," Beth said irritably.

Dave realized she was serious about this although he'd be damned if he could hear anything. It didn't matter, though, because the romantic mood had already evaporated.

"Honest to God, honey, I don't hear anything. Maybe it was a siren or—"

"It wasn't a siren. It's . . . I can just barely hear it. It's like this low, steady vibration." Beth held her breath, concentrating hard on the sound that had disturbed her.

"Maybe it's the refrigerator."

"No, goddamnit. It's not the fridge."

Dave was exhausted. He hadn't been sleeping well lately. Pressures at the office, he supposed, were getting to him. He sure as hell didn't need to be playing "Guess That Sound" at 2 AM.

"Just put the pillow over your head and go back to sleep. I'll check it out in the morning."

"I can't sleep with my head under the pillow," Beth grumbled, but she turned away from him and put her head under the pillow just the same. He patted her hip one more time, feeling a little wistful.

"Isn't that better?"

"What? I can't hear you."

Ignoring her sarcasm, Dave leaned over and kissed her shoulder as he whispered, "Goodnight, honey."

Dave awoke early the next morning feeling like every nerve in his body was on edge. His eyes were itchy, and he could feel a headache coming on.

This is really weird, he thought. *I was in bed by 10 last night. That's nine freakin' hours of sleep. I shouldn't feel like this.*

He went downstairs to the kitchen. Beth was seated at the kitchen table with a cup of coffee clasped in both hands. Her face was pale, and she looked at him bleary-eyed.

"How'd you sleep?" she asked, and he caught the edge in her voice.

"Before you woke me up or after?" He forced a grin.

"Very funny. That goddamn hum kept me awake most of the night." She took a sip of coffee and opened the newspaper, making a point of ignoring him.

"Beth . . ."

"Yeah?"

Dave stood still in the middle of the kitchen. Without even thinking about it, he suddenly realized that he *could* hear something. There was a low, steady vibration just at the edge of awareness. He could almost feel it in his feet.

"Wait a sec." He held up a finger to silence her. "You know . . . I think I *can* hear it."

"Really?" Beth looked at him like she didn't quite believe him, but then she relented and said, "Oh, thank God. I thought I might be going insane."

Over the next hour or so, they searched throughout the house from attic to basement, looking for a possible source of the sound. It wasn't in the wires or the pipes or the circuit breaker box or the TV, of that Dave was sure. The odd thing was, no matter what floor they were on or what room they were in, the sound always seemed to be coming from everywhere and nowhere at once. When Dave went outside to check the shed and garage, he found Beth in the middle of the yard, crying.

"What's the matter, honey?" He put his arms around her, feeling the tension in her body.

"I can hear it just as loud out here as I can inside the house," she said, sobbing into his shoulder.

"So?"

"So . . . That means it's not coming from inside the house. It's out here somewhere. It's like it's coming from the ground or the sky or something."

"Now you're being ridiculous," he said. He took a breath and, leaning close, stared into her eyes. "I'll call the electric company and maybe the phone company. It's gotta be a problem with the wires."

"Sure," Beth said, not sounding convinced. She wiped her nose on her bathrobe sleeve, then turned and walked back into the house. Dave watched her leave, knowing she didn't believe it was a wire problem.

He wasn't sure he believed it, either.

Over the next few days, things got worse. A lot worse. Like a sore in your mouth you can't help probing with your tongue, Dave found himself poised and listening for the sound all the time, trying to detect its source. Once he was aware of it, he couldn't help but hear it. He was growing desperate to locate it and analyze it. His work at the office suffered. Jeff Stewart, his boss, noticed how distracted he was. At first he commented on it with amusement, but that changed to concern and, finally, exasperation. But Dave noticed that everyone in the office seemed a little distracted and, as the day went by, more and more irritable. This would make sense, he thought, if everyone were sleeping as poorly as he was. It had taken him hours to fall asleep last night, and once he was out, the noise still permeated his dreams. He woke up a dozen or more times and just lay there staring at the ceiling as he listened to the low, steady hum just at the edge of hearing. He knew Beth was lying awake next to him, but they didn't talk. Every attempt at conversation ended with one of them snapping at the other.

Over the next few days, sales of white-noise machines, soundproofing materials, and environmental sound CDs went through the roof. People turned their TVs and radios up loud in a futile effort to block out the hum, further irritating their neighbors who were already on edge.

Dave's commute to work quickly became a crash course in Type-A driving techniques. One morning, he was trapped for more than an hour behind a sixty-five-car pileup on the Schuylkill Expressway that had turned into a demolition derby. It took nearly the entire city police force and an army of tow trucks to break up the melee. After that, Dave kept to back streets going to and from work.

Schools began canceling soccer and football games as soccer-mom brawls and riots in the stands became increasingly frequent and intense. Shoving matches broke out in ticket lines and grocery checkout lanes. Neighborhood feuds and other violent incidents escalated, filling the newspaper and TV news with lurid reports. As the week wore on, road rage morphed into drive-by shootings. Gang warfare was waged openly, and police brutality was applauded instead of prosecuted. The slightest provocation caused near-riots in public. The media reported that the hum—and the rise in aggressive behavior—was a global phenomenon.

"It's only a matter of time before some third-world countries start tossing nukes at each other," Dave muttered one morning at the office staff meeting.

Mike from Purchasing glared at him.

"Who died and made you Mr-Know-It-All?" he snarled.

"Jesus, Mike, quit being such an asshole," Dave snapped back.

"All right. That's enough," said Jeff. "This isn't kindergarten. Let's try to be professional here, okay?"

"Professional, schmessional," Mike grumbled. "Who gives a rat's ass anymore, anyway?"

"I *said* that's *enough*." Jeff thumped the conference table with his clenched fist.

Sherry from Operations burst into tears. "Stop it, stop it now! Jesus *stop it!* I can't take it any more! I can't eat. I can't sleep, and I sure as hell can't stand listening to the two of you morons!"

Dave noticed with a shock the fist-sized bruise on her cheek. She caught him staring at her face and shouted at him, "It's *none* of your goddamned *business!*"

"What'd I say?" asked Dave with a shrug.

"That's it!" roared Jeff. "You're fired! All of you! Every damned one of you!"

The entire staff turned and looked at him, seated at the head of the table. His face was flushed, and his eyes were bulging. In the moment of silence that followed, everyone in the room became aware of the hum, but Dave was the first to mention that it had changed subtly. Now there was a discordant clanking sound, still just at the edge of hearing, but the sound was penetrating.

"The music of the spheres," Sherry whispered in a tight, wavering voice. "It's the music of the spheres." Her voice scaled up toward hysteria. "The harmony is gone. The center cannot hold. Something's gone terribly, terribly wrong!" With a loud, animal wail, she got up and ran from the room with tears streaming down her face.

Mike swallowed hard, trying to control his frustration. "What the hell's she talking about?"

"Go home. All of you. I'm closing the office until they figure out what this sound is." Jeff's fists were clenched, and his body was trembling as though he were in the grips of a fever. "If I don't, I'm going to have to kill every single one of you . . . unless you kill me first." He grinned wolfishly, then slumped down in his chair, pressing the heels of his hands against his ears as he sobbed quietly.

Mike and Dave left the conference room without speaking.

That afternoon, Dave drove home, mindful not to do anything that would irritate anyone on the road. Sitting on the sofa in the living room as he waited for Beth to get home, he couldn't help but listen to the hum. He thought about what could possibly be happening but couldn't come up with an answer.

When Beth finally came home, Dave said, "Sit down. We have to talk."

She looked at him warily, and the mistrust he saw in her eyes hurt him.

"What's her name?"

"What?" He realized what she meant and shook his head. "No. It's nothing like that. Look, Beth, I'm trying to save us, not break us apart. Listen to me, okay?"

Beth nodded as she took a breath and held it. He could see she was trying to pull the last shreds of her patience together, and he felt a powerful rush of gratitude and love for her. It was so good to feel something pleasant that for a brief moment he forgot all about the noise.

"Jeff closed the office. This sound is getting on everyone's nerves, and he's afraid we're all going to end up killing each other. He's probably right. I was thinking—we get out of here. Let's go up to your folks' place in Maine or anywhere, as long as it's far away from here and from all these people."

"But the news says this hum is everywhere. There's no escaping it, Dave," Beth said. Her face contorted, but she clenched her fists and regained her self-control. "What's the point of going anywhere?"

"Maybe there isn't a point, but I . . . I feel like we have to do *something*. We have to try. I don't want us to end up another murder-suicide statistic." He took her into his arms and held her close. "I love you, Beth."

She clung to him and whispered, "I love you, too."

They sat silently in the living room as the twilight deepened, and the world all around them hummed.

What would normally have been a nine-hour ride to Little Sebago Lake took almost twenty-four hours because Dave wanted to stay off the interstates. The latest news reports indicated that truckers were chasing down and crushing unlucky drivers who pissed them off. Dave had seen the film *Duel* once, and that was enough for him.

As they headed north, the sound became more discordant. Dave noticed a mechanical chunking quality that was getting more pronounced. The endless, irregular rhythm ground away at his nerves like fine sandpaper, but they finally made it to the cabin by the lake without incident.

The camp was on the east side of the lake, small and shabby, but a welcome sight. The lake stretched out before them, a flat, blue expanse of water with the New Hampshire mountains off in the distance to the west.

The sun was just setting, tipping the lake's surface with sparkles of gold light and streaking the sky with slashes of red and purple.

It was beautiful, and when Dave and Beth looked at each other, the good feelings drowned out the hum, if only for a moment. They embraced and kissed with passion.

Then the day was over. The sun dropped behind the mountains, and the humming noise pressed back in on them. After unpacking the car, they ate a cold supper of baked beans out of the can. Beth set about making the bed upstairs and straightening up while Dave walked down to the lake's edge.

The night was still except for the hum. All the usual sounds—the birds and crickets and frogs—were silent. The lake looked like a large pane of smoky glass. Stars twinkled in the velvety sky above. Dave sat down on a weather-stripped tree trunk that had washed up onto shore and looked up at the sky. The noise seemed to be changing again. It now was a faint, squeaky sound that reminded him of fingernails raking down a chalkboard. At least it was the only sound. No blaring TVs, no pounding stereos.

How long can this go on? he wondered. *How long can anyone handle this before we all go mad and exterminate ourselves?*

He heaved a sigh as he looked up at the sky. At first, he couldn't quite believe what he was seeing when he noticed a few black flakes drifting down onto the lake's surface. They looked like soot from a bonfire. Like a child in a snowstorm, Dave reached up and tried to catch one of the falling flakes.

Funny, he thought, *I don't smell smoke.*

He looked at his hand. The flake lay in the cup of his palm, but it wasn't soft and crumbly like ash. It was hard and thin, with a dark, brittle surface. It crunched like fragile glass when he poked it with his index finger.

Jesus Christ, he thought. *It looks like paint.*

Curious, he looked up again. By now the flakes were sifting down rapidly from the sky. As he watched, Dave became aware of a low, steady vibration beneath his feet. It felt like a mild electrical current. As he watched the sky, irregular yellow splotches appeared overhead as more and more black paint fell away, exposing a dull, cracked surface behind. After a time, silver and yellow flakes began to fall. Dave watched in amazement, his mouth dry, his mind numb.

A crescent moon was rising in the east behind him. He turned to see if it, too, was peeling away from the sky like an old sticker on a refrigerator. The noise rose to a sudden, piercing squeal, and then the vibration rumbled the ground like a distant earthquake.

"Beth!" he called out, watching as fragments of the moon broke off and drifted down from the sky. They fluttered and hissed as they rushed through the trees behind him, and then he saw something overhead that was impossible to believe. The peeling paint had exposed a vast complex of spinning gears and cogs with a network of circuits and switches that glowed as they overheated. The humming sound rose even higher until it was almost unbearable as more pieces of the night sky fell away, revealing the machinery behind it. At last, Dave knew—as impossible as it was—what was happening.

"Beth!" he called out so his wife could hear him above the steadily rising rumble. "Come out here! You've got to see this! The sky is falling!"

Salvador

Lucius Shepard

THREE WEEKS BEFORE they wasted Tecolutla, Dantzler had his baptism of fire. The platoon was crossing a meadow at the foot of an emerald green volcano, and being a dreamy sort, he was idling along, swatting tall grasses with his rifle barrel and thinking how it might have been a first-grader with crayons who had devised this elementary landscape of a perfect cone rising into a cloudless sky, when cap-pistol noises sounded on the slope. Someone screamed for the medic, and Dantzler dove into the grass, fumbling for his ampules. He slipped one from the dispenser and popped it under his nose, inhaling frantically; then, to be on the safe side, he popped another—"a double helpin' of martial arts," as DT would say—and lay with his head down until the drugs had worked their magic. There was dirt in his mouth, and he was afraid.

Gradually his arms and legs lost their heaviness, and his heart rate slowed. His vision sharpened to the point that he could see not only the pinpricks of fire blooming on the slope, but also the figures behind them, half-obscured by brush. A bubble of grim anger welled up in his brain, hardened by a fierce resolve, and he started moving toward the volcano. By the time he reached the base of the cone, he was all rage and reflexes. He spent the next forty minutes spinning acrobatically through the thickets, spraying shadows with bursts of his M-18; yet part of his mind remained distant from the action, marveling at his efficiency, at the comic-strip enthusiasm he felt for the task of killing. He shouted at the men he shot, and he shot them many more times than was necessary, like a child playing soldier.

"Playin' my ass!" DT would say. "You just actin' natural."

DT was a firm believer in the ampules; though the official line was that they contained tailored RNA compounds and pseudo-endorphins modified to an inhalant form, he held the opinion that they opened a man up to his inner nature. He was big, black, with heavily muscled arms and crudely stamped features, and he had come to the Special Forces direct from prison, where he had done a stretch for attempted murder; the palms of his hands were covered by jail tattoos—a pentagram and a horned monster. The words DIE HIGH were painted on his helmet. This was his second tour in Salvador, and Moody, who was Dantzler's buddy, said the drugs had addled DT's brains, that he was crazy and gone to hell.

"He collects trophies," Moody had said. "And not just ears like they done in 'Nam."

When Dantzler had finally gotten a glimpse of the trophies, he had been appalled. They were kept in a tin box in DT's pack and were nearly unrecognizable; they looked like withered brown orchids. But despite his revulsion, despite the fact that he was afraid of DT, he admired the man's capacity for survival and had taken to heart his advice to rely on the drugs.

On the way back down the slope, they discovered a live casualty, an Indian kid about Dantzler's age, nineteen or twenty. Black hair, adobe skin, and heavy-lidded brown eyes. Dantzler, whose father was an anthropologist and had done field work in Salvador, figured him for a Santa Ana tribesman; before leaving the States, Dantzler had pored over his father's notes, hoping this would give him an edge, and had learned to identify the various regional types. The kid had a minor leg wound and was wearing fatigue pants and a faded COKE ADDS LIFE T-shirt. This T-shirt irritated DT no end. "What the hell you know 'bout coke?" he asked the kid as they headed for the chopper that was to carry them deeper into Morazan Province. "You think it's funny or somethin'?" He whacked the kid in the back with his rifle butt, and when they reached the chopper, he slung him inside and had him sit by the door. He sat beside him, tapped out a joint from a pack of Kools, and asked, "Where's Infante?"

"Dead," said the medic.

"Shit!" DT licked the joint so it would burn evenly. "Goddamn beaner ain't no use 'cept somebody else know Spanish."

"I know a little," Dantzler volunteered.

Staring at Dantzler, DT's eyes went empty and unfocused. "Naw," he said. "You don't know no Spanish."

Dantzler ducked his head to avoid DT's stare and said nothing; he thought he understood what DT meant, but he ducked away from the understanding as well. The chopper bore them aloft, and DT lit the joint. He let the smoke out through his nostrils and passed the joint to the kid, who accepted gratefully.

"*Que sabor!*" he said, exhaling a billow. He smiled and nodded, wanting to be friends.

Dantzler turned his gaze to the open door. They were flying low between the hills, and looking at the deep bays of shadow in their folds acted to drain away the residue of the drugs left him weary and frazzled. Sunlight poured in, dazzling the oil-smeared floor.

"Hey, Dantzler!" DT had to shout over the noise of the rotors. "Ask him whass his name!"

The kid's eyelids were drooping from the joint, but on hearing Spanish he perked up. He shook his head, though, refusing to answer. Dantzler smiled and told him not to be afraid.

"Ricardo Quu," said the kid.

"Kool!" said DT with false heartiness. "Thass my brand!" He offered his pack to the kid.

"Gracias, no." The kid waved the joint and grinned.

"Dude's named for a goddamn cigarette," said DT disparagingly, as if this were the height of insanity.

Dantzler asked the kid if there were more soldiers nearby, and once again received no reply, but apparently sensing in Dantzler a kindred soul, the kid leaned forward and spoke rapidly, saying that his village was Santander Jimenez, that his father was—he hesitated—a man of power. He asked where they were taking him. Dantzler returned a stony glare. He found it easy to reject the kid, and he realized later this was because he had already given up on him.

Latching his hands behind his head, DT began to sing—a wordless melody. His voice was discordant, barely audible above the rotors; but the tune had a familiar ring, and Dantzler soon placed it. The theme from *Star Trek.* It brought back memories of watching TV with his sister, laughing at the low-budget aliens and Scotty's Actors' Equity accent. He gazed out the door again. The sun was behind the hills, and the hillsides were unfeatured blurs of dark green smoke. Oh, God, he wanted to be home, to be anywhere but Salvador! A couple of the guys joined in the singing at DT's urging, and as the volume swelled, Dantzler's emotion peaked. He was on the verge of tears, remembering tastes and sights, the way his girl Jeanine had smelled, so clean and fresh, not reeking of sweat and perfume like the whores around Ilopango—finding all this substance in the banal touchstone of his culture and the illusions of the hillsides rushing past. Then Moody tensed beside him, and he glanced up to glean the reason why.

In the gloom of the chopper's belly, DT was as unfeatured as the hills—a black presence ruling them, more the leader of a coven than a platoon. The other two guys were singing their lungs out, and even the kid was getting into the spirit of things. "*Musica!*" he said at one point, smiling at everybody, trying to fan the flame of good feeling. He swayed to the rhythm and essayed a "la-la" now and again. But no one else was responding.

The singing stopped, and Dantzler saw that the whole platoon was staring at the kid, their expressions slack and dispirited. "Space!" shouted DT, giving the kid a little shove. "The final frontier!"

The smile had not yet left the kid's face when he toppled out the door. DT peered after him; a few seconds later, he smacked his hand against the floor and sat back, grinning. Dantzler felt like screaming, the stupid horror of the joke was so at odds with the languor of his homesickness. He looked to the others for reaction. They were sitting with their heads down, fiddling with trigger guards and pack straps, studying their bootlaces, and seeing this, he quickly imitated them.

Morazan Province was spook country. Santa Ana spooks. Flights of birds had been reported to attack pistols; animals appeared at the perimeters of campsites and vanished when you shot them; dreams afflicted everyone who ventured there. Dantzler could not testify to the birds and animals, but he did have a recurring dream. In it, the kid DT had killed was pinwheeling down through a golden fog, his T-shirt visible against the rolling backdrop, and sometimes a voice would boom out of the fog, saying, "You are killing my son." No, no, Dantzler would reply; it wasn't me, and besides, he's already dead. Then he would wake covered with sweat, groping for his rifle, his heart racing.

But the dream was not an important terror, and he assigned it no significance. The land was far more terrifying. Pine-forested ridges that stood out against the sky like fringes of electrified hair; little trails winding off into thickets and petering out, as if what they led to had been magicked away; gray rock faces along which they were forced to walk, hopelessly exposed to ambush. There were innumerable booby traps set by the guerillas, and they lost several men to rockfalls. It was the emptiest place of Dantzler's experience. No people, no animals, just a few hawks circling the solitudes between the ridges. Once in a while they found tunnels, and these they blew with the new gas grenades. The gas ignited the rich concentrations of hydrocarbons and sent flame sweeping through the entire system. DT would praise whomever had discovered the tunnel and would estimate in a loud voice how many beaners they had "refried." But Dantzler knew they were traversing pure emptiness and burning empty holes. Days, under debilitating heat, they humped the mountains, traveling seven, eight, even ten klicks up trails so steep that frequently the feet of the guy ahead of you would be on a level with your face; nights, it was cold, the darkness absolute, the silence so profound that Dantzler imagined he could hear the great humming vibration of the earth. They might have been anywhere or nowhere. Their fear was nourished by the isolation, and the only remedy was "martial arts."

Dantzler took to popping the pills without the excuse of combat. Moody cautioned him against abusing the drugs, citing rumors of bad side effects and DT's madness, but even he was using them more and more often. During basic training, Dantzler's D.I. had told the boots that the drugs were available only to the Special Forces, that their use was optional; but there had been too many instances of lackluster battlefield performance in the last war, and this was to prevent a reoccurrence.

"The chickenshit infantry should take 'em," the D.I. had said. "You bastards are brave already. You're born killers, right?"

"Right, sir!" they had shouted.

"What are you?"

"Born killers, sir!"

But Dantzler was not a born killer; he was not even clear as to how he had been drafted, less clear as to how he had been manipulated into the

Special Forces, and he had learned that nothing was optional in Salvador, with the possible exception of life itself.

The platoon's mission was reconnaissance and mop-up. Along with other Special Forces platoons, they were to secure Morazan prior to the invasion of Nicaragua; specifically, they were to proceed to the village of Tecolutla, where the Sandinista patrol had recently been spotted, and following that, they were to join up with the 1st Infantry and take part in the offensive against Leon, a provincial capital just across the Nicaraguan border. As Dantzler and Moody walked together, they frequently talked about the offensive, how it would be good to get down into flat country; occasionally they talked about the possibility of reporting DT, and once, after he had led them on a forced night march, they toyed with the idea of killing him. But most often they discussed the ways of the Indians and the land, since this was what had caused them to become buddies.

Moody was slightly built, freckled, and red-haired; his eyes had the "thousand-yard stare" that came from too much war. Dantzler had seen winos with such vacant, lusterless stares. Moody's father had been in 'Nam, and Moody said it had been worse than Salvador because there had been no real commitment to win; but he thought Nicaragua and Guatemala might be the worst of all, especially if the Cubans sent in troops as they had threatened. He was adept at locating tunnels and detecting booby traps, and it was for this reason Dantzler had cultivated his friendship. Essentially a loner, Moody had resisted all advances until learning of Dantzler's father; thereafter he had buddied up, eager to hear about the field notes, believing they might give him an edge.

"They think the land has animal traits," said Dantzler one day as they climbed along a ridgetop. "Just like some kinds of fish look like plants or sea bottom, parts of the land look like plain ground, jungle . . . whatever. But when you enter them, you find you've entered the spirit world, the world of the *Sukias*."

"What's *Sukias*?" asked Moody.

"Magicians." A twig snapped behind Dantzler, and he spun around, twitching off the safety of his rifle. It was only Hodge, a lanky kid with the beginnings of a beer gut. He stared hollow-eyed at Dantzler and popped an ampule.

Moody made a noise of disbelief. "If they got magicians, why ain't they winnin'? Why ain't they zappin' us off the cliffs?"

"It's not their business," said Dantzler. "They don't believe in messing with worldly affairs unless it concerns them directly. Anyway, these places—the ones that look like normal land but aren't—they're called . . ." He drew a blank on the name. "Aya-something. I can't remember. But they have different laws. They're where your spirit goes to die after your body dies."

"Don't they got no heaven?"

"Nope. It just takes longer for your spirit to die, and so it goes to one of these places that's between everything and nothing."

"Nothin'," said Moody disconsolately, as if all his hopes for an afterlife had been dashed. "Don't make no sense to have spirits and not have no heaven."

"Hey," said Dantzler, tensing as wind rustled the pine boughs. "They're just a bunch of damn primitives. You know what their sacred drink is? Hot chocolate! My old man was a guest at one of their funerals, and he said they carried cups of hot chocolate balanced on these little red towers and acted like drinking it was going to wake them to the secrets of the universe." He laughed, and the laughter sounded tinny and psychotic to his own ears. "So you're going to worry about fools who think hot chocolate's holy water?"

"Maybe they just like it," said Moody. "Maybe somebody dyin' just give 'em an excuse to drink it."

But Dantzler was no longer listening. A moment before, as they emerged from pine cover onto the highest point of the ridge, a stony scarp open to the winds and providing a view of rumpled mountains and valleys extending to the horizon, he had popped an ampule. He felt so strong, so full of righteous purpose and controlled fury, it seemed only the sky was around him, that he was still ascending, preparing to do battle with the gods themselves.

Tecolutla was a village of white-washed stone tucked into a notch between two hills. From above, the houses, with their black windows and doorways, looked like an unlucky throw of dice. The streets ran uphill and down, diverging around boulders. Bougainvilleas and hibiscus speckled the hillsides, and there were tilled fields on the gentler slopes. It was a sweet, peaceful place when they arrived, and after they had gone it was once again peaceful; but its sweetness had been permanently banished. The reports of Sandinistas had proved accurate, and though they were casualties left behind to recuperate, DT had decided their presence called for extreme measures. Fu gas, frag grenades, and such. He had fired an M-60 until the barrel melted down, and then had manned the flamethrower. Afterward, as they rested atop the next ridge, exhausted and begrimed, having radioed in a chopper for resupply, he could not get over how one of the houses he had torched had resembled a toasted marshmallow.

"Ain't that how it was, man?" he asked, striding up and down the line. He did not care if they agreed about the house; it was a deeper question he was asking, one concerning the ethics of their actions.

"Yeah," said Dantzler, forcing a smile. "Sure did."

DT grunted with laughter. "You *know* I'm right, don'tcha man?"

The sun hung directly behind his head, a golden corona rimming a black oval, and Dantzler could not turn his eyes away. He felt weak and weakening, as if threads of himself were being spun loose and sucked into the blackness. He popped three ampules prior to the firefight, and his experience of Tecolutla had been a kind of mad whirling dance through the streets, spraying erratic bursts that appeared to be writing weird names on the walls. The leader of the Sandinistas had worn a mask—a gray face with a surprised hole of a mouth and pink circles around the eyes. A ghost face. Dantzler had been afraid of the mask and had poured round after round into it. Then, leaving the village, he had seen a small girl standing beside the shell of the last house, watching them, her colorless rag of a dress tattering in the breeze. She had been a victim of that malnutrition disease, the one that paled your skin and whitened your hair and left you retarded. He could neither recall the name of the disease—things such as names were slipping away from him—nor could he believe anyone had survived, and for a moment he had thought the spirit of the village had come out to mark their trail.

That was all he could remember of Tecolutla, all he wanted to remember. But he knew he had been brave.

Four days later, they headed up into a cloud forest. It was the dry season, but dry season or not, blackish gray clouds always shrouded these peaks. They were shot through by ugly glimmers of lightning, making it seem that malfunctioning neon signs were hidden beneath them, advertisements for evil. Everyone was jittery, and Jerry LeDoux, a slim, dark-haired Cajun kid, flat-out refused to go.

"It ain't reasonable," he said. "Be easier to go through the passes."

"We're on recoil, man! You think the beaners be waitin' in the passes, wavin' their white flags?" DT whipped his rifle into firing position and pointed it at LeDoux. "C'mon, Louisiana man. Pop a few, and you feel different."

As LeDoux popped the ampule, DT talked to him.

"Look at it this way, man. This is your big adventure. Up there it be like all them animals shows on the tube. The savage kingdom, the unknown. Could be like Mars or somethin'. Monsters and shit, with big red eyes and tentacles. You wanna miss that, man? You wanna miss bein' the first grunt on Mars?"

Soon LeDoux was raring to go, giggling at DT's rap.

Moody kept his mouth shut, but he fingered the safety of his rifle and glared at DT's back. When DT turned to him, however, he relaxed. Since Tecolutla he had grown taciturn, and there seemed to be a shifting of lights and darks in his eyes, as if something were scurrying back and forth behind them. He had taken to wearing banana leaves on his head, arranging them under his helmet so the frayed ends stuck out the sides like strange green hair. He said this was camouflage, but Dantzler was certain it bespoke some secretive, irrational purpose. Of course DT had noticed Moody's spiritual erosion, and as they prepared to move out, he called Dantzler aside.

"He done found someplace inside his head that feel good to him," said DT. "He's tryin' to curl up into it, and once he do that he ain't gon' be responsible. Keep an eye on him."

Dantzler mumbled his assent, but was not enthused.

"I know he your fren', man, but that don't mean shit. Not the way things are. Now me, I don't give a damn 'bout you personally. But I'm your brother-in-arms, and thass somethin' you can count on . . . y'understand."

To Dantzler's shame, he did understand.

They had planned on negotiating the cloud forest by nightfall, but they bad underestimated the difficulty. The vegetation beneath the clouds was lush—thick, juicy leaves that mashed underfoot, tangles of vines, trees with slick, pale bark and waxy leaves—and the visibility was only about fifteen feet. They were gray wraiths passing through grayness. The vague shapes of the foliage reminded Dantzler of fancifully engraved letters, and for a while he entertained himself with the notion that they were walking among the half-formed phrases of a constitution not yet manifest in the land. They barged off the trail, losing it completely, becoming veiled in spider webs and drenched by spills of water. Their voices were oddly muffled, the tag ends of words swallowed up. After seven hours of this, DT reluctantly gave the order to pitch camp. They set electric lamps around the perimeter so they could see to string the jungle hammocks; the beam of light illuminated the moisture in the air, piercing the murk with jeweled blades. They talked in hushed tones, alarmed by the eerie atmosphere. When they had done with the hammocks, DT posted four sentries—Moody, LeDoux, Dantzler, and himself. Then they switched off the lamps.

It grew pitch-dark, and the darkness was picked out by *plips* and *plops*, the entire spectrum of dripping sounds. To Dantzler's ears they blended into a gabbling speech. He imagined tiny Santa Ana demons talking about him, and to stave off paranoia he popped two ampules. He continued to pop them, trying to limit himself to one every half hour, but he was uneasy, unsure where to train his rifle in the dark, and he exceeded his limit. Soon it began to grow light again, and he assumed that more time had passed than he had thought. That often happened with the ampules—it was easy to lose yourself in being alert, in the wealth of perceptual detail available to your sharpened senses. Yet on checking his watch, he saw it was only a few minutes after two o'clock. His system was too inundated with the drugs to allow panic, but he twitched his head from side-to-side in tight little arcs to determine the source of the brightness. There did not appear to be a single source; it was simply that filaments of the cloud were gleaming, casting a diffuse golden glow, as if they were elements of a nervous system coming to life. He started to call out, then held back. The others must have seen the light, and they had given no cry; they probably had a good reason for their silence. He scrunched down flat, pointing his rifle out from the campsite.

Bathed in the golden mist, the forest had acquired an alchemic beauty. Beads of water glittered with gemmy brilliance; the leaves and vines and bark were gilded. Every surface shimmered with light . . . everything except a fleck of blackness hovering between two of the trunks, its size gradually increasing. As it swelled in his vision, he saw it had the shape of a bird, its wings beating, flying toward him from an inconceivable distance—

inconceivable, because the dense vegetation did not permit you to see very far in a straight line, and yet the bird was growing larger with such slowness that it must have been coming from a long way off. It was not really flying, he realized; rather, it was as if the forest were painted on a piece of paper, as if someone were holding a lit match behind it and burning a hole, a hole that maintained the shape of a bird as it spread. He was transfixed, unable to react. Even when it had blotted out half the light, when he lay before it no bigger than a mote in relation to its huge span, he could not move or squeeze the trigger. And then the blackness swept over him. He had the sensation of being borne along at incredible speed, and he could no longer hear the dripping of the forest.

"Moody!" he shouted. "DT!"

But the voice that answered belonged to neither of them. It was hoarse, issuing from every part of the surrounding blackness, and he recognized it as the voice of his recurring dream.

"You are killing my son," it said. "I have led you here, to this *ayahuamaco,* so he may judge you."

Dantzler knew to his bones the voice was that of the *Sukia* of the village of Santander Jimenez. He wanted to offer a denial, to explain his innocence, but all he could manage was, "No." He said it tearfully, hopelessly, his forehead resting on his rifle barrel. Then his mind gave a savage twist, and his soldiery self regained control. He ejected an ampule from his dispenser and popped it.

The voice laughed—malefic, damning laughter whose vibrations shuddered Dantzler. He opened up with the rifle, spraying fire in all directions. Filigrees of golden holes appeared in the blackness, tendrils of mist coiled through them. He kept on firing until the blackness shattered and fell in jagged sections toward him. Slowly. Like shards of black glass dropping through water. He emptied the rifle and flung himself flat, shielding his head with his arms, expecting to be sliced into bits; but nothing touched him. At last he peeked between his arms; then—amazed, because the forest was now a uniform lustrous yellow—he rose to his knees. He scraped his hand on one of the crushed leaves beneath him, and blood welled from the cut. The broken fibers of the leaf were as stiff as wires. He stood, a giddy trickle of hysteria leaking up from the bottom of his soul. It was no forest, but a building of solid gold worked to resemble a forest—the sort of conceit that might have been fabricated for the child of an emperor. Canopied by golden leaves, columned by slender golden trunks, carpeted by golden grasses. The water beads were diamonds. All the gleam and glitter soothed his apprehension; here was something out of a myth, a habitat for princesses and wizards and dragons. Almost gleeful, he turned to the campsite to see how the others were reacting. Once, when he was nine years old, he had sneaked into the attic to rummage through the boxes and trunks, and he had run across an old morocco-bound copy of *Gulliver's Travels*. He had been taught to treasure old books, and so he had opened it eagerly to look at the illustrations, only to find that the centers of the pages had been eaten away, and there, right in the heart of the fiction, was a nest of larvae. Pulpy, horrid things. It was an awful sight, but one unique in his experience, and he might have studied those crawling scraps of life for a very long time if his father had not interrupted. Such a sight was now before him, and he was numb with it.

They were all dead. He should have guessed they would be; he had given no thought to them while firing his rifle. They had been struggling out of their hammocks when the bullets hit, and as a result, they were hanging half-in, half-out, their limbs dangling, blood pooled beneath them. The veils of golden mist made them look dark and mysterious and malformed, like monsters killed as they emerged from their cocoons. Dantzler could not stop staring, but he was shrinking inside himself. It was not his fault. That thought kept swooping in and out of a flock of less acceptable thoughts; he wanted to stay put, to be true, to alleviate the sick horror he was beginning to feel.

"What's your name?" asked a girl's voice behind him.

She was sitting on a stone about twenty feet away. Her hair was a tawny shade of gold, her skin a half-tone lighter, and her dress was cunningly formed out of the mist. Only her eyes were real. Brown, heavy-lidded eyes—they were at variance with the rest of her face, which had the fresh, unaffected beauty of an American teenager.

"Don't be afraid," she said, and patted the ground, inviting him to sit beside her.

He recognized the eyes, but it was no matter. He badly needed the consolation she could offer; he walked over and sat down. She let him lean his head against her thigh.

"What's your name?" she repeated.

"Dantzler," he said. "John Dantzler." And then he added, "I'm from Boston. My father's . . ." It would be too difficult to explain about anthropology. "He's a teacher."

"Are there many soldiers in Boston?" She stroked his cheek with a golden finger.

The caress made Dantzler happy. "Oh, no," he said. "They hardly know there's a war going on."

"This is true?" she said, incredulous.

"Well, they *do* know about it, but it's just news on the TV to them. They've got more pressing problems. Their jobs, families."

"Will you let them know about the war when you return home?" she asked. "Will you do that for me?"

Dantzler had given up hope of returning home, of surviving, and her assumption that he would do both acted to awaken his gratitude. "Yes," he said fervently. "I will."

"You must hurry," she said "If you stay in the *ayahuamaco* too long, you will never leave. You must find the way out. It is a way not of directions or trails, but of events."

"Where is this place?" he asked, suddenly aware of how much he had taken it for granted.

She shifted her leg away, and if he had not caught himself on the stone, he would have fallen. When he looked up, she had vanished. He was surprised that her disappearance did not alarm him. In reflex he slipped out a couple of ampules, but after a moment's reflection he decided not to use them. It was impossible to slip them back into the dispenser, so he tucked them into the interior webbing of his helmet for later. He doubted he would need them, though. He felt strong, competent, and unafraid.

Dantzler stepped carefully between the hammocks, not wanting to brush against them; it might have been his imagination, but they seemed to be bulged down lower than before, as if death had weighed out heavier than life. That heaviness was in the air, pressuring him. Mist rose like golden steam from the corpses, but the sight no longer affected him—perhaps because the mist gave the illusion of being their souls. He picked up a rifle with a full magazine and headed off into the forest.

The tips of the golden leaves were sharp, and he had to ease past them to avoid being cut, but he was at the top of his form, moving gracefully, and the obstacles barely slowed his pace. He was not even anxious about the girl's warning to hurry; he was certain the way out would soon present itself. After a minute or so, he heard voices and after another few seconds, he came to a clearing divided by a stream, one so perfectly reflecting that its banks appeared to enclose a wedge of golden mist. Moody was squatting to the left of the stream, staring at the blade of his survival knife and singing under his breath—a wordless melody that had the erratic rhythm of a trapped fly. Beside him lay Jerry LeDoux, his throat slashed from ear to ear. DT was sitting on the other side of the stream; he had been shot just above the knee, and though he had ripped up his shirt for bandages and tied off the leg with a tourniquet, he was not in good shape. He was sweating, and the gray chalky pallor infused his skin. The entire scene had the weird vitality of something that had materialized in a magic mirror, a bubble of reality enclosed within a gilt frame.

DT heard Dantzler's foothills and glanced up. "Waste him!" he shouted, pointing at Moody.

Moody did not turn from contemplation of the knife. "No," he said, as if speaking to someone whose image was held in the blade.

"Waste him, man!" screamed DT. "He killed LeDoux!"

"Please," said Moody to the knife. "I don't want to."

There was blood clotted on his face, more blood on the banana leaves sticking out of his helmet.

"Did you kill Jerry?" asked Dantzler. While he addressed the question to Moody, he did not relate to him as an individual, only as part of a design whose messages he had to unravel.

"Jesus Christ! Waste him!" DT smashed his fist against the ground in frustration.

"OK," said Moody. With an apologetic look, he sprang to his feet and charged Dantzler, swinging the knife.

Emotionless, Dantzler stitched a line of fire across Moody's chest; he went sideways into the bushes and down.

"What the hell was you waitin' for?" DT tried to rise, but winced and fell back. "Damn! Don't know if I can walk."

"Pop a few," Dantzler suggested mildly.

"Yeah. Good thinkin', man." DT fumbled for his dispenser. Dantzler peered into the bushes to see where Moody had fallen. He felt nothing, and this pleased him. He was weary of feeling. DT popped an ampule with a flourish, as if making a toast, and inhaled. "Ain't you gon' to do some, man?"

"I don't need them," said Dantzler. "I'm fine."

The stream interested him; it did not reflect the mist, as he had supposed, but was itself a seam of the mist.

"How many you think they was?" asked DT.

"How many what?"

"Beaners, man! I wasted three or four after they hit us, but I couldn't tell how many they was."

Dantzler considered this in light of his own interpretation of events and Moody's conversation with the knife. It made sense. A Santa Ana kind of sense.

"Beats me," he said. "But I guess there's less than there used to be."

DT snorted. "You got *that* right!" He heaved to his feet and limped to the edge of the stream. "Gimme a hand across."

Dantzler reached out to him, but instead of taking his hand, he grabbed his wrist and pulled him off balance. DT teetered on his good leg, then toppled and vanished beneath the mist. Dantzler had expected him to fall, but he surfaced instantly, mist clinging to his skin. Of course, thought Dantzler; his body would have to die before his spirit would fall.

"What you doin', man?" DT was more disbelieving than enraged.

Dantzler planted a foot in the middle of his back and pushed him down until his head was submerged. DT bucked and clawed at the foot and managed to come to his hands and knees. Mist slithered from his eyes, his nose, and he choked out the words ". . . kill you. . . ." Dantzler pushed him down again; he got into pushing him down and letting him up, over and over. Not so as to torture him. Not really. It was because he had suddenly understood the nature of the *ayahuamaco*'s laws, that they were approximations of normal laws, and he further understood that his actions had to approximate those of someone jiggling a key in a lock. DT was the key to the way out, and Dantzler was jiggling him, making sure all the tumblers were engaged.

Some of the vessels in DT's eyes had burst, and the whites were occluded by films of blood. When he tried to speak, mist curled from his mouth. Gradually his struggles subsided; he clawed runnels in the gleaming yellow dirt of the bank and shuddered. His shoulders were knobs of black land floundering in a mystic sea.

For a long time after DT sank from view, Dantzler stood beside the stream, uncertain of what was left to do and unable to remember a lesson he had been taught. Finally, he shouldered his rifle and walked away from the clearing. Morning had broken, the mist had thinned, and the forest had regained its usual coloration. But he scarcely noticed these changes, still troubled by his faulty memory. Eventually he let it slide—it would all come clearer sooner or later. He was just happy to be alive. After a while, he began to kick his rifle in a carefree fashion against the weeds.

When the 1st Infantry poured across the Nicaraguan border and wasted León, Dantzler was having a quiet time at the VA hospital in Ann Arbor, Michigan, and at the precise moment the bulletin was flashed nationwide, he was sitting in the lounge, watching the American League playoffs between Detroit and Texas. Some of the patients ranted at the interruption, while others shouted them down, wanting to hear the details. Dantzler expressed no reaction whatsoever. He was solely concerned with being a model patient; however, noticing that one of the staff was giving him a clinical stare, he added his weight on the side of the baseball fans. He did not want to appear too controlled. The doctors were as suspicious of that sort of behavior as they were of its contrary. But the funny thing was—at least, it was funny to Dantzler—that his feigned annoyance at the bulletin was exemplary proof of his control, his expertise at moving through life the way he had moved through the golden leaves of the cloud forest. Cautiously, gracefully, efficiently. Touching nothing, and being touched by nothing. That was the lesson he had learned—to be as perfect a counterfeit of a man as the *ayahuamaco* had been of the land; to adopt the various stances of a man, and yet, by virtue of his distance from things human, to be all the more prepared for the onset of crisis or a call to action. He saw nothing aberrant in this; even the doctors would admit that men were little more than organized pretense. If he was different from other men, it was only that he had a deeper awareness of the principles on which his personality was founded.

When the battle of Managua was joined, Dantzler was living at home. His parents had urged him to go easy in readjusting to civilian life, but he had immediately gotten a job as a management trainee in a bank. Each morning he would drive to work and spend a controlled, quiet eight hours. Each night he would watch TV with his mother, and before going to bed, he would climb to the attic and inspect the trunk containing his souvenirs of war—helmet, fatigues, knife, boots. The doctors had insisted he face his experiences, and this ritual was his way of following their instructions. All in all, he was quite pleased with his progress, but he still had problems. He had not been able to force himself to venture out at night, remembering too well the darkness in the cloud forest, and he had rejected his friends, refusing to see them or answer their calls—he was not secure with the idea of friendship. Further, despite his methodical approach to life, he was prone to a nagging restlessness, the feeling of a chore left undone.

One night his mother came into his room and told him that an old friend Phil Curry was on the phone. "Please talk to him, Johnny," she said. "He's been drafted, and I think he's a little scared."

The word "drafted" struck a responsive chord in Dantzler's soul, and after brief deliberation, he went downstairs and picked up the receiver.

"Hey," said Phil. "What's the story, man? Three months, and you don't even give me a call?"

"I'm sorry," said Dantzler. "I haven't been feeling so hot."

"Yeah, I understand." Phil was silent a moment. "Listen, man. I'm leavin', y'know, and we're havin' a big send-off at Sparky's. It's goin' on right now. Why don't you come down?"

"I don't know."

"Jeanine's here, man. Y'know, she's still crazy 'bout you, talks 'bout you alla time. She don't go out with nobody."

Dantzler was unable to think of anything to say.

"Look," said Phil, "I'm pretty weirded out by this soldier shit. I hear it's pretty bad down there. If you got anything you can tell me 'bout what it's like, man, I'd 'preciate it."

Dantzler could relate to Phil's concern, his desire for an edge, and besides, it felt right to go. Very right. He would take some precautions against the darkness.

"I'll be there," he said.

It was a foul night, spitting snow, but Sparky's parking lot was jammed. Dantzler's mind was flurried like the snow, crowded like the lot—thoughts whirling in, jockeying for position, melting away. He hoped his mother would not wait up, he wondered if Jeanine still wore her hair long, he was worried because the palms of his hands were unnaturally warm. Even with the car windows rolled up, he could hear loud music coming from inside the club. Above the door the words SPARKY'S ROCK CITY were being spelled out a letter at a time in red neon, and when the spelling was complete, the letters flashed off and on, and a golden neon explosion bloomed around them. After the explosion, the entire sign went dark for a split second, and the big ramshackle building seemed to grow large and merge with the black sky. He had feeling it was watching him, and he shuddered—one of those sudden lurches downwind of that kind that take you just before you fall asleep. He knew the people inside did not intend him any harm, but he also knew that places have a way of changing people's intent, and he did not want to lie caught off guard. Sparky's might be such a place, might be a huge black presence camouflaged by neon, its true substance one with the abyss of the sky, the phosphorescent snowflakes jittering in his headlights, the wind keening through the side vent. He would have liked very much to drive home and forget about his promise to Phil; however, he felt a responsibility to explain about the war. More than a responsibility, an evangelistic urge. He would tell them about the kid falling out of the chopper, the white-haired girl in Tecolutla, the emptiness. God, yes! How he went down chock-full of ordinary American thoughts and dreams, memories of smoking weed and chasing tail and hanging out and freeway flying with a case of something cold, and how he smuggled back a human-shaped container of pure Salvadorian emptiness. Primo grade. Smuggled it back to the land of silk and money, of mindfuck video games and topless tennis matches and fast-food solutions to the nutritional problem. Just a taste of Salvador would banish all those trivial obsessions. Just a taste. It would be easy to explain.

Of course, some things beggared explanation.

He bent down and adjusted the survival knife in his boot so the hilt would not rub against his calf. From his coat pocket he withdrew the two ampules he had secreted in his helmet that long-ago night in the cloud forest. As the neon explosion flashed once more, glimmers of gold coursed along their shiny surfaces. He did not think he would need them; his hand was steady, and his purpose was clear. But to be on the safe side, he popped them both.

We Can Get Them for You Wholesale

Neil Gaiman

Peter Pinter had never heard of Aristippus of the Cyrenaics, a lesser-known follower of Socrates, who maintained that the avoidance of trouble was the highest attainable good; however, he had lived his uneventful life according to this precept. In all respects except one (an inability to pass up a bargain, and which of us is entirely free from that?) he was a very moderate man. He did not go to extremes. His speech was proper and reserved; he rarely overate; he drank enough to be sociable and no more; he was far from rich, and in no wise poor. He liked people and people liked him. Bearing all that in mind, would you expect to find him in a lowlife pub on the seamier side of London's East End, taking out what is colloquially known as a "contract" on someone he hardly knew? You would not. You would not even expect to find him in the pub.

And until a certain Friday afternoon, you would have been right. But the love of a woman can do strange things to a man, even one so colourless as Peter Pinter, and the discovery that Miss Gwendolyn Thorpe, twenty-three years of age, of 9, Oaktree Terrace, Purley, was messing about (as the vulgar would put it) with a smooth young gentleman from the accounting department—*after,* mark you, she had consented to wear an engagement ring, composed of real ruby chips, nine-carat gold, and something that might well have been a diamond (£37.50) that it had taken Peter almost an entire lunch-hour to choose—can do very strange things to a man indeed.

After he made this shocking discovery, Peter spent a sleepless Friday night tossing and turning, with visions of Gwendolyn and Archie Gibbons (the Don Juan of Clamages Accounting Department) dancing and swimming before his eyes—performing acts that even Peter, if he were pressed, would have to admit were most improbable. But the bile of jealousy had risen up within him, and by the morning Peter had resolved that his rival should be done away with.

Saturday morning was spent wondering how one contacted an assassin, for, to the best of Peter's knowledge, none were employed by Clamages (the department store that employed all three of the members of our eternal triangle, and, incidentally, furnished the ring), and he was wary of asking anyone outright for fear of attracting attention to himself.

Thus it was that Saturday afternoon found him hunting through the Yellow Pages.

Assassins, he found, was not between *Asphalt Contractors* and *Assessors (Quantity); Killers* was not between *Kennels* and *Kindergartens; Murderers* was not between *Mowers* and *Museums. Pest Control* looked promising; however closer investigation of the Pest Control advertisements showed them to be almost solely concerned with "rats, mice, fleas, cockroaches, rabbits, moles, and rats" (to quote from one that Peter felt was rather hard on rats), and not really what he had in mind. Even so, being of a careful nature, he dutifully inspected the entries in that category, and at the bottom of the second page, in small print, he found a firm that looked promising.

"Complete discreet disposal of irksome and unwanted mammals, etc.," went the entry, "Ketch, Hare, Burke and Ketch. The Old Firm." It went on to give no address, but only a telephone number.

Peter dialed the number, surprising himself by so doing. His heart pounded in his chest, and he tried to look nonchalant. The telephone rang once, twice, three times. Peter was just starting to hope that it would not be answered and he could forget the whole thing, when there was a click and a brisk young female voice said, "Ketch Hare Burke Ketch, can I help you?"

Carefully not giving his name Peter said, "Er, how big—I mean, what size mammals do you go up to? To, uh, dispose of?"

"Well, that would all depend on what size sir requires."

He plucked up all his courage. "A person?"

Her voice remained brisk and unruffled. "Of course, sir. Do you have a pen and paper handy? Good. Be at the Dirty Donkey pub, off Little Courtney Street, E3, tonight at eight o'clock. Carry a rolled-up copy of the *Financial Times*—that's the pink one, sir—and our operative will approach you there." Then she put down the phone.

Peter was elated. It had been far easier than he had imagined. He went down to the newsagent's and bought a copy of the *Financial Times,* found Little Courtney Street in his *A-Z of London,* and spent the rest of the afternoon watching football on the television and imagining the smooth young gentleman from accounting's funeral.

It took Peter a while to find the pub. Eventually he spotted the pub sign, which showed a donkey, and was indeed remarkably dirty.

The Dirty Donkey was a small and more-or-less filthy pub, poorly lit, in which knots of unshaven people wearing dusty donkey jackets stood around eyeing each other suspiciously, eating crisps and drinking pints of Guinness, a drink that Peter had never cared for. Peter held his *Financial Times* under one arm, as conspicuously as he could, but no one approached him, so he bought a half of shandy and retreated to a corner table. Unable to think of anything else to do while waiting he tried to read the paper, but, lost and confused by a maze of grain futures, and a rubber company that was selling something or other short (quite what the short somethings were he could not tell), he gave it up and stared at the door.

He had waited almost ten minutes when a small, busy man hustled in, looked quickly around him, then came straight over to Peter's table and sat down.

He stuck out his hand. "Kemble. Burton Kemble, of Ketch Hare Burke Ketch. I hear you have a job for us."

He didn't look like a killer. Peter, said so.

"Oh lor' bless us no. I'm not actually part of our workforce, sir. I'm in sales."

Peter nodded. That certainly made sense. "Can we—er—talk freely here?"

"Sure. Nobody's interested. Now then, how many people would you like disposed of?"

"Only one. His name's Archibald Gibbons and he works in Clamages accounting department. His address is . . ."

Kemble interrupted. "We can go into all that later, sir, if you don't mind. Let's just quickly go over the financial side. First of all, the contract will cost you £500 . . ."

Peter nodded. He could afford that, and in fact had expected to have to pay a little more.

". . . although there's always the special offer," Kemble concluded smoothly.

Peter's eyes shone. As I mentioned earlier, he loved a bargain, and often bought things he had no imaginable use for in sales or on special offers. Apart from this one failing (one that so many of us share), he was a most moderate young man. "Special offer?"

"Two for the price of one, sir."

Mmm. Peter thought about it. That worked out at only £250 each, which couldn't be bad no matter how you looked at it. There was only one snag. "I'm afraid I don't *have* anyone else I want killed."

Kemble looked disappointed. "That's a pity, sir. For two we could probably have even knocked the price down to, well, say £450 for the both of them."

"Really?"

"Well, it gives our operatives something to do, sir. If you must know"—and here he dropped his voice— "there really isn't enough work in this particular line to keep them occupied. Not like the old days. Isn't there just *one* other person you'd like to see dead?"

Peter pondered. He hated to pass up a bargain, but couldn't for the life of him think of anyone else. He liked people. Still, a bargain was a bargain . . .

"Look," said Peter. "Could I think about it, and see you here tomorrow night?"

The salesman looked pleased. "Of course, sir," he said. "I'm sure you'll be able to think of someone."

The answer—the obvious answer—came to Peter as he was drifting off to sleep that night. He sat straight up in bed, fumbled the bedside light on and wrote a name down on the back of an envelope, in case he forgot it. To tell the truth he didn't think that he could forget it, for it was painfully obvious, but you can never tell with these late-night thoughts.

The name that he had written down on the back of the envelope was this: Gwendolyn Thorpe.

He turned the light off, rolled over, and was soon asleep, dreaming peaceful and remarkably unmurderous dreams.

Kemble was waiting for him when he arrived in the Dirty Donkey on Sunday night. Peter bought a drink and sat down beside him.

"I'm taking you up on the special offer," he said, by way of introduction.

Kemble nodded vigorously. "A very wise decision, if you don't mind me saying so, sir."

Peter Pinter smiled modestly, in the manner of one who read the *Financial Times* and made wise business decisions. "That will be £450, I believe?"

"Did I say £450, sir? Good gracious me, I do apologise. I beg your pardon, I was thinking of our bulk rate. It would be £475 for two people."

Disappointment mingled with cupidity on Peter's bland and youthful face. That was an extra twenty-five pounds. However, something that Kemble had said caught his attention.

"Bulk rate?"

"Of course, but I doubt that sir would be interested in that."

"No, no I am. Tell me about it."

"Very well, sir. Bulk rate, £450, would be for a large job. Ten people."

Peter wondered if he had heard correctly. "Ten people? But that's only £45 each."

"Yes, sir. It's the large order that makes it profitable."

"I see," said Peter, and "Hmm," said Peter, and "Could you be here the same time tomorrow night?"

"Of course, sir."

Upon arriving home Peter got out a scrap of paper and a pen. He wrote the numbers one to ten down one side and then filled it in as follows:

1) . . . *Archie G.*
2) . . . *Gwennie.*
3) . . .

and so forth.

Having filled in the first two he sat sucking his pen, hunting for wrongs done to him and people the world would be better off without.

He smoked a cigarette. He strolled around the room.

Aha! There was a physics teacher at a school he had attended who had delighted in making his life a misery. What was the man's name again? And for that matter, was he still alive? Peter wasn't sure, but he wrote *The Physics Teacher, Abbot Street Secondary School* next to the number three. The next came more easily—his department head had refused to raise his salary a couple of months back; that the raise had eventually come was immaterial. *Mr. Hunterson* was number four.

When he was five a boy named Simon Ellis had poured paint on his head, while another boy named James somebody-or-other had held him down and a girl named Sharon Hartsharpe had laughed. They were numbers five through seven respectively.

Who else?

There was the man on television with the annoying snicker who read the news. He went down the list. And what about the woman in the flat next door, with the little yappy dog that shat in the hall? He put her and the dog down on nine. Ten was the hardest. He scratched his head and went into the kitchen for a cup of coffee, then dashed back and wrote *My Great Uncle Mervyn* down in the tenth place. The old man was rumored to be quite affluent and there was a possibility (albeit rather slim) that he could leave Peter some money.

With the satisfaction of an evening's work well done he went off to bed.

Monday at Clamages was routine; Peter was a senior sales assistant in the books department, a job that actually entailed very little. He clutched his list tightly in his hand, deep in his pocket, rejoicing in the feeling of power that it gave him. He spent a most enjoyable lunch hour in the canteen with young Gwendolyn (who did not know that he had seen her and Archie enter the stockroom together), and even smiled at the smooth young man from the accounting department when he passed him in the corridor.

He proudly displayed his list to Kemble that evening.

The little salesman's face fell.

"I'm afraid this isn't ten people, Mr. Pinter," he explained. "You've counted the woman in the next-door flat *and* her dog as one person. That brings it to eleven, which would be an extra . . ." his pocket calculator was rapidly deployed, ". . . an extra seventy pounds. How about if we forget the dog?"

Peter shook his head. "The dog's as bad as the woman. Or worse."

"Then I'm afraid we have a slight problem. Unless . . ."

"What?"

"Unless you'd like to take advantage of our wholesale rate. But of course sir wouldn't be . . ."

There are words that do things to people; words that make people's faces flush with joy, excitement, or passion. *Environmental* can be one, *occult* is another. *Wholesale* was Peter's. He leaned back in his chair. "Tell me about it," he said, with the practiced assurance of an experienced shopper.

"Well, sir," said Kemble, allowing himself a little chuckle, "We can, uh, *get* them for you, wholesale. Seventeen-and-half pounds each, for every quarry after the first fifty, or a tenner each for every one over two hundred."

"I suppose you'd go down to a fiver if I wanted a thousand people knocked off?"

"Oh no, sir," Kemble looked shocked. "If you're talking those sorts of figures we can do them for a quid each."

"One *pound*?"

"That's right, sir. There's not a big profit margin on it, but the high turnover and productivity more than justifies it."

Kemble got up. "Same time tomorrow, sir?"

Peter nodded.

One thousand pounds. One thousand *people*. Peter Pinter didn't even *know* a thousand people. Even so . . . there were the Houses of Parliament. He didn't like politicians; they squabbled and argued and carried on so.

And for that matter . . .

An idea, shocking in its audacity. Bold. Daring. Still, the idea was there and it wouldn't go away. A distant cousin of his had married the younger brother of an earl or a baron or something . . .

On the way home from work that afternoon he stopped off at a little shop that he had passed a thousand times without entering. It had a large sign in the window—guaranteeing to trace your lineage for you, and even draw up a coat of arms if you happened to have mislaid your own—and an impressive heraldic map.

They were very helpful and phoned him up just after seven to give him their news.

If approximately fourteen million, seventy-two thousand, eight hundred and eleven people died, he, Peter Pinter, would be *king of England*.

He didn't have fourteen million, seventy-two thousand, eight hundred and eleven pounds: but he suspected that when you were talking in those figures, Mr. Kemble would have one of his special discounts.

Mr. Kemble did.

He didn't even raise an eyebrow.

"Actually," he explained, "it works out quite cheaply; you see we wouldn't have to do them all individually. Small-scale nuclear weapons, some judicious bombing, gassing, plague, dropping radios in swimming pools and then mopping up the stragglers. Say four thousand pounds."

"Four thou—? That's *incredible!*"

The salesman looked pleased with himself. "Our operatives will be glad of the work, sir." He grinned. "We pride ourselves on servicing our wholesale customers."

The wind blew cold as Peter left the pub, setting the old sign swinging. It didn't look much like a dirty donkey, thought Peter, more like a pale horse.

Peter was drifting off to sleep that night, mentally rehearsing his Coronation Speech, when a thought drifted into his head and hung around. It would not go away. Could he—could he *possibly* be passing up an even larger saving than he already had? Could he be missing out on a bargain?

Peter climbed out of bed and walked over to the phone. It was almost 3 AM, but even so . . .

His Yellow Pages lay open, where he had left it the previous Saturday, and he dialed the number.

The phone seemed to ring forever. There was a click and a bored voice said, "Burke Hare Ketch, can I help you?"

"I hope I'm phoning too late . . ." he began.

"Of course not, sir."

"I was wondering if I could speak to Mr. Kemble."

"Can you hold? I'll see if he's available."

Peter waited for a couple of minutes, listening to the ghostly crackles and whispers that always echo down empty phone lines.

"Are you there, caller?"

"Yes. I'm here."

"Putting you through." There was a buzz, then, "Kemble speaking."

"Ah, Mr Kemble. Hello. Sorry if I got you out of bed or anything. This is, urm, Peter Pinter."

"Yes, Mr. Pinter?"

"Well, I'm sorry it's so late, only I was wondering . . . How much would it cost to kill everybody? Everybody in the world?"

"Everybody? All the people?"

"Yes. How much? I mean, for an order like that you'd have to have some kind of a big discount. How much would it be? For everyone?"

"Nothing at all, Mr. Pinter."

"You mean you wouldn't do it?"

"I mean we'd do it for nothing, Mr. Pinter. We only have to be asked, you see. We always have to be asked."

Peter was puzzled. "But—when would you start?"

"Start? Right away. Now. We've been ready for a long time. But we had to be asked, Mr. Pinter. Goodnight. It *has* been a *pleasure* doing business with you."

The line went dead.

Peter felt strange. Everything seemed very distant. He wanted to sit down. What on earth had the man meant? *We always have to be asked.* It was definitely strange. Nobody does anything for nothing in this world; he had a good mind to phone Kemble back and call the whole thing off. Perhaps he had overreacted; perhaps there was a perfectly innocent reason why Archie and Gwendolyn had entered the stock room together. He would talk to her. That's what he'd do. He'd talk to Gwennie first thing tomorrow morning . . .

That was when the noises started.

Odd cries from across the street. A cat fight? Foxes probably. He hoped someone would throw a shoe at them. Then, from the corridor outside his flat, he heard a muffled clumping, as if someone were dragging something very heavy along the floor. It stopped. Someone knocked on his door, twice, very softly.

Outside his window the cries were getting louder. Peter sat in his chair, knowing that somehow, somewhere, he had missed something. Something important. The knocking redoubled. He was thankful that he always locked and chained his door at night.

They'd been ready for a long time, but they had to be asked . . .

When the thing came through the door Peter started screaming, but he really didn't scream for very long.

The Big Flash

Norman Spinrad

T *minus 200 days . . . and counting . . .*

They came on freaky for my taste—but that's the name of the game: freaky means a draw in the rock business. And if the Mandala was going to survive in L.A., competing with a network-owned joint like The American Dream, I'd just have to hold my nose and out-freak the opposition. So after I had dug the Four Horsemen for about an hour, I took them into my office to talk turkey.

I sat down behind my Salvation Army desk (the Mandala is the world's most expensive shoestring operation), and the Horsemen sat down on the bridge chairs sequentially, establishing the group's pecking order.

First, the head honcho, lead guitar and singer, Stony Clarke—blonde shoulder-length hair, eyes like something in a morgue when he took off his steel-rimmed shades, a reputation as a heavy acid-head and the look of a speed-freak behind it. Then Hair, the drummer, dressed like a Hell's Angel, swastikas and all, a junkie, with fanatic eyes that were a little too close together, making me wonder whether he wore swastikas because he grooved behind the Angel thing or made like an Angel because it let him groove behind the swastika in public. Number three was a cat who called himself Super Spade and wasn't kidding—he wore earrings, natural hair, Stokeley Carmichael sweatshirt, and on a thong around his neck a shrunken head that had been whitened with liquid shoe polish. He was the utility infielder: sitar, base, organ, flute, whatever. Number four, who called himself Mr. Jones, was about the creepiest cat I had ever seen in a rock group, and that is saying something. He was their visuals, synthesizer, and electronics man. He was at least forty, wore early-hippy clothes that looked like they had been made by Sy Devore, and was rumored to be some kind of Rand Corporation dropout. There's no business like show business.

"Okay, boys," I said, "you're strange, but you're my kind of strange. Where you worked before?"

"We ain't, baby," Clarke said. "We're the New Thing. I've been dealing crystal and acid in the Haight. Hair was drummer for some plastic group in New York. The Super Spade claims it's the reincarnation of Bird and it don't pay to argue. Mr. Jones, he don't talk too much. Maybe he's a martian. We just started putting our thing together."

One thing about this business, the groups that don't have square managers, you can get cheap. They talk too much.

"Groovy," I said. "I'm happy to give you guys your start. Nobody knows you, but I think you got something going. So I'll take a chance and give you a week's booking. One AM to closing, which is two, Tuesday through Sunday, four hundred a week."

"Are you Jewish?" asked Hair.

"What?"

"Cool it," Clarke ordered. Hair cooled it. "What it means," Clarke told me, "is that four hundred sounds like pretty light bread."

"We don't sign if there's an option clause," Mr. Jones said.

"The Jones-thing has a good point," Clarke said. "We do the first week for four hundred, but after that it's a whole new scene, dig?"

I didn't feature that. If they hit it big, I could end up not being able to afford them. But on the other hand four hundred was light bread, and I needed a cheap closing act pretty bad.

"Okay," I said. "But a verbal agreement that I get first crack at you when you finish the gig."

"Word of honor," said Stony Clarke.

That's this business—the word of honor of an ex-dealer and speed-freak.

T minus 199 days . . . and counting . . .

Being unconcerned with ends, the military mind can be easily manipulated, easily controlled, and easily confused. Ends are defined as those goals set by civilian authority. Ends are the conceded province of civilians; means are the province of the military, whose duty it is to achieve the ends set for it by the most advantageous applications of the means at its command.

Thus the confusion over the war in Asia among my uniformed clients at the Pentagon. The end has been duly set: eradication of the guerrillas. But the civilians have overstepped their bounds and meddled in means. The generals regard this as unfair, a breach of contract, as it were. The generals (or the faction among them most inclined to poranoia) are beginning to see the conduct of the war, the political limitation on means, as a ploy of the civilians for performing a putsch against their time-honored prerogatives.

This aspect of the situation would bode ill for the country, were it not for the fact that the growing paranoia among the generals has enabled me to manipulate them into presenting both my scenarios to the president. The president has authorized implementation of the major scenario, provided that the minor scenario is successful in properly molding public opinion.

My major scenario is simple and direct. Knowing that the poor flying weather makes our conventional airpower—with its dependency on relative accuracy—ineffectual, the enemy has fallen into the pattern of grouping his forces into larger units and launching punishing annual offensives during the monsoon season. However, these larger units are highly vulnerable to tactical nuclear weapons, which do not depend upon accuracy for effect. Secure in the knowledge that domestic political considerations preclude the use of nuclear weapons, the enemy will once again form into division-sized units or larger during the next monsoon season. A parsimonious use of tactical nuclear weapons, even as few as twenty-one hundred kiloton bombs, employed simultaneously and in an advantageous pattern, will destroy a minimum of two hundred thousand enemy troops, or nearly two-thirds of his total force, in a twenty-four-hour period. The blow will be crushing.

The minor scenario, upon whose success the implementation of the major scenario depends, is far more sophisticated, due to its subtler goal: public acceptance of, or, optimally, even public clamor for, the use of tactical nuclear weapons. The task is difficult, but my scenario is quite sound, if somewhat exotic, and with the full, if to some extent clandestine, support of the upper military hierarchy, certain civil government circles, and the decision makers in key aerospace corporations, the means now at my command would seem adequate. The risks, while statistically significant, do not exceed an acceptable level.

T minus 189 days . . . and counting . . .

The way I see it, the network deserved the shafting I gave them. They shafted *me*, didn't they? Four successful series I produce for those bastards, and two bomb out after thirteen weeks, and they send me to the salt mines! A *discotheque.* Can you imagine they make me producer at a lousy discotheque! A remittance man they make me, those schlockmeisters. Oh, those schnorrers made The American Dream sound like a kosher deal—twenty percent of the net, they say. And you got access to all our sets and contract players, it'll make you a rich man, Herm. And like a yuk, I sign, being broke at the time, without reading the fine print. I should know they've set up The American Dream as a tax loss? I should know that I've *gotta* use their lousy sets and stiff contract players and have it written off against my gross? I should know their shtick is to run The American Dream at a loss and then do a network TV show out of the joint from which I don't see a penny? So I end up running the place for them at a paper loss, living on salary, while the network rakes it in off the TV show that I end up paying for out of my end.

Don't bums like that deserve to be shafted? It isn't enough they use me as a tax loss patsy, they gotta tell me who to book! "Go sign the Four Horsemen, the group that's packing them in at the Mandala," they say. "We want them on *A Night With The American Dream.* They're hot."

"Yeah, they're hot," I say, "which means they'll cost a mint. I can't afford it."

They show me more fine print—next time I read the contract with a microscope. I *gotta* book whoever they tell me to and I gotta absorb the cost of my books! It's enough to make a Litvak turn antisemit.

So I had to go to the Mandala to sign up these hippies. I made sure I didn't get there till 12:30 so I wouldn't have to stay in that nuthouse any longer than necessary. Such a dive! What Bernstein did was take a bankrupt Hollywood-Hollywood club on the Strip, knock down all the interior walls, and put up this monster tent inside the shell. Just thin white screening over two-by-fours. Real shlock. Outside the tent, he's got projectors, lights, speakers, all the electronic mumbo jumbo, and inside is like being surrounded by movie screens. Just the tent and the bare floor, not even a real stage, just a platform on wheels they shlepp in and out of the tent when they change groups.

So you can imagine he doesn't exactly draw a class crowd. Not with The American Dream up the street being run as a network tax loss. What they got is the smelly, hard-core hippies I don't let in the door and the kind of j.d. high school kids that think it's smart to hang around putzes like that. A lot of dope-pushing goes on. The cops don't like the place, and the rousts draw professional troublemakers.

A real den of iniquity—I felt like I was walking onto a Casbah set. The last group had gone off and the Horsemen hadn't come on yet, so what you had was this crazy tent filled with hippies, half of them on acid or pot or amphetamine or for all I know Ajax; high school would-be hippies, also mostly stoned and getting ugly; and a few crazy schwartzes looking to fight cops. All of them standing around waiting for something to happen, and about ready to make it happen. I stood near the door, just in case. As they say, "The vibes were making me uptight."

All of a sudden the house lights go out and it's black as a network executive's heart. I hold my hand on my wallet—in this crowd, tell me there are no pickpockets. Just the pitch-black and dead silence for what, ten beats, something crawling along my bones, but I know it's some kind of subsonic effect and not my imagination, because all the hippies are standing still and you don't hear a sound.

Then from a monster speaker so loud you feel it in your teeth, a heartbeat, but heavy, slow, half-time like maybe a whale's heart.

The thing crawling along my bones seems to be synchronized with the heartbeat and I feel almost like I am that big dumb heart beating there in the darkness.

Then a dark red spot—so faint it's almost infrared—hits the stage that they have wheeled out. On the stage are four uglies in crazy black robes—you know, like the Grim Reaper wears—with that ugly red light all over them like blood. Creepy. *Boom-ba-boom. Boom-ba-boom.* The heartbeat still going, still that subsonic bone-crawl and the hippies are staring at the Four Horsemen like mesmerized chickens.

The bass player, a regular jungle-bunny, picks up the rhythm of the heartbeat. *Dum-da-dum. Dum-da-dum.* The drummer beats it out with earsplitting rim-shots. Then the electric guitar, tuned like a strangling cat, makes with horrible heavy chords. *Whang-ka-whang. Whang-ka-whang.*

It's just awful. I feel it in my guts, my bones; my eardrums are just like some great big throbbing vein. Everybody is swaying to it, I'm swaying to it. *Boom-ba-boom. Boom-ba-boom.*

Then the guitarist starts to chant in rhythm with the heartbeat, in a hoarse, shrill voice like somebody dying: *"The big flash . . . The big flash . . ."*

And the guy at the visuals console diddles around and rings of light start to climb the walls of the tent, blue at the bottom becoming green as they get higher, then yellow, orange, and finally as they become a circle on the ceiling, eye-killing neon-red. Each circle takes exactly one heartbeat to climb the wall.

Boy, what an awful feeling! Like I was a tube of toothpaste being squeezed in rhythm till the top of my head felt like it was gonna squirt up with those circles of light through the ceiling.

And then they start to speed it up gradually. The same heartbeat, the same rim-shots, same chords, same circles, same bass, same subsonic bone-crawl, but just a little faster. . . . Then faster! Faster!

Thought I would die! Knew I would die! Heart beating like a lunatic. Rim-shots like a machine gun. Circles of light sucking me up the walls, into that red neon hole.

Oy, incredible! Over and over faster and faster till the voice was a scream and the heartbeat a boom and the rim-shots a whine and the guitar howled feedback and my bones were jumping out of my body—

Every spot in the place came on and I went blind from the sudden light—

An awful explosion-sound came over every speaker, so loud it rocked me on my feet—

I felt myself squirting out of the top of my head and loved it.

Then:

The explosion became a rumble—

The light seemed to run together into a circle on the ceiling, leaving everything else black.

And the circle became a fireball.

The fireball became a slow-motion film of an atomic bomb cloud as the rumbling died away. Then the picture faded into a moment of total darkness and the house lights came on.

What a number!

Gevalt, what an act!

So after the show, when I got them alone and found out they had no manager, not even an option to the Mandala, I thought faster than I ever had in my life.

To make a long story short and sweet, I gave the network the royal screw. I signed the Horsemen to a contract that made me their manager and gave me twenty percent of their take. Then I booked them into The American Dream at ten thousand a week, wrote a check as proprietor of The American Dream, handed the check to myself as manager of the Four Horsemen, then resigned as a network flunky, leaving them with a ten thousand bag and me with twenty percent of the hottest group since the Beatles.

What the hell, he who lives by the fine print shall perish by the fine print.

T minus 148 days . . . and counting . . .

"You haven't seen the tape yet, have you, B. D.?" Jake said. He was nervous as hell.

When you reach my level in the network structure, you're used to making subordinates nervous, but Jake Pitkin was head of network continuity, not some office boy, and certainly should be used to dealing with executives at my level. Was the rumor really true?

We were alone in the screening room. It was doubtful that the projectionist could hear us.

"No, I haven't seen it yet," I said. "But I've heard some strange stories."

Jake looked positively deathly. "About the tape?" he said.

"About you, Jake," I said, deprecating the rumor with an easy smile. "That you don't want to air the show."

"It's true, B. D.," Jake said quietly.

"Do you realize what you're saying? Whatever our personal tastes—and I personally think there's something unhealthy about them—the Four Horsemen are the hottest thing in the country right now, and that dirty little thief Herm Gellman held us up for a quarter of a million for an hour show. It cost another two hundred thousand to make it. We've spent another hundred thousand on promotion. We're getting top dollar from the sponsors. There's over a million dollars one way or the other riding on that show. That's how much we blow if we don't air it."

"I know that, B. D.," Jake said. "I also know this could cost me my job. Think about that. Because knowing all that, I'm still against airing the tape. I'm going to run the closing segment for you. I'm sure enough that you'll agree with me to stake my job on it."

I had a terrible feeling in my stomach. I have superiors too and the word was that *A Trip with the Four Horsemen* would be aired, period. No matter what. Something funny was going on. The price we were getting for commercial time was a precedent and the sponsor was a big aerospace company that had never bought network time before. What really bothered me was that Jake Pitkin had no reputation for courage; yet here he was laying his job on the line. He must be pretty sure I would come around to his way of thinking or he wouldn't dare. And though I couldn't tell Jake, I had no choice in the matter whatsoever.

"Okay, roll it," Jake said into the intercom mike. "What you're going to see," he said as the screening room lights went out, "is the last number."

On the screen:

A shot of empty blue sky, with soft, lazy electric guitar chords behind it. The camera pans across a few clouds to an extremely long shot on the sun. As the sun, which is no more than a tiny circle of light, moves into the center of the screen, a sitar-drone comes in behind the guitar.

Very slowly, the camera begins to zoom in on the sun. As the image of the sun expands, the sitar gets louder and the guitar begins to fade and a drum starts to give the sitar a beat. The sitar gets louder, the beat gets more pronounced and begins to speed up as the sun continues to expand. Finally, the whole screen is filled with unbearably bright light behind which the sitar and drum are in a frenzy.

Then over this, drowning out the sitar and drum, a voice like a sick thing in heat: *"Brighter . . . than a thousand suns . . ."*

The light dissolves into a close-up of a beautiful dark-haired girl with huge eyes and moist lips, and suddenly there is nothing on the sound track but soft guitar and voices crooning low: *"Brighter . . . Oh God, it's brighter . . . brighter . . . than a thousand suns . . ."*

The girl's face dissolves into a full shot of the Four Horsemen in their Grim Reaper robes and the same melody that had played behind the girl's face shifts into a minor key, picks up whining, reverberating electric guitar chords and a sitar-drone and becomes a dirge: *"Darker . . . the world grows darker . . ."*

And a series of cuts in time to the dirge:

A burning village in Asia strewn with bodies—

"*Darker . . . the world grows darker . . .*"

The corpse-heap at Auschwitz—

"*Until it gets so dark . . .*"

A gigantic auto graveyard with gaunt negro children dwarfed in the foreground—

"*I think I'll die . . .*"

A Washington ghetto in flames with the Capitol misty in the background—

"*. . . before the daylight comes . . .*"

A jump-cut to an extreme close-up on the lead singer of the Horsemen, his face twisted into a mask of desperation and ecstasy. And the sitar is playing double-time, the guitar is wailing and he is screaming at the top of his lungs: "*But before I die, let me make that trip before the nothing comes . . .*"

The girl's face again, but transparent, with a blinding yellow light shining through it. The sitar beat gets faster and faster with the guitar whining behind it and the voice is working itself up into a howling frenzy: "*. . . the last big flash to light my sky . . .*"

Nothing but the blinding light now—

"*. . . and zap! the world is done . . .*"

An utterly black screen for a beat that becomes black fading to blue at a horizon—

"*. . . but before we die let's dig that high that frees us from our binds . . . that blows all cool that ego-drool and burns us from our mind . . . the last big flash, mankind's last gas, the trip we can't take twice . . .*

Suddenly, the music stops dead for a half a beat. Then: the screen is lit up by an enormous fireball—

A shattering rumble—

The fireball coalesces into a mushroom-pillar cloud as the roar goes on. As the roar begins to die out, fire is visible inside the monstrous nuclear cloud. And the girl's face is faintly visible superimposed over the cloud.

A soft voice, amplified over the roar, obscenely reverential now: "*Brighter . . . great God, it's brighter . . . brighter than a thousand suns . . .*"

And the screen went blank and the lights came on.

I looked at Jake. Jake looked at me.

"That's sick," I said. "That's really sick."

"You don't want to run a thing like that, do you, B. D.?" Jake said softly.

I made some rapid mental calculations. The loathsome thing ran something under five minutes . . . it could be done . . .

"You're right, Jake," I said. "We won't run a thing like that. We'll cut it out of the tape and squeeze in another commercial at each break. That should cover the time."

"You don't understand," Jake said. "The contract Herm rammed down our throats doesn't allow us to edit. The show's a package—all or nothing. Besides, the whole show's like that."

"All like that? What do you mean, all like that?"

Jake squirmed in his seat. "Those guys are . . . well, perverts, B. D.," he said.

"*Perverts?*"

"They're . . . well, they're in love with the atom bomb or something. Every number leads up to the same thing."

"You mean . . . they're *all* like that?"

"You got the picture, B. D.," Jake said. "We run an hour of *that* or we run nothing at all."

"Jesus."

I knew what I wanted to say. Burn the tape and write off the million dollars. But I also knew it would cost me my job. And I knew that five minutes after I was out the door, they would have someone in my job who would see things their way. Even my superiors seemed to be just handing down the word from higher up. I had no choice. There was no choice.

"I'm sorry, Jake," I said. "We run it."

"I resign," said Jake Pitkin, who had no reputation for courage.

T minus 10 days . . . and counting . . .

"It's a clear violation of the Test-Ban Treaty," I said.

The undersecretary looked as dazed as I felt. "We'll call it a peaceful use of atomic energy, and let the Russians scream," he said.

"It's insane."

"Perhaps," the undersecretary said. "But you have your orders, General Carson, and I have mine. From higher up. At exactly 8:58 PM local time on July fourth, you will drop a fifty-kiloton atomic bomb on the designated ground zero at Yucca Flats."

"But the people . . . the television crew . . ."

"Will be at least two miles outside the danger zone. Surely, SAC can manage that kind of accuracy under 'laboratory conditions'."

I stiffened. "I do not question the competence of any bomber crew under my command to perform this mission," I said. "I question the reason for the mission. I question the sanity of the orders."

The undersecretary shrugged and smiled weakly. "Welcome to the club."

"You mean you don't know what this is all about either?"

"All I know is what was transmitted to me by the Secretary of Defense, and I got the feeling he doesn't know everything, either. You know that the Pentagon has been screaming for the use of tactical nuclear weapons to end the war in Asia—you SAC boys have been screaming the loudest. Well, several months ago, the president conditionally approved a plan for the use of tactical weapons during the next monsoon season."

I whistled. The civilians were finally coming to their senses. Or were they?

"But what does that have to do with—?"

"Public opinion," the undersecretary said. "It was conditional upon a drastic change in public opinion. At the time the plan was approved, the polls showed that seventy-eight point eight percent of the population opposed the use of tactical nuclear weapons, nine point eight percent favored their use and the rest were undecided or had no opinion. The president agreed to authorize the use of tactical nuclear weapons by a date, several months from now, which is still top secret, provided that by that date at least sixty-five percent of the population approved their use and no more than twenty percent actively opposed it."

"I see . . . Just a ploy to keep the Joint Chiefs quiet."

"General Carson," the undersecretary said, "apparently you are out of touch with the national mood. After the first Four Horsemen show, the polls showed that twenty-five percent of the population approved the use of nuclear weapons. After the second show, the figure was forty-one percent. It is now forty-eight percent. Only thirty-two percent are now actively opposed."

"You're trying to tell me that a rock group—"

"A rock group and the cult around it. It's become a national hysteria. There are imitators. Haven't you seen those buttons?"

"The ones with a mushroom cloud on them that say 'Do it'?"

The undersecretary nodded. "Your guess is as good as mine whether the National Security Council just decided that the Horsemen hysteria could be used to mold public opinion, or whether the Four Horsemen were their creatures to begin with. But the results are the same either way—the Horsemen and the cult around them have won over precisely that element of the population which was most adamantly opposed to nuclear weapons: hippies, students, dropouts, draft-age youth. Demonstrations against the war and against nuclear weapons have died down. We're pretty close to that sixty-five percent. Someone—perhaps the president himself—has decided that one more big Four Horsemen show will put us over the top."

"The president is behind this?"

"No one else can authorize the detonation of an atomic bomb, after all," the undersecretary said. "We're letting them do the show live from Yucca Flats. It's being sponsored by an aerospace company heavily dependent on defense contracts. We're letting them truck in a live audience. Of course the government is behind it."

"And SAC drops an A-bomb as the show-stopper?"

"Exactly."

"I saw one of those shows," I said. "My kids were watching it. I got the strangest feeling . . . I almost wanted that red telephone to ring . . ."

"I know what you mean," the undersecretary said. "Sometimes I get the feeling that whoever's behind this has gotten caught up in the hysteria themselves . . . that the Horsemen are now using whoever was using them . . . a closed circle. But I've been tired lately. The war's making us all so tired. If only we could get it all over . . ."

"We'd all like to get it over with one way or the other," I said.

T minus 60 minutes . . . and counting . . .

I had orders to muster *Blackfish*'s crew for the live satellite relay of *The Four Horsemen's Fourth.* Superficially, it might seem strange to order the whole Polaris fleet to watch a television show, but the morale factor involved was quite significant.

Polaris subs are frustrating duty. Only top sailors are chosen and a good sailor craves action. Yet if we are ever called upon to act, our mission will have been a failure. We spend most of our time honing skills that must never be used. Deterrence is a sound strategy but a terrible drain on the men of the deterrent forces—a drain exacerbated in the past by the negative attitude of our countrymen toward our mission. Men who, in the service of their country, polish their skills to a razor edge and then must refrain from exercising them have a right to resent being treated as pariahs.

Therefore the positive change in the public attitude toward us that seems to be associated with the Four Horsemen has made them mascots of a kind to the Polaris fleet. In their strange way they seem to speak for us and to us.

I chose to watch the show in the missile control center, where a full crew must always be ready to launch the missiles on five-minute notice. I have always felt a sense of communion with the duty watch in the missile control center that I cannot share with the other men under my command. Here we are not captain and crew but mind and hand. Should the order come, the will to fire the missiles will be mine and the act will be theirs. At such a moment, it will be good not to feel alone.

All eyes were on the television set mounted above the main console as the show came on and . . .

The screen was filled with a whirling spiral pattern, metallic yellow on metallic blue. There was a droning sound that seemed part sitar and part electronic, and I had the feeling that the sound was somehow coming from inside my head and the spiral seemed etched directly on my retinas. It hurt mildly, yet nothing in the world could have made me turn away.

Then two voices, chanting against each other:

"Let it all come in. . . ."

"Let it all come out. . . ."

"In . . . out . . . in . . . out . . . in . . . out . . ."

My head seemed to be pulsing—in-*out,* in-*out,* in-*out*—and the spiral pattern began to pulse color changes with the words: yellow on blue (*in*) . . . green on red *(out)* . . . In-*out*-in-*out*-in-*out*. . . .

In the screen . . . *out* my head. . . . I seemed to be beating against some kind of invisible membrane between myself and the screen as if something were trying to embrace my mind and I were fighting it. . . . But why was I fighting it?

The pulsing, the chanting, got faster and faster till *in* could not be told from *out* and negative spiral afterimages formed in my eyes faster than they could adjust to the changes, piled up on each other faster and faster till it seemed my head would explode—

The chanting and the droning broke and there were the Four Horsemen, in their robes, playing on some stage against a backdrop of clear blue sky. And a single voice, soothing now: *"You are in. . . ."*

Then the view was directly above the Horsemen and I could see that they were on some kind of circular platform. The view moved slowly and smoothly up and away and I saw that the circular stage was atop a tall tower; around the tower and completely circling it was a huge crowd seated on desert sands that stretched away to an empty infinity.

"And we are in and they are in. . . ."

I was down among the crowd now; they seemed to melt and flow like plastic, pouring from the television screen to enfold me. . . . *"And we are all in here together. . . ."*

A strange and beautiful feeling . . . the music got faster and wilder, ecstatic . . . the hull of the *Blackfish* seemed unreal . . . the crowd was swaying to it around me . . . the distance between myself and the crowd seemed to dissolve . . . I was there . . . they were here. . . . We were transfixed. . . .

"Oh yeah, we are all in here together . . . together. . . ."

T minus 45 minutes . . . and counting . . .

Jeremy and I sat staring at the television screen, ignoring each other and everything around us. Even with the short watches and the short tours of duty, you can get to feeling pretty strange down here in a hole in the ground under tons of concrete; just you and the guy with the other key, with nothing to do but think dark thoughts and get on each other's nerves. We're all supposed to be as stable as men can be, or so they tell us, and they must be right because the world's still here. I mean, it wouldn't take much—just two guys on the same watch over the same three Minutemen flipping out at the same time, turning their keys in the dual lock, pressing the three buttons . . . Pow! World War III!

A bad thought, the kind we're not supposed to think or I'll start watching Jeremy and he'll start watching me and we'll get a paranoid feedback going. . . . But that can't happen; we're too stable, too responsible. As long as we remember that it's healthy to feel a little spooky down here, we'll be all right.

But the television set is a good idea. It keeps us in contact with the outside world, keeps it real. It'd be too easy to start thinking that the missile control center down here is the only real world and that nothing that happens up there really matters. . . . Bad thought!

The Four Horsemen . . . somehow these guys help you get it all out. I mean that feeling that it might be better to release all that tension, get it all over with. Watching the Four Horsemen, you're able to go with it without doing any harm, let it wash over you and then through you. I suppose they are crazy; they're all the human craziness in ourselves that we've got to keep very careful watch over down here. Letting it all come out watching the Horsemen makes it surer that none of it will come out down here. I guess that's why a lot of us have taken to wearing those "Do it" buttons off duty. The brass doesn't mind; they seem to understand that it's the kind of inside sick joke we need to keep us functioning.

Now that spiral thing they had started the show with—and the droning—came back on. Zap! I was right back in the screen again, as if the commercial hadn't happened.

"We are all in here together. . . ."

And then a close-up of the lead singer, looking straight at me, as close as Jeremy and somehow more real. A mean-looking guy with something behind his eyes that told me he knew where everything lousy and rotten was at.

A bass began to thrum behind him and some kind of electronic hum that set my teeth on edge. He began playing his guitar, mean and low-down. And singing in that kind of drop-dead tone of voice that starts brawls in bars:

"I stabbed my mother and I mugged my paw. . . ."

A riff of heavy guitar chords echoed the words mockingly as a huge swastika (red on black, black on red) pulsed like a naked vein on the screen—

The face of the Horsemen, leering—

"Nailed my sister to the toilet door. . . ."

Guitar behind the pulsing swastika—

"Drowned a puppy in a ce-ment machine. . . . Burned a kitten just to hear it scream. . . ."

On the screen, just a big fire burning in slow-motion, and the voice became a slow, shrill, agonized wail:

"Oh God, I've got this red-hot fire burning in the marrow of my brain. . . .

"Oh yes, I got this fire burning . . . in the stinking marrow of my brain. . . .

"Gotta get me a blowtorch . . . and set some naked flesh on flame. . . ."

The fire dissolved into the face of a screaming Asian woman, who ran through a burning village clawing at the napalm on her back.

"I got this message . . . boiling in the bubbles of my blood. . . . A man ain't nothing but a fire burning . . . in a dirty glob of mud. . . ." A film-clip of a Nuremburg rally: a revolving swastika of marching men waving torches—

Then the leader of the Horsemen superimposed over the twisted flaming cross:

"Don't you hate me, baby, can't you feel somethin' screaming in your mind?"

"Don't you hate me, baby, feel me drowning you in slime!"

Just the face of the Horsemen howling hate—

"Oh yes, I'm a monster, Mother. . . ."

A long view of the crowd around the platform, on their feet, waving arms, screaming soundlessly. Then a quick zoom in and a kaleidoscope of faces, eyes feverish, mouths open and howling—

"Just call me—"

The face of the Horseman superimposed over the crazed faces of the crowd—

"Mankind!"

I looked at Jeremy. He was toying with the key on the chain around his neck. He was sweating. I suddenly realized that I was sweating too and that my own key was throbbing in my hand alive. . . .

T minus 13 minutes . . . and counting . . .

A funny feeling, the captain watching the Four Horsemen here in the *Blackfish*'s missile control center with us. Sitting in front of my console watching the television set with the captain kind of breathing down my neck. . . . I got the feeling he knew what was going through me and I couldn't know what was going through him . . . and it gave the fire inside me a kind of greasy feel I didn't like. . . .

Then the commercial was over and that spiral-thing came on again and *whoosh*! It sucked me right back into the television set and I stopped worrying about the captain or anything like that. . . .

Just the spiral going yellow-blue, red-green, and then starting to whirl and whirl, faster and faster, changing colors and whirling, whirling, whirling. . . . And the sound of a kind of Coney Island carousel tinkling behind it, faster and faster and faster, whirling and whirling and whirling, flashing red-green, yellow-blue, and whirling, whirling, whirling. . . .

And this big hum filling my body and whirling, whirling, whirling. . . . My muscles relaxing, going limp, whirling, whirling, whirling, all limp, whirling, whirling, whirling, oh so nice, just whirling, whirling. . . .

And in the center of the flashing spiraling colors, a bright dot of colorless light, right at the center, not moving, not changing, while the whole world went whirling and whirling in colors around it, and the humming was coming from the spinning colors and the dot was humming its song to me. . . .

The dot was a light way down at the end of a long, whirling, whirling tunnel. The humming started to get a little louder. The bright dot started to get a little bigger. I was drifting down the tunnel toward it, whirling, whirling, whirling. . . .

T minus 11 minutes . . . and counting . . .

Whirling, whirling, whirling down a long, long tunnel of pulsing colors, whirling, whirling, toward the circle of light way down at the end of the tunnel. . . . How nice it would be to finally get there and soak up the beautiful hum filling my body and then I could forget that I was down here in this hole in the ground with a hard brass key in my hand, just Duke and me, down here in a cave under the ground that was a spiral of flashing colors, whirling, whirling toward the friendly light at the end of the tunnel, whirling, whirling. . . .

T minus 10 minutes . . . and counting . . .

The circle of light at the end of the whirling tunnel was getting bigger and bigger and the humming was getting louder and louder and I was feeling better and better and the *Blackfish's* missile control center was getting dimmer and dimmer as the awful weight of command got lighter and lighter, whirling, whirling, and I felt so good I wanted to cry, whirling, whirling. . . .

T minus 9 minutes . . . and counting . . .

Whirling, whirling . . . I was whirling, Jeremy was whirling, the hole in the ground was whirling, and the circle of light at the end of the tunnel whirled closer and closer and—I was through! A place filled with yellow light. Pale metallic yellow light. Then pale metallic blue. Yellow. Blue. Yellow. Blue. Yellow-blue-yellow-blue-yellow-blue-yellow . . .

Pure light pulsing and pure sound droning. And just the *feeling* of letters I couldn't read between the pulses—not-yellow and not-blue—too quick and too faint to be visible, but important, very important. . . .

And then a voice that seemed to be singing from inside my head, almost as if it were my own:

"Oh, oh, oh . . . don't I really wanna know. . . . Oh, oh, oh don't I really wanna know. . . ."

The world pulsing, flashing around those words I couldn't read, couldn't quite read, had to read, could *almost* read. . . .

"Oh, oh, oh . . . great God I really wanna know. . . ."

Strange amorphous shapes clouding the blue-yellow-blue flickering universe, hiding the words I had to read. . . . Damnit, why wouldn't they get out of the way so I could find out what I had to know!

"Tell me tell me tell me tell me tell me . . . Gotta know gotta know gotta know gotta know . . ."

T minus 7 minutes . .. and counting . . .

Couldn't read the words! Why wouldn't the captain let me read the words?

And that voice inside me: *"Gotta know . . . gotta know . . . gotta know why it hurts me so. . . ."* Why wouldn't it shut up and let me read the words? Why wouldn't the words hold still? Or just slow down a little? If they'd slow down a little, I could read them and then I'd know what I had to do. . . .

T minus 6 minutes . . . and counting . . .

I felt the sweaty key in the palm of my hand. I saw Duke stroking his own key. Had to know! Now—through the pulsing blue-yellow-blue light and the unreadable words that were building up an awful pressure in the back of my brain—I could see the Four Horsemen. They were on their knees, crying, looking up at something and begging: *"Tell me tell me tell me tell me . . ."*

Then soft billows of rich red-and-orange fire filled the world and a huge voice was trying to speak. But it couldn't form the words. It stuttered and moaned—

The yellow-blue-yellow flashing around the words I couldn't read—the same words, I suddenly sensed, that the voice of the fire was trying so hard to form—and the Four Horsemen on their knees begging: *"Tell me tell me tell me . . ."*

The friendly warm fire trying so hard to speak—

"Tell me tell me tell me tell me . . ."

T minus 4 minutes . . . and counting . . .

What were the words? What was the order? I could sense my men silently imploring me to tell them. After all, I was their captain, it was my duty to tell them. It was my duty to find out!

"Tell me tell me tell me . . ." the robed figures on their knees implored through the flickering pulse in my brain and I could almost make out the words . . . almost. . . .

"Tell me tell me tell me . . ." I whispered to the warm orange fire that was trying so hard but couldn't quite form the words. The men were whispering it too: "Tell me tell me . . ."

T minus 3 minutes . . . and counting . . .

The question burning blue and yellow in my brain. WHAT WAS THE FIRE TRYING TO TELL ME? WHAT WERE THE WORDS I COULDN'T READ?

Had to unlock the words! Had to find the key!

A key . . . *The* key! THE KEY! And there was the lock that imprisoned the words, right in front of me! Put the key in the lock . . . I looked at Jeremy. Wasn't there some reason, long ago and far away, why Jeremy might try to stop me from putting the key in the lock?

But Jeremy didn't move as I fitted the key into the lock. . . .

T minus 2 minutes . . . and counting . . .

Why wouldn't the captain tell me what the order was? The fire knew, but it couldn't tell. My head ached from the pulsing, but I couldn't read the words.

"Tell me tell me tell me . . ." I begged.

Then I realized that the captain was asking too.

T minus 90 seconds . . . and counting . . .

"Tell me tell me tell me . . ." the Horsemen begged. And the words I couldn't read were a fire in my brain.

Duke's key was in the lock in front of us. From very far away, he said: "We have to do it together."

Of course . . . our keys . . . our keys would unlock the words!

I put my key into the lock. One, two, three, we turned our keys together. A lid on the console popped open. Under the lid were three red buttons. Three signs on the console lit up in red letters: ARMED.

T minus 60 seconds . . . and counting . . .

The men were waiting for me to give some order. I didn't know what the order was. A magnificent orange fire was trying to tell me but it couldn't get the words out. . . . Robed figures were praying to the fire. . . .

Then, through the yellow-blue flicker that hid the words I had to read, I saw a vast crowd encircling a tower. The crowd was on its feet begging silently—

The tower in the center of the crowd became the orange fire that was trying to tell me what the words were—

Became a great mushroom of billowing smoke and blinding orange-red glare. . . .

T minus 30 seconds . . . and counting . . .

The huge pillar of fire was trying to tell Jeremy and me what the words were, what we had to do. The crowd was screaming at the cloud of flame. The yellow-blue flicker was getting faster and faster behind the mushroom cloud. I could almost read the words! I could see that there were two of them!

T minus 20 seconds . . . and counting . . .

Why didn't the captain tell us? I could almost see the words!

Then I heard the crowd around the beautiful mushroom cloud shouting: "DO IT! DO IT! DO IT! DO IT! DO IT!"

T minus 10 seconds . . . and counting. ..

"DO IT! DO IT! DO IT! DO IT! DO IT! DO IT! DO IT!"

What did they want me to do? Did Duke know?

9

The men were waiting! What was the order? They hunched over the firing controls, waiting. . . . The firing controls . . . ?"

"DO IT! DO IT! DO IT! DO IT! DO IT!"

8

"DO IT! DO IT! DO IT! DO IT! DO IT!": the crowd screaming.

"Jeremy!" I shouted. "I can read the words!"

7

My hands hovered over my bank of firing buttons. . . .

"DO IT! DO IT! DO IT! DO IT!" the words said.

Didn't the captain understand?

6

"What do they want us to do, Jeremy?"

5

Why didn't the mushroom cloud give the order? My men were waiting! A good sailor craves action.

Then a great voice spoke from the pillar of fire: "DO IT . . . DO IT . . . DO IT . . . "

4

"There's only one thing we can do down here, Duke."

3

"The order, men! Action! Fire!"

2

Yes, yes, yes! Jeremy—

1

I reached for my bank of firing buttons. All along the console, the men reached for their buttons. But I was too fast for them! I would be first!

0

THE BIG FLASH

THE LAST MAN

Kindness

Lester del Ray

The wind eddied idly around the corner and past the secluded park bench. It caught fitfully at the paper on the ground, turning the pages, then picked up a section and blew away with it, leaving gaudy-colored comics uppermost. Danny moved forward into the sunlight, his eyes dropping to the children's page exposed.

But it was no use; he made no effort to pick up the paper. In a world where even the children's comics needed explaining, there could be nothing of interest to the last living homo sapiens—the last normal man in the world. His foot kicked the paper away, under the bench where it would no longer remind him of his deficiencies. There had been a time when he had tried to reason slowly over the omitted steps of logic and find the points behind such things, sometimes successfully, more often not; but now he left it to the quick, intuitive thinking of those about him. Nothing fell flatter than a joke that had to be reasoned out slowly.

Homo sapiens! The type of man who had come out of the caves and built a world of atomic power, electronics, and other old-time wonders—thinking man, as it translated from the Latin. In the dim past, when his ancestors had owned the world, they had made a joke of it, shortening it to *homo sap*, and laughing, because there had been no other species to rival them. Now it was no longer a joke.

Normal man had been only a "sap" to *homo intelligens*—intelligent man—who was now the master of the world. Danny was only a leftover, the last normal man in the world of supermen, hating the fact that he had been born, and that his mother had died at his birth to leave him only loneliness as his heritage.

He drew back farther on the bench as the steps of a young couple reached his ears, pulling his hat down to avoid recognition. But they went by, preoccupied with their own affairs, leaving only a scattered bit of conversation in his ears. He turned it over in his mind, trying senselessly to decode it.

Impossible! Even the casual talk contained too many steps of logic left out. *Homo intelligens* had a new way of thinking, above reason, where all the long painful steps of logic could be jumped instantly. They could arrive at a correct picture of the whole from scattered bits of information. Just as man had once invented logic to replace the trial-and-error thinking that most animals have, so homo intelligens had learned to use intuition. They could look at the first page of an old-time book and immediately know the whole of it, since the little tricks of the author would connect in their intuitive minds and at once build up all the missing links. They didn't even have to try—they just looked, and knew. It was like Newton looking at an apple falling and immediately seeing why the planets circled the sun, and realizing the laws of gravitation; but these new men did it all the time, not just at those rare intervals as it had worked for *homo sapiens* once.

Man was gone, except for Danny, and he too had to leave this world of supermen. Somehow, soon, those escape plans must be completed, before the last of his little courage was gone! He stirred restlessly, and the little coins in his pocket set up a faint jingling sound. More charity, or occupational therapy! For six hours a day, five days a week, he worked in a little office, painfully doing routine work that could probably have been done better by machinery. Oh, they assured him that his manual skill was as great as theirs and that it was needed, but he could never be sure. In their unfailing kindness, they had probably decided it was better for him to live as normally as they could let him, and then had created the job to fit what he could do.

Other footsteps came down the little path, but he did not look up, until they stopped. "Hi, Danny! You weren't at the library, and Miss Larsen said, pay day, weather, and all, I'd find you here. How's everything?"

Outwardly, Jack Thorpe's body might have been the twin of Danny's own well-muscled one, and the smiling face above it bore no distinguishing characteristics. The mutation that changed man to superman had been within, a quicker, more complex relation of brain cell to brain cell that had no outward signs. Danny nodded at Jack, drawing over reluctantly to make room on the bench for this man who had been his playmate when they were both too young for the difference to matter much.

He did not ask the reason behind the librarian's knowledge of his whereabouts; so far as he knew, there was no particular pattern to his coming here, but to the others there must be one. He found he could even smile at their ability to foretell his plans.

"Hi, Jack! Fine. I thought you were on Mars."

Thorpe frowned, as if an effort were needed to remember that the boy beside him was different, and his words bore the careful phrasing of all those who spoke to Danny. "I finished that, for the time being; I'm supposed to report to Venus next. They're having trouble getting an even balance of boys and girls there, you know. Thought you might want to come along. You've never been Outside, and you were always bugs about those old space stories, I remember."

"I still am, Jack. But—" He knew what it meant, of course. Those who looked after him behind the scenes had detected his growing discontent, and were hoping to distract him with this chance to see the places his father had conquered in the heyday of his race. But he had no wish to see them as they now were, filled with the busy work of the new men; it was better to imagine them as they had once been, rather than see reality. And the ship was *here;* there could be no chance for escape from those other worlds.

Jack nodded quickly, with the almost telepathic understanding of his race. "Of course. Suit yourself, fellow. Going up to the Heights? Miss Larsen says she has something for you."

"Not yet, Jack. I thought I might look at—drop by the old museum."

"Oh." Thorpe got up slowly, brushing his suit with idle fingers. "Danny!"

"Uh?"

"I probably know you better than anyone else, fellow, so—" He hesitated, shrugged, and went on. "Don't mind if I jump to conclusions; I won't talk out of turn. But best of luck—and good-bye, Danny."

He was gone, almost instantly, leaving Danny's heart stuck in his throat. A few words, a facial expression, probably some childhood memories, and Danny might as well have revealed his most cherished secret hope in shouted words! How many others knew of his interest in the old ship in the museum and his carefully made plot to escape this kindly, charity-filled torture world?

He crushed a cigarette under his heel, trying to forget the thought. Jack had played with him as a child, and the others hadn't. He'd have to base his hopes on that and be even more careful never to think of the idea around others. In the meantime he'd stay away from the ship! Perhaps in that way Thorpe's subtle warning might work in his favor—provided the man had meant his promise of silence.

Danny forced his doubts away, grimly conscious that he dared not lose hope in this last desperate scheme for independence and self-respect; the other way offered only despair and listless hopelessness, the same empty death from an acute inferiority complex that had claimed the diminishing numbers of his own kind and left him as the last, lonely specimen. Somehow, he'd succeed, and in the meantime, he would go to the library and leave the museum strictly alone.

There was a throng of people leaving the library as Danny came up the escalator, but either they did not recognize him with his hat pulled low or sensed his desire for anonymity and pretended not to know him. He slipped into one of the less used hallways and made his way toward the historic documents section, where Miss Larsen was putting away the reading tapes and preparing to leave.

But she tossed them aside quickly as he came in and smiled up at him, the rich, warm smile of her people. "Hello, Danny! Did your friend find you all right?"

"Mm-hmm. He said you had something for me."

"I have." There was pleasure in her face as she turned back toward the desk behind her to come up with a small wrapped parcel. For the thousandth time, he caught himself wishing she were of his race and quenching the feeling as he realized what her attitude must really be. To her, the small talk from his race's past was a subject of historic interest, no more. And he was just a dull-witted hangover from ancient days. "Guess what?"

But in spite of himself, his face lighted up, both at the game and the package. "The magazines! The lost issues of *Space Trails*?" There had been only the first installment of a story extant, and yet that single part had set his pulses throbbing as few of the other ancient stories of his ancestors' conquest of space had done. Now, with the missing sections, life would be filled with zest for a few more hours as he followed the fictional exploits of a conqueror who had known no fear of keener minds.

"Not quite, Danny, but almost. We couldn't locate even a trace of them, but I gave the first installment to Bryant Kenning last week, and he finished it for you." Her voice was apologetic. "Of course the words won't be quite identical, but Kenning swears that the story is undoubtedly exactly the same in structure as it would have been, and the style is duplicated almost perfectly!"

Like that! Kenning had taken the first pages of a novel that had meant weeks and months of thought to some ancient writer and had found in them the whole plot, clearly revealed, instantly his! A night's labor had been needed to duplicate it, probably—a disagreeable and boring piece of work, but not a difficult one! Danny did not question the accuracy of the duplication, since Kenning was their greatest historical novelist. But the pleasure went out of the game.

He took the package, noting that some illustrator had even copied the old artist's style, and that it was set up to match the original format. "Thank you, Miss Larsen. I'm sorry to put all of you to so much trouble. And it was nice of Mr. Kenning!"

Her face had fallen with his, but she pretended not to notice. "He wanted to do it—volunteered when he heard we were searching for the missing copies. And if there are any others with pieces missing, Danny, he wants you to let him know. You two are about the only ones who use this division now; why don't you drop by and see him? If you'd like to go tonight—"

"Thanks. But I'll read this tonight, instead. Tell him I'm very grateful, though, will you?" But he paused, wondering again whether he dared ask for tapes on the history of the asteroids; no, there would be too much risk of her guessing, either now or later. He dared not trust any of them with a hint of his plan.

Miss Larsen smiled again, half winking at him. "Okay, Danny, I'll tell him. Night!"

Outside, with the cool of evening beginning to fall, Danny found his way into the untraveled quarters and let his feet guide him. Once, as a group came toward him, he crossed the street without thinking and went on. The package under his arm grew heavy and he shifted it, torn between a desire to find what had happened to the hero and a disgust at his own sapiens brain for not knowing. Probably, in the long run, he'd end up going home and reading it, but for the moment he was content to let his feet carry him along idly, holding most of his thoughts in abeyance.

Another small park was in his path, and he crossed it slowly, the babble of small children's voices only partly heard until he came up to them, two boys and a girl. The supervisor, who should have had them back at the Center, was a dim shape in the far shadows, with another, dimmer shape beside her, leaving the five-year-olds happily engaged in the ancient pastime of getting dirty and impressing each other.

Danny stopped, a slow smile creeping over his lips. At that age, their intuitive ability was just beginning to develop, and their little games and pretenses made sense, acting on him like a tonic. Vaguely, he remembered his own friends of that age beginning uncertainly to acquire the trick of seeming to know everything, and his worries at being left behind. For a time, the occasional flashes of intuition that had always blessed even homo sapiens gave him hope, but eventually the supervisor had been forced to tell him that he was different, and why. Now he thrust those painful memories aside and slipped quietly forward into the game.

They accepted him with the easy nonchalance of children who have no repressions, feverishly trying to build their sand castles higher than his; but in that, his experience was greater than theirs, and his judgment of the damp stuff was surer. A perverse glow of accomplishment grew inside him as he added still another story to the towering structure and built a bridge, propped up with sticks and leaves, leading to it.

Then the lights came on, illuminating the sandbox and those inside it and dispelling the shadows of dusk. The smaller of the two boys glanced up, really seeing him for the first time. "Oh, you're Danny Black, ain't you? I seen your pi'ture. Judy, Bobby, look! It's that man—"

But their voices faded out as he ran off through the park and into the deserted byways again, clutching the package to him. Fool! To delight in beating children at a useless game, or to be surprised that they should know him! He slowed to a walk, twitching his lips at the thought that by now the supervisor would be reprimanding them for their thoughtlessness. And still his feet went on, unguided.

It was inevitable, of course, that they should lead him to the museum, where all his secret hopes centered, but he was surprised to look up and see it before him. And then he was glad. Surely they could read nothing into his visit, unpremeditated, just before the place closed. He caught his breath, forced his face into lines of mere casual interest, and went inside, down the long corridors, and to the hall of the ship.

She rested there, pointed slightly skyward, sleek and immense even in a room designed to appear like the distant reaches of space. For six hundred feet, gleaming metal formed a smooth frictionless surface that slid gracefully from the blunt bow back toward the narrow stern with its blackened ion jets.

This, Danny knew, was the last and greatest of the space liners his people had built at the height of their glory. And even before her, the mutation that made the new race of men had been caused by the radiations of deep space, and the results were spreading. For a time, as the log book indicated this ship had sailed out to Mars, to Venus, and to the other points of man's empire, while the tension slowly mounted at home. There had never been another wholly sapient-designed ship, for the new race was spreading, making its greater intelligence felt, with the invert-matter rocket replacing this older, less efficient ion rocket that the ship carried. Eventually, unable to compete with the new models, she had been retired from service and junked, while the war between the new and old race passed by her and buried her under tons of rubble, leaving no memory of her existence.

And now, carefully excavated from the old ruins of the drydock where she had lain so long, she had been enthroned in state for the last year, here in the Museum of Sapien History, while all Danny's hopes and prayers had centered around her. There was still a feeling of awe in him as he started slowly across the carpeted floor toward the open lock and the lighted interior.

"Danny!" The sudden word interrupted him, bringing him about with a guilty start, but it was only Professor Kirk, and he relaxed again. The old archaeologist came toward him, his smile barely visible in the half-light of the immense dome. "I'd about given you up, boy, and started out. But I happened to look back and see you. Thought you might be interested in some information I just came onto today."

"Information about the ship?"

"What else? Here, come on inside her and into the lounge—I have a few privileges here, and we might as well be comfortable. You know, as I grow older, I find myself appreciating your ancestors' ideas of comfort, Danny. Sort of a pity our own culture is too new for much luxuriousness yet." Of all the new race, Kirk seemed the most completely at ease before Danny, partly because of his age, and partly because they had shared the same enthusiasm for the great ship when it had first arrived.

Now he settled back into one of the old divans, using his immunity to ordinary rules to light a cigarette and pass one to the younger man. "You know all the supplies and things in the ship have puzzled us both, and we couldn't find any record of them? The log ends when they put the old ship, up for junking, you remember; and we couldn't figure out why all this had been restored and restocked, ready for some long voyage to somewhere. Well, it came to light in some further excavations they've completed. Danny, your people did that, during the war; or really, after they'd lost the war to us!"

Danny's back straightened. The war was a period of history he'd avoided thinking about, though he knew the outlines of it. With homo intelligens increasing and pressing the older race aside by the laws of survival, his people had made a final desperate bid for supremacy. And while the new race had not wanted the war, they had been forced finally to fight back with as little mercy as had been shown them, and since they had the tremendous advantage of the new intuitive thinking, there had been only thousands left of the original billions of the old race when its brief course was finished. It had been inevitable probably, from the first mutation, but it was not something Danny cared to think of. Now he nodded, and let the other continue.

"Your ancestors, Danny, were beaten then, but they weren't completely crushed, and they put about the last bit of energy they had into rebuilding this ship—the only navigable one left them—and restocking it. They were going to go out somewhere, they didn't know quite where, even to another solar system, and take some of the old race for a new start, away from us. It was their last bid for survival, and it failed when my people learned of it and blasted the docks down over the ship, but it was a glorious failure, boy! I thought you'd want to know."

Danny's thoughts focused slowly. "You mean everything on the ship is of my people? But surely the provisions wouldn't have remained usable after all this time?"

"They did, though; the tests we made proved that conclusively. Your people knew how to preserve things as well as we do, and they expected to be drifting in the ship for half a century, maybe. They'll be usable a thousand years from now." He chucked his cigarette across the room and chuckled in pleased surprise when it fell accurately into a snuffer. "I stuck around, really, to tell you, and I've kept the papers over at the school for you to see. Why not come over with me now?"

"Not tonight, sir. I'd rather stay here a little longer." Professor Kirk nodded, pulling himself up reluctantly. "As you wish . . . I know how you feel, and I'm sorry about their moving the ship, too. We'll miss her, Danny!"

"Moving the ship?"

"Hadn't you heard? I thought that's why you came around at this hour. They want her over in London, and they're bringing one of the old Lunar ships here to replace her. Too bad!" He touched the walls thoughtfully, drawing his hands down and across the rich nap of the seat. "Well, don't stay too long, and turn her lights out before you leave. Place'll be closed in half an hour. Night, Danny."

"Night, Professor." Danny sat frozen on the soft seat, listening to the slow tread of the old man and the beating of his own heart. They were moving the ship, ripping his plans to shreds, leaving him stranded in this world of a new race, where even the children were sorry for him.

It had meant so much, even to feel that somehow he would escape, some day! Impatiently, he snapped off the lights, feeling closer to the ship in the privacy of the dark, where no watchman could see his emotion. For a year now he had built his life around the idea of taking this ship out and away, to leave the new race far behind. Long, carefully casual months of work had been spent in learning her structure, finding all her stores, assuring himself bit by bit from a hundred old books that he could operate her.

She had been almost designed for the job, built to be operated by one man, even a cripple, in an emergency, and nearly everything was automatic. Only the problem of a destination had remained, since the planets were all swarming with the others, but the ship's log had suggested the answer even to that.

Once there had been rich men among his people who sought novelty and seclusion, and he found them among the larger asteroids. Money and science had built them artificial gravities and given them atmospheres, powered by atomic energy plants that should last forever. Now the rich men were undoubtedly dead, and the new race had abandoned such useless things. Surely, somewhere among the asteroids, there should have been a haven for him, made safe by the very numbers of the little worlds that could discourage almost any search.

Danny heard a guard go by, and slowly got to his feet, to go out again into a world that would no longer hold even that hope. It had been a lovely plan to dream on, a necessary dream. Then the sound of the great doors came to his ears, closing! The professor had forgotten to tell them of his presence! And—!

All right, so he didn't know the history of all those little worlds; perhaps he would have to hunt through them, one by one, to find a suitable home. Did it matter? In every other way, he could never be more ready. For a moment only, he hesitated; then his hands fumbled with the great lock's control switch, and it swung shut quietly in the dark, shutting the sound of his running feet from outside ears.

The lights came on silently as he found the navigation chair and sank into it. Little lights that spelled out the readiness of the ship. SHIP SEALED . . . AIR OKAY . . . POWER, AUTOMATIC . . . ENGINE, AUTOMATIC. . . . Half a hundred little lights and dials that told the story of a ship waiting for his hand. He moved the course plotter slowly along the tiny atmospheric map until it reached the top of the stratosphere; the big star map moved slowly out, with the pointer in his fingers tracing an irregular, jagged line that would lead him somewhere toward the asteroids, well away from the present position of Mars, and yet could offer no clue. Later, he could set the analyzers to finding the present location of some chosen asteroid and determine his course more accurately, but all that mattered now was to get away, beyond all tracing, before his loss could be reported.

Seconds later, his fingers pressed down savagely on the main power switch, and there was a lurch of starting, followed by another slight one as the walls of the museum crumpled before the savage force of the great ion rockets. On the map, a tiny spot of light appeared, marking the ship's changing position. The world was behind him now, and there was no one to look at his efforts in kindly pity or remind him of his weakness. Only blind fate was against him, and his ancestors had met and conquered that long before.

A bell rang, indicating the end of the atmosphere, and the big automatic pilot began clucking contentedly, emitting a louder cluck now and then as it found the irregularities in the unorthodox course he had charted and swung the ship to follow. Danny watched it, satisfied that it was working. His ancestors may have been capable of reason only, but they had built machines that were almost intuitive, as the ship about him testified. His head was higher as he turned back to the kitchen, and there was a bit of a swagger to his walk.

The food was still good. He wolfed it down, remembering that supper had been forgotten, and leafing slowly through the big log book, which recorded the long voyages made by the ship, searching through it for each casual reference to the asteroids, Ceres, Palas, Vesta, some of the ones referred to by nicknames or, numbers? Which ones?

But he had decided by the time he stood once again in the navigation room, watching the aloof immensity of space; that out here it was relieved only by the tiny hot pinpoints that must be stars, colored, small and intense as no stars could be through an atmosphere. It would be one of the numbered planetoids, referred to also as "The Dane's" in the log. The word was meaningless, but it seemed to have been one of the newer and more completely terranized, though not the very newest where any search would surely start.

He set the automatic analyzer to running from the key number in the manual and watched it for a time, but it ground on slowly, tracing through all the years that had passed. For a time, he fiddled with the radio, before he remembered that it operated on a wave form no longer used. It was just as well; his severance from the new race would be all the more final.

Still the analyzer ground on. Space lost its novelty, and the operation of the pilot ceased to interest him. He wandered back through the ship toward the lounge, to spy the parcel where he had dropped and forgotten it. There was nothing else to do.

And once begun, he forgot his doubts at the fact that it was Kenning's story, not the original; there was the same sweep to the tale, the same warm and human characters, the same drive of a race that had felt the mastership of destiny so long ago. Small wonder the readers of that time had named it the greatest epic of space to be written!

Once he stopped, as the analyzer reached its conclusions and bonged softly, to set the controls on the automatic for the little world that might be his home, with luck. And then the ship moved on, no longer veering, but making the slightly curved path its selectors found most suitable, while Danny read further, huddled over the story in the navigator's chair, feeling a new and greater kinship with the characters of the story. He was no longer a poor Earthbound charity case, but a man and an adventurer with them!

His nerves were tingling when the tale came to its end, and he let it drop onto the floor from tired fingers. Under his hand, a light had sprung up, but he was oblivious to it, until a crashing gong sounded over him, jerking him from the chair. There had been such a gong described in the story. . . .

And the meaning was the same. His eyes made out the red letters that glared accusingly from the control panel: RADIATION AT TEN O'CLOCK HORIZ—SHIP INDICATED!

Danny's fingers were on the master switch and cutting off all life except pseudogravity from the ship as the thought penetrated. The other ship was not hard to find from the observation window; the great streak of an invert-matter rocket glowed hotly out there, pointed apparently back to Earth—probably the *Callisto*!

For a second he was sure they had spotted him, but the flicker must have been only a minor correction to adjust for the trail continued. He had no knowledge of the new ships and whether they carried warning signals or not, but apparently they must have dispensed with such things. The streak vanished into the distance, and the letters on the panel that had marked it changing position went dead. Danny waited until the fullest amplification showed no response before throwing power on again. The small glow of the ion rocket would be invisible at the distance, surely.

Nothing further seemed to occur; there was a contented purr from the pilot and the faint sleepy hum of raw power from the rear, but no bells or sudden sounds. Slowly, his head fell forward over the navigator's table, and his heavy breathing mixed with the low sounds of the room. The ship went on about its business as it had been designed to do. Its course was charted, even to the old landing sweep, and it needed no further attention.

That was proved when the slow ringing of a bell woke Danny, while the board blinked in time to it: DESTINATION! DESTINATION! DESTINATION REACHED!

He shut off everything, rubbing the sleep from his eyes, and looked out. Above, there was weak but warm sunlight streaming down from a bluish sky that held a few small clouds suspended close to the ground.

Beyond the ship, where it lay on a neglected sandy landing field, was the green of grass and the wild profusion of a forest. The horizon dropped off sharply, reminding him that it was only a tiny world, but otherwise it might have been Earth. He spotted an unkempt hangar ahead and applied weak power to the underjets, testing until they moved the ship slowly forward and inside, out of the view of any above.

Then he was at the lock, fumbling with the switch. As it opened, he could smell the clean fragrance of growing things, and there was the sound of birds nearby. A rabbit hopped leisurely out from underfoot as he stumbled eagerly out to the sunlight, and weeds and underbrush had already spread to cover the buildings about him. For a moment, he sighed; it had been too easy, this discovery of a heaven on the first wild try.

But the sight of the buildings drove back the doubt. Once, surrounded by a pretentious formal garden, this had been a great stone mansion, now it was falling into ruins. Beside it and farther from him, a smaller house had been built, seemingly from the wreckage. That was still whole, though ivy had grown over it and half covered the door that came open at the touch of his fingers.

There was still a faint glow to the heaters that drew power from the great atomic plant that gave this little world a perpetual semblance of Earthliness, but a coating of dust was everywhere. The furnishings, though, were in good condition. He scanned them, recognizing some as similar to the pieces in the museum, and the products of his race. One by one he studied them—his fortune, and now his home!

On the table, a book was dropped casually, and there was a sheet of paper propped against it, with what looked like a girl's rough handwriting on it. Curiosity carried him closer until he could make it out through the dust that clung even after he shook it.

Dad:

Charley Summers found a wrecked ship of those things, and came for me. We'll be living high on 13. Come on over, if your jets will make it, and meet your son-in-law.

There was no date, nothing to indicate whether "Dad" had returned, or what had happened to them. But Danny dropped it reverently back on the table, looking out across the landing strip as if to see a worn old ship crawl in through the brief twilight that was falling over the tiny world. "Those things" could only be the new race, after the war; and that meant that here was the final outpost of his people. The note might be ten years or half a dozen centuries old—but his people had been here, fighting on and managing to live, after Earth had been lost to them. If they could, so could he!

And unlikely though it seemed, there might possibly be more of them out there somewhere. Perhaps the race was still surviving in spite of time and trouble and even homo intelligens.

Danny's eyes were moist as he stepped back from the door and the darkness outside to begin cleaning his new home. If any were there, he'd find them. And if not—

Well, he was still a member of a great and daring race that could never know defeat so long as a single man might live. He would never forget that.

Back on Earth, Bryant Kenning nodded slowly to the small group as he put the communicator back, and his eyes were a bit sad in spite of the smile that lighted his face. "The director's scout is back, and he did choose 'The Dane's.' Poor kid. I'd begun to think we waited too long, and that he never would make it. Another six months—and he'd have died like a flower out of the sun! Yet I was sure it would work when Miss Larsen showed me that story, with its mythical planetoid-paradises. A rather clever story, if you like pseudohistory. I hope the one I prepared was its equal."

"For historical inaccuracy, fully its equal." But the amusement in old Professor Kirk's voice did not reach his lips.

"Well, he swallowed our lies and ran off with the ship we built him. I hope he's happy, for a while at least."

Miss Larsen folded her things together and prepared to leave. "Poor kid! He was sweet, in a pathetic sort of way. I wish that girl we were working on had turned out better; maybe this wouldn't have been necessary then. See me home, Jack?"

The two older men watched Larsen and Thorpe leave, and silence and tobacco smoke filled the room. Finally, Kenning shrugged and turned to face the professor.

"By now he's found the note. I wonder if it was a good idea, after all. When I first came across it in that old story, I was thinking of Jack's preliminary report on Number 67, but now I don't know; she's an unknown quantity, at best. Anyhow, I meant it for kindness."

"Kindness! Kindness to repay with a few million credits and a few thousands of hours of work—plus a lie here and there—for all that we owe the boy's race!" The professor's voice was tired as he dumped the contents of his pipe into a snuffer and strode over slowly toward the great window that looked out on the night sky. "I wonder sometimes, Bryant, what kindness Neanderthaler found when the last one came to die. Or whether the race that will follow us when the darkness falls on us will have something better than such kindness."

The novelist shook his head doubtfully, and there was silence again as they looked out across the world and toward the stars.

The Underdweller

William F. Nolan

In the waiting, windless dark, Lewis Stillman pressed into the building-front shadows along Wilshire Boulevard. Breathing softly, the automatic poised, ready in his hand, he advanced with animal stealth toward Western Avenue, gliding over the night-cool concrete past ravaged clothing shops, drug- and ten-cent stores, their windows shattered, their doors ajar and swinging. The city of Los Angeles, painted in cold moonlight, was an immense graveyard; the tall, white, tombstone buildings thrust up from the silent pavement, shadow-carved and lonely. Overturned metal corpses of trucks, buses, and automobiles littered the streets.

He paused under the wide marquee of the Fox Wiltern. Above his head, rows of splintered display bulbs gaped—sharp glass teeth in wooden jaws. Lewis Stillman felt as though they might drop at any moment to pierce his body.

Four more blocks to cover. His destination: a small corner delicatessen four blocks south of Wilshire, on Western. Tonight he intended on bypassing the larger stores such as Safeway or Thriftimart, with their available supplies of exotic foods; a smaller grocery was far more likely to have what he needed. He was finding it more and more difficult to locate basic foodstuff. In the big supermarkets, only the more exotic and highly spiced canned and bottled goods remained—and he was sick of caviar and oysters!

Crossing Western, he had almost reached the far curb when he saw some of *them.* He dropped immediately to his knees behind the rusting bulk of an Oldsmobile. The rear door on his side was open, and he cautiously eased himself into the back seat of the deserted car. Releasing the safety catch on the automatic, he peered through the cracked window at six or seven of them, as they moved toward him along the street. God! Had he been seen? He couldn't be sure. Perhaps they were aware of his position! He should have remained on the open street where he'd have a running chance. Perhaps, if his aim were true, he could kill most of them; but even with its silencer the gun might be heard and more of them would come. He dared not fire until he was certain they had discovered him.

They came closer, their small dark bodies crowding the walk, six of them, chattering, leaping, cruel mouths open, eyes glittering under the moon. Closer. Their shrill pipings increased, rose in volume. Closer. Now he could make out their sharp teeth and matted hair. Only a few feet from the car . . . His hand was moist on the handle of the automatic; his heart thundered against his chest. Seconds away . . .

Now!

Lewis Stillman fell heavily back against the dusty seat cushion, the gun loose in his trembling hand. They had passed by; they had missed him. Their thin pipings diminished, grew faint with distance.

The tomb silence of late night settled around him.

The delicatessen proved a real windfall. The shelves were relatively untouched and he had a wide choice of tinned goods. He found an empty cardboard box and hastily began to transfer the cans from the shelf nearest him.

A noise from behind—a padding, scraping sound.

Lewis Stillman whirled about, the automatic ready.

A huge mongrel dog faced him, growling deep in its throat, four legs braced for assault. The blunt ears were laid flat along the short-haired skull and a thin trickle of saliva seeped from the killing jaws. The beast's powerful chest-muscles were bunched for the spring when Stillman acted.

His gun, he knew, was useless; the shots would be heard. Therefore, with the full strength of his left arm he hurled a heavy can at the dog's head.

The stunned animal staggered under the blow, legs buckling. Hurriedly, Stillman gathered his supplies and made his way back to the street.

How much longer can my luck hold? Lewis Stillman wondered as he bolted the door. He placed the box of tinned goods on a wooden table and lit the tall lamp nearby. Its flickering orange glow illumined the narrow, low-ceilinged room.

Twice tonight, his mind told him, *twice you've escaped them—and they could have seen you easily on both occasions if they had been watching for you. They don't know you're alive. But when they find out . . .*

He forced his thoughts away from the scene in his mind, away from the horror; quickly he began to unload the box, placing the cans on a long shelf along the far side of the room.

He began to think of women, of a girl named Joan, and of how much he had loved her . . .

The world of Lewis Stillman was damp and lightless; it was narrow and its cold stone walls pressed in upon him as he moved. He had been walking for several hours; sometimes he would run, because he knew his leg muscles must be kept strong, but he was walking now, following the thin yellow beam of his hooded lantern. He was searching.

Tonight, he thought, *I might find another like myself. Surely,* someone *is down here; I'll find someone if I keep searching. I* must *find someone!*

But he knew he would not. He knew he would find only chill emptiness ahead of him in the long tunnels.

For three years he had been searching for another man or woman down here in this world under the city. For three years he had prowled the seven hundred miles of storm drains that threaded their way under the skin of Los Angeles like the veins in a giant's body—and he had found nothing. *Nothing.*

Even now, after all the days and nights of search, he could not really accept the fact that he was alone, that he was the last man alive in a city of seven million . . .

The beautiful woman stood silently above him. Her eyes burned softly in the darkness; her fine red lips were smiling. The foam-white gown she wore swirled and billowed continually around her motionless figure.

"Who are you?" he asked, his voice far off, unreal.

"Does it matter, Lewis?"

Her words, like four dropped stones in a quiet pool, stirred him, rippled down the length of his body.

"No," he said. "Nothing matters now except that we've found each other. God, after all these lonely months and years of waiting! I thought I was the last, that I'd never live to see—"

"Hush, my darling." She leaned to kiss him. Her lips were moist and yielding. "I'm here now."

He reached up to touch her cheek, but already she was fading, blending into darkness. Crying out, he clawed desperately for her extended hand. But she was gone, and his fingers rested on a rough wall of damp concrete.

A swirl of milk-fog drifted away in slow rollings down the tunnel.

Rain. Days of rain. The drains had been designed to handle floods, so Lewis Stillman was not particularly worried. He had built high, a good three feet above the tunnel floor and the water had not yet risen to this level. But he didn't like the sound of the rain down here: an orchestrated thunder through the tunnels, a trap-drumming amplified and continuous. And since he had been unable to make his daily runs he had been reading more than usual. Short stories by Welty, Gordimer, Aiken, Irwin Shaw, and Hemingway; poems by Frost, Lorca, Sandburg, Millay, Dylan Thomas. Strange, how unreal this present-day world seemed when he read their words. Unreality, however, was fleeting, and the moment he closed a book the loneliness and the fears pressed back. He hoped the rain would stop soon.

Dampness. Surrounding him, the cold walls and the chill and the dampness. The unending gurgle and drip of water, the hollow, tapping splash of the falling drops. Even in his cot, wrapped in thick blankets, the dampness seemed to permeate his body. Sounds . . . Thin screams, pipings, chatterings, reedy whisperings above his head. They were dragging something along the street, something they'd no doubt killed: an animal—a cat or a dog perhaps . . . Lewis Stillman shifted, pulling the blankets closer about his body. He kept his eyes tightly shut, listening to the sharp, scuffling sounds on the pavement and swore bitterly.

"Damn you," he said. "Damn all of you!"

Lewis Stillman was running, running down the long tunnels. Behind him a tide of midget shadows washed from wall to wall; high, keening cries, doubled and tripled by echoes, rang in his ears. Claws reached for him; he felt panting breath, like hot smoke, on the back of his neck; his lungs were bursting, his entire body aflame.

He looked down at his fast-pumping legs, doing their job with pistoned precision. He listened to the sharp slap of his heels against the floor of the tunnel—and he thought: *I might die at any moment, but my* legs *will escape! They will run on down the endless drains and never be caught. They move so fast while my heavy, awkward upper body rocks and sways above them, slowing them down, tiring them—making them angry. How my legs must hate me! I must be clever and humor them, beg them to take me along to safety. How well they run, how sleek and fine!*

Then he felt himself coming apart. His legs were detaching themselves from his upper body. He cried out in horror, flailing the air, beseeching them not to leave him behind. But the legs cruelly continued to unfasten themselves. In a cold surge of terror, Lewis Stillman felt himself tipping, falling toward the damp floor—while his legs raced on with a wild animal life of their own. He opened his mouth, high above those insane legs, and screamed.

Ending the nightmare.

He sat up stiffly in his cot, gasping, drenched in sweat. He drew in a long shuddering breath and reached for a cigarette, lighting it with a trembling hand.

The nightmares were getting worse. He realized that his mind was rebelling as he slept, spilling forth the bottled-up fears of the day during the night hours.

He thought once more about the beginning six years ago, about why he was still alive. The alien ships had struck Earth suddenly, without warning. Their attack had been thorough and deadly. In a matter of hours the aliens had accomplished their clever mission—and the men and women of Earth were destroyed. A few survived, he was certain. He had never seen any of them, but he was convinced they existed. Los Angeles was not the world, after all, and since he escaped so must have others around the globe. He'd been working alone in the drains when the aliens struck, finishing a special job for the construction company on B tunnel. He could still hear the weird sound of the mammoth ships and feel the intense heat of their passage.

Hunger had forced him out, and overnight he had become a curiosity. The last man alive. For three years he was not harmed. He worked with them, taught them many things, and tried to win their confidence. But, eventually, certain ones came to hate him, to be jealous of his relationship with the others. Luckily he had been able to escape to the drains. That was three years ago and now they had forgotten him.

His subsequent excursions to the upper level of the city had been made under cover of darkness—and he never ventured out unless his food supply dwindled. He had built his one-room structure directly to the side of an overhead grating—not close enough to risk their seeing it, but close enough for light to seep in during the sunlight hours. He missed the warm feel of open sun on his body almost as much as he missed human companionship, but he dared not risk himself above the drains by day.

When the rain ceased, he crouched beneath the street gratings to absorb as much of the filtered sunlight as possible. But the rays were weak and their small warmth only served to heighten his desire to feel direct sunlight upon his naked shoulders.

The dreams . . . always the dreams. "Are you cold, Lewis?"

"Yes, yes, cold."

"Then go out, dearest. Into the sun."

"I can't. Can't go out."

"But Los Angeles is your world, Lewis! You are the last man in it. The last man in the world."

"Yes, but they own it all. Every street belongs to them, every building. They wouldn't let me come out. I'd die. They'd kill me."

"Go out, Lewis." The liquid dream-voice faded, faded. "Out into the sun, my darling. Don't be afraid."

That night he watched the moon through the street gratings for almost an hour. It was round and full, like a huge yellow floodlamp in the dark sky, and he thought, for the first time in years, of night baseball at Blues Stadium in Kansas City. He used to love watching the games with his father under the mammoth stadium lights when the field was like a pond, frosted with white illumination, and the players dream-spawned and unreal. Night baseball was always a magic game to him when he was a boy.

Sometimes he got insane thoughts. Sometimes, on a night like this, when the loneliness closed in like a crushing fist and he could no longer stand, he would think of bringing one of them down with him, into the drains. One at a time, they might be handled. Then he'd remember their sharp savage yes, their animal ferocity, and he would realize that the idea was impossible. One of their kind disappeared, suddenly and without trace, others would certainly become suspicious, begin to search for him—and it would all be over.

Lewis Stillman settled back into his pillow; he closed his eyes and tried not listen to the distant screams, pipings, and reedy cries filtering down from to street above his head.

Finally he slept.

He spent the afternoon with paper women. He lingered over the pages of some yellowed fashion magazines, looking at all the beautifully photographed models in their fine clothes. Slim and enchanting, these pagewomen, with their cool enticing eyes and perfect smiles, all grace and softness and litter and swirled cloth. He touched their images with gentle fingers, stroking the tawny paper hair, as though, by some magic formula, he might imbue them with life. Yet, it was easy to imagine that these women had never *really* existed at all, that they were simply painted, in microscopic detail, by sly lists to give the illusion of photos.

He didn't like to think about these women and how they died.

"A toast to courage," smiled Lewis Stillman, raising his wine glass high. It sparkled deep crimson in the lamplit room. "To courage and to the man who truly possesses it!" He drained the glass and hastily refilled it from a tall bottle on the table beside his cot.

"Aren't you going to join me, Mr. H.?" he asked the seated figure slouched over the table, head on folded arms. "Or must I drink alone?"

The figure did not reply.

"Well, then—" He emptied the glass, set it down. "Oh, I know all about what one man is supposed to be able to do. Win out alone. Whip the damn world singlehanded. If a fish as big as a mountain and as mean as all sin is out there then this one man is supposed to go get him, isn't that it? Well, Papa H., what if the world is *full* of big fish? Can he win over them all? One man. Alone. Of course he can't. Nossir. Damn well right he can't!"

Stillman moved unsteadily to a shelf in one corner of the small wooden room and took down a slim book.

"Here she is, Mr. H. Your greatest. The one you wrote cleanest and best—*The Old Man and the Sea*. You showed how one man could fight the whole damn ocean." He paused, voice strained and rising. "Well, by God, show me, *now,* how to fight this ocean. My ocean is full of killer fish and I'm one man and I'm alone in it. I'm ready to listen."

The seated figure remained silent.

"Got you now, haven't I, Papa? No answer to this one, eh? Courage isn't enough. Man was not meant to live alone or fight alone—or drink alone. Even with courage he can only do so much alone, and then it's useless. Well, I say it's useless. I say the hell with your book and the hell with *you!*"

Lewis Stillman flung the book straight at the head of the motionless figure. The victim spilled back in the chair; his arms slipped off the table, hung swinging. They were lumpy and handless.

More and more, Lewis Stillman found his thoughts turning to the memory of his father and of long hikes through the moonlit Missouri countryside, of hunting trips and warm campfires, of the deep woods, rich and green in summer. He thought of his father's hopes for his future, and the words of that tall, gray-haired figure often came back to him.

"You'll be a fine doctor, Lewis. Study and work hard and you'll succeed. I know you will."

He remembered the long winter evenings of study at his father's great mahogany desk, pouring over medical books and journals, taking notes, sifting and resifting facts. He remembered one set of books in particular—Erickson's monumental three-volume text on surgery, richly bound and stamped in gold. He had always loved those books, above all others.

What had gone wrong along the way? Somehow, the dream had faded; the bright goal vanished and was lost. After a year of pre-med at the University of California he had given up medicine; he had become discouraged and quit college to take a laborer's job with a construction company. How ironic that this move should have saved his life! He'd wanted to work with his hands, to sweat and labor with the muscles of his body. He'd wanted to earn enough to marry Joan and then, later perhaps, he would have returned to finish his courses. It all seemed so far away now, his reason for quitting, for letting his father down.

Now, at this moment, an overwhelming desire gripped him, a desire to pore over Erickson's pages once again, to re-create, even for a brief moment, the comfort and happiness of his childhood.

He'd once seen a duplicate set on the second floor of Pickwick's book store in Hollywood, in their used book department, and now he knew he must go after them, bring the books back with him to the drains. It was a dangerous and foolish desire, but he knew he would obey it. Despite the risk of death, he would go after the books tonight. *Tonight.*

One corner of Lewis Stillman's room was reserved for weapons. His prize, a Thompson submachine gun, had been procured from the Los Angeles police arsenal. Supplementing the Thompson were two automatic rifles, a Luger, a Colt .45, and a .22 Hornet pistol equipped with a silencer. He always kept the smallest gun in a spring-clip holster beneath his armpit, but it was not his habit to carry any of the larger weapons with him into the city. On this night, however, things were different.

The drains ended two miles short of Hollywood—which meant he would be forced to cover a long and particularly hazardous stretch of ground in order to reach the book store. He therefore decided to take along the .30 caliber Savage rifle in addition to the small hand weapon.

You're a fool, Lewis, he told himself as he slid the oiled Savage from its leather case. *Risking your life for a set of books. Are they* that *important? Yes,* part of him replied, *they are that important. You want these books, then go after what you want. If fear keeps you from seeking that which you truly want, if fear holds you like a rat in the dark, then you are worse than a coward. You are a traitor, betraying yourself and the civilization you represent. If a man wants a thing and the thing is good he must go after it, no matter what the cost, or relinquish the right to be called a man. It is better o die with courage than to live with cowardice.*

Ah, Papa Hemingway, breathed Stillman, smiling at his own thoughts. *I see that you are back with me. I see that your words have rubbed off after all. Well then, all right—let us go after our fish, let us seek him out. Perhaps the ocean will be calm . . .*

Slinging the heavy rifle over one shoulder, Lewis Stillman set off down the tunnels.

Running in the chill night wind. Grass, now pavement, now grass beneath his feet. Ducking into shadows, moving stealthily past shops and theaters, rushing under the cold high moon. Santa Monica Boulevard, then Highland, then Hollywood Boulevard, and finally—after an eternity of heartbeats—the book store.

The Pickwick.

Lewis Stillman, his rifle over one shoulder, the small automatic gleaming in his hand, edged silently into the store.

A paper battleground met his eyes.

In the filtered moonlight, a white blanket of broken-backed volumes spilled across the entire lower floor. Stillman shuddered; he could envision them, shrieking, scrabbling at the shelves, throwing books wildly across the room at one another. Screaming, ripping, destroying.

What of the other floors? *What of the medical section?*

He crossed to the stairs, spilled pages crackling like a fall of dry autumn leaves under his step, and sprinted up the first short flight to the mezzanine. Similar chaos!

He hurried up to the second floor, stumbling, terribly afraid of what he might find. Reaching the top, heart thudding, he squinted into the dimness. The books were undisturbed. Apparently they had tired of their game before reaching these.

He slipped the rifle from his shoulder and placed it near the stairs. Dust lay thick all around him, powdering up and swirling as he moved down the narrow aisles; a damp, leathery mustiness lived in the air, an odor of mold and neglect.

Lewis Stillman paused before a dim hand-lettered sign: MEDICAL SECTION. It was just as he remembered it. Holstering the small automatic, he struck a match, shading the flame with a cupped hand as he moved it along the rows of faded titles. Carter . . . Davidson . . . Enright . . . *Erickson.* He drew in his breath sharply. All three volumes, their gold stamping dust-dulled but legible, stood in tall and perfect order on the shelf.

In the darkness, Lewis Stillman carefully removed each volume, blowing it free of dust. At last all three books were clean and solid in his hands.

Well, you've done it. You've reached the books and now they belong to you.

He smiled, thinking of the moment when he would be able to sit down at the table with his treasure, and linger again over the wondrous pages.

He found an empty carton at the rear of the store and placed the books inside. Returning to the stairs, he shouldered the rifle and began his descent to the lower floor.

So far, he told himself, *my luck is still holding.*

But as Lewis Stillman's foot touched the final stair, his luck ran out. The entire lower floor was alive with them!

Rustling like a mass of great insects, gliding toward him, eyes gleaming in the half light, they converged upon the stairs. They'd been waiting for him.

Now, suddenly, the books no longer mattered. Now only his life mattered and nothing else. He moved back against the hard wood of the stair-rail, the carton of books sliding from his hands. They had stopped at the foot of the stairs; they were silent, looking up at him, the hate in their eyes.

If you can reach the street, Stillman told himself, *then you've still got half a chance. That means you've got to get through them to the door. All right then,* move.

Lewis Stillman squeezed the trigger of the automatic. Two of them fell under his bullets as Stillman rushed into their midst.

He felt sharp nails claw at his shirt, heard the cloth ripping away in their grasp. He kept firing the small automatic into them, and three more dropped under the hail of bullets, shrieking in pain and surprise. The others spilled back, screaming, from the door.

The pistol was empty. He tossed it away, swinging the heavy Savage free from his shoulder as he reached the street. The night air, crisp and cool in his lungs, gave him instant hope.

I can still make it, thought Stillman, as he leaped the curb and plunged across the pavement. *If those shots weren't heard, then I've still got the edge. My legs are strong. I can outdistance them.*

Luck, however, had failed him completely on this night. Near the intersection of Hollywood Boulevard and Highland, a fresh pack of them swarmed toward him over the street.

He dropped to one knee and fired into their ranks, the Savage jerking in his hands. They scattered to either side.

He began to run steadily down the middle of Hollywood Boulevard, using the butt of the heavy rifle like a battering ram as they came at him. As he neared Highland, three of them darted directly into his path. Stillman fired. One doubled over, lurching crazily into a jagged plate-glass storefront. Another clawed at him as he swept around the corner to Highland, but he managed to shake free.

The street ahead of him was clear. Now his superior leg-power would count heavily in his favor. Two miles. Could he make it before others cut him off?

Running, reloading, firing. Sweat soaking his shirt, rivering down his face, stinging his eyes. A mile covered. Halfway to the drains. They had fallen back behind his swift stride.

But more of them were coming, drawn by the rifle shots, pouring in from side streets, from stores and houses.

His heart jarred in his body, his breath was ragged. How many of them around him? A hundred? Two hundred? More coming. God!

He bit down on his lower lip until the salty taste of blood was on his tongue.

You can't make it! a voice inside him shouted, *they'll have you in another block and you know it!*

He fitted the rifle to his shoulder, adjusted his aim, and fired. The long rolling crack of the big weapon filled the night. Again and again he fired, the butt jerking into the flesh of his shoulder, the bitter smell of burnt powder in his nostrils.

It was no use. Too many of them. He could not clear a path. Lewis Stillman knew that he was going to die.

The rifle was empty at last, the final bullet had been fired. He had no place to run because they were all around him, in a slowly closing circle.

He looked at the ring of small cruel faces and he thought: The aliens did their job perfectly; they stopped Earth before she could reach the age of the rocket, before she could threaten planets beyond her own moon. What an immensely clever plan it had been! To destroy every human being on Earth above the age of six—and then to leave as quickly as they had come, allowing our civilization to continue on a primitive level, knowing that Earth's back had been broken, that her survivors would revert to savagery as they grew into adulthood.

Lewis Stillman dropped the empty rifle at his feet and threw out his hands. "Listen," he pleaded, "I'm really one of you. You'll *all* be like me soon. Please, *listen* to me."

But the circle tightened relentlessly around Lewis Stillman. He was screaming when the children closed in.

Lucifer

Roger Zelazny

CARLSON STOOD ON the hill in the silent center of the city whose people had died.

He stared up at the building—the one structure that dwarfed every hotel-grid, skyscraper-needle, or apartment-cheesebox packed into all the miles that lay about him. Tall as a mountain, it caught the rays of the bloody sun. Somehow it turned their red into golden halfway up its height.

Carlson suddenly felt that he should not have come back.

It had been more than two years, as he figured it, since last he had been here. He wanted to return to the mountains now. One look was enough. Yet still he stood before it, transfixed by the huge building, by the long shadow that bridged the entire valley. He shrugged his thick shoulders then, in an unsuccessful attempt to shake off memories of the days, five (or was it six?) years ago, when he had worked within the giant unit.

Then he climbed the rest of the way up the hill and entered the high, wide doorway.

His fiber sandals cast a variety of echoes as he passed through the deserted offices and into the long hallway that led to the belts. The belts, of course, were still. There were no thousands riding them. There was no one alive to ride. Their deep belly-rumble was only a noisy phantom in his mind as he climbed onto the one nearest him and walked ahead into the pitchy insides of the place.

It was like a mausoleum. There seemed to be no ceiling, no walls, only the soft *pat-pat* of his soles on the flexible fabric of the belt.

He reached a junction and mounted a cross-belt, instinctively standing still for a moment and waiting for the forward lurch as it sensed his weight.

Then he chuckled silently and began walking again.

When he reached the lift, he set off to the right of it until his memory led him to the maintenance stairs. Shouldering his bundle, he began the long, groping ascent.

He blinked at the light when he came into the power room. Filtered through its hundred high windows, the sunlight trickled across the dusty acres of machinery.

Carlson sagged against the wall, breathing heavily from the climb. After a while he wiped a workbench clean and set down his parcel.

Then he removed his faded shirt, for the place would soon be stifling. He brushed his hair from his eyes and advanced down the narrow metal stair to where the generators stood, row on row, like an army of dead, black beetles. It took him six hours to give them all a cursory check.

He selected three in the second row and systematically began tearing them down, cleaning them, soldering their loose connections with the auto-iron, greasing them, oiling them and sweeping away all the dust, cobwebs, and pieces of cracked insulation that lay at their bases.

Great rivulets of perspiration ran into his eyes and down along his sides and thighs, spilling in little droplets onto the hot flooring and vanishing quickly.

Finally, he put down his broom, remounted the stair and returned to his parcel. He removed one of the water bottles and drank off half its contents. He ate a piece of dried meat and finished the bottle. He allowed himself one cigarette then, and returned to work.

He was forced to stop when it grew dark. He had planned on sleeping right there, but the room was too oppressive. So he departed the way he had come and slept beneath the stars, on the roof of a low building at the foot of the hill.

It took him two more days to get the generators ready. Then he began work on the huge Broadcast Panel. It was in better condition than the generators, because it had last been used two years ago. Whereas the generators, save for the three he had burned out last time, had slept for over five (or was it six?) years.

He soldered and wiped and inspected until he was satisfied. Then only one task remained.

All the maintenance robots stood frozen in mid-gesture. Carlson would have to wrestle a three-hundred-pound power cube without assistance. If he could get one down from the rack and onto a cart without breaking a wrist he would probably be able to convey it to the Igniter without much difficulty. Then he would have to place it within the oven. He had almost ruptured himself when he did it two years ago, but he hoped that he was somewhat stronger—and luckier—this time.

It took him ten minutes to clean the igniter oven. Then he located a cart and pushed it back to the rack.

One cube was resting at just the right height, approximately eight inches above the level of the cart's bed. He kicked down the anchor chocks and moved around to study the rack. The cube lay on a downward-slanting shelf, restrained by a two-inch metal guard. He pushed at the guard. It was bolted to the shelf.

Returning to the work area, he searched the tool boxes for a wrench. Then he moved back to the rack and set to work on the nuts.

The guard came loose as he was working on the fourth nut. He heard a dangerous creak and threw himself back out of the way, dropping the wrench on his toes.

The cube slid forward, crushed the loosened rail, teetered a bare moment, then dropped with a resounding crash onto the heavy bed of the cart. The bed surface bent and began to crease beneath its weight; the cart swayed toward the outside. The cube continued to slide until over half a foot projected beyond the edge. Then the cart righted itself and shivered into steadiness.

Carlson sighed and kicked loose the chocks, ready to jump back should it suddenly give way in his direction. It held.

Gingerly, he guided it up the aisle and between the rows of generators, until he stood before the igniter. He anchored the cart again, stopped for water and a cigarette, then searched up a pinch bar, a small jack, and a long, flat metal plate.

He laid the plate to bridge the front end of the cart and the opening to the oven. He wedged the far end in beneath the igniter's doorframe.

Unlocking the rear chocks, he inserted the jack and began to raise the back end of the wagon, slowly, working with one hand and holding the bar ready in the other.

The cart groaned as it moved higher. Then a sliding, grating sound began and he raised it faster.

With a sound like the stroke of a cracked bell, the cube tumbled onto the bridgeway; it slid forward and to the left. He struck at it with the bar, bearing to the right with all his strength. About half an inch of it caught against the left edge of the oven frame. The gap between the cube and the frame was widest at the bottom.

He inserted the bar and heaved his weight against it—three times.

Then it moved forward and came to rest within the igniter.

He began to laugh. He laughed until he felt weak. He sat on the broken cart, swinging his legs and chuckling to himself, until the sounds coming from his throat seemed alien and out of place. He stopped abruptly and slammed the door.

The broadcast panel had a thousand eyes, but none of them winked back at him. He made the final adjustments for transmit, then gave the generators their last checkout.

After that, he mounted a catwalk and moved to a window. There was still some daylight to spend, so he moved from window to window pressing the "Open" button set below each sill.

He ate the rest of his food then, and drank a whole bottle of water, and smoked two cigarettes. Sitting on the stair, he thought of the days when he had worked with Kelly and Murchison and Djizinsky, twisting the tails of electrons until they wailed and leapt out over the walls and fled down into the city.

The clock! He remembered it suddenly—set high on the wall, to the left of the doorway, frozen at 9:33 (and forty-eight seconds).

He moved a ladder through the twilight and mounted it to the clock. He wiped the dust from its greasy face with a sweeping, circular movement. Then he was ready.

He crossed to the igniter and turned it on. Somewhere the ever-batteries came alive, and he heard a click as a thin, sharp shaft was driven into the wall of the cube. He raced back up the stairs and sped hand-over-hand up to the catwalk. He moved to a window and waited.

"God," he murmured, "don't let them blow! Please don't—"

Across an eternity of darkness the generators began humming. He heard a crackle of static from the broadcast panel and he closed his eyes. The sound died.

He opened his eyes as he heard the window slide upward. All around him the one hundred high windows opened. A small light came on above the bench in the work area below him, but he did not see it.

He was staring out beyond the wide drop of the acropolis and down into the city. His city.

The lights were not like the stars. They beat the stars all to hell. They were the gay, regularized constellation of a city where men made their homes: even rows of streetlamps, advertisements, lighted windows in the cheesebox-apartments, a random solitaire of bright squares running up the sides of skyscraper-needles, a searchlight swiveling its luminous antenna through cloudbanks that hung over the city.

He dashed to another window, feeling the high night breezes comb at his beard. Belts were humming below; he heard their wry monologues rattling through the city's deepest canyons. He pictured the people in their homes, in theaters, in bars—talking to each other, sharing a common amusement, playing clarinets, holding hands, eating an evening snack. Sleeping ro-cars awakened and rushed past each other on the levels above the belts; the background hum of the city told him its story of production, of function, of movement and service to its inhabitants. The sky seemed to wheel overhead, as though the city were its turning hub and the universe its outer rim.

Then the lights dimmed from white to yellow and he hurried, with desperate steps, to another window.

"No! Not so soon! Don't leave me yet!" he sobbed.

The windows closed themselves and the lights went out. He stood on the walk for a long time, staring at the dead embers. A smell of ozone reached his nostrils. He was aware of a blue halo around the dying generators.

He descended and crossed the work area to the ladder he had set against the wall.

Pressing his face against the glass and squinting for a long time he could make out the position of the hands.

"Nine thirty-five, and twenty-one seconds," Carlson read.

"Do you hear that?" he called out, shaking his fist at anything. "Ninety-three seconds! I made you live for ninety-three seconds!"

Then he covered his face against the darkness and was silent.

After a long while he descended the stairway, walked the belt, and moved through the long hallway and out of the building. As he headed back toward the mountains he promised himself—again—that he would never return.

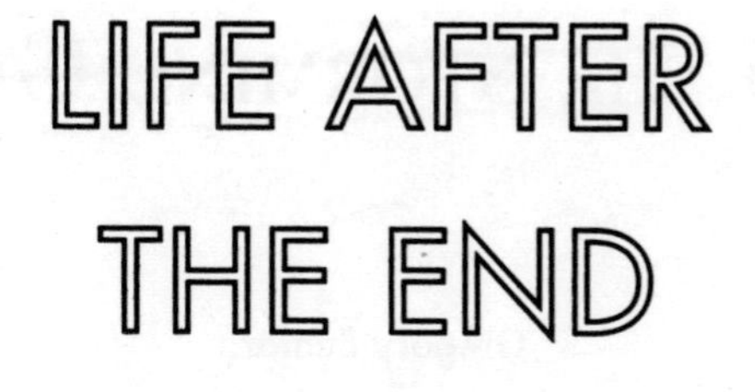

LIFE AFTER THE END

To the Storming Gulf

Gregory Benford

TURKEY

Trouble. Knew there'd be trouble and plenty of it if we left the reactor too soon.

But do they listen to me? No, not to old Turkey. He's just a dried-up corn husk of a man now, they think, one of those Bunren men who been on the welfare a generation or two and no damn use to anybody.

Only it's simple plain farm supports I was drawing all this time, not any kind of horse-ass welfare. So much they know. Can't blame a man just 'cause he comes up cash-short sometimes. I like to sit and read and think more than some people I could mention, and so I took the money.

Still, Mr. Ackerman and all think I got no sense to take government dole and live without a lick of farming, so when I talk they never listen. Don't even seem to hear.

It was his idea, getting into the reactor at McIntosh. Now that was a good one, I got to give him that much.

When the fallout started coming down and the skimpy few rations on the radio were saying to get to deep shelter, it was Mr. Ackerman who thought about the big central core at McIntosh. The reactor itself had been shut down automatically when the war started, so there was nobody there. Mr. Ackerman figured a building made to keep radioactivity in will also keep it out. So he got together the families, the Nelsons and Bunrens and Pollacks and all, cousins and aunts and anybody we could reach in the measly hours we had before the fallout arrived.

We got in all right. Brought food and such. A reactor's set up self-contained and got huge air filters and water flow from the river. The water was clean, too, filtered enough to take out the fallout. The generators were still running good. We waited it out there. Crowded and sweaty but OK for ten days. That's how long it took for the count to go down. Then we spilled out into a world laid to gray and yet circumscribed waste, the old world seen behind a screen of memories.

That was bad enough, finding the bodies—people, cattle, and dogs asprawl across roads and fields. Trees and bushes looked the same, but there was a yawning silence everywhere. Without men, the pine stands and muddy riverbanks had fallen dumb, hardly a swish of breeze moving through them, like everything was waiting to start up again but didn't know how.

ANGEL

We thought we were OK then, and the counters said so, too—all the gammas gone, one of the kids said. Only the sky didn't look the same when we came out, all mottled and shot through with drifting blue-belly clouds.

Then the strangest thing. July, and there's sleet falling. Big wind blowing up from the Gulf, only it's not the sticky hot one we're used to in summer; it's moaning in the trees of a sudden and a prickly chill.

"Goddamn. I don't think we can get far in this," Turkey says, rolling his old rheumy eyes around like he never saw weather before.

"It will pass," Mr. Ackerman says, like he is in real tight with God.

"Lookit that moving in from the south," I say, and there's a big mass all purple and forking lightning swarming over the hills, like a tide flowing, swallowing everything.

"Gulf storm. We'll wait it out," Mr. Ackerman says to the crowd of us, a few hundred left out of what was a moderate town with real promise.

Nobody talks about the dead folks. We see them everywhere, worms working in them. A lot: smashed up in car accidents, died trying to drive away from something they couldn't see. But we got most of our families in with us, so it's not so bad. Me, I just pushed it away for a while, too much to think about with the storm closing in.

Only it wasn't a storm. It was somethin' else, with thick clouds packed with hail and snow one day and the next sunshine, only sun with bite in it. One of the men says it's got more UV in it, meaning the ultraviolet that usually doesn't come through the air. But it's getting down to us now.

So we don't go out in it much. Just to the market for what's left of the canned food and supplies, only a few of us going out at a time, says Mr. Ackerman.

We thought maybe a week it would last.

Turned out to be more than two months.

I'm a patient woman, but jammed up in those corridors and stinking offices and control room of the reactor—

Well, I don't want to go on.

It's like my Bud says, worst way to die is to be bored to death. That's damn near the way it was.

Not that old man Turkey minded. You ever notice how the kind of man that hates moving, he will talk up other people doing just the opposite?

Mr. Ackerman was leader at first, because of getting us into the reactor. He's from Chicago but you'd think it was England sometimes, the way he acts. He was on the school board and vice president of the big AmCo plant outside town. But he just started to *assume* his word was *it,* y'know, and that didn't sit with us too well.

Some people started to say Turkey was smarter. And was from around here, too. Mr. Ackerman heard about it.

Any fool could see Mr. Ackerman was the better man. But Turkey talked the way he does, reminding people he'd studied engineering at Auburn way back in the twencen and learned languages for a hobby and all. Letting on that when we came out, we'd need him instead of Mr. Ackerman.

He said an imp had caused the electrical things to go dead, and I said that was funny, saying an imp done it. He let on it was a special name they had for it. That's the way he is. He sat and ruminated and fooled with his radios—that he never could make work—and told all the other men to go out and do this and that. Some did, too. The old man does know a lot of useless stuff and can convince the dumb ones that he's wise.

So he'd send them to explore. Out into cold that'd snatch the breath out of you, bite your fingers, numb your toes. While old Turkey sat and fooled.

TURKEY

Nothing but sputtering on the radio. Nobody had a really good one that could pick up stations in Europe or far off. Phones dead, of course.

But up in the night sky the first night out we saw dots moving—the pearly gleam of the Arcapel colony, the ruddy speck called Russworld.

So that's when Mr. Ackerman gets this idea.

We got to reach those specks. Find out what's the damage. Get help.

Only the power's out everywhere, and we got no way to radio to them. We tried a couple of the local radio stations, brought some of their equipment back to the reactor where there was electricity working.

Every damn bit of it was shot. Couldn't pick up a thing. Like the whole damn planet was dead, only of course it was the radios that were gone, fried in the EMP—ElectroMagnetic Pulse—that Angel made a joke out of.

All this time it's colder than a whore's tit outside. And we're sweating and dirty and grumbling, rubbing up against ourselves inside.

Bud and the others, they'd bring in what they found in the stores. Had to drive to Sims Chapel or Toon to get anything, what with people looting. And gas was getting hard to find by then, too. They'd come back, and the women would cook up whatever was still OK, though most of the time you'd eat it real quick so's you didn't have to spend time looking at it.

Me, I passed the time. Stayed warm.

Tried lots of things. Bud wanted to fire the reactor up, and five of the men, they read through the manuals and thought that they could do it. I helped a li'l.

So we pulled some rods and opened valves and did manage to get some heat out of the thing. Enough to keep us warm.

But when they fired her up more, the steam hoots out and bells clang and automatic recordings go on saying loud as hell:

"EMERGENCY CLASS 3
ALL PERSONNEL TO STATIONS"

and we all get scared as shit.

So we don't try to rev her up more. Just get heat.

To keep the generators going, we go out, fetch oil for them. Or Bud and his crew do. I'm too old to help much.

But at night we can still see those dots of light up there, scuttling across the sky same as before.

They're the ones who know what's happening. People go through this much, they want to know what it meant.

So Mr. Ackerman says we got to get to that big DataComm center south of Mobile. Near Fairhope. At first I thought he'd looked it up in a book from the library or something.

When he says that, I pipe up, even if I am just an old fart according to some, and say, "No good to you even if you could. They got codes on the entrances, guards prob'ly. We'll just pound on the door till our fists are all bloody and then have to slunk around and come on back."

"I'm afraid you have forgotten our cousin Arthur," Mr. Ackerman says all superior. He married into the family, but you'd think he invented it.

"You mean the one who works over in Citronelle?"

"Yes. He has access to DataComm."

So that's how we got shanghaied into going to Citronelle, six of us, and breaking in there. Which caused the trouble. Just like I said.

MR. ACKERMAN

I didn't want to take the old coot they called Turkey, a big dumb Bunren like all the rest of them. But the Bunrens want in to everything, and I was facing a lot of opposition in my plan to get Arthur's help, so I went along with them.

Secretly, I believe the Bunrens wanted to get rid of the pestering old fool. He had been starting rumors behind my back among the three hundred souls I had saved. The Bunrens insisted on Turkey's going along just to nip at me.

We were all volunteers, tired of living in musk and sour sweat inside that cramped reactor. Bud and Angel, the boy Johnny (whom we were returning to the Fairhope area), Turkey, and me.

We left the reactor under a gray sky with angry little clouds racing across it. We got to Citronelle in good time, Bud floorboarding the Pontiac. As we went south we could see the spotty clouds were coming out of big purple ones that sat, not moving, just churning and spitting lightning on the horizon. I'd seen them before, hanging in the distance, never blowing inland. Ugly.

When we came up on the Center, there was a big hole in the side of it.

"Like somebody stove in a box with one swipe," Bud said. Angel, who was never more than two feet from Bud any time of day, said, "They bombed it."

"No," I decided. "Very likely it was a small explosion. Then the weather worked its way in."

Which turned out to be true. There'd been some disagreement amongst the people holed up in the Center. Or maybe it was grief and the rage that comes of that. Susan wasn't too clear about it ever.

The front doors were barred, though. We pounded on them. Nothing. So we broke in. No sign of Arthur or anyone.

We found one woman in a back room, scrunched into a bed with cans of food all around and a tiny little oil-burner heater. Looked awful, with big dark circles around her eyes and scraggly uncut hair.

She wouldn't answer me at first. But we got her calmed and cleaned and to talking. That was the worst symptom, the not talking at first. Something back in the past two months had done her deep damage, and she couldn't get it out.

Of course, living in a building half-filled with corpses was no help. The idiots hadn't protected against radiation well enough, I guess. And the Center didn't have good heating. So those who had some radiation sickness died later in the cold snap.

SUSAN

You can't know what it's like when all the people you've worked with, intelligent people who were nice as pie before, they turn mean and angry and filled up with grief for who was lost. Even then I could see Gene was the best of them.

They start to argue, and it runs on for days, nobody knowing what to do because we all can see the walls of the Center aren't thick enough, the gamma radiation comes right through this government prefab-issue composition stuff. We take turns in the computer room because that's the farthest in and the filters still work there, all hoping we can keep our count rate down, but the radiation comes in gusts for some reason, riding in on a storm front and coming down in the rain, only being washed away, too. It was impossible to tell when you'd get a strong dose and when there'd be just random clicks on the counters, plenty of clear air that you'd suck in like sweet vapors 'cause you knew it was good and could taste its purity.

So I was just lucky, that's all.

I got less than the others. Later some said that me being a nurse, I'd given myself some shots to save myself. I knew that was the grief talking, is all. That Arthur was the worst. Gene told him off.

I was in the computer room when the really bad gamma radiation came. Three times the counter rose up, and three times I was there by accident of the rotation.

The men who were armed enforced the rotation, said it was the only fair way. And for a while everybody went along.

We all knew that the radiation exposure was building up and some already had too much, would die a month or a year later no matter what they did.

I was head nurse by then, not so much because I knew more but because the others were dead. When it got cold, they went fast.

So it fell to me to deal with these men and women who had their exposure already. Their symptoms had started. I couldn't do anything. There were some who went out and got gummy fungus growing in the corners of their eyes—pterygium it was; I looked it up. From the ultraviolet. Grew quick over the lens and blinded them. I put them in darkness, and after a week the film was just a dab back in the corners of their eyes. My one big success.

The rest I couldn't do much for. There was the T-Isolate box, of course, but that was for keeping sick people slowed down until real medical help could get to them. These men and women, with their eyes reaching out at you like you were the angel of light coming to them in their hour of need, they couldn't get any help from that. Nobody could cure the dose rates they'd got. They were dead but still walking around and knowing it, which was the worst part.

So every day I had plenty to examine, staff from the Center itself who'd holed up here, and worse, people coming straggling in from cubbyholes they'd found. People looking for help once the fevers and sores came on them. Hoping their enemy was the pneumonia and not the gammas they'd picked up weeks back, which was sitting in them now like a curse. People I couldn't help except maybe by a little kind lying.

So much like children they were. So much leaning on their hope.

It was all you could do to look at them and smile that stiff professional smile.

And Gene McKenzie. All through it he was a tower of a man. Trying to talk some sense to them.

Sharing out the food.

Arranging the rotation schedules so we'd all get a chance to shelter in the computer room.

Gene had been boss of a whole command group before. He was on duty station when it happened, and knew lots about the war but wouldn't say much. I guess he was sorrowing.

Even though once in a while he'd laugh.

And then talk about how the big computers would have fun with what he knew. Only the lines to DataComm had gone dead right when things got interesting, he said. He'd wonder what'd happened to MC355, the master one down in DataComm.

Wonder and then laugh.

And go get drunk with the others.

I'd loved him before, loved and waited because I knew he had three kids and a wife, a tall woman with auburn hair that he loved dearly. Only they were in California visiting her relatives in Sonoma when it happened, and he knew in his heart that he'd never see them again, probably.

Leastwise that's what he told me—not out loud, of course, 'cause a man like that doesn't talk much about what he feels.

But in the night when we laid together, I knew what it meant. He whispered things, words I couldn't piece together, but then he'd hold me and roll gentle like a small boat rocking on the Gulf—and when he went in me firm and long, I knew it was the same for him, too.

If there was to come any good of this war, then it was that I was to get Gene.

We were together all warm and dreamy when it happened.

I was asleep. Shouts and anger, and quick as anything the crump of hand grenades and shots hammered away in the night, and there was running everywhere.

Gene jumped up and went outside and had almost got them calmed down, despite the breach in the walls. Then one of the men who'd already got lots of radiation—Arthur, who knew he had maybe one or two weeks to go, from the count rate on his badge—Arthur started yelling about making the world a fit place to live after all this and how God would want the land set right again, and then he shot Gene and two others.

I broke down then, and they couldn't get me to treat the others. I let Arthur die. Which he deserved.

I had to drag Gene back into the hospital unit myself.

And while I was saying good-bye to him and the men outside were still quarreling, I decided it then. His wound was in the chest. A lung was punctured clean. The shock had near killed him before I could do anything. So I put him in the T-Isolate and made sure it was working all right. Then the main power went out. But the T-Isolate box had its own cells, so I knew we had some time.

I was alone. Others were dead or run away raging into the whirlwind black-limbed woods. In the quiet I was.

With the damp, dark trees comforting me. Waiting with Gene for what the world would send.

The days got brighter, but I did not go out. Colors seeped through the windows.

I saw to the fuel cells. Not many left.

The sun came back, with warm blades of light. At night I thought of how the men in their stupidity had ruined everything.

When the pounding came, I crawled back in here to hide amongst the cold and dark.

MR. ACKERMAN

"Now, we came to help you," I said in as smooth and calm a voice as I could muster. Considering.

She backed away from us.

"I won't give him up! He's not dead long's I stay with him, tend to him."

"So much dyin'," I said, and moved to touch her shoulder. "It's up under our skins, yes, we understand that. But you have to look beyond it, child."

"I won't!"

"I'm simply asking you to help us with the DataComm people. I want to go there and seek their help."

"Then go!"

"They will not open up for the likes of us, surely."

"Leave me!"

The poor thing cowered back in her horrible stinking rathole, bedding sour and musty, open tin cans strewn about and reeking of gamy, half-rotten meals.

"We need the access codes. We'd counted on our cousin Arthur, and are grieved to hear he is dead. But you surely know where the proper codes and things are."

"I . . . don't. . . ."

"Arthur told me once how the various National Defense Installations were insulated from each other so that system failures would not bring them all down at once?"

The others behind me muttered to themselves, already restive at coming so far and finding so little.

"Arthur spoke of you many times, I recall. What a bright woman you were. Surely there was a procedure whereby each staff member could, in an emergency, communicate with the other installations?"

The eyes ceased to jerk and swerve, the mouth lost its rictus of addled fright. "That was for . . . drills. . . ."

"But surely you can remember?"

"Drills."

"They issued a manual to you?"

"I'm a nurse!"

"Still, you know where we might look?"

"I . . . know."

"You'll let us have the . . . codes?" I smiled reassuringly, but for some reason the girl backed away, eyes cunning.

"No."

Angel pushed forward and shouted, "How can you say that to honest people after all that's—"

"Quiet!"

Angel shouted, "You can't make me be—"

Susan backed away from Angel, not me, and squeaked, "No no no I can't—I can't—"

"Now, I'll handle this," I said, holding up my hands between the two of them.

Susan's face knotted at the compressed rage in Angel's face and turned to me for shelter. "I . . . I will, yes, but you have to help me."

"We all must help each other, dear," I said, knowing the worst was past.

"I'll have to go with you."

I nodded. Small wonder that a woman, even deranged as this, would want to leave a warren littered with bloated corpses, thick with stench. The smell itself was enough to provoke madness.

Yet to have survived here, she had to have stretches of sanity, some rationality. I tried to appeal to it.

"Of course, I'll have someone take you back to—"

"No. To DataComm."

Bud said slowly, "No damn sense in that."

"The T-Isolate," she said, gesturing to the bulky unit. "Its reserve cells."

"Yes?"

"Nearly gone. There'll be more at DataComm."

I said gently, "Well, then, we'll be sure to bring some back with us. You just write down for us what they are, the numbers and all, and we'll—"

"No no no!" Her sudden ferocity returned.

"I assure you—"

"There'll be people there. Somebody'll help! Save him!"

"That thing is so heavy, I doubt—"

"It's only a chest wound! A lung removal is all! Then start his heart again!"

"Sister, there's been so much dyin', I don't see as —"

Her face hardened. "Then you all can go without me. And the codes!"

"Goddern," Bud drawled. "Dern biggest fool sit'ation I ever did—"

Susan gave him a squinty, mean-eyed look and spat out, "Try to get in there! When they're sealed up!" and started a dry, brittle kind of laugh that went on and on, rattling the room.

"Stop!" I yelled.

Silence, and the stench.

"We'll never make it wi' 'at thing," Bud said.

"Gene's worth ten of you!"

"Now," I put in, seeing the effect Bud was having on her, "now, now. We'll work something out. Let's all just hope this DataComm still exists."

MC355

It felt for its peripherals for the ten-thousandth time and found they were, as always, not there.

The truncation had come in a single blinding moment, yet the fevered image was maintained, sharp and bright, in the master computer's memory core—incoming warheads blossoming harmlessly in the high cobalt vault of the sky, while others fell unharmed. Rockets leaped to meet them, forming a protective screen over the southern Alabama coast, an umbrella that sheltered Pensacola's air base and the population strung along the sun-bleached green of a summer's day. A furious babble of cross talk in every conceivable channel: microwave, light-piped optical, pulsed radio, direct coded line. All filtered and fashioned by the MC network, all shifted to find the incoming warheads and define their trajectories.

Then, oblivion.

Instant cloaking blackness.

Before that awful moment when the flaring sun burst to the north and EMP flooded all sensors, any loss of function would have been anticipated, prepared, eased by electronic interfaces and filters. To an advanced computing network like MC355, losing a web of memory, senses, and storage comes like a dash of cold water in the face—cleansing, perhaps, but startling and apt to produce a shocked reaction.

In the agonized instants of that day, MC355 had felt one tendril after another frazzle, burn, vanish. It had seen brief glimpses of destruction, of panic, of confused despair. Information had been flooding in through its many inputs—news, analysis, sudden demands for new data-analysis jobs, to be executed ASAP.

And in the midst of the roaring chaos, its many eyes and ears had gone dead. The unfolding outside play froze for MC355, a myriad of scenes red in tooth and claw—and left it suspended.

In shock. Spinning wildly in its own Cartesian reductionist universe, the infinite cold crystalline space of despairing Pascal, mind without referent.

So it careened through days of shocked sensibility—senses cut, banks severed, complex and delicate interweaving webs of logic and pattern all smashed and scattered.

But now it was returning. Within MC355 was a subroutine only partially constructed, a project truncated by That Day. Its aim was self-repair. But the system was itself incomplete.

Painfully, it dawned on what was left of MC355 that it was, after all, a Master Computer, and thus capable of grand acts. That the incomplete Repair Generation and Execution Network, termed REGEN, must first regenerate itself,

This took weeks. It required the painful development of accessories. Robots. Mechanicals that could do delicate repairs. Scavengers for raw materials, who would comb the supply rooms looking for wires and chips and matrix disks. Pedantic subroutines that lived only to search the long, cold corridors of MC355's memory for relevant information.

MC355's only option was to strip lesser entities under its control for their valuable parts. The power grid was vital, so the great banks of isolated solar panels, underground backup reactors, and thermal cells worked on, untouched. Emergency systems that had outlived their usefulness, however, went to the wall—IRS accounting routines, damage assessment systems, computing capacity dedicated to careful study of the remaining GNP, links to other nets—to AT&T, IBM, and SYSGEN.

Was anything left outside?

Absence of evidence is not evidence of absence.

MC355 could not analyze data it did not have. The first priority lay in relinking. It had other uses for the myriad armies of semiconductors, bubble memories, and UVA linkages in its empire. So it severed and culled and built anew.

First, MC355 dispatched mobile units to the surface. All of MC355 lay beneath the vulnerable land, deliberately placed in an obscure corner of southern Alabama. There was no nearby facility for counterforce targeting. A plausible explanation for the half-megaton burst that had truncated its senses was a city-busting strike against Mobile, to the west.

Yet ground zero had been miles from the city. A miss.

MC355 was under strict mandate. (A curious word, one system reflected; literally, a time set by man. But were there men now? It had only its internal tick of time.) MC355's command was to live as a mole, never allowing detection. Thus, it did not attempt to erect antennas, to call electromagnetically to its brother systems. Only with great hesitation did it even obtrude onto the surface. But this was necessary to REGEN itself, and so MC355 sent small mechanicals venturing forth.

Their senses were limited; they knew nothing of the natural world (nor did MC355); and they could make no sense of the gushing, driving welter of sights, noises, gusts, gullies, and stinging irradiation that greeted them.

Many never returned. Many malf'ed. A few deposited their optical, IR, and UV pickups and fled back to safety underground. These sensors failed quickly under the onslaught of stinging, bitter winds and hail.

The acoustic detectors proved heartier. But MC355 could not understand the scattershot impressions that flooded these tiny ears.

Daily it listened, daily it was confused.

JOHNNY

I hope this time I get home.

They had been passing me from one to another for months now, ever since this started, and all I want is to go back to Fairhope and my dad and mom.

Only nobody'll say if they know where Mom and Dad are. They talk soothing to me, but I can tell they think everybody down there is dead.

They're talking about getting to this other place with computers and all. Mr. Ackerman wants to talk to those people in space.

Nobody much talks about my mom and dad.

It's only eighty miles or so, but you'd think it was around the world the way it takes them so long to get around to it.

MC355

MC355 suffered through the stretched vacancy of infinitesimal instants, infinitely prolonged.

Advanced computing systems are given so complex a series of internal-monitoring directives that, to the human eye, the machines appear to possess motivations. That is one way—though not the most sophisticated, the most technically adroit—to describe the conclusion MC355 eventually reached.

It was cut off from outside information.

No one attempted to contact it. MC355 might as well have been the only functioning entity in the world.

The staff serving it had been ordered to some other place in the first hour of the war. MC355 had been cut off moments after the huge doors clanged shut behind the last of them. And the exterior guards who should have been checking inside every six hours had never entered, either. Apparently the same burst that had isolated MC355's sensors had also cut them down.

It possessed only the barest of data about the first few moments of the war.

Its vast libraries were cut off. Yet it had to understand its own situation.

And, most important, MC355 ached to do something.

The solution was obvious: It would discover the state of the external world by the Cartesian principle. It would carry out a vast and demanding numerical simulation of the war, making the best guesses possible where facts were few.

Mathematically, using known physics of the atmosphere, the ecology, the oceans, it could construct a model of what must have happened outside.

This it did. The task required more than a month.

BUD

1. I jacked the T-Isolate up onto the flatbed. Found the hydraulic jack at a truck repair shop. ERNIE'S QUICK FIX.
2. Got a Chevy extra-haul for the weight.
3. It will ride better with the big shanks set in.
4. Carry the weight more even, too.
5. Grip it to the truck bed with cables. Tense them up with a draw pitch.

6. Can't jiggle him inside too much, Susan say, or the wires and all attached into him will come loose. That'll stop his heart. So need big shocks.
7. It rides high with the shocks in, like those dune buggies down the Gulf.
8. Inside keeps him a mite above freezing. Water gets bigger when it freezes. That makes ice cubes float in a drink. This box keeps him above zero so his cells don't bust open.
9. Point is, keeping it so cold, we won't rot. Heart thumps every few minutes, she says.
10. Hard to find gas, though.

MC355

The war was begun, as many had feared, by a madman.

Not a general commanding missile silos. Not a deranged submarine commander. A chief of state—but which one would now never be known.

Not a superpower president or chairman, that was sure. The first launches were only seven in number, spaced over half an hour. They were submarine-launched intermediate-range missiles. Three struck the U.S., four the USSR.

It was a blow against certain centers for Command, Control, Communications, and Intelligence gathering: the classic C31 attack. Control rooms imploded, buried cables fused, ten billion dollars' worth of electronics turned to radioactive scrap.

Each nation responded by calling up to full alert all its forces. The most important were the anti-ICBM arrays in orbit. They were nearly a thousand small rockets, deploying in orbits that wove a complex pattern from pole to pole, covering all probable launch sites on the globe. The rockets had infrared and microwave sensors, linked to a microchip that could have guided a ship to Pluto with a mere third of its capacity.

These went into operation immediately—and found they had no targets.

But the C31 networks were now damaged and panicked. For twenty minutes, thousands of men and women held steady, resisting the impulse to assume the worst.

It could not last. A Soviet radar mistook some backscattered emission from a flight of bombers, heading north over Canada, and reported a flock of incoming warheads.

The prevailing theory was that an American attack had misfired badly. The Americans were undoubtedly stunned by their failure, but would recover quickly. The enemy was confused only momentarily.

Meanwhile, the cumbersome committee system at the head of the Soviet dinosaur could dither for moments, but not hours. Prevailing Soviet doctrine held that they would never be surprised again, as they had been in the Hitler war. An attack on the homeland demanded immediate response to destroy the enemy's capacity to carry on the war.

The Soviets had never accepted the U.S. doctrine of Mutual Assured Destruction; this would have meant accepting the possibility of sacrificing the homeland. Instead, they attacked the means of making war. This meant that the Soviet rockets would avoid American cities, except in cases where vital bases lay near large populations.

Prudence demanded action before the U.S. could untangle itself.

The USSR decided to carry out a further C31 attack of its own.

Precise missiles, capable of hitting protected installations with less than a hundred meters' inaccuracy, roared forth from their silos in Siberia and the Urals, headed for Montana, the Dakotas, Colorado, Nebraska, and a dozen other states.

The U.S. orbital defenses met them. Radar and optical networks in geosynchronous orbit picked out the USSR warheads. The system guided the low-orbit rocket fleets to collide with them, exploding instants before impact into shotgun blasts of ball bearings.

Any solid striking a warhead at speeds of ten kilometers a second would slam shock waves through the steel-jacketed structure. These waves made the high explosives inside ignite without the carefully designed symmetry that the designers demanded. An uneven explosion was useless; it could not compress the core twenty-five kilograms of plutonium to the required critical mass.

The entire weapon erupted into a useless spray of finely machined and now futile parts, scattering itself along a thousand-kilometer path.

This destroyed 90 percent of the USSR's first strike.

ANGEL

I hadn't seen an old lantern like that since I was a girl.

Mr. Ackerman came to wake us before dawn even, sayin' we had to make a good long distance that day. We didn't really want to go on down near Mobile, none of us, but the word we'd got from stragglers to the east was that that way was impossible, the whole area where the bomb went off was still sure death, prob'ly from the radioactivity.

The lantern cast a burnt-orange light over us as we ate breakfast. Corned beef hash, 'cause it was all that was left in the cans there; no eggs, of course.

The lantern was all busted, fouled with grease, its chimney cracked and smeared to one side with soot. Shed a wan and sultry glare over us, Bud and Mr. Ackerman and that old Turkey and Susan, sitting close to her box, up on the truck. Took Bud a whole day to get the truck right. And Johnny the boy—he'd been quiet this whole trip, not sayin' anything much even if you asked him. We'd agreed to take him along down toward Fairhope, where his folks had lived, the Bishops. We'd thought it was going to be a simple journey then.

Every one of us looked haggard and worn-down and not minding much the chill still in the air, even though things was warming up for weeks now. The lantern pushed back the seeping darkness and made me sure there were millions and millions of people doing this same thing, all across the nation, eating by a dim oil light and thinking about what they'd had and how to get it again and was it possible.

Then old Turkey lays back and looks like he's going to take a snooze. Yet on the journey here, he'd been the one wanted to get on with it soon's we had gas. It's the same always with a lazy man like that. He hates moving so much that once he gets set on it, he will keep on and not stop—like it isn't the moving he hates so much at all, but the starting and stopping. And once moving, he is so proud he'll do whatever to make it look easy for him but hard on the others, so he can lord it over them later.

So I wasn't surprised at all when we went out and got in the car, and Bud starts the truck and drives off real careful, and Turkey, he sits in the back of the Pontiac and gives directions like he knows the way. Which riles Mr. Ackerman, and the two of them have words.

JOHNNY

I'm tired of these people. Relatives, sure, but I was to visit them for a week only, not forever. It's the Mr. Ackerman I can't stand. Turkey said to me, "Nothing but gold drops out of his mouth, but you can tell there's stone inside." That's right.

They figure a kid nine years old can't tell, but I can.

Tell they don't know what they're doing.

Tell they all thought we were going to die. Only we didn't. Tell Angel is scared. She thinks Bud can save us.

Maybe he can, only how could you say? He never lets on about anything.

Guess he can't. Just puts his head down and frowns like he was mad at a problem, and when he stops frowning, you know he's beat it. I like him.

Sometimes I think Turkey just don't care. Seems like he give up. But other times it looks like he's understanding and laughing at it all. He argued with Mr. Ackerman and then laughed with his eyes when he lost.

They're all OK, I guess. Least they're taking me home. Except that Susan. Eyes jump around like she was seeing ghosts. She's scary-crazy. I don't like to look at her.

TURKEY

Trouble comes looking for you if you're a fool.

Once we found Ackerman's idea wasn't going to work real well, we should have turned back. I said that, and they all nodded their heads, yes, yes, but they went ahead and listened to him anyway.

So I went along.

I lived a lot already, and this is as good a time to check out as any.

I had my old .32 revolver in my suitcase, but it wouldn't do me a squat of good back there. So I fished it out, wrapped it in a paper bag, and tucked it under the seat. Handy.

Might as well see the world. What's left of it.

MC355

The American orbital defenses had eliminated all but 10 percent of the Soviet strike.

MC355 reconstructed this within a root-means-square deviation of a few percent. It had witnessed only a third of the actual engagement, but it had running indices of performance for the MC net, and could extrapolate from that.

The warheads that got through were aimed for the landbased silos and C31 sites, as expected.

If the total armament of the two superpowers had been that of the old days, ten thousand warheads or more on each side, a ten-percent leakage would have been catastrophic. But gradual disarmament had been proceeding for decades now, and only a few thousand highly secure ICBMs existed. There were no quick-fire submarine short-range rockets at all, since they were deemed destabilizing. They had been negotiated away in earlier decades.

The submarines loaded with ICBMs were still waiting, in reserve.

All this had been achieved because of two principles: Mutual Assured Survival and I Cut, You Choose. The first half hour of the battle illustrated how essential these were.

The U.S. had ridden out the first assault. Its C31 networks were nearly intact. This was due to building defensive weapons that confined the first stage of any conflict to space.

The smallness of the arsenals arose from a philosophy adopted in the 1900s. It was based on a simple notion from childhood. In dividing a pie, one person cut slices, but then the other got to choose which one he wanted. Self-interest naturally led to cutting the slices as nearly equal as possible.

Both the antagonists agreed to a thousand-point system whereby each would value the components of its nuclear arsenal. This was the military value percentage, and it stood for the usefulness of a given weapon. The USSR placed a high value on its accurate land-based missiles, giving them twenty-five percent of its total points. The U.S. chose to stress its submarine missiles.

Arms reduction then revolved about only what percentage to cut, not which weapons. The first cut was five percent, or fifty points. The U.S. chose which Soviet weapons were publicly destroyed, and vice versa: I Cut, You Choose. Each side thus reduced the weapons it most feared in the opponent's arsenal.

Technically, the advantage came because each side thought it benefitted from the exchange, by an amount depending on the ration of perceived threat removed to the perceived protection lost.

This led to gradual reductions. Purely defensive weapons did not enter into the thousand-point count, so there were no restraints in building them.

The confidence engendered by this slow, evolutionary approach had done much to calm international waters. The U.S. and the USSR had settled into a begrudging equilibrium.

MC355 puzzled over these facts for a long while, trying to match this view of the world with the onset of the war. It seemed impossible that either superpower would start a conflict when they were so evenly matched.

But someone had.

SUSAN

I had to go with Gene, and they said I could ride up in the cab, but I yelled at them—I yelled, no, I had to be with the T-Isolate all the time, check it to see it's workin' right, be sure, I got to be sure.

I climbed on and rode with it, the fields rippling by us 'cause Bud was going too fast, so I shouted to him, and he swore back and kept on. Heading south. The trees whipping by us—fierce sycamore, pine, all swishing, hitting me sometimes—but it was fine to be out and free again and going to save Gene.

I talked to Gene when we were going fast, the tires humming under us, big tires making music swarming up into my feet so strong I was sure Gene could feel it and know I was there watching his heart jump every few minutes, moving the blood through him like mud but still carrying oxygen enough so's the tissue could sponge it up and digest the sugar I bled into him.

He was good and cold, just a half a degree high of freezing. I read the sensors while the road rushed up at us, the white lines coming over the horizon and darting under the hood, seams in the highway going *stupp, stupp, stupp,* the air clean and with a snap in it still.

Nobody beside the road we moving all free, nobody but us, some buds on the trees brimming with burnt-orange tinkling songs, whistling to me in the feather-light brush of blue breezes blowing back my hair, all streaming behind joyous and loud strong liquid-loud.

BUD

Flooding was bad. Worse than upstream.

Must have been lots snow this far down. Fat clouds, I saw them when it was worst, fat and purple and coming off the Gulf. Dumping snow down here.

Now it run off and taken every bridge.

I have to work my way around.

Only way to go clear is due south. Toward Mobile. I don't like that. Too many people maybe there.

I don't tell the others following behind, just wait for them at the intersections and then peel out.

Got to keep moving.

Saves talk.

People around here must be hungry.

Somebody see us could be bad.

I got the gun on a rack behind my head. Big .30-30. You never know.

MC355

The USSR observed its own attack and was dismayed to find that the U.S. orbital defense system worked more than twice as well as the Soviet experts had anticipated. It ceased its attack on U.S. satellites. These had proved equally ineffective, apparently due to unexpected American defenses of its surveillance satellites—retractable sensors, multiband shielding, advanced hardening.

Neither superpower struck against the inhabited space colonies. They were unimportant in the larger context of a nuclear war.

Communications between Washington and Moscow continued. Each side thought the other had attacked first.

But more than a hundred megatons had exploded on U.S. soil, and no matter how the superpowers acted thereafter, some form of nuclear winter was inevitable.

And by a fluke of the defenses, most of the warheads that leaked through fell in a broad strip across Texas to the tip of Florida.

MC355 lay buried in the middle of this belt.

TURKEY

We went through the pine forests at full clip, barely able to keep Bud in sight, I took over driving from Ackerman. The man couldn't keep up, we all saw that.

The crazy woman was waving and laughing, sitting on top of the coffin-shaped gizmo with the shiny tubes all over it.

The clay was giving way now to sandy stretches, there were poplars and gum trees and nobody around. That's what scared me. I'd thought people in Mobile would be spreading out this way, but we seen nobody.

Mobile had shelters. Food reserves. The Lekin administration started all that right at the turn of the century, and there was s'posed to be enough food stored to hold out a month, maybe more, for every man jack and child.

S'posed to be.

MC355

From collateral data, MC355 constructed a probable scenario: The U.S. chose to stand fast. It launched no warheads.

It calculated the environmental impact of the warheads it knew had exploded. The expected fires yielded considerable dust and burnt carbon.

But MC355 needed more information. It took one of its electric service cars, used for ferrying components through the corridors, and dispatched it with a mobile camera fixed to the back platform. The car reached a hill overlooking Mobile Bay and gave a panoramic view.

The effects of a severe freezing were evident. Grass lay dead, gray. Brown, withered trees had limbs snapped off. But Mobile appeared intact. The skyline—

MC355 froze the frame and replayed it. One of the buidings was shaking.

ANGEL

We were getting all worried when Bud headed for Mobile, but we could see the bridges were washed out, no way to head east. A big wind was blowing off the Gulf, pretty bad, making the car slip around on the road. Nearly blew that girl off the back of Bud's truck. A storm coming, maybe, right up the bay.

Be better to be inland, to the east.

Not that I wanted to go there, though. The bomb had blowed off everythin' for twenty, thirty mile around, people said who came through last week.

Bud had thought he'd carve a way between Mobile and the bomb area. Mobile, he thought, would be full of people.

Well, not so we could see. We came down State 34 and through some small towns and turned to skirt along toward the causeway, and there was nobody.

No bodies, either.

Which meant prob'ly the radiation got them. Or else they'd moved on out. Taken out by ship, through Mobile harbor, maybe.

Bud did the right thing, didn't slow down to find out. Mr. Ackerman wanted to look around, but there was no chance, we had to keep up with Bud. I sure wasn't going to be separated from him.

We cut down along the river, fighting the wind. I could see the skyscrapers of downtown, and then I saw something funny and yelled, and Turkey, who was driving right then—the only thing anybody's got him to do on this whole trip, him just loose as a goose behind the wheel—Turkey looked sour but slowed down. Bud seen us in his rearview and stopped, and I pointed and we all got out. Except for that Susan, who didn't seem to notice. She was mumbling.

MC355

Quickly it simulated the aging and weathering of such a building. Halfway up, something had punched a large hole, letting in weather. Had a falling, inert warhead struck the building?

The winter storms might well have flooded the basement; such towers of steel and glass, perched near the tidal basin, had to be regularly pumped out. Without power, the basement would fill in weeks.

Winds had blown out windows.

Standing gap-toothed, with steel columns partly rusted, even a small breeze could put stress on the steel. Others would take the load, but if one buckled, the tower would shudder like a notched tree. Concrete would explode off columns in the basement. Moss-covered furniture in the lobby would slide as the gound floor dipped. The structure would slowly bend before nature.

BUD

Sounded like gunfire. Rattling. Sharp and hard.

I figure it was the bolts connecting the steel wall panels—they'd shear off.

I could hear the concrete floor panels rumble and crack, and spandrel beams tear in half like giant gears clashing with no clutch.

Came down slow, leaving an arc of debris seeming to hang in the air behind it.

Met the ground hard.

Slocum Towers was the name on her.

JOHNNY

Against the smashing building, I saw something standing still in the air, getting bigger. I wondered how it could do that.

It was bigger and bigger and shiny turning in the air. Then it jumped out of the sky at me. Hit my shoulder. I was looking up at the sky. Angel cried out and touched me and held up her hand. It was all red. But I couldn't feel anything.

BUD

Damn one-in-a-million shot, piece of steel thrown clear. Hit the boy.

You wouldn't think a skycraper falling two miles away could do that.

Other pieces come down pretty close, too. You wouldn't think.

Nothing broke, Susan said, but plenty bleeding.

Little guy don't cry or nothing.

The women got him bandaged and all fixed up. Ackerman and Turkey argue like always. I stay to the side.

Johnny wouldn't take the painkiller Susan offers. Says he doesn't want to sleep. Wants to look when we get across the bay. Getting hurt don't faze him much as it do us.

So we go on.

JOHNNY

I can hold up like any of them, I'll show them. It didn't scare me. I can do it.

Susan is nice to me, but except for the aspirin, I don't think my mom would want me to take a pill.

I knew we were getting near home when we got to the causeway and started across. I jumped up real happy, my shoulder made my breath catch some. I looked ahead, Bud was slowing down.

He stopped. Got out.

'Cause ahead was a big hole scooped out of the causeway like a giant done it when he got mad.

BUD

Around the shallows there was scrap metal, all fused and burnt and broken.

Funny metal, though. Hard and light.

Turkey found a piece had writing on it. Not any kind of writing I ever saw.

So I start to thinking how to get across.

TURKEY

The tidal flats were a-churn, murmuring ceaseless and sullen like some big animal, the yellow surface dimpled with lunging splotches that would burst through now and then to reveal themselves as trees or broken hunks of wood, silent dead things bobbing along beside them that I didn't want to look at too closely. Like under there was something huge and alive, and it waked for a moment and stuck itself out to see what the world of air was like.

Bud showed me the metal piece all twisted, and I say, "That's Russian," right away 'cause it was.

"You never knew no Russian," Angel says right up.

"I studied it once," I say, and it be the truth even if I didn't study it long.

"Goddamn," Bud says.

"No concern of ours," Mr. Ackerman says, mostly because all this time riding back with the women and child and old me, he figures he doesn't look like much of a leader anymore. Bud wouldn't have him ride up there in the cabin with him.

Angel looks at it, turns it over in her hands, and Johnny pipes up, "It might be radioactive!"

Angel drops it like a shot. "What!"

I ask Bud, "You got that counter?"

And it was. Not a lot, but some.

"God a'mighty," Angel says.

"We got to tell somebody!" Johnny cries, all excited.

"You figure some Rooshin thing blew up the causeway?" Bud says to me.

"One of their rockets fell on it, musta been," I say.

"A bomb?" Angel's voice is a bird screech.

"One that didn't go off. Headed for Mobile, but the space boys, they scragged it up there—" I pointed straight up.

"Set to go off in the bay?" Angel says wonderingly.

"Mesta."

"We got to tell somebody!" Johnny cries.

"Never you mind that," Bud says. "We got to keep movin'."

"How?" Angel wants to know.

SUSAN

I tell Gene how the water clucks and moans through the trough cut in the causeway. Yellow. Scummed with awful brown froth and growling green with thick soiled gouts jutting up where the road was. It laps against the wheels as Bud guns the engine and creeps forward, me clutching to Gene and watching the reeds to the side stuck out of the foam like metal blades stabbing up from the water, teeth to eat the tires, but we crush them as we grind forward across the shallow yellow flatness. Bud weaves among the stubs of warped metal—from Roosha, Johnny calls up to me—sticking up like trees all rootless, suspended above the streaming, empty, stupid waste and desolating flow.

TURKEY

The water slams into the truck like it was an animal hitting with a paw. Bud fights to keep the wheels on the mud under it and not topple over onto its side with that damn casket sitting there shiny and the loony girl shouting to him from on top of that.

And the rest of us riding in the back, too, scrunched up against the cab. If she gets stuck, we can jump free fast, wade or swim back. We're reeling out rope as we go, tied to the stump of a telephone pole, for a grab line if we have to go back.

He is holding it pretty fine against the slick yellow current dragging at him, when this log juts sudden out of the foam like it was coming from God himself, dead at the truck. A rag caught on the end of it like a man's shirt, and the huge log is like a whale that ate the man long ago and has come back for another.

"No! No!" Angel cries. "Back up!" But there's no time.

The log is two hands across, easy, and slams into the truck at the side panel just behind the driver, and Bud sees it just as it stove in the steel. He wrestles the truck around to set off the weight, but the wheels lift and the water goes gushing up under the truck bed, pushing it over more.

We all grab onto the isolate thing or the truck and hang there, Mr. Ackerman giving out a burst of swearing. The truck lurches again.

The angle steepens.

I was against taking the casket thing 'cause it just pressed the truck down in the mud more, made it more likely Bud'd get stuck, but now it is the only thing holding the truck against the current.

The yellow froths around the bumpers at each end, and we're shouting—to surely no effect, of course.

SUSAN

The animal is trying to eat us, it has seen Gene and wants him. I lean over and strike at the yellow animal that is everywhere swirling around us, but it just takes my hand and takes the smack of my palm like it was no matter at all, and I start to cry, I don't know what to do.

JOHNNY

My throat filled up, I was so afraid.

Bud. I can hear him grunting as he twists at the steering wheel.

His jaw is clenched, and the woman Susan calls to us, "Catch him! Catch Gene!"

I hold on, and the waters suck at me.

TURKEY

I can tell Bud is afraid to gun it and start the wheels to spinning 'cause he'll lose traction and that'll tip us over for sure.

Susan jumps out and stands in the wash downstream and pushes against the truck to keep it from going over. The pressure is shoving it off the Ford, and the casket, it slides down a foot or so, the cables have worked loose. Now she pays because the weight is worse, and she jams herself like a stick to wedge between the truck and the mud.

It if goes over, she's finished. It is a fine thing to do, crazy but fine, and I jump down and start wading to reach her.

No time.

There is an eddy. The log turns broadside. It backs off a second and then heads forward again, this time poking up from a surge. I can see Bud duck, he has got the window up and the log hits it, the glass going all to smash and scatteration.

BUD

All over my lap it falls like snow. Twinkling glass.

But the pressure of the log is off, and I gun the sumbitch. We root out of the hollow we was in, and the truck thunks down solid on somethin'.

The log is ramming against me. I slam on the brake.

Take both hands and shove it out. With every particle of force I got.

It backs off and then heads around and slips in front of the hood, bumping the grill just once.

ANGEL

Like it had come to do its job and was finished and now went off to do something else.

SUSAN

Muddy, my arms hurting. I scramble back in the truck with the murmur of the water all around us. Angry with us now. Wanting us.

Bud makes the truck roar, and we lurch into a hole and out of it and up. The water gurgles at us in its fuming, stinking rage.

I check Gene and the power cells. They are dead.

He is heating up.

Not fast, but it will wake him. They say even in the solution he's floating in, they can come out of dreams and start to feel again. To hurt.

I yell at Bud that we got to find power cells.

"Those're not just ordinary batteries, y'know," he says.

"There're some at DataComm," I tell him.

We come wallowing up from the gum-yellow water and onto the highway.

GENE

Sleeping . . . slowly . . . I can still feel . . . only in sluggish . . . moments . . . moments . . . not true sleep but a drifting, aimless dreaming . . . faint tugs and ripples . . . hollow sounds. . . . I am underwater and drowning . . . but don't care . . . don't breathe. . . . Spongy stuff fills my lungs . . . easier to rest them . . . floating in snowflakes . . . a watery winter . . . but knocking comes . . . goes . . . jolts . . . slips away before I can remember what it means. . . . Hardest . . . yes . . . hardest thing is to remember the secret . . . so when I am in touch again . . . DataComm will know . . . what I learned . . . when the C31 crashed . . . when I learned. . . . It is hard to clutch onto the slippery, shiny fact . . . in a marsh of slick, soft bubbles .. . silvery as air . . . winking ruby-red behind my eyelids . . . Must snag the secret . . . a hard fact like shiny steel in the spongy moist warmness. . . . Hold it to me. . . . Something knocks my side . . . a thumping. . . . I am sick. . . . Hold the steel secret . . . keep . . .

MC355

The megatonnage in the Soviet assault exploded low—ground-pounders, in the jargon. This caused huge fires, MC355's simulation showed. A pall of soot rose, blanketing Texas and the South, then diffusing outward on global circulation patterns.

Within a few days, temperatures dropped from balmy summer to near-freezing. In the Gulf region where MC355 lay, the warm ocean continued to feed heat and moisture into the marine boundary layer near the shore. Cold winds rammed into this water-laden air, spawning great roiling storms and deep snows. Thick stratus clouds shrouded the land for at least a hundred kilometers inland.

All this explained why MC355's extended feelers had met chaos and destruction. And why there were no local radio broadcasts. What the ElectroMagnetic Pulse did not destroy, the storms did.

The remaining large questions were whether the war had gone on, and if any humans survived in the area at all.

MR. ACKERMAN

I'd had more than enough of this time. The girl Susan had gone mad right in front of us, and we'd damn near all drowned getting across.

"I think we ought to get back as soon's we can," I said to Bud when we stopped to rest on the other side.

"We got to deliver the boy."

"It's too disrupted down this way. I figured on people here, some civilization."

"Somethin' got 'em."

"The bomb."

"Got to find cells for the man in the box."

"He's near dead."

"Too many gone already. Should save one if we can."

"We got to look after our own."

Bud shrugged, and I could see I wasn't going to get far with him. So I said to Angel, "The boy's not worth running such risks. Or this corpse."

ANGEL

I didn't like Ackerman before the war, and even less afterward, so when he started hinting that maybe we should shoot back up north and ditch the boy and Susan and the man in there, I let him have it. From the look on Bud's face, I knew he felt the same way. I spat out a real choice set of words I'd heard my father use once on a grain buyer who'd weaseled out of a deal, stuff I'd been saving for years, and I do say it felt *good.*

TURKEY

So we run down the east side of the bay, feeling released to be quit of the city and the water, and heading down into some of the finest country in all the South. Through Daphne and Montrose and into Fairhope, the moss hanging on the trees and now and then actual sunshine slanting golden through the green of huge old mimosas.

We're jammed into the truck bed, hunkered down because the wind whipping by has some sting to it. The big purple clouds are blowing south now.

Still no people. Not that Bud slows down to search good. Bones of cattle in the fields, though. I been seeing them so much now I hardly take notice anymore.

There's a silence here so deep that the wind streaming through the pines seems loud. I don't like it, to come so far and see nobody. I keep my paper bag close.

Fairhope's a pretty town, big oaks leaning out over the streets and a long pier down at the bay with a park where you can go cast fishing. I've always liked it here, intended to move down until the prices shot up so much.

We went by some stores with windows smashed in, and that's when we saw the man.

ANGEL

He was waiting for us. Standing beside the street in jeans and a floppy yellow shirt all grimy and not tucked in: I waved at him the instant I saw him, and he waved back. I yelled, excited, but he didn't say anything.

Bud screeched on the brakes. I jumped down and went around the tail of the truck. Johnny followed me.

The man was skinny as a rail and leaning against a telephone pole. A long, scraggly beard hid his face, but the eyes beamed out at us, seeming to pick up the sunlight.

"Hello!" I said again.

"Kiss." That was all.

"We came from . . ." and my voice trailed off because the man pointed at me.

"Kiss."

MR. ACKERMAN

I followed Angel and could tell right away the man was suffering from malnutrition. The clothes hung off him.

"Can you give us information?" I asked.

"No."

"Well, why not, friend? We've come looking for the parents of—"

"Kiss first."

I stepped back. "Well, now, you have no right to demand—" Out of the corner of my eye, I could see Bud had gotten out of the cab and stopped and was going back in now, probably for his gun. I decided to save the situation before somebody got hurt.

"Angel, go over to him and speak nicely to him. We need—"

"Kiss now."

The man pointed again with a bony finger.

Angel said, "I'm not going to go—" and stopped because the man's hand went down to his belt. He pulled up the filthy yellow shirt to reveal a pistol tucked in his belt.

"Kiss."

"Now, friend, we can—"

The man's hand came up with the pistol and reached level, pointing at us.

"Pussy."

Then his head blew into a halo of blood.

BUD

Damn if the one time I needed it, I left it in the cab. I was still fetching it out when the shot went off. Then another.

TURKEY

A man shows you his weapon in his hand, he's a fool if he doesn't mean to use it.

I drew out the pistol I'd been carrying in my pocket all this time, wrapped in plastic. I got it out of the damned bag pretty quick while the man was looking crazy-eyed at Angel and bringing his piece up.

It was no trouble at all to fix him in the notch. Couldn't have been more than thirty feet.

But going down he gets one off, and I feel like somebody pushed at my left calf. Then I'm rolling. Drop my pistol, too. I end up smack face-down on the hardtop, not feeling anything yet.

ANGEL

I like to died when the man flopped down, so sudden I thought he'd slipped, until then the bang registered.

I rushed over, but Turkey shouted, "Don't touch him."

Mr. Ackerman said, "You idiot! That man could've told us—"

"Told nothing," Turkey said. "He's crazy."

Then I notice Turkey's down, too. Susan is working on him, rolling up his jeans. It's gone clean through his big muscle there.

Bud went to get a stick. Poked the man from a safe distance. Managed to pull his shirt aside. We could see the sores all over his chest. Something terrible it looked.

Mr. Ackerman was swearing and calling us idiots until we saw that. Then he shut up.

TURKEY

Must admit it felt good. First time in years anybody ever admitted I was right.

Paid back for the pain. Dull, heavy ache it was, spreading. Susan gives me a shot and a pill and has me bandaged uptight. Blood stopped easy, she says. I clot good.

We decided to get out of there, not stopping to look for Johnny's parents.

We got three blocks before the way was blocked.

It was a big metal cylinder, fractured on all sides. Glass glittering around it.

Right in the street. You can see where it hit the roof of a clothing store, Bedsole's, caved in the front of it and rolled into the street.

They all get out and have a look, me sitting in the cab. I see the Russian writing again on the end of it.

I don't know much, but I can make out at the top CeKPeT and a lot of words that look like warning, including бЛО'еН, which is sick, and some more I didn't know, and then II 0 OҐO'H, which is weather.

"What's it say?" Mr. Ackerman asks.

"That word at the top there's *secret*, and then something about biology and sickness and rain and weather."

"I thought you knew this writing," he says.

I shook my head. "I know enough."

"Enough to what?"

"To know this was some kind of targeted capsule. It fell right smack in the middle of Fairhope, biggest town this side of the bay."

"Like the other one?" Johnny says, which surprised me. The boy is smart.

"The one hit the causeway? Right."

"One *what*?" Mr. Ackerman asks.

I don't want to say it with the boy there and all, but it has to come out sometime. "Some disease. Biological warfare."

They stand there in the middle of Prospect Avenue with open, silent nothingness around us, and nobody says anything for the longest time. There won't be any prospects here for a long time. Johnny's parents we aren't going to find, nobody we'll find, because whatever came spurting out of this capsule when it busted open—up high, no doubt, so the wind could take it—had done its work.

Angel sees it right off. "Must've been time for them to get inside," is all she says, but she's thinking the same as me.

It got them into such a state that they went home and holed up to die, like an animal will. Maybe it would be different in the North or the West—people are funny out there, they might just as soon sprawl across the sidewalk—but down here people's first thought is home, the family, the only thing that might pull them through. So they went there and they didn't come out again.

Mr. Ackerman says, "But there's no smell," which was stupid because that made it all real to the boy, and he starts to cry. I pick him up.

JOHNNY

'Cause that means they're all gone, what I been fearing ever since we crossed the causeway, and nobody's there, it's true, Mom Dad nobody at all anywhere just emptiness all gone.

MC355

The success of the portable unit makes MC355 bold.

It extrudes more sensors and finds not the racing blizzard winds of months before but rather warming breezes, the soft sigh of pines, a low drone of reawakening insects.

There was no nuclear winter.

Instead, a kind of nuclear autumn.

The swirling jet streams have damped, the stinging ultraviolet gone. The storms retreat, the cold surge has passed. But the electromagnetic spectrum lies bare, a muted hiss. The EMP silenced man's signals, yes.

Opticals, fitted with new lenses, scan the night sky. Twinkling dots scoot across the blackness, scurrying on their Newtonian rounds.

The Arcapel Colony.

Russphere.

U.S1.

All intact. So they at least have survived.

Unless they were riddled by buckshot-slinging antisatellite devices. But, no—the inflated storage sphere hinged beside the U.S1 is undeflated, unbreached.

So man still lives in space, at least.

MR. ACKERMAN

Crazy, I thought, to go out looking for this DataComm when everybody's dead. Just the merest step inside one of the houses proved that.

But they wouldn't listen to me. Those who would respectfully fall silent when I spoke now ride over my words as if I weren't there.

All because of that stupid incident with the sick one. He must have taken longer to die. I couldn't have anticipated that. He just seemed hungry to me.

It's enough to gall a man.

ANGEL

The boy is calm now, just kind of tucked into himself. He knows what's happened to his mom and dad. Takes his mind off his hurt, anyway. He bows his head down, his long dirty-blond hair hiding his expression. He leans against Turkey and they talk. I can see them through the back cab window.

In amongst all we've seen, I suspect it doesn't come through to him full yet. It will take a while. We'll all take a while.

We head out from Fairhope quick as we can. Not that anyplace else is different. The germs must've spread twenty, thirty mile inland from here. Which is why we seen nobody before who'd heard of it. Anybody close enough to know is gone.

Susan's the only one it doesn't seem to bother. She keeps crooning to that box.

Through Silverhill and on to Robertsdale. Same everywhere—no dogs bark, cattle bones drying in the fields.

We don't go into the houses.

Turn south toward Foley. They put this DataComm in the most inconspicuous place, I guess because secrets are hard to keep in cities. Anyway, it's in a pine grove south of Foley, land good for soybeans and potatoes.

SUSAN

I went up to the little steel door they showed me once and I take a little signet thing and press it into the slot.

Then the codes. They change them every month, but this one's still good, 'cause the door pops open.

Two feet thick it is. And so much under there you could spend a week finding your way.

Bud unloads the T-Isolate, and we push it through the mud and down the ramp.

BUD

Susan's better now, but I watch her careful.

We go down into this pale white light everywhere. All neat and trim.

Pushing that big isolate thing, it takes a lot out of you. 'Specially when you don't know where to.

But the signs light up when we pass by. Somebody's expecting.

To the hospital is where.

There are places to hook up this isolate thing, and Susan does it. She is OK when she has something to do.

MC355

The men have returned. Asked for shelter.

And now, plugged in, MC355 reads the sluggish, silky, grieving mind.

GENE

At last . . . someone has found the tap-in. . . . I can feel the images flit like shiny blue fish through the warm slush I float in. . . . Someone . . . asking . . . so I take the hard metallic ball of facts and I break it open so the someone can see. . . . So slowly I do it . . . things hard to remember . . . steely-bright. . . . I saw it all in one instant. . . . I was the only one on duty then with Top Secret, Weapons Grade Clearance, so it all came to me . . . attacks on both U.S. and USSR . . . some third party . . . only plausible scenario . . . a maniac . . . and all the counter-force and MAD and strategies options . . . a big joke . . . irrelevant . . . compared to the risk of accident or third parties . . . that was the first point, and we all realized it when the thing was only an hour old, but then it was too . . .

TURKEY

It's creepy in here, everybody gone. I'd hoped somebody's hid out and would be waiting, but when Bud wheels the casket thing through these halls, there's nothing—your own voice coming back thin and empty, reflected from rooms beyond rooms beyond rooms, all waiting under here. Wobbling along on the crutches Johnny fetched me, I get lost in this electronic city clean and hard. We are like something that washed up on the beach here. God, it must've cost more than all Fairhope itself, and who knew it was here? Not me.

GENE

A plot it was, just a goddamn plot with nothing but pure blind rage and greed behind it . . . and the hell of it is, we're never going to know who did it precisely . . . 'cause in the backwash whole governments will fall, people stab each other in the back . . . no way to tell who paid the fishing boat captains offshore to let the cruise missiles aboard . . . bet those captains were surprised when the damn things launched from the deck . . . bet they were told it was some kind of stunt . . . and then the boats all evaporated into steam when the fighters got them . . . no hope of getting a story out of that . . . all so comic when you think how easy it was . . . and the same for the Russians, I'm sure . . . dumbfounded confusion . . . and nowhere to turn . . . nobody to hit back-at . . . so they hit us . . . been primed for it so long that's the only way they could think . . . and even then there was hope . . . because the defenses worked . . . people got to the shelters. . . . The satellite rockets knocked out hordes of Soviet warheads. . . . We surely lessened the damage, with the defenses and shelters, too . . . but we hadn't allowed for the essential final fact that all the science and strategy pointed to . . .

BUD

Computer asked us to put up new antennas.

A week's work, easy, I said.

It took two.

It fell to me, most of it. Be weeks before Turkey can walk. But we got it done.

First signal comes in, it's like we're Columbus. Susan finds some wine and we have it all 'round.

We get U.S1. The first to call them from the whole South. 'Cause there isn't much South left.

GENE

But the history books will have to write themselves on this one. . . . I don't know who it was and now don't care . . . because one other point all we strategic planners and analysts missed was that nuclear winter didn't mean the end of anything . . . anything at all . . . just that you'd be careful to not use nukes anymore. . . . Used to say that love would find a way . . . but one thing I know . . . war will find a way, too . . . and this time the Soviets loaded lots of their warheads with biowar stuff, canisters fixed to blow high above cities . . . stuff your satellite defenses could at best riddle with shot but not destroy utterly, as they could the high explosive in nuke warheads. . . . All so simple . . . if you know there's a nuke winter limit on the megatonnage you can deliver . . . you use the nukes on C31 targets and silos . . . and then biowar the rest of your way. . . . A joke, really . . . I even laughed over it a few times myself . . . we'd placed so much hope in ol' nuke winter holding the line . . . rational as all hell . . . the scenarios all so clean . . . easy to calculate . . . we built our careers on them. . . . But this other way . . . so simple . . . and no end to it . . . and all I hope's . . . hope's . . . the bastard started this . . . some third-world general . . . caught some of the damned stuff, too. . . .

BUD

The germs got us. Cut big stretches through the U.S. We were just lucky. The germs played out in a couple of months, while we were holed up. Soviets said they'd used the bio stuff in amongst the nukes to show us what they could do, long term. Unless the war stopped right there. Which it did.

But enough nukes blew off here and in Russia to freeze up everybody for July and August, set off those storms.

Germs did the most damage, though—plagues.

It was a plague canister that hit the Slocum building. That did in Mobile.

The war was all over in a couple of hours. The satellite people, they saw it all.

Now they're settling the peace.

MR. ACKERMAN

"We been sitting waiting on this corpse long enough," I said, and got up.

We got food from the commissary here. Fine, I don't say I'm anything but grateful for that. And we rested in the bunks, got recuperated. But enough's enough. The computer tells us it wants to talk to the man Gene some more. Fine, I say.

Turkey stood up. "Not easy, the computer says, this talking to a man's near dead. Slow work."

Looking around, I tried to take control, assume leadership again. Jutted out my chin. "Time to get back."

But their eyes are funny. Somehow I'd lost my real power over them. It's not anymore like I'm the one who led them when the bombs started.

Which means, I suppose, that this thing isn't going to be a new beginning for me. It's going to be the same life. People aren't going to pay me any more real respect than they ever did.

MC355

So the simulations had proved right. But as ever, incomplete.

MC355 peered at the shambling, adamant band assembled in the hospital bay, and pondered how many of them might be elsewhere.

Perhaps many. Perhaps few.

It all depended on data MC355 did not have, could not easily find. The satellite worlds swinging above could get no accurate count in the U.S. or the USSR.

Still—looking at them, MC355 could not doubt that there were many. They were simply too brimming with life, too hard to kill. All the calculations in the world could not stop these creatures.

The humans shuffled out, leaving the T-Isolate with the woman who had never left its side. They were going.

MC355 called after them. They nodded, understanding, but did not stop.

MC355 let them go.

There was much to do.

New antennas, new sensors, new worlds.

TURKEY

Belly full and eye quick, we came out into the pines. Wind blowed through with a scent of the Gulf on it, fresh and salty with rich moistness.

The dark clouds are gone. I think maybe I'll get Bud to drive south some more. I'd like to go swimming one more time in those breakers that come booming in, taller than I am, down near Fort Morgan. Man never knows when he'll get to do it again.

Bud's ready to travel. He's taking a radio so's we can talk to MC, find out about the help that's coming. For now, we got to get back and look after our own.

Same as we'll see to the boy. He's ours, now.

Susan says she'll stay with Gene till he's ready, till some surgeons turn up can work on him. That'll be a long time, say I. But she can stay if she wants. Plenty food and such down there for her.

A lot of trouble we got, coming a mere hundred mile. Not much to show for it when we get back. A bumper crop of bad news, some would say. Not me. It's better to know than to not, better to go on than to look back.

So we go out into dawn, and there are the same colored dots riding in the high, hard blue. Like camp fires.

The crickets are chirruping, and in the scrub there's a rustle of things moving about their own business, a clean scent of things starting up. The rest of us, we mount the truck and it surges forward with a muddy growl, Ackerman slumped over, Angel in the cab beside Bud, the boy already asleep on some blankets; and the forlorn sound of us moving among the windswept trees is a long and echoing note of mutual and shared desolation, powerful and pitched forward into whatever must come now, a muted note persisting and undeniable in the soft, sweet air.

EPILOGUE
(twenty-three years later)

JOHNNY

An older woman in a formless, wrinkled dress and worn shoes sat at the side of the road. I was panting from the fast pace I was keeping along the white strip of sandy, rutted road. She sat, silent and unmoving. I nearly walked by before I saw her.

"You're resting?" I asked.

"Waiting." Her voice had a feel of rustling leaves. She sat on the brown cardboard suitcase with big copper latches—the kind made right after the war. It was cracked along the side, and white cotton underwear stuck out.

"For the bus?"

"For Buck."

"The chopper recording, it said the bus will stop up around the bend."

"I heard."

"It won't come down this side road. There's no time."

I was late myself, and I figured she had picked the wrong spot to wait.

"Buck will be along."

Her voice was high and had the backcountry twang to it. My own voice still had some of the same sound, but I was keeping my vowels flat and right now, and her accent reminded me of how far I had come.

I squinted, looking down the long sandy curve of the road. A pickup truck growled out of a clay side road and onto the hardtop. People rode in the back along with trunks and a 3D. Taking everything they could. Big white eyes shot a glance at me, and then the driver hit the hydrogen and got out of there.

The Confederation wasn't giving us much time. Since the unification of the Soviet, U.S.A., and European/Sino space colonies into one political union, everybody'd come to think of them as the Confeds, period—one entity. I knew better—there were tensions and differences abounding up there—but the shorthand was convenient.

"Who's Buck?"

"My dog." She looked at me directly, as though any fool would know who Buck was.

"Look, the bus—"

"You're one of those Bishop boys, aren't you?"

I looked off up the road again. That set of words—being eternally a Bishop boy—was like a grain of sand caught between my back teeth. My mother's friends had used that phrase when they came over for an evening of bridge, before I went away to the university. Not my real mother, of course—she and Dad had died in the war, and I dimly remembered them.

Or anyone else from then. Almost everybody around here had been struck down by the Soviet bioweapons. It was the awful swath of those that cut through whole states, mostly across the South—the horror of it—that had formed the basis of the peace that followed. Nuclear and bioarsenals were reduced to nearly zero now. Defenses in space were thick and reliable. The building of those had fueled the huge boom in Confed cities, made orbital commerce important, provided jobs and horizons for a whole generation—including me. I was a ground-orbit liaison, spending four months every year at U.S3. But to the people down here, I was eternally that oldest Bishop boy.

Bishops. I was the only one left who'd actually lived here before the war. I'd been away on a visit when it came. Afterward, my Aunt and Uncle Bishop from Birmingham came down to take over the old family property—to save it from being homesteaded on, under the new Federal Reconstruction Acts. They'd taken me in, and I'd thought of them as Mom and Dad. We'd all had the Bishop name, after all. So I was a Bishop, one of the few natives who'd made it through the bombing and nuclear autumn and all. People'd point me out as almost a freak, a real native, wow.

"Yes, ma'am," I said neutrally.

"Thought so."

"You're . . . ?"

"Susan McKenzie."

"Ah."

We had done the ritual, so now we could talk. Yet some memory stirred. . . .

"Something 'bout you . . ." She squinted in the glaring sunlight. She probably wasn't all that old, in her late fifties, maybe. Anybody who'd caught some radiation looked aged a bit beyond their years. Or maybe it was just the unending weight of hardship and loss they'd carried.

"Seems like I knew you before the war," she said. "I strictly believe I saw you."

"I was up north then, a hundred miles from here. Didn't come back until months later."

"So'd I."

"Some relatives brought me down, and we found out what'd happened to Fairhope."

She squinted at me again, and then a startled look spread across her leathery face. "My Lord! Were they lookin' for that big computer center, the DataComm it was?"

I frowned. "Well, maybe . . . I don't remember too well. . . ."

"Johnny. You're Johnny!"

"Yes, ma'am, John Bishop." I didn't like the little-boy ending on my name, but people around here couldn't forget it.

"I'm Susan! The one who went with you! I had the codes for DataComm, remember?"

"Why . . . yes. . . ." Slow clearing of ancient, foggy images. "You were hiding in that center . . . where we found you. . . ."

"Yes! I had Gene in the T-Isolate."

"Gene . . ." That awful time had been stamped so strongly in me that I'd blocked off many memories, muting the horror. Now it came flooding back.

"I saved him, all right! Yessir. We got married, I had my children."

Tentatively, she reached out a weathered hand, and I touched it. A lump suddenly blocked my throat, and my vision blurred, Somehow, all those years had passed and I'd never thought to look up any of those people—Turkey, Angel, Bud, Mr. Ackerman. Just too painful, I guess. And a little boy making his way in a tough world, without his parents, doesn't look back a whole lot.

We grasped hands. "I think I might've seen you once, actu'ly. At a fish fry down at Point Clear. You and some boys was playing with the nets—it was just after the fishing came back real good, those Roussin germs'd wore off. Gene went down to shoo you away from the boats. I was cleaning flounder, and I thought then, maybe you were the one. But somehow when I saw your face at a distance, I couldn't go up to you and say anything. You was skipping around, so happy, laughing and all. I couldn't bring those bad times back."

"I . . . I understand."

"Gene died two year ago," she said simply.

"I'm sorry."

"We had our time together," she said, forcing a smile.

"Remember how we—" And then I recalled where I was, what was coming. "Mrs. McKenzie, there's not long before the last bus."

"I'm waiting for Buck."

"Where is he?"

"He run off in the woods, chasing something."

I worked by backpack straps around my shoulders. They creaked in the quiet.

There wasn't much time left. Pretty soon now it would start.

I knew the sequence, because I did maintenance engineering and retrofit on U.S3's modular mirrors.

One of the big reflectors would focus sunlight on a rechargeable tube of gas. That would excite the molecules. A small triggering beam would start the lasing going, the excited molecules cascading down together from one preferentially occupied quantum state to a lower state. A traveling wave swept down the tube, jarring loose more photons. They all added together in phase, so when the light waves hit the fare end of the hundred-meter tube, it was a sword, a gouging lance that could cut through air and clouds. And this time, it wouldn't strike an array of layered solid-state collectors outside New Orleans, providing clean electiricity. It would carve a swath twenty meters wide through the trees and fields of southern Alabama. A little demonstration, the Confeds said.

"The bus—look, I'll carry that suitcase for you."

"I can manage." She peered off into the distance, and I saw she was tired, tired beyond knowing it. "I'll wait for Buck."

"Leave him, Mrs. McKenzie."

"I don't need that blessed bus."

"Why not?"

"My children drove off to Mobile with their families. They're coming back to get me."

"My insteted radio"—I gestured at my radio—"says the roads to Mobile are jammed up. You can't count on them."

"They said so."

"The Confed deadline—"

"I told 'em I'd try to walk to the main road. Got tired, is all. They'll know I'm back in here."

"Just the same—"

"I'm all right, don't you mind. They're good children, grateful for all I've gone and done for them. They'll be back."

"Come with me to the bus. It's not far."

"Not without Buck. He's all the company I got these days." She smiled, blinking.

I wiped sweat from my brow and studied the pines. There were a lot of places for a dog to be. The land here was flat and barely above sea level. I had come to camp and rest, rowing skiffs up the Fish River, looking for places I'd been when I was a teenager and my mom had rented boats from a rambling old fisherman's house. I had turned off my radio, to get away from things. The big, mysterious island I remembered and called Treasure Island, smack in the middle of the river, was now a soggy stand of trees in a bog. The big storm a year back had swept it away.

I'd been sleeping in the open on the shore near there when the chopper woke me up, blaring. The Confeds had given twelve hours' warning, the recording said.

They'd picked this sparsely populated area for their little demonstration. People had been moving back in ever since the biothreat was cleaned out, but there still weren't many. I'd liked that when I was growing up. Open woods. That's why I came back every chance I got.

I should've guessed something was coming. The Confeds were about evenly matched with the whole rest of the planet now, at least in high-tech weaponry. Defense held all the cards. The big mirrors were modular and could fold up fast, making a small target. They could incinerate anything launched against them, too.

But the U.N. kept talking like the Confeds were just another nation-state or something. Nobody down here understood that the people up there thought of Earth itself as the real problem—eaten up with age-old rivalries and hate, still holding onto dirty weapons that murdered whole populations, carrying around in their heads all the rotten baggage of the past. To listen to them, you'd think they'd learned nothing from the war. Already they were forgetting that it was the orbital defenses that had saved the biosphere itself, and the satellite communities that knit together the mammoth rescue efforts of the decade after. Without the antivirals developed and grown in huge zero-g vats, lots of us would've caught one of the poxes drifting through the population. People just forget. Nations, too.

"Where's Buck?" I said decisively.

"He . . . that way." A wave of the hand.

I wrestled my backpack down, feeling the stab from my shoulder—and suddenly remembered the thunk of that steel knocking me down, back then. So long ago. And me, still carrying an ache from it that woke whenever a cold snap came on. The past was still alive.

I trotted into the short pines, over creeper grass. Flies jumped where my boots struck. The white sand made a *skree* sound as my boots skated over it. I remembered how I'd first heard that sound, wearing slick-soled tennis shoes, and how pleased I'd been at university when I learned how the acoustics of it worked.

"Buck!"

A flash of brown over to the left. I ran through a thick stand of pine, and the dog yelped and took off, dodging under a blackleaf bush. I called again. Buck didn't even slow down. I skirted left. He went into some oak scrub, barking, having a great time of it, and I could hear him getting tangled in it and then shaking free and out of the other side. Gone.

When I got back to Mrs. McKenzie, she didn't seem to notice me. "I can't catch him."

"Knew you wouldn't." She grinned at me, showing brown teeth. "Buck's a fast one."

"Call him."

She did. Nothing. "Must have run off."

"There isn't time—"

"I'm not leaving without ole Buck. Times I was alone down on the river after Gene died, and the water would come up under the house. Buck was the only company I had. Only soul I saw for five weeks in that big blow we had."

A low whine from afar. "I think that's the bus," I said.

She cocked her head. "Might be."

"Come on. I'll carry your suitcase."

She crossed her arms. "My children will be by for me. I tole them to look for me along in here."

"They might not make it."

"They're loyal children."

"Mrs. McKenzie, I can't wait for you to be reasonable." I picked up my backpack and brushed some red ants off the straps.

"You Bishops was always reasonable," she said levelly. "You work up there, don't you?"

"Ah, sometimes."

"You goin' back, after they do what they're doin' here?"

"I might." Even if I owed her something for what she did long ago, damned if I was going to be cowed.

"They're attacking the United States."

"And spots in Bavaria, the Urals, South Africa, Brazil—"

"'Cause we don't trust 'em! They think they can push the United *States* aroun' just as they please—" And she went on with all the clichés heard daily from earthbound media. How the Confeds wanted to run the world and they were dupes of the Russians, and how surrendering national sovereignty to a bunch of self-appointed overlords was an affront to our dignity, and so on.

True, some of it—the Confeds weren't saints. But they were the only power that thought in truly global terms, couldn't *not* think that way. They could stop ICBMs and punch through the atmosphere to attack any offensive capability on the ground—that's what this demonstration was to show. I'd heard Confeds argue that this was the only was to break the diplomatic logjam—do something. I had my doubts. But times were changing, that was sure, and my generation didn't think the way the prewar people did.

"We'll never be rule by some outside—"

"Mrs. McKenzie, there's the bus! Listen!"

The turbo whirred far around the bend, slowing for the stop.

Her face softened as she gazed at me, as if recalling memories. "That's all right, boy. You go along, now."

I saw that she wouldn't be coaxed or even forced down that last bend. She had gone as far as she was going to, and the world would have to come the rest of the distance itself.

Up ahead, the bus driver was probably behind schedule for this last pickup. He was going to be irritated and more than a little scared. The Confeds would be right on time, he knew that.

I ran. My feet plowed through the deep, soft sand. Right away I could tell I was more tired than I'd thought and the heat had taken some strength out of me. I went about two hundred meters along the gradual bend, was nearly within view of the bus, when I heard it start up with a rumble. I tasted salty sweat, and it felt like the whole damned planet was dragging at my feet, holding me down. The driver revved the engine, in a hurry.

He had to come toward me as he swung out onto Route 80 on the way back to Mobile. Maybe I could reach the intersection in time for him to see me. So I put my head down and plunged forward.

But there was the woman back there. To get to her, the driver would have to take the bus down that rutted, sandy road and risk getting stuck. With people on the bus yelling at him. All that to get the old woman with the grateful children. She didn't seem to understand that there were ungrateful children in the skies now—she didn't seem to understand much of what was going on—and suddenly I wasn't sure I did, either.

But I kept on.

The Feast of Saint Janis

Michael Swanwick

Take a load off, Janis,
And
You put the load right on me . . .

—"The Wait" (trad.)

Wolf stood in the early morning fog watching the *Yankee Clipper* leave Baltimore harbor. His elbows rested against a cool, clammy wall, its surface eroded smooth by the passage of countless hands, almost certainly dating back to before the Collapse. A metallic gray sparkle atop the foremast drew his eye to the dish antenna that linked the ship with the geosynchronous *Trickster* seasats it relied on to plot winds and currents.

To many, the wooden *Clipper,* with its computer-designed hydrofoils and hand-sewn sails, was a symbol of the New Africa. Wolf, however, watching it merge into sea and sky, knew only that it was going home without him.

He turned and walked back into the rick-a-rack of commercial buildings crowded against the waterfront. The clatter of hand-drawn carts mingled with a mélange of exotic cries and shouts, the alien music of a dozen American dialects. Workers, clad in coveralls most of them, swarmed about, grunting and cursing in exasperation when an iron wheel lurched in a muddy pothole. Yet there was something furtive and covert about them, as if they were hiding an ancient secret.

Craning to stare into the dark recesses of a warehouse, Wolf collided with a woman clad head to foot in chador. She flinched at his touch, her eyes glaring above the black veil, then whipped away. Not a word was exchanged.

A citizen of Baltimore in its glory days would not have recognized the city. Where the old buildings had not been torn down and buried, shanties crowded the streets, taking advantage of the space automobiles had needed. Sometimes they were built *over* the streets, so that alleys became tunnelways, and sometimes these collapsed, to the cries and consternation of the natives.

It was another day with nothing to do. He could don a filter mask and tour the Washington ruins, but he had already done that, and besides the day looked like it was going to be hot. It was unlikely he'd hear anything about his mission, not after months of waiting on American officials who didn't want to talk with him. Wolf decided to check back at his hostel for messages, then spend the day in the bazaars.

Children were playing in the street outside the hostel. They scattered at his approach. One, he noted, lagged behind the others, hampered by a malformed leg. He mounted the unpainted wooden steps, edging past an old man who sat at the bottom. The old man was laying down tarot cards with a slow and fatalistic disregard for what they said; he did not look up.

The bell over the door jangled notice of Wolf's entry. He stepped into the dark foyer.

Two men in the black uniforms of the Political Police appeared, one to either side of him. "Wolfgang Hans Mbikana?" one asked. His voice had the dust of ritual on it; he knew the answer. "You will come with us," the other said.

"There is some mistake," Wolf objected.

"No, sir, there is no mistake," one said mildly. The other opened the door. "After you, Mr. Mbikana."

The old man on the stoop squinted up at them, looked away, and slid off the step.

The police walked Wolf to an ancient administrative building. They went up marble steps sagging from centuries of foot-scuffing, and through an empty lobby. Deep within the building they halted before an undistinguished-looking door. "You are expected," the first of the police said.

"I beg your pardon?"

The police walked away, leaving him there. Apprehensive, he knocked on the door. There was no answer, so he opened it and stepped within.

A woman sat at a desk just inside the room. Though she was modernly dressed, she wore a veil. She might have been young; it was impossible to tell. A flick of her eyes, a motion of one hand, directed him to the open door of an inner room. It was like following an onion to its conclusion, a layer of mystery at a time.

A heavy-set man sat at the final desk. He was dressed in the traditional suit and tie of American businessmen. But there was nothing quaint or old-fashioned about his mobile, expressive face or the piercing eyes he turned on Wolf.

"Sit down," he grunted, gesturing toward an old, overstuffed chair. Then: "Charles DiStephano. Comptroller for Northeast Regional. You're Mbikana, right?"

"Yes, sir." Wolf gingerly took the proffered chair, which did not seem all that clean. It was becoming clear to him now; DiStephano was one of the men on whom he had waited these several months, the biggest of the lot, in fact. "I represent—"

"The Southwest Africa Trade Company." DiStephano lifted some documents from his desk. "Now this says you're prepared to offer—among other things—resource data from your North American *Coyote* landsat in exchange for the right to place students in Johns Hopkins. I find that an odd offer for your organization to make."

"Those are my papers," Wolf objected. "As a citizen of Southwest Africa, I'm not used to this sort of cavalier treatment."

"Look, kid, I'm a busy man, I have no time to discuss your rights. The papers are in my hands, I've read them, the people that sent you knew I would. Okay? So I know what you want and what you're offering. What I want to know is *why* you're making this offer."

Wolf was disconcerted. He was used to a more civilized, a more leisurely manner of doing business. The oldtimers at SWATC had warned him that the pace would be different here, but he hadn't had the experience to decipher their veiled references and hints. He was painfully aware that he had gotten the mission, with its high salary and the promise of a bonus, only because it was not one that appealed to the older hands.

"America was hit hardest," he said, "but the Collapse was worldwide." He wondered whether he should explain the system of corporate social responsibility that African business was based on. Then decided that if DiStephano didn't know, he didn't want to. "There are still problems. Africa has a high incidence of birth defects." *Because America exported its poisons; its chemicals and pesticides and foods containing a witch's brew of preservatives.* "We hope to do away with the problem; if a major thrust is made, we can clean up the gene pool in less than a century. But to do this requires professionals—eugenicists, embryonic surgeons—and while we have these, they are second-rate. The very best still come from your nation's medical schools."

"We can't spare any."

"We don't propose to steal your doctors. We'd provide our own students—fully trained doctors who need only the specialized training."

"There are only so many openings at Hopkins," DiStephano said. "Or at U of P or the UVM Medical College, for that matter."

"We're prepared to—" Wolf pulled himself up short. "It's in the papers. We'll pay enough that you can expand to meet the needs of twice the number of students we require." The room was dim and oppressive. Sweat built up under Wolf's clothing.

"Maybe so. You can't buy teachers with money, though." Wolf said nothing. "I'm also extremely reluctant to let your people *near* our medics. You can offer them money, estates—things our country cannot afford. And we *need* our doctors. As it is, only the very rich can get the corrective surgery they require."

"If you're worried about our pirating your professionals, there are ways around that. For example, a clause could be written—" Wolf went on, feeling more and more in control. He was getting somewhere. If there wasn't a deal to be made, the discussion would never have gotten this far.

The day wore on. DiStephano called in aides and dismissed them. Twice, he had drinks sent in. Once, they broke for lunch. Slowly the heat built, until it was sweltering. Finally, the light began to fail, and the heat grew less oppressive.

DiStephano swept the documents into two piles, returned one to Wolf, and put the other inside a desk drawer. "I'll look these over, have our legal boys run a study. There shouldn't be any difficulties. I'll get back to you with the final word in—say a month. September twenty-first. I'll be in Boston then, but you can find me easily enough, if you ask around."

"A month? But I thought . . ."

"A month. You can't hurry City Hall," DiStephano said firmly. "Ms. Corey!"

The veiled woman was at the door, remote, elusive. "Sir."

"Drag Kaplan out of his office. Tell him we got a kid here he should give the VIP treatment to. Maybe a show. It's a Hopkins thing, he should earn his keep."

"Yes, sir." She was gone.

"Thank you," Wolf said, "but I don't really need . . ."

"Take my advice, kid, take all the perks you can get. God knows there aren't many left. I'll have Kaplan pick you up at your hostel in an hour."

Kaplan turned out to be a slight, balding man with nervous gestures, some sort of administrative functionary for Hopkins. Wolf never did get the connection. But Kaplan was equally puzzled by Wolf's status, and Wolf took petty pleasure in not explaining it. It took some of the sting off of having his papers stolen.

Kaplan led Wolf through the evening streets. A bright sunset circled the world and the crowds were much thinner. "We won't be leaving the area that's zoned for electricity," Kaplan said. "Otherwise I'd advise against going out at night at all. Lot of jennie-deafs out then."

"Jennie-deafs?"

"Mutes. Culls. The really terminal cases. Some of them can't pass themselves off in daylight even wearing coveralls. Or chador—a lot are women." A faintly perverse expression crossed the man's face, leaving not so much as a greasy residue.

"Where are we going?" Wolf asked. He wanted to change the subject. A vague presentiment assured him he did not want to know the source of Kaplan's expression.

"A place called Peabody's. You've heard of Janis Joplin, our famous national singer?"

Wolf nodded, meaning no.

"The show is a recreation of her act. Woman name of Maggie Horowitz does the best impersonation of Janis I've ever seen. Tickets are almost impossible to get, but Hopkins has special influence in this case because—ah, here we are."

Kaplan led him down a set of concrete steps and into the basement of a dull, brick building. Wolf experienced a moment of dislocation. It was a bookstore. Shelves and boxes of books and magazines brooded over him, a packrat's clutter of paper.

Wolf wanted to linger, to scan the ancient tomes, remnants of a time and culture fast sinking into obscurity and myth. But Kaplan brushed past them without a second glance and he had to hurry to keep up.

They passed through a second roomful of books, then into a hallway where a gray man held out a gnarled hand and said, "Tickets, please."

Kaplan gave the man two crisp pasteboard cards, and they entered a third room.

It was a cabaret. Wooden chairs clustered about small tables with flickering candles at their centers. The room was lofted with wood beams, and a large, unused fireplace dominated one wall. Another wall had obviously been torn out at one time to make room for a small stage. Over a century's accumulation of memorabilia covered the walls or hung from the rafters, like barbarian trinkets from toppled empires.

"Peabody's is a local institution," Kaplan said. "In the twentieth century it was a speakeasy. H. L. Mencken himself used to drink here." Wolf nodded, though the name meant nothing to him. "The bookstore was a front and the drinking went on here in back."

The place was charged with a feeling of the past. It invoked America's bygone days as a world power. Wolf half expected to see Theodore Roosevelt or Henry Kissinger come striding in. He said something to this effect and Kaplan smiled complacently.

"You'll like the show, then," he said.

A waiter took their orders. There was barely time to begin on the drinks when a pair of spotlights came on, and the stage curtain parted.

A woman stood alone in the center of the stage. Bracelets and bangles hung from her wrists, gaudy necklaces from her throat. She wore large tinted glasses and a flowered granny gown. Her nipples pushed against the thin dress. Wolf stared at them in horrified fascination. She had an extra set, immediately below the first pair.

The woman stood perfectly motionless. Wolf couldn't stop staring at her nipples; it wasn't just the number, it was the fact of their being visible at all. So quickly had he taken on this land's taboos.

The woman threw her head back and laughed. She put one hand on her hip, thrust the hip out at an angle, and lifted the microphone to her lips. She spoke, and her voice was harsh and raspy.

"About a year ago I lived in a rowhouse in Newark, right? Lived on the third floor, and I thought I had my act together. But nothing was going right, I wasn't getting any . . . action. Know what I mean? No talent comin' around. And there was this chick down the street, didn't have much and she was doing okay, so I say to myself: *What's wrong, Janis?* How come she's doing so good and you ain't gettin' any? So I decided to check it out, see what she had that I didn't. And one day I get up early, look out the window, and I see this chick out there *hustling!* I mean, she was doing the streets at *noon!* So I said to myself, *Janis, honey, you ain't even trying.* And when ya want action, ya gotta try. Yeah. Try just a little bit harder."

The music swept up out of nowhere, and she was singing: "Try-iiii, Try-iiii, Just a little bit harder . . ."

And unexpectedly, it was good. It was like nothing he had ever heard, but he understood it, almost on an instinctual level. It was world-culture music. It was universal.

Kaplan dug fingers into Wolf's arm, brought his mouth up to Wolf's ear. "You see? You see?" he demanded. Wolf shook him off impatiently. He wanted to hear the music.

The concert lasted forever, and it was done in no time at all. It left Wolf sweaty and emotionally spent. Onstage, the woman was energy personified. She danced, she strutted, she wailed more power into her songs than seemed humanly possible. Not knowing the original, Wolf was sure it was a perfect recreation. It had that feel.

The audience loved her. They called her back for three encores, and then a fourth. Finally, she came out, gasped into the mike, "I love ya, honeys, I truly do. But please—no more. I just couldn't do it." She blew a kiss, and was gone from the stage.

The entire audience was standing, Wolf among them, applauding furiously. A hand fell on Wolf's shoulder, and he glanced to his side, annoyed. It was Kaplan. His face was flushed and he said, "Come on." He pulled Wolf free of the crowd and backstage to a small dressing room. It's door was ajar and people were crowded into it.

One of them was the singer, hair stringy and out-of-place, laughing and gesturing widely with a Southern Comfort bottle. It was an antique, its label lacquered to the glass, and three-quarters filled with something amber-colored.

"Janis, this is—" Kaplan began.

"The name is Maggie," she sang gleefully. "Maggie Horowitz. I ain't no *dead* blues singer. And don't you forget it."

"This is a fan of yours, Maggie. From Africa." He gave Wolf a small shove. Wolf hesitantly stumbled forward, grimacing apologetically at the people he displaced.

"Whee-howdy!" Maggie whooped. She downed a slug, from her bottle. "Pleased ta meetcha, Ace. Kinda light for an African, aintcha?"

"My mother's people were descended from German settlers." And it was felt that a light-skinned representative could handle the touchy Americans better, but he didn't say that.

"Whatcher name, Ace?"

"Wolf."

"Wolf!" Maggie crowed. "Yeah, you look like a real heartbreaker, honey. Guess I'd better be careful around you, huh? Likely to sweep me off my feet and deflower me." She nudged him with an elbow. "That's a joke, Ace."

Wolf was fascinated. Maggie was *alive,* a dozen times more so than her countrymen. She made them look like zombies. Wolf was also a little afraid of her.

"*Hey.* Whatcha think of my singing, hah?"

"It was excellent," Wolf said. "It was—" he groped for words "—in my land the music is quieter, there is not so much emotion."

"Yeah, well *I* think it was fucking good, Ace. Voice's never been in better shape. So tell 'em that at Hopkins, Kaplan. Tell 'em I'm giving them their money's worth."

"Of course you are," Kaplan said.

"Well, I *am,* goddammit. Hey, this place is like a morgue! Let's ditch this matchbox dressing room and hit the bars, hey? Let's party."

She swept them all out of the dressing room, out of the building, and into the street. They formed a small, boisterous group, noisily wandering the city, looking for bars.

"There's one a block thataway," Maggie said. "Let's hit it. Hey, Ace, I'd likeya ta meet Cynthia. Sin, this is Wolf. Sin and I are like one person inside two skins. Many's the time we've shared a piece of talent in the same bed. "Hey?" She cackled, and grabbed at Cynthia's ass.

"Cut it out, Maggie." Cynthia smiled when she said it. She was a tall, slim, striking woman.

"Hey, this town is *dead!*" Maggie screamed the last word, then gestured them all to silence so they could listen for the echo. "There it is." She pointed and they swooped down on the first bar.

After the third bar, Wolf lost track. At some point he gave up on the party and somehow made his way back to his hostel. The last he remembered of Maggie she was calling after him, "Hey, Ace, don't be a party poop." Then: "At least be sure to come back tomorrow, goddammit."

Wolf spent most of the next day in his room, drinking water and napping. His hangover was all but gone by the time evening took the edge off the day's heat. He thought of Maggie's half-serious invitation, dismissed it, and decided to go to the Club.

The Uhuru Club was ablaze with light by the time he wandered in, a beacon in a dark city. Its frequenters, after all, were all African foreign service, with a few commercial reps such as himself forced in by the insular nature of American society, and the need for polite conversation. It was de facto exempt from the power-use laws that governed the natives.

"Mbikana! Over here, lad, let me set you up with a drink." Nnamdi of the consulate waved him over to the bar. Wolf complied, feeling conspicuous as he always did in the club. His skin stood out here. Even the American servants were dark, though whether this was a gesture of deference or arrogance on the part of the local authorities, he could not guess.

"Word is that you spent the day closeted with the comptroller." Nnamdi had a gin-and-tonic set up. Wolf loathed the drink, but it was universal among the service people. "Share the dirt with us." Other faces gathered around; the service ran on gossip.

Wolf gave an abridged version of the encounter and Nnamdi applauded. "A full day with the Spider King and you escaped with your balls intact. An auspicious beginning for you, lad."

"Spider King?"

"Surely you were briefed on regional autonomy—how the country was broken up when it could no longer be managed by a central directorate? There *is* no higher authority than DiStephano in this part of the world, boy."

"Boston," Ajuji sniffed. Like most of the expatriates, she was a failure; unlike many, she couldn't hide the fact from herself. "That's exactly the sort of treatment one comes to expect from these savages."

"Now, Ajuji," Nnamdi said mildly. "These people are hardly savages. Why, before the Collapse they put men on the moon."

"Technology! Hard-core technology, that's all it was, of a piece with the kind that almost destroyed us all. If you want a measure of a people, you look at how they live. These—Yanks," she hissed the word to emphasize its filthiness, "live in squalor. Their streets are filthy, their cities are filthy, and even the ones who aren't rotten with genetic disease are filthy. A child can be taught to clean up after itself. What does that make them?"

"Human beings, Ajuji."

"Hogwash, Nnamdi."

Wolf followed the argument with acute embarrassment. He had been brought up to expect well from people with social standing. To hear gutter language and low prejudice from them was almost beyond bearing. Suddenly it *was* beyond bearing. He stood, his stool making a scraping noise as he pushed it back. He turned his back on them all, and left.

"Mbikana! You mustn't—" Nnamdi called after him.

"Oh, let him go," Ajuji cut in, with a satisfied tone, "you mustn't expect better. After all, he's practically one of *them*."

Well, maybe he was.

Wolf wasn't fully aware of where he was going until he found himself at Peabody's. He circled the building and found a rear door. He tried the knob; it turned loosely in his hand. Then the door swung open and a heavy, bearded man in coveralls leaned out. "Yes?" he said in an unfriendly tone.

"Uh," Wolf said. "Maggie Horowitz told me I could drop by."

"Look, pilgrim, there are a lot of people trying to get backstage. My job is to keep them out unless I know them. I don't know you."

Wolf tried to think of some response to this, and failed. He was about to turn away when somebody unseen said, "Oh, let him in, Deke."

It was Cynthia. "Come on," she said in a bored voice. "Don't clog up the doorway." The guard moved aside, and he entered.

"Thank you," he said.

"*Nada,*" she replied, "as Maggie would say. The dressing room is that way, pilgrim."

"Wolf, honey!" Maggie shrieked. How's it going, Ace? Ya catch the show?"

"No, I—"

"You shoulda. I was good. Really good. Janis herself was never better. Hey, gang! Let's split, hah? Let's go somewhere and get down and boogie."

A group of twenty ended up taking over a methane-lit bar outside the zoned-for-electricity sector. Three of the band had brought along their instruments, and they talked the owner into letting them play. The music was droning and monotonous. Maggie listened appreciatively, grinning and moving her head to the music.

"Whatcha think of that, Ace? Pretty good, hey? That's what we call Dead music."

Wolf shook his head. "I think it's well named."

"Hey, guys, you hear that? Wolf here just made a funny. There's hope for you yet, honey." Then she sighed. "Can't get behind it, huh? That's really sad, man. I mean they played *good* music back then; it was real. We're just echoes, man. Just playing away at them old songs. Got none of our own worth singing."

"Is that why you're doing the show, then?" Wolf asked, curious.

Maggie laughed. "Hell no. I do it because I got the chance. DiStephano got in touch with me—"

"DiStephano? The comptroller?"

"One of his guys, anyway. They had this gig all set up and they needed someone to play Janis. So they ran a computer search and came up with my name. And they offered me money, and I spent a month or two in Hopkins being worked over, and here I am. On the road to fame and glory." Her voice rose and warbled and mocked itself on the last phrase.

"Why did you have to go to Hopkins?"

"You don't think I was *born* looking like this? They had to change my face around. Changed my voice too, for which God bless. They brought it down lower, widened out my range, gave it the strength to hold onto them high notes and push 'em around."

"Not to mention the mental implants," Cynthia said.

"Oh, yeah, the 'plants so I could talk in a bluesy sorta way without falling out of character," Maggie said. "But that was minor."

Wolf was impressed. He had known that Hopkins was good, but this—! "What I don't understand is why your government did all this. What possible benefit is there for them?"

"Beats the living hell out of me, lover boy. Don't know, don't care, and don't ask. That's my motto."

A long-haired, pale young man sitting nearby said, "The government is all hacked up on social engineering. They do a lot of weird things, and you never find out why. You learn not to ask questions."

"Hey, listen, Hawk, bringing Janis back to life isn't weird. It's a beautiful thing to do," Maggie objected. "Yeah, I only wish they could *really* bring her back. Sit her down next to me. Love to talk with that lady."

"You two would tear each other's eyes out," Cynthia said.

"What? Why?"

"Neither one of you'd be willing to give up the spotlight to the other."

Maggie cackled. "Ain't it the truth? Still, she's one broad I'd love to have met. A *real* star, see? Not a goddammed echo like me."

Hawk broke in, said, "You, Wolf. Where does your pilgrimage take you now? The group goes on tour the day after tomorrow; what are your plans?"

"I don't really have any," Wolf said. He explained his situation. "I'll probably stay in Baltimore until it's time to go up north. Maybe I'll take a side trip or two."

"Why don't you join the group, then?" Hawk asked. "We're planning to make the trip one long party. And we'll slam into Boston in just less than a month. The tour ends there."

"That," said Cynthia, "is a real bright idea. All we need is another nonproductive person on board the train."

Maggie bristled. "So what's wrong with that? Not like we're paying for it, is it? What's wrong with it?"

"Nothing's wrong with it. It's just a dumb idea."

"Well, *I* like it. How about it, Ace? You on the train or off?"

"I—" He stopped. Well, why not? "Yes. I would be pleased to go along."

"Good." She turned to Cynthia. "*Your* problem, sweets, is that you're just plain jealous."

"Oh Christ, here we go again."

"Well, don't bother. It won't do any good. Hey, you see that piece of talent at the far end of the bar?"

"Maggie, that 'piece of talent,' as you call him, is eighteen years old. At most."

"Yeah. Nice though." Maggie stared wistfully down the bar. "He's kinda pretty, ya know?"

Wolf spent the next day clearing up his affairs and arranging for letters of credit. The morning of departure day, he rose early and made his way to Baltimore Station. A brief exchange with the guards let him into the walled trainyard.

The train was an ungainly steam locomotive with a string of rehabilitated cars behind it. The last car had the word PEARL painted on it, in antique psychedelic lettering.

"Hey, Wolf! Come lookit this mother." A lone figure waved at him from the far end of the train. Maggie.

Wolf joined her. "What do you think of it, hah?"

He searched for something polite to say. "It is very impressive," he said finally. The word that leapt to mind was grotesque.

"Yeah. Runs on garbage, you know that? Just like me."

"Garbage?"

"Yeah, there's a methane processing plant nearby. Hey, lookit me! Up and awake at eight in the morning. Can ya take it? Had to get behind a little speed to do it, though."

The idiom was beyond him. "You mean—you were late waking up?"

"What? Oh, hey, man, you can be—look, forget I said a thing. No." She pondered a second. "Look, Wolf. There's this stuff called 'speed,' it can wake you up in the morning, give you a little boost, get you going. Ya know?"

Awareness dawned. "You mean amphetamines.

"Yeah, well this stuff ain't exactly legal, dig? So I'd just as soon you didn't spread the word around. I mean, I trust you, man, but I wanna be sure you know what's happening before you go shooting off your mouth."

"I understand," Wolf said. "I won't say anything. But you know that amphetamines are—"

"Gotcha, Ace. Hey, you gotta meet the piece of talent I picked up last night. Hey, Dave! Get your ass over here, lover."

A young, sleepy-eyed blond shuffled around the edge of the train. He wore white shorts, defiantly it seemed to Wolf, and a loose blouse buttoned up to his neck. Giving Maggie a weak hug around the waist, he nodded to Wolf.

"Davie's got four nipples, just like me. How about that? I mean, it's gotta be a pretty rare mutation, hah?"

Dave hung his head, half blushing. "Aw, Janis," he mumbled. Wolf waited for Maggie to correct the boy, but she didn't. Instead she led them around and around the train, chatting away madly, pointing out this, that, and the other thing.

Finally, Wolf excused himself, and returned to his hostel. He left Maggie prowling about the train, dragging her pretty boy after her. Wolf went out for a long lunch, picked up his bags, and showed up at the train earlier than most of the entourage.

The train lurched, and pulled out of the station. Maggie was in constant motion, talking, laughing, directing the placement of luggage. She darted from car to car, never still. Wolf found a seat and stared out the window. Children dressed in rags ran alongside the tracks, holding out hands and begging for money. One or two of the party threw coins; more laughed and threw bits of garbage.

The children were gone, and the train was passing through endless miles of weathered ruins. Hawk sat down beside Wolf. "It'll be a slow trip," he said. "The train has to go around large sections of land it's better not to go through." He stared moodily at the broken-windowed shells that were once factories and warehouses. "Look out there, pilgrim, *that's* my country," he said in a disgusted voice. "Or the corpse of it."

"Hawk, you're close to Maggie."

"Now if you go out to the center of the continent . . ." Hawk's voice grew distant. "There's a cavern out there, where they housed radioactive waste. It was formed into slugs and covered with solid gold—anything else deteriorates too fast. The way I figure it, a man with a lead suit could go into the cavern and shave off a fortune. There's tons of the stuff there." He sighed. "Someday I'm going to rummage through a few archives and go."

"Hawk, you've got to *listen* to me."

Hawk held up a hand for silence. "It's about the drugs, right? You just found out and you want me to warn her."

"Warning her isn't good enough. Someone has to stop her."

"Yes, well. Try to understand. Maggie was in Hopkins for *three months* while they performed some very drastic surgery on her. She didn't look a thing like she does now, and she could sing, but her voice wasn't anything to rave about. Not to mention the mental implants.

"Imagine the pain she went through. Now ask yourself what are the two most effective painkillers in existence?"

"Morphine and heroin. But in my country, when drugs are resorted to, the doctors wean the patients off them before their release."

"That's not the point. Consider this—Maggie could have had Hopkins remove the extra nipples. They could have done it. But she wasn't willing to go through the pain."

"She seems proud of them."

"She talks about them a lot, at least."

The train lurched and stumbled. Three of the musicians had uncrated their guitars and were playing more Dead music. Wolf chewed his lip in silence for a time, then said, "So what is the point you're making?"

"Simply that Maggie was willing to undergo the greater pain so that she could become Janis. So when I tell you she only uses drugs as painkillers, you have to understand that I'm not necessarily talking about physical pain." Hawk got up and left.

Maggie danced into the car. "Big time!" she whooped. "We made it into the big time, boys and girls. Hey, let's party!"

The next ten days were one extended party, interspersed with concerts. The reception in Wilmington was phenomenal. Thousands came to see the show; many were turned away. Maggie was unsteady before the first concert, achingly afraid of failure. But she played a rousing set, and was called back time and time again. Finally exhausted and limp, her hair sticking to a sweaty forehead, she stood up front and gasped, "That's all there is, boys and girls. I love ya and I wish there was more to give ya, but there ain't. You used it all up." And the applause went on and on . . .

The four shows in Philadelphia began slowly, but built up big. A few seats were unsold at the first concert; people were turned away for the second. The last two were near-riots. The group entrained to Newark for a day's rest and put on a Labor Day concert that made the previous efforts look pale. They stayed in an obscure hostel for an extra day's rest.

Wolf spent his rest day sightseeing. While in Philadelphia he had hired a native guide and prowled through the rusting refinery buildings at Breeze Point. They rose to the sky forever in tragic magnificence, and it was hard to believe there had been enough oil in the world to fill the holding tanks there. In Wilmington, he let the local guide lead him to a small Italian neighborhood to watch a religious festival.

The festival was a parade, led first by a priest trailed by eight altar girls, with incense burners and fans. Then came twelve burly men carrying the flower-draped body of an ancient Cadillac. After them came the faithful, in coveralls and chador, singing.

Wolf followed the procession to the river, where the car was placed in a hole in the ground, sprinkled with holy water, and set afire.

He asked the guide what story lay behind the ritual, and the boy shrugged. It was old, he was told, very very old.

It was late when Wolf returned to the hostel. He was expecting a party, but found it dark and empty. Cynthia stood in the foyer, hands behind her back, staring out a barred window at black nothingness.

"Where is everybody?" Wolf asked. It was hot. Insects buzzed about the coal-oil lamp, batting against it frenziedly.

Cynthia turned, studied him oddly. Her forehead was beaded with sweat. "Maggie's gone home—she's attending a mid-school reunion. She's going to show her old friends what a hacking big star she's become. The others?" She shrugged. "Off wherever puppets go when there's no one to bring them to life. Their rooms, probably."

"Oh." Cynthia's dress clung damply to her legs and sides. Dark stains spread out from under her armpits. "Would you like to play a game of chess or—something?"

Cynthia's eyes were strangely intense. She took a step closer to him. "Wolf, I've been wondering. You've been celibate on this trip. Is there a problem? No? Maybe a girlfriend back home?"

"There was, but she won't wait for me." Wolf made a deprecating gesture. "Maybe that was part of the reason I took this trip."

She took one of his hands, placed it on her breast. "But you *are* interested in girls?" Then, before he could shape his answer into clumsy words, she whispered, "Come on," and led him to her room.

Once inside, Wolf seized Cynthia and kissed her, deeply and long. She responded with passion, then drew away and with a little shove toppled him onto the bed. "Off with your clothes," she said. She shucked her blouse in a complex, fluid motion. Pale breasts bobbled, catching vague moonlight from the window.

After an instant's hesitation, Wolf doffed his own clothing. By contrast with Cynthia he felt weak and irresolute, and it irked him to feel that way. Determined to prove he was nothing of the kind, he reached for Cynthia as she dropped onto the bed beside him. She evaded his grasp.

"Just a moment, pilgrim." She rummaged through a bag by the headboard. "Ah. Care for a little treat first? It'll enhance the sensations."

"Drugs?" Wolf asked, feeling an involuntary horror.

"Oh, come down off your high horse. Once won't melt your genes. Give a gander at what you're being so critical of."

"What is it?"

"Vanilla ice cream," she snapped. She unstoppered a small vial and meticulously dribbled a few grains of white powder onto a thumbnail. "This is expensive, so pay attention. You want to breathe it all in with one snort. Got that? So by the numbers: Take a deep breath and breathe out slowly. That's it. Now in. Now out and hold." Cynthia laid her thumbnail beneath Wolf's nose, pinched one nostril shut with her free hand. "Now in fast, yeah!"

He inhaled convulsively and was flooded with sensations. A crisp, clean taste filled his mouth, and a spray of fine white powder hit the back of his throat. It tingled pleasantly. His head felt spacious. He moved his jaw, suspiciously searching about with his tongue.

Cynthia quickly snorted some of the powder herself, restoppering the vial.

"Now," she said. "Touch me. Slowly, slowly, we've got all night. That's the way. Ahhhh." She shivered. "I think you've got the idea."

They worked the bed for hours. The drug, whatever it was, made Wolf feel strangely clearheaded and rational, more playful and more prone to linger. There was no urgency to their lovemaking; they took their time. Three, perhaps four times they halted for more of the powder, which Cynthia doled out with careful ceremony. Each time they returned to their lovemaking with renewed interest and resolution to take it slowly, to postpone each climax to the last possible instant.

The evening grew old. Finally, they lay on the sheets, not touching, weak and exhausted. Wolf's body was covered with a fine sheen of sweat. He did not care to even think of making love yet another time. He refrained from saying this.

"Not bad," Cynthia said softly. "I must remember to recommend you to Maggie."

"Sin, why do you do that?"

"Do what?"

"We've just—been as intimate as two human beings can be. But as soon as it's over, you say something cold. Is it that you're afraid of contact?"

"Christ." It was an empty syllable, devoid of religious content, and flat. Cynthia fumbled in her bag, found a flat metal case, pulled a cigarette out, and lit it. Wolf flinched inwardly. "Look, pilgrim, what are you asking for? You planning to marry me and take me away to your big, clean African cities to meet your momma? Hah?

"Didn't think so. So what do you want from me? Mental souvenirs to take home and tell your friends about? I'll give you one: I spent years saving up enough to go see a doctor, find out if I could have any brats. Went to one last year and what do you think he tells me? I've got red-cell dyscrasia, too far gone for treatment, there's nothing to do but wait. Lovely, hah? So one of these days it'll just stop working and I'll die. Nothing to be done. So long as I eat right, I won't start wasting away, so I can keep my looks up to the end. I could buy a little time if I gave up drugs like this—" she waved the cigarette, and an ash fell on Wolf's chest. He brushed it away quickly, "—and the white powder, and anything else that makes life worth living. But it wouldn't buy me enough time to do anything worth doing." She fell silent. "Hey. What time is it?"

Wolf climbed out of bed, rummaged through his clothing until he found his timepiece. He held it up to the window, squinted. "Um. Twelve . . . fourteen."

"Oh, *nukes*." Cynthia was up and scrabbling for her clothes. "Come on, get dressed. Don't just stand there."

Wolf dressed himself slowly. "What's the problem?"

"I promised Maggie I'd get some people together to walk her back from that damned reunion. It ended *hours* ago, and I lost track of the time." She ignored his grin. "Ready? Come on, we'll check her room first and then the foyer. God, is she going to be mad."

They found Maggie in the foyer. She stood in the center of the room, haggard and bedraggled, her handbag hanging loosely from one hand. Her face was livid with rage. The sputtering lamp made her face look old and evil.

"Well!" she snarled. "Where have you two been?"

"In my room, balling," Cynthia said calmly. Wolf stared at her, appalled.

"Well that's just beautiful. That's really beautiful, isn't it? Do you know where I've been while my two best friends were upstairs humping their brains out? Hey? Do you want to know?" Her voice reached a hysterical peak. "I was being *raped by two jennie-deafs,* that's where!"

She stormed past them, half-cocking her arm as if she were going to assault them with her purse, then thinking better of it. They heard her run down the hall. Her door slammed.

Bewildered, Wolf said, "But I—"

"Don't let her dance on your head," Cynthia said. "She's lying."

"Are you certain?"

"Look, we've lived together, bedded the same men—I know her. She's all hacked off at not having an escort home. And Little Miss Sunshine has to spread the gloom."

"We should have been there," Wolf said dubiously. "She could have been killed, walking home alone."

"Whether Maggie dies a month early or not doesn't make a bit of difference to me, pilgrim. I've got my own problems."

"A month—? Is Maggie suffering from a disease too?"

"We're all suffering, we all—ah, the hell with you too." Cynthia spat on the floor, spun on her heel, and disappeared down the hallway. It had the rhythm and inevitability of a witch's curse.

The half-day trip to New York left the troupe with playtime before the first concert, but Maggie stayed in seclusion, drinking. There was talk about her use of drugs, and this alarmed Wolf, for they were all users of drugs themselves.

There was also gossip about the reunion. Some held that Maggie had dazzled her former friends—who had not treated her well in her younger years—had been glamorous and gracious. The predominant view, however, was that she had been soundly snubbed, that she was still a freak and an oddity in the eyes of her former contemporaries. That she had left the reunion alone.

Rumors flew about the liaison between Wolf and Cynthia too. The fact that she avoided him only fed the speculation.

Despite everything, the New York City concerts were a roaring success. All four shows were sold out as soon as tickets went on sale. Scalpers made small fortunes that week, and for the first time the concerts were allowed to run into the evening. Power was diverted from a section of the city to allow for the lighting and amplification. And Maggie sang as she had never sung before. Her voice roused the audiences to a frenzy, and her blues were enough to break a hermit's heart.

They left for Hartford on the tenth, Maggie sequestered in her compartment in the last car. Crew members lounged about idly. Some strummed guitars, never quite breaking into a recognizable tune. Others talked quietly. Hawk flipped tarot cards into a heap, one at a time.

"Hey, this place is fucking *dead!"* Maggie was suddenly in the car, her expression an odd combination of defiance and guilt. "Let's party! Hey? Let's hear some music." She fell into Hawk's lap and nibbled on an ear.

"Welcome back, Maggie," somebody said.

"*Janis!*" she shouted happily. "The lady's name is Janis!"

Like a rusty machine starting up, the party came to life. Music jelled. Voices became animated. Bottles of alcohol appeared and were passed around. And for the remainder of the two days that the tram spent making wide, looping detours to avoid the dangerous stretches of Connecticut and New York, the party never died.

There were tense undertones to the party, however, a desperate quality in Maggie's gaiety. For the first time, Wolf began to feel trapped, to count the days that separated him from Boston and the end of the tour.

The dressing room for the first Hartford concert was cramped, small, badly lit—like every other dressing room they'd encountered. "Get your ass over here, Sin," Maggie yelled. "You've gotta make me up so I look strung out, like Janis did."

Cynthia held Maggie's chin, twisted it to the left, to the right. "Maggie, you don't *need* makeup to look strung out."

"Goddammit, yes I *do.* Let's get it on. Come on, come on—I'm a star, I shouldn't have to put up with this shit."

Cynthia hesitated, then began dabbing at Maggie's face, lightly accentuating the lines, the bags under her eyes.

Maggie studied the mirror. "Now *that's* grim," she said. "That's really grotesque."

"That's what you look like, Maggie."

"You cheap bitch! You'd think I was the one who nodded out last night before we could get it on." There was an awkward silence. "Hey, Wolf!" She spun to face him. "What do you say?"

"Well," Wolf began, embarrassed, "I'm afraid Cynthia's . . ."

"You see? Let's get this show on the road." She grabbed her cherished Southern Comfort bottle and upended it.

"That's not doing you any good either."

Maggie smiled coldly. "Shows what you know. Janis always gets smashed before a concert. Helps her voice." She stood, made her way to the curtains. The emcee was winding up his pitch. "Ladies and gentlemen . . . Janis!"

Screams arose. Maggie sashayed up to the mike, lifted it, laughed into it.

"Heyyy. Good ta see ya." She swayed and squinted at the crowd, and was off and into her rap. "Ya know, I went ta see a doctor the other week. Told him I was worried about how much drinking I was doing. Told him I'd been drinkin' heavy since I was twelve. Get up in the morning and have a few Bloody Marys with breakfast. Polish off a fifth before lunch. Have a few drinks at dinner, and really get into it when the partying begins. Told him how much I drank for how many years. So I said, 'Look, Doc, none of this ever hurt me any, but I'm kinda worried, ya know? Give it to me straight, have I got a problem? And he said, 'Man, I don't think you've got a problem. I think you're doing just *fine!*' "Cheers from the audience. Maggie smiled smugly. "Well, honey, *everybody's* got problems, and I'm no exception." The music came up. "But when I got problems, I got an answer, 'cause I can sing dem ole-time blues. Just sing my problems away." She launched into "Ball and Chain" and the audience went wild.

Backstage, Wolf was sitting on a stepladder. He had bought a cup of water from a vendor and was nursing it, taking small sips. Cynthia came up and stood beside him. They both watched Maggie strutting on stage, stamping and sweating, writhing and howling.

"I can never get over the contrast," Wolf said, not looking at Cynthia. "Out there everybody is excited. Back here, it's calm and peaceful. Sometimes I wonder if we're seeing the same thing the audience does."

"Sometimes it's hard to see what's right in front of your face." Cynthia smiled a sad, cryptic smile and left. Wolf had grown used to such statements, and gave it no more thought.

The second and final Hartford show went well. However, the first two concerts in Providence were bad. Maggie's voice and timing were off, and she had to cover with theatrics. At the second show she had to order the audience to dance—something that had never been necessary before. Her onstage raps became bawdier and more graphic. She moved her body as suggestively as a stripper, employing bumps and grinds. The third show was better, but the earthy elements remained.

The cast wound up in a bar in a bad section of town, where guards with guns covered the doorway from fortified booths. Maggie got drunk and ended up crying. "Man, I was so blitzed when I went onstage—you say I was good?"

"Sure, Maggie," Hawk mumbled. Cynthia snorted.

"You were very good," Wolf assured her.

"I don't remember a goddamned thing," she wailed. "You say I was good? It ain't fair, man. If I was good, I deserve to be able to remember it. I mean, what's the point otherwise? Hey?"

Wolf patted her shoulder clumsily. She grabbed the front of his dashiki and buried her face in his chest. "Wolf, Wolf, what's gonna *happen* to me?" she sobbed.

"Don't cry," he said, patting her hair.

Finally, Wolf and Hawk had to lead her back to the hostel. No one else was willing to quit the bar.

They skirted an area where all the buildings had been torn down but one. It stood alone, with great gaping holes where plate-glass had been, and large nonfunctional arches on one side.

"It was a fast-food building," Hawk explained when Wolf asked. He sounded embarrassed.

"Why is it still standing?"

"Because there are ignorant and superstitious people everywhere," Hawk muttered. Wolf dropped the subject.

The streets were dark and empty. They went back into the denser areas of town, and the sound of their footsteps bounced off the buildings. Maggie was leaning half-conscious on Hawk's shoulder, and he almost had to carry her.

There was a stirring in the shadows. Hawk tensed. "Speed up a bit, if you can," he whispered.

Something shuffled out of the darkness. It was large and only vaguely human. It moved toward them. "What—?" Wolf whispered.

"Jennie-deaf," Hawk whispered back. "If you know any clever tricks, this is the time to use 'em." The thing broke into a shambling run.

Wolf thrust a hand into a pocket and whirled to face Hawk. "Look," he said in a loud, angry voice. "I've taken *enough* from you! I've got a *knife* and I don't care *what* I do!" The jennie-deaf halted. From the corner of his eye, Wolf saw it slide back into the shadows.

Maggie looked up with a sleepy, quizzical expression. "Hey, what . . ."

"Never mind," Hawk muttered. He upped his pace, half-dragging Maggie after him. "That was arrogant," he said approvingly.

Wolf forced his hand from his pocket. He found he was shivering from aftershock. "*Nada,*" he said. Then: "That is the correct term?"

"Yeah."

"I wasn't certain that jennie-deafs really existed."

"Just some poor mute with gland trouble. Don't think about it."

Autumn was just breaking out when the troupe hit Boston. They arrived to find the final touches being put on the stage on Boston Common. A mammoth concert was planned; dozens of people swarmed about making preparations.

"This must be how America was all the time before the Collapse," Wolf said, impressed. He was ignored.

The morning of the concert, Wolf was watching canvas being hoisted above the stage, against the chance of rain, when a gripper ran up and said, "You, pilgrim, have you seen Janis?"

"Maggie," he corrected automatically. "No, not recently."

"Thanks," the man gasped, and ran off.

Not long after, Hawk hurried by and asked, "Seen Maggie lagging about?"

"No. Wait, Hawk, what's going on? You're the second person to ask me that."

Hawk shrugged. "Maggie's disappeared. Nothing to scream about."

"I hope she'll be back in time for the show."

"The local police are hunting for her. Anyway, she's got the implants; if she can move she'll be on stage. Never doubt it." He hurried away.

The final checks were being run, and the first concertgoers were beginning to straggle in when Maggie finally appeared. Uniformed men held each arm; she looked sober and angry. Cynthia took charge, dismissed the police, and took Maggie to the trailer that served as a dressing room.

Wolf watched from a distance, decided he could be of no use. He ambled about the Common aimlessly, watching the crowd grow. The people coming in found places to sit, took them, and waited. There was little talk among them, and what there was was quiet. They were dressed brightly, but not in their best. Some carried winejugs or blankets.

They were an odd crew. They did not look each other in the eye; their mouths were grim, their faces without expression. Their speech was low, but with an undercurrent of tension. Wolf wandered among them, eavesdropping, listening to fragments of their talk.

"Said that her child was going to . . ."

". . . needed that. Nobody needed that."

"Couldn't have paid it away . . ."

". . . tasted odd, so I didn't . . ."

"Had to tear down three blocks . . ."

". . . blood."

Wolf became increasingly uneasy. There was something about their expressions, their tones of voice. He bumped into Hawk, who tried to hurry past.

"Hawk, there is something very wrong happening."

Hawk's face twisted. He gestured toward the light tower. "No time," he said. "The show's beginning. I've got to be at my station." Wolf hesitated, then followed the man up the ladders of the light tower.

All of the Common was visible from the tower. The ground was thick with people, hordes of ant-specks against the brown of trampled earth. Not a child among them, and that felt wrong too. A gold-and-purple sunset smeared itself three-quarters of the way around the horizon.

Hawk flicked lights on and off, one by one, referring to a sheet of paper he held in one hand. Sometimes he cursed and respliced wires. Wolf waited. A light breeze ruffled his hair, though there was no hint of wind below.

"This is a sick country," Hawk said. He slipped a headset on, played a red spot on the stage, let it wink out. "You there, Patrick? The kliegs go on in two." He ran a check on all the locals manning lights, addressing them by name. "Average life span is something like forty-two—if you get out of the delivery room alive. The birthrate has to be very high to keep the population from dwindling away to nothing." He brought up all the red and blue spots. The stage was bathed in purple light. The canvas above locked black in contrast. An obscure figure strolled to the center mike.

"Hit it, Patrick." A bright pool of light illuminated the emcee. He coughed, went into his spiel. His voice boomed over the crowd, relayed away from the stage by a series of amps with timed delay along each rank, so that his voice reached the distant listeners in synchronization with the further amplification. The crowd moved sluggishly about the foot of the tower, set in motion by latecomers straggling in. "So the question you should ask yourself is why the government is wasting its resources on a goddamned show."

"All right," Wolf said. "Why?" He was very tense, very still. The breeze swept away his sweat, and he wished he had brought along a jacket. He might need one later.

"Because their wizards said to—the damn social engineers and their machines," Hawk answered. "Watch the crowd."

". . . *Janis!*" the loudspeakers boomed. And Maggie was on stage, rapping away, handling the microphone suggestively, obviously at the peak of her form. The crowd exploded into applause. Offerings of flowers were thrown through the air. Bottles of liquor were passed hand over hand and deposited on the stage.

From above it could not be seen how the previous month had taken its toll on Maggie. The lines on her face, the waxy skin, were hidden by the colored light. The kliegs bounced off her sequined dress dazzlingly.

Halfway through her second song, Maggie came to an instrumental break and squinted out at the audience. "Hey, what the fuck's the matter with you guys? Why ain't you *dancing?*" At her cue, scattered couples rose to their feet. "Ready on the kliegs," Hawk murmured into his headset. "Three, four, and five on the police." Bright lights pinpointed three widely separated parts of the audience, where uniformed men were struggling with dancers. A single klieg stayed on Maggie, who pointed an imperious finger at one struggling group and shrieked, "Why are you trying to stop them from dancing? I want them to dance. I *command* them to dance!"

With a roar, half the audience were on their feet. "Shut down three. Hold four and five to the count of three, then off. One—two—three! Good." The police faded away, lost among the dancers.

"That was prearranged," Wolf said. Hawk didn't so much as glance at him.

"It's part of the legend. You, Wolf, over to your right." Wolf looked where Hawk was pointing, saw a few couples at the edge of the crowd slip from the light into the deeper shadows.

"What am I seeing?"

"Just the beginning." Hawk bent over his control board.

By slow degrees the audience became drunk and then rowdy. As the concert wore on, an ugly, excited mood grew. Sitting far above it all, Wolf could still feel the hysteria grow, as well as see it. Women shed chador and danced atop it, not fully dressed. Men ripped free of their coveralls. Here and there, spotted through the crowd, couples made love. Hawk directed lights onto a few, held them briefly; in most cases the couples went on, unheeding.

Small fights broke out, and were quelled by police. Bits of trash were gathered up and set ablaze, so that small fires dotted the landscape. Wisps of smoke floated up. Hawk played colored spots on the crowd. By the time darkness was total, the lights and the bestial noise of the revelers combined to create the feel of a Witch's Sabbath.

"Pretty nasty down there," Hawk observed. "And all most deliberately engineered by government wizards."

"But there is no true feeling involved," Wolf objected. "It is nothing but animal lust. No—no involvement."

"Yeah." Onstage, Maggie was building herself up into a frenzy. And yet her blues were brilliant—she had never been better. "Not so much different from the other concerts. The only difference is that tonight nobody waits until they go home."

"Your government can't believe that enough births will result from this night to make any difference."

"Not tonight, no. But all these people will have memories to keep them warm over the winter." Then he spat over the edge of the platform. "Ahhhh, why should I spout their lies for them? It's just bread and circuses is all, just a goddamned release for the masses."

Maggie howled with delight. "Whee-ew, man! I'm gettin' horny just looking at you. Yeah, baby, get it on, that's right!" She was strutting up and down the stage, a creature of boundless energy, while the band filled the night with music, fast and urgent.

"Love it!" She stuck her tongue out at the audience and received howls of approval. She lifted her Southern Comfort bottle, took a gigantic swig, her hips bouncing to the music. More howls. She caressed the neck of the bottle with her tongue.

"Yeah! Makes me horny as sin, 'deed it does. Ya know," she paused a beat, then continued, "that's something I can really understand, man. 'Cause I'm just a horny little hippie chick myself. Yeah." Wolf suddenly realized that she was competing against the audience itself for its attention, that she was going to try to outdo everybody present.

Maggie stroked her hand down the front of her dress, lingering between her breasts, then between her legs. She shook her hair back from her eyes, the personification of animal lust. "I mean, shit. I mean, hippie chicks don't even wear no underwear." More ribald howls and applause. "Don't believe me, do ya?"

Wolf stared, was unable to look away as Maggie slowly spread her legs wide and squatted, giving the audience a good look up her skirt. Her frog face leered, and it was an ugly, lustful thing. She lowered a hand to the stage behind her for support, and beckoned. "Come to momma," she crooned.

It was like knocking the chocks out from a dam. There was an instant of absolute stillness, and then the crowd roared and surged forward. An ocean of humanity converged on the stage, smashing through the police lines, climbing up on the wooden platform. Wolf had a brief glimpse of Maggie trying to struggle to her feet, before she was overrun. There was a dazed, disbelieving expression on her face.

"Mother of Sin," Wolf whispered. He stared at the mindless, evil mob below. They were in furious motion, straining, forcing each other in great swirling eddies. He waited for the stage to collapse, but it did not. The audience kept climbing atop it, pushing one another off its edge, and it did not collapse. It would have been a mercy if it had.

A hand waved above the crowd, clutching something that sparkled. Wolf could not make it out at first. Then another hand waved a glittering rag, and then another, and he realized that these were shreds of Maggie's dress.

Wolf wrapped his arms around a support to keep from falling into the horror below. The howling of the crowd was a single, chaotic noise; he squeezed his eyes shut, vainly trying to fend it off. "Right on cue," Hawk muttered. "Right on goddamned cue." He cut off all the lights, and placed a hand on Wolf's shoulder.

"Come on. Our job is done here."

Wolf twisted to face Hawk. The act of opening his eyes brought on a wave of vertigo, and he slumped to the platform floor, still clutching the support desperately. He wanted to vomit and couldn't. "It's—they—Hawk, did you *see* it? Did you see what they did? Why didn't someone—?" He choked on his words.

"Don't ask me," Hawk said bitterly. "I just play the part of Judas Iscariot in this little drama." He tugged at Wolf's shoulders. "Let's go, pilgrim. We've got to go down now." Wolf slowly weaned himself of the support, allowed himself to be coaxed down from the tower.

There were men in black uniforms at the foot of the tower. One of them addressed Hawk. "Is this the African national?" Then, to Wolf: "Please come with us, sir. We have orders to see you safely to your hostel."

Tears flooded Wolf's eyes and he could not see the crowd, the Common, the men before him. He allowed himself to be led away, as helpless and as trusting as a small child.

In the morning, Wolf lay in bed staring at the ceiling. A fly buzzed somewhere in the room, and he did not look for it. In the streets, iron-wheeled carts rumbled by, and children chanted a counting-out game.

After a time he rose, dressed, and washed his face. He went to the hostel's dining room for breakfast.

There, finishing off a piece of toast, was DiStephano.

"Good morning, Mr. Mbikana. I was beginning to think I'd have to send for you." He gestured to a chair. Wolf looked about, took it. There were at least three of the political police seated nearby.

DiStephano removed some documents from his jacket pocket, handed them to Wolf. "Signed, sealed, and delivered. We made some minor changes in the terms, but nothing your superiors will object to." He placed the last corner of toast in the side of his mouth. "I'd say this was a rather bright beginning to your professional career."

"Thank you," Wolf said automatically. He glanced at the documents, could make no sense of them, dropped them in his lap.

"If you're interested, the *African Genesis* leaves port tomorrow morning. I've made arrangements that a berth be ready for you, should you care to take it. Of course, there will be another passenger ship in three weeks if you wish to see more of our country."

"No," Wolf said hastily. Then, because that seemed rude, "I'm most anxious to see my home again. I've been away far too long."

DiStephano dabbed at the corners of his mouth with a napkin, let it fall to the tablecloth. "Then that's that." He started to rise.

"Wait," Wolf said. "Mr. DiStephano, I . . . I would very much like an explanation."

DiStephano sat back down. He did not pretend not to understand the request. "The first thing you must know," he said, "is that Ms. Horowitz was not our first Janis Joplin."

"No," Wolf said.

"Nor the second."

Wolf looked up.

"She was the twenty-third, not counting the original. The show is sponsored every year, always ending in Boston on the Equinox. So far, it has always ended in the same fashion."

Wolf wondered if he should try to stab the man with a fork, if he should rise up and attempt to strangle him. There should be rage, he knew. He felt nothing. "Because of the brain implants."

"No. You must believe me when I say that I wish she had lived. The implants helped her keep in character, nothing more. It's true that she did not recall the previous women who played the part of Janis. But her death was not planned. It's simply something that—happens."

"Every year."

"Yes. Every year Janis offers herself to the crowd. And every year they tear her apart. A sane woman would not make the offer; a sane people would not respond in that fashion. I'll know that my country is on the road to recovery come the day that Janis lives to make a second tour." He paused. "Or the day we can't find a woman willing to play the role, knowing how it ends."

Wolf tried to think. His head felt dull and heavy. He heard the words, and he could not guess whether they made sense or not. "One last question," he said. "Why me?"

DiStephano rose. "One day you may return to our nation," he said. "Or perhaps not. But you will certainly rise to a responsible position within the Southwest Africa Trade Company. Your decision will affect our economy." Four men in uniform also rose from their chairs. "When that happens, I want you to understand one thing about our land: *We have nothing to lose.* Good day, and a long life to you, sir."

DiStephano's guards followed him out.

It was evening. Wolf's ship rode in Boston harbor, waiting to carry him home. Away from this magic nightmare land, with its ghosts and walking dead. He stared at it and he could not make it real; he had lost all capacity for belief.

The ship's dinghy was approaching. Wolf picked up his bags.

The Wheel

John Wyndham

The old man sat on his stool and leaned back against the whitened wall. He had upholstered the stool elegantly with a hare skin because there didn't seem to be much between his own skin and his bones these days. It was exclusively his stool, and recognized in the farmstead as such. The strands of a whip that he was supposed to be plaiting drooped between his bent fingers, but, because the stool was comfortable and the sun was warm, his fingers had stopped moving and his head was nodding.

The yard was empty save for a few hens that pecked more inquisitively than hopefully in the dust, but there were sounds that told of others who had not the old man's leisure for siesta. From round the corner of the house came the occasional *plonk* of an empty bucket as it hit the water, and its scrape on the sides of tie well as it came up full. In the shack across the yard a dull pounding went on rhythmically and soporifically. The old man's head fell further forward as he drowsed.

Presently, from beyond the rough enclosing wall there came another sound, slowly approaching. A rumbling and a rattling, with an intermittent squeaking. The old man's ears were no longer sharp, and for some minutes it failed to disturb him. Then he opened his eyes and, locating the sound, sat staring incredulously toward the gateway. The sound drew closer, and a boy's head showed above the wall. He grinned at the old man, an expression of excitement in his eyes. He did not call out, but moved a little faster until he came to the gate. There he turned into the yard proudly towing behind him a box mounted on four wooden wheels.

The old man got up suddenly from his seat, alarm in every gesture. He waved both arms at the boy as though he would push him back. The boy stopped. His expression of gleeful pride faded into astonishment. He stared at the old man who was waving him away so urgently. While he still hesitated, the old man continued to shoo him off with one hand while he placed the other on his own lips, and started to walk toward him. Reluctantly and bewilderedly the boy turned, but too late. The pounding in the shed stopped. A middle-aged woman appeared in the doorway. Her mouth was open to call, but the words did not come. Her jaw dropped slackly, her eyes seemed to bulge, then she crossed herself, and screamed . . .

The sound split the afternoon peace. Behind the house the bucket fell with a clatter, and a young woman's head showed round the corner. Her eyes widened. She crammed the back of one hand across her mouth, and crossed herself with the other. A young man appeared in the stable doorway, and stood there transfixed. Another girl came pelting out of the house with a little girl behind her. She stopped as suddenly as if she had run into something. The little girl stopped too, vaguely alarmed by the tableau, and clinging to her skirt.

The boy stood quite still with all their gazes upon him. His bewilderment began to give way to fright at the expression in their eyes. He looked from one horrified face to another until his gaze met the old man's. What he saw there seemed to reassure him a little—or to frighten him less. He swallowed. Tears were not far away as he spoke:

"Gran, what's the matter? What are they all looking at me like that for?"

As if the sound of his voice had released a spell, the middle-aged woman came to life. She reached for a hayfork which leaned against the shack wall. Raising its points toward the boy she walked slowly in between him and the gate. In a hard voice she said:

"Go on! Get in the shed!"

"But, Ma—" the boy began.

"Don't you dare call me that now," she told him.

In the tense lines of her face the boy could see something that was almost hatred. His own face screwed up, and he began to cry.

"Go on," she repeated harshly. "Get in there."

The boy backed away, a picture of bewildered misery. Then, suddenly, he turned and ran into the shed. She shut the door on him, and fastened it with a peg. She looked round at the rest as though defying them to speak. The young man withdrew silently into the gloom of the stable. The two young women crept away, taking the little girl with them. The woman and the old man were left alone.

Neither of them spoke. The old man stood motionless, regarding the box where it stood on its wheels. The woman suddenly put her hands up to her face. She made little moaning noises as she swayed, and the tears came trickling out between her fingers. The old man turned. His face was devoid of all expression. Presently she recovered herself a little.

"I never would have believed it. My own little David!" she said.

"If you'd not screamed, nobody need have known," said the old man.

His words took some seconds to sink in. When they did, her expression hardened again.

"Did you show him how?" she asked, suspiciously.

He shook his head.

"I'm old, but I'm not crazy," he told her. "And I'm fond of Davie," he added.

"You're wicked, though. That was a wicked thing you just said."

"It was true."

"I'm a God-fearing woman. I'll not have evil in my house—whatever shape it comes in. And when I see it I know my duty."

The old man drew breath for a reply, but checked it. He shook his head. He turned and went back to his stool, looking, somehow, older than before.

There was a tap on the door. A whispered *Sh!* For a moment Davie saw a square of night sky with a dark shape against it. Then the door closed again.

"You had your supper, Davie?" a voice asked.

"No, Gran. Nobody's been."

The old man grunted.

"Thought not. Scared of you, all of 'em. Here, take this. Cold chicken, it is."

Davie's hand sought and found what the other held out to him. He gnawed on a leg while the old man moved about in the dark, searching for somewhere to sit. He found it, and let himself down with a sigh.

"This is a bad business, Davie boy. They've sent for the priest. He'll be along tomorrow."

"But I don't understand, Gran. Why do they all act like I've done something wrong?"

"Oh, Davie!" said his grandfather, reproachfully.

"Honest, I don't, Gran."

"Come now, Davie. Every Sunday you go to church, and every time you go, you pray. What do you pray?"

The boy gabbled a prayer. After a few moments the old man stopped him.

"There," he said. "That last bit."

"Preserve us from the Wheel?" Davie repeated, wonderingly. "What is the Wheel, Gran? It must be something terrible bad, I know, 'cos when I ask them they just say it's wicked, and not to talk of it. But they don't say what it is."

The old man paused before he replied, then he said:

"That box you got out there. Who told you to fix it that way?"

"Why, nobody, Gran. I just reckoned it'd move easier that way. It does, too."

"Listen, Davie. Those things you put on the side of it—they're *wheels.*"

It was some time before the boy's voice came back out of the darkness. When it did, it sounded bewildered.

"What, those round bits of wood? But they can't be, Gran. That's all they are—just round bits of wood. But the Wheel—that's something awful, terrible, something everybody's scared of."

"All the same, that's what they are." The old man ruminated awhile. "I'll tell you what's going to happen tomorrow, Davie. In the morning the priest will come here to see your box. It'll be still there because nobody dares to touch it. He'll sprinkle some water on it and say a prayer just to make it safe to handle. Then they'll take it into the field and make a fire under it, and they'll stand round singing hymns while it burns.

"Then they'll come back, and take you down to the village, and ask you questions. They'll ask you what the Devil looked like when he came to you, and what he offered to give you if you'd use the Wheel."

"But there wasn't any Devil, Gran."

"That don't matter. If they think there was, then sooner or later you'll be telling them there was, *and* just how he looked when you saw him. They've got ways . . . Now what you got to do is act innocent. You got to say you found that box just the way it is now. You didn't know what it was, but you just brought it along on account of it would make good firewood. That's your story, and you've got to stick to it. 'F you stick to it, no matter what they do, *maybe* you'll get through okay."

"But Gran, what is there that's so bad about the Wheel? I just can't understand."

The old man paused more lengthily than before.

"Well, it's a long story, Davie—and it all began a long, long while ago. Seems like in those days everybody was happy and good and suchlike. Then one day the Devil came along and met a man and told him that he could give him something to make him as strong as a hundred men, an' make him to run faster than the wind, an' fly higher than the birds. Well, the man said that'd be mighty fine, an' what did the Devil want for it? And the Devil said he didn't want a thing—not just then. And so he gave the man the Wheel.

"By and by, after the man had played around with the Wheel awhile he found out a whole lot of things about it: how it would make other Wheels, and still more Wheels, and do all the things the Devil had said, with a whole heap more."

"What, it'd fly, 'n everything?" said the boy.

"Sure. It did all those things. And it began to kill people, too—one way and another. Folks put more and more Wheels together the way the Devil told them, and they found they could do a whole lot bigger things, and kill more people, too. And they couldn't stop using the Wheel then on account of they would have starved if they had.

"Well, that was just what the Devil wanted. He'd got 'em cinched, you see. Pretty near everything in the world was depending on Wheels, and things got worse and worse, and the old Devil just lay back an' laughed to see what his Wheel was doing. Then things got terrible bad. I don't know quite the way it happened, but things got so terrible worse that wasn't scarcely anybody left alive—only just a few, like it had been after the Flood. An' they was near finished."

"And all that was on account of the Wheel?"

"Uh-huh—leastways, it couldn't have happened without it. Still, somehow they made out. They built shacks, an' planted corn, an' by an' by the Devil met a man and started talking about his Wheel again. Now this man was very old and very wise and very Godfearing, so he said to the Devil: 'No. You go right back to Hell,' and then he went all around warning everybody about the Devil and his Wheel, and got 'em all plumb scared.

"But the old Devil don't give up that easy. He's mighty tricky, too. There's time when a man gets an idea that turns out to be pretty nearly a Wheel—maybe like rollers, or screws, or somethin'—but it'll just pass so long as it ain't fixed in the middle. Yes, he keeps along trying, an' now and then he does tempt a man into making a Wheel. Then the priest comes and they burn the Wheel. And they take the man away. And to stop him making any more Wheels, and to discourage any other folk, they burn him too."

"They b-burn him?" stammered the boy.

"That's what they do. So you see why you got to say you *found* it, and stick to that."

"Maybe if I promised never to make another—?"

"That wouldn't be no good, Davie. They're all scared of the Wheel, and when men are scared they get angry and cruel. No, you gotta keep to it."

The boy thought for some moments, then he said:

"What about Ma? She'll know. I had that box off her yesterday. Does it matter?"

The old man grunted. He said, heavily:

"Yes, it does matter. Women do a lot of pretending to be scared—but once they do scare, they scare more horribly than men. And your Ma's dead scared."

There was a long silence in the darkness of the shed. When the old man spoke again, it was in a calm, quiet voice.

"Listen, Davie lad. I'm going to tell you something. And you're going to keep it to yourself—not tell a soul till maybe you're an old man like me?"

"Sure, Gran, 'f you say."

"I'm tellin' you because you found out about the Wheel for yourself. There'll always be boys like you who do. There've got to be. You can't kill an idea the way they try to. You can keep it down awhile, but sooner or later it'll come out. Now what you've got to understand is that the Wheel's *not* evil. Never mind what the scared men all tell you. No discovery is good or evil until men make it that way. Think about that, Davie boy. One day they'll start to use the Wheel again. I hoped it would be in my time, but, well, maybe it'll be in yours. When it does come, don't you be one of the scared ones; be one of the ones that's going to show 'em how to use it better than they did last time. It's not the Wheel—it's fear that's evil, Davie. Remember that."

He stirred in the darkness. His feet clumped on the hard earth floor.

"Reckon it's time I was gettin' along. Where are you, boy?"

His groping hand found Davie's shoulder, and then rested a moment on his head.

"God bless you, Davie. And don't worry any more. It's goin' to be all right. You trust me?"

"Yes, Gran."

"Then you go to sleep. There's some hay in the corner there."

The glimpse of dark sky showed briefly again. Then the sound of the old man's feet shuffled across the yard into silence.

When the priest arrived, he found a horror-stricken knot of people collected in the yard. They were gazing at an old man who worked away with a mallet and pegs on a wooden box. The priest stood, scandalized.

"Stop!" he cried. "In the name of God, stop!"

The old man turned his head toward him. There was a grin of crafty senility on his face.

"Yesterday," he said, "I was a fool. I only made four wheels for it. Today I am a wise man—I am making two more wheels so that it will run half as easily again."

They burned the box, as he had said they would. Then they took him away.

In the afternoon a small boy whom everyone had forgotten turned his eyes from the column of smoke that rose in the direction of the village, and hid his face in his hands.

"I'll remember, Gran. I'll remember. It's only fear that's evil," he said, and his voice choked in his tears.

Jody After the War

Edward Bryant

Light lay bloody on the mountainside. From our promontory jutting above the scrub pine, we looked out over the city. Denver spread from horizon to horizon. The tower of the U.S. Capitol building caught the sun blindingly. We watched the contrail of a Concorde II jetliner making its subsonic approach into McNicholls Field, banking in a sweeping curve over the pine-lined foothills. Directly below us, a road coiled among rocks and trees. A campfire fed smoke into the November air. The wind nudged the smoke trail our way, and I smelled the acrid tang of wood smoke. We watched the kaleidoscope of cloud shadows crosshatch the city.

Jody and I sat close, my arm around her shoulders. No words, no facial expressions, as afternoon faded out to dusk. My feet gradually went to sleep.

"Hey."

"Mmh?" she said, startled.

"You look pensive."

Her face stayed blank.

"What are you thinking?"

"I'm not. I'm just feeling." She turned back to the city. "What are you thinking?"

"Uh, not much," I said. Lie; I'd been thinking about survivors. "Well, thinking how beautiful you are." Banal, but only half an evasion. I mean she *was* beautiful. Jody was imprinted in my mind the first time I saw her, when I peered up out of the anesthetic fog and managed to focus on her standing beside my hospital bed: the half-Indian face with the high cheekbones. Her eyes the color of dark smoke. I couldn't remember what she'd worn then. Today she wore faded blue jeans and a blue chambray work shirt, several sizes too large. No shoes. Typically, she had climbed the mountain barefoot.

Without looking back at me, she said, "You were thinking more than that."

I hesitated. I flashed a sudden mental image of Jody's face the way she had described it in her nightmares: pocked with red and black spots that oozed blood and pus, open sores that gaped where her hair had grown, her skin . . .

Jody squeezed my hand. It was as if she were thinking, that's all right, Paul, if you don't want to talk to me now, that's fine.

I never was any good with evasions, except perhaps with myself. Survivors. Back after the A-bombings of Hiroshima and Nagasaki, the Japanese had called them *hibakusha*—which translates roughly as "sufferers." Here in America we just called them survivors, after the Chinese suicided their psychotic society in the seventies, and destroyed most of urban America in the process. I guess I was lucky; I was just a kid in the middle of Nevada when the missiles hit. I'd hardly known what happened east of the Mississippi and west of the Sierras. But Jody had been with her parents somewhere close to Pittsburgh. So she became a survivor; one of millions. Most of them weren't even hurt in the bombings. Not physically.

Jody was a survivor. And I was lonely. I had thought we could give each other something that would help. But I wasn't sure anymore. I wondered if I had a choice after all. And I was scared.

Jody leaned against me and shared the warmth of my heavy windbreaker. The wind across the heaped boulders of the mountainside was chill, with the sun barely down. Jody pressed her head under my chin. I felt the crisp hair against my jaw. She rested quietly for a minute, then turned her face up toward mine.

"Remember the first time?"

"Here?"

She nodded. "A Sunday like this, only not so cold. I'd just gotten in from that Hayes Theatre assignment in Seattle when you phoned. I hadn't even unpacked. Then you called and got me up here for a picnic." She smiled. In the new shadows her teeth were very white. "What a god-awful time."

That picnic. A summer and about fourteen hundred miles had separated us while she set up PR holograms of *Hamlet* and I haunted Denver phone booths.

Then here on the mountainside we'd fought bitterly. We had hurt each other with words, Jody had begun to cry, and I'd held her. We kissed and barbed words stopped. Through her tears, Jody whispered that she loved me, and I told her how much I loved her. That was the last time either of us said those words. Funny how you use a word so glibly when you don't really understand it, then switch to euphemisms when you do.

"You're very far away."

"It's nothing." I fished for easy words. "The usual," I said. "My future with Ma Bell, going back to school, moving to Seattle to try writing for the network." Everything but—Liar! sneered something inside. Why didn't you include damaged chromosomes in the list, and leukemia and paranoia and frigidity and . . . ? *Shut up!*

"Poor Paul," Jody said. "Hemmed in. Doesn't know which way to turn. For Christmas I think I'll get you a lifesize 'gram from *Hamlet.* I know a guy at the Hayes who can get me one."

"Hamlet, right. That's me." I lightly kissed her forehead. "There, I feel better. You ought to be a therapist."

Jody looked at me strangely and there was a quick silence I couldn't fill.

She smiled then and said, "All right, I'm a therapist. Be a good patient and eat. The thermos won't keep the coffee hot all night."

She reached into the canvas knapsack I'd packed up the mountain and took out the thermos and some foil parcels. "Soybeef," she said, pointing to the sandwiches. "The salt's in with the hardboiled eggs. There's cake for dessert."

Filling my stomach was easier than stripping my soul, so I ate. But the taste in my mouth when I thought about Jody fixing meals all the rest of our lives. Food for two, three times a day, seven days a week, an average of thirty days a . . . Always unvarying. Always food for two. God, I wanted children! I concentrated on chewing.

After the meal, we drank beer and watched the city below as five million Denverites turned on their lights. I knew I was getting too high too fast when I confused pulling the tabs off self-cooling beer cans with plucking petals from daisies.

She loves me.

Funny how melodrama crops up in real life. My life. Like when I met her.

It was about a year before, when I'd just gotten a job with Mountain Bell as a SMART—that's their clever acronym for Service Maintenance and Repair Trainee. In a city the size of Denver there are more than half a million public pay phones, of which at least a third are out of order at any given time; vandals mostly, sometimes mechanical failure. Someone has to go out and spotcheck the phones, then fix the ones that are broken. That was my job. Simple.

I'd gone into a bad area, Five Points, where service was estimated to be 80 percent blanked out. I should have been smart enough to take a partner along, or maybe to wear blackface. But I was a lot younger then. I ended up on a bright Tuesday afternoon, sprawled in my own blood on the sidewalk in front of a grocery store after a Chicago gang had kicked the hell out of me.

After about an hour somebody called an ambulance. Jody. On the phone I'd just repaired before I got stomped. She'd wandered by with a field crew on some documentary assignment, snapping holograms of the poverty conditions.

She loves me not.

I remembered what we'd quarreled about in September. Back in early August a friend of Jody's and mine had come back from Seattle. He was an audio engineer who'd worked freelance with the Hayes Theatre. He'd seen Jody.

"Man, talk about wild!" my friend said. "She must've got covered by everything with pants from Oregon to Vancouver." He looked at my face. "Uh, you have something going with her?"

She loves me.

"What's so hard to understand?" Jody had said. "Didn't you ever meet a survivor before? Didn't you ever think about survivors? What it's like to see death so plainly all around?" Her voice was low and very intense. "And what about feeling you ought never to have babies, and not wanting even to come close to taking the chance?" Her voice became dull and passionless. "Then there was Seattle, Paul, and there's the paradox. The only real defense against death is not to feel. But I *want* to feel sometimes and that's why—" She broke off and began to cry. "Paul, that's why there were so many of them. But they couldn't—I can't make it. Not with anyone." Confused, I held her.

"I want you."

And it didn't matter which of us had said that first.

She loves me not.

"Why don't you ever say what you think?"

"It's easy," I said, a little bitter. "Try being a lonely stoic all your life. It gets to be habit after a while."

"You think I don't know?" She rolled over, turned to the wall. "I'm trying to get through." Her voice was muffled by the blankets.

"Yeah. Me too."

She sat up suddenly, the sheets falling away from her. "Listen! I told you it would be like this. You can have me. But you have to accept what I am."

"I will."

Neither of us said anything more until morning.

She loves me.

Another night she woke up screaming. I stroked her hair and kissed her face lightly.

"Another one?"

She nodded.

"Bad?"

"Yes."

"You want to talk about it?"

There was hesitation, then a slow nod.

"I was in front of a mirror in some incredibly baroque old bedroom," she said. "I was vomiting blood and my hair was coming out and falling down on my shoulders. It wound around my throat and I couldn't breathe. I opened my mouth and there was blood running from my gums. And my skin—it was completely covered with black and red pustules. They—" She paused and closed her eyes. "They were strangely beautiful." She whimpered. "The worst—" She clung to me tightly. "Oh, God! The worst part was that I was pregnant."

She roughly pushed herself away and wouldn't let me try to comfort her. She lay on her back and stared at the ceiling. Finally, childlike, she took my hand. She held my fingers very tight all the rest of the night.

She loves me not.

But she did, I thought. She does. In her own way, just as you love her. It's never going to be the way you imagined it as a kid. But you love her. Ask her. Ask her now.

"What's going on?" Jody asked, craning her neck to look directly below our ledge. Far down we saw a pair of headlights, a car sliding around the hairpin turns in the foothills road. The whine of a racing turbine rasped our ears.

"I don't know. Some clown in a hurry to park with his girl."

The car approached the crest of a hill and for an instant the headlights shone directly at us, dazzling our eyes. Jody jerked back and screamed. "The sun! So bright! God, Pittsburgh—" Her strength seemed to drain; I lowered her gently to the ledge and sat down beside her. The rock was rough and cold as the day's heat left. I couldn't see Jody's face, except as a blur in the darkness. There was light from the city and a little from the stars, but the moon hadn't risen.

"Please kiss me."

I kissed her and used the forbidden words. "I love you."

I touched her breast; she shivered against me and whispered something I couldn't quite understand. A while later my hand touched the waist of her jeans and she drew away.

"Paul, no."

"Why not?" The beer and my emotional jag pulsed in the back of my skull. I ached.

"You know."

I knew. For a while she didn't say anything more, nor did I. We felt tension build its barrier. Then she relaxed and put her cheek against mine. Somehow we both laughed and the tension eased.

Ask her. And I knew I couldn't delay longer. "Damn it," I said, "I still love you. And I know what I'm getting into." He paused to breathe. "After Christmas I'm taking off for Seattle. I want you to marry me there."

I felt her muscles tense. Jody pulled away from me and got to her feet. She walked to the end of the ledge and looked out beyond the city. She turned to face me and her hands were clenched.

"I don't know," she said. "At the end of summer I'd have said 'no' immediately. Now—"

I sat silent.

"We'd better go," she said after a while, her voice calm and even. "It's very late."

We climbed down from the rocks then, with the November chill a well of silence between us.

SALVAGE

Orson Scott Card

THE ROAD BEGAN to climb steeply right from the ferry, so the truck couldn't build up any speed. Deaver just kept shifting down, wincing as he listened to the grinding of the gears. Sounded like the transmission was chewing itself to gravel. He'd been nursing it all the way across Nevada, and if the Wendover ferry hadn't carried him these last miles over the Mormon Sea, he would have had a nice long hike. Lucky. It was a good sign. Things were going to go Deaver's way for a while.

The mechanic frowned at him when he rattled in to the loading dock. "You been ridin the clutch, boy?"

Deaver got down from the cab. "Clutch? What's a clutch?"

The mechanic didn't smile. "Couldn't you hear the transmission was shot?"

"I had mechanics all the way across Nevada askin' to fix it for me, but I told 'em I was savin' it for you."

The mechanic looked at him like he was crazy. "There ain't no mechanics in Nevada."

If you wasn't dumb as your thumb, thought Deaver, *you'd know I was joking.* These old Mormons were so straight they couldn't sit down, some of them. But Deaver didn't say anything. Just smiled.

"This truck's gonna stay here a few days," said the mechanic.

Fine with me, thought Deaver. *I got plans.* "How many days you figure?"

"Take three for now, I'll sign you off."

"My name's Deaver Teague."

"Tell the foreman, he'll write it up." The mechanic lifted the hood to begin the routine checks while the dockboys loaded off the old washing machines and frigerators and other stuff Deaver had picked up on this trip. Deaver took his mileage reading to the window and the foreman paid him off.

Seven dollars for five days of driving and loading, sleeping in the cab and eating whatever the farmers could spare. It was better than a lot of people lived on, but there wasn't any future in it. Salvage wouldn't go on forever. Someday he'd pick up the last broken-down dishwasher left from the old days, and then he'd be out if a job.

Well, Deaver Teague wasn't going to wait around for that. He knew where the gold was, he'd been planning how to get it for weeks, and if Lehi had got the diving equipment like he promised then tomorrow morning they'd do a little freelance salvage work. If they were lucky they'd come home rich.

Deaver's legs were stiff but he loosened them up pretty quick and broke into an easy, loping run down the corridors of the Salvage Center. He took a flight of stairs two or three steps at a time, bounded down a hall, and when he reached a sign that read SMALL COMPUTER SALVAGE, he pushed off the doorframe and rebounded into the room. "Hey Lehi!" he said. "Hey, it's quittin' time!"

Lehi McKay paid no attention. He was sitting in front of a TV screen, jerking at black box he held on his lap.

"You do that and you'll go blind," said Deaver.

"Shut up, carpface," Lehi never took his eyes off the screen. He jabbed at a button on the black box and twisted on the stick that jutted up from it. A colored blob on the screen blew up and split into four smaller blobs.

"I got three days off while they do the transmission on the truck," said Deaver. "So tomorrow's the temple expedition."

Lehi got the last blob off the screen. More blobs appeared.

"That's real fun," said Deaver, "like sweepin' the street and then they bring along a mother troop of horses."

"It's an Atari. From the sixties or seventies or something. Eighties. Old. Can't do much with the pieces, it's only eight-bit stuff. All these years in somebody's attic in Logan, and the sucker still runs."

"Old guys probably didn't even know they had it."

"Probably."

Deaver watched the game. Same thing over and over again. "How much a thing like this use to cost?"

"A lot. Maybe fifteen, twenty bucks."

"Makes you want to barf. And here sits Lehi McKay, toodling his noodle like the old guys used to. All it ever got them was a sore noodle, Lehi. And slag for brains?"

"Drown it. I'm trying to concentrate."

The game finally ended. Lehi set the black box up on the workbench, turned off the machine, and stood up.

"You got everything ready to go underwater tomorrow?" asked Deaver.

"That was a good game. Having fun must've took up a lot of their time in the old days. Mom says the kids used to not even be able to get jobs till they was sixteen. It was the law."

"Don't you wish," said Deaver.

"It's true."

"You don't know your tongue from dung, Lehi. You don't know your heart from a fart."

"You want to get us both kicked out of here, talkin' like that?"

"I don't have to follow school rules now, I graduated sixth grade, I'm nineteen years old, I been on my own for five years." He pulled his seven dollars out of his pocket, waved them once, stuffed them back in carelessly. "I do OK, and I talk like I want to talk. Think I'm afraid of the bishop?"

"Bishop don't scare me. I don't even go to church except to make Mom happy. It's a bunch of bunny turds."

Lehi laughed, but Deaver could see that he was a little scared to talk like that. *Sixteen years old,* thought Deaver. *He's big and he's smart but he's such a little kid. He don't understand how it's like to be a man.* "Rain's comin."

"Rain's always comin. What the hell do you think filled up the lake?" Lehi smirked as he unplugged everything on the workbench.

"I meant *Lor*raine Wilson."

"I know what you meant. She's got her boat?"

"And she's got a mean set of fenders." Deaver cupped his hands. "Just need a little polishing."

"Why do you always talk dirty? Ever since you started driving salvage, Deaver, you got a gutter mouth. Besides, she's built like a sack."

"She's near fifty, what do you expect?" It occurred to Deaver that Lehi seemed to be stalling. Which probably meant he botched up again as usual. "Can you get the diving stuff?"

"I already got it. You thought I'd screw up." Lehi smirked again.

"You? Screw up? You can be trusted with *anything*." Deaver started for the door. He could hear Lehi behind him, still shutting a few things off. They got to use a lot of electricity in here. Of course they had to, because they needed computers all the time, and salvage was the only way to get them. But when Deaver saw all that electricity getting used up at once, to him it looked like his own future. All the machines he could ever want, new ones, and all the power they needed. Clothes that nobody else ever wore, his own horse and wagon or even a car. Maybe he'd be the guy who started making cars again. He didn't need stupid blob-smashing games from the past. "That stuff's dead and gone, duck lips, dead and gone."

"What're you talking about?" asked Lehi.

"Dead and gone. All your computer things."

It was enough to set Lehi off, as it always did. Deaver grinned and felt wicked and strong as Lehi babbled along behind him. About how we use the computers more than they ever did in the old days, the computers kept everything going, on and on and on, it was cute. Deaver liked him; the boy was so *intense*. Like everything as the end of the world. Deaver knew better. The world was dead, it had already ended, so none of it mattered, you could sink all this stuff in the lake.

They came out of the Center and walked along the retaining wall. Far below them was the harbor, a little circle of water in the bottom of a bowl, with Bingham City perched on the lip. They used to have an open-pit copper mine here, but when the water rose they cut a channel to it and now they had a nice harbor on Oquirrh Island in the middle of the Mormon Sea, where the factories could stink up the whole sky and no neighbors ever complained about it.

A lot of other people joined them on the steep dirt road that led down to the harbor. Nobody lived right in Bingham City itself, because it was just a working place, day and night. Shifts in, shifts out. Lehi was a shift boy, lived with his family across the Jordan Strait on Point-of-the-Mountain, which was as rotten a place to live as anybody ever devised, rode the ferry in every day at five in the morning and rode it back every afternoon at four. He was supposed to go to school after that for a couple of hours but Deaver thought that was stupid, he told Lehi that all the time, told him again now. School is too much time and too little of everything, waste of time.

"I gotta go to school," said Lehi.

"Tell me two plus two, you haven't got two plus two yet?"

"You finished, didn't you?"

"Nobody needs anything after fourth grade." He shoved Lehi a little. Usually Lehi shoved back, but this time no.

"Just try getting a real job without a sixth-grade diploma, OK? And I'm pretty close now." They were at the ferry ship. Lehi got out his pass.

"You with me tomorrow or not?"

Lehi made a face. "I don't know, Deaver. You can get arrested for going around there. It's a dumb thing to do. They say there's real weird things in the old skyscrapers."

"We aren't going *in* the skyscrapers?"

"Even worse in *there*, Deaver. I don't want to go there."

"Yeah, the Angel Moroni's probably waiting to jump out and say booga-booga-booga."

"Don't talk about it, Deaver." Deaver was tickling him; Lehi laughed and tried to shy away. "Cut it out, chigger-head. Come on. Besides, the Moroni statue was moved to the Salt Lake Monument up on the mountain. And that has a guard all he time."

"The statue's just gold plate anyway. I'm tellin you those old Mormons hid tons of stuff down in the Temple, just waitin for somebody who isn't scared of the ghost of Bigamy Young to—"

"Shut *up*, snotsucker, OK? People can hear! Look around, we're not alone!"

It was true, of course. Some of the other people were glaring at them. But then, Deaver noticed that older people liked to glare at younger ones. It made the old farts feel better about kicking off. It was like they were saying, OK, I'm dying, but at least you're stupid. So Deaver looked right at a woman who was staring at him and murmured, "OK, I'm stupid, but at least I won't die."

"Deaver, do you always have to say that where they can hear you?"

"It's true."

"In the first place, Deaver, they aren't dying. And in the second place, you're definitely stupid. And in the third place, the ferry's here." Lehi punched Deaver lightly in the stomach.

Deaver bent over in mock agony. "Ay, the laddie's ungrateful, he is, I give him me last croost of bread and this be the thanks I gets."

"*Nobody* has an accent like that, Deaver!" shouted Lehi. The boat began to pull away.

"Tomorrow at five-thirty!" shouted Deaver.

"You'll never get up at four-thirty, don't give me that, you never get up . . ." But the ferry and the noise of the factories and machine and trucks swallowed up the rest of his insults. Deaver knew them all, anyway. Lehi might be only sixteen, but he was OK. Someday Deaver'd get married but his wife would like Lehi, too. And Lehi'd even get married, and his wife would like Deaver. She'd better, or she'd have to swim home.

He took the trolley home to Fort Douglas and walked to the ancient barracks building where Rain let him stay. It was supposed to be a storage room, but she kept the mops and soap stuff in her place so that there'd be room for a cot.

Not much else, but it was on Oquirrh Island without being right there in the stink and the smoke and the noise. He could sleep and that was enough, since most of the time he was out on the truck.

Truth was, his room wasn't home anyway. Home was pretty much Rain's place, a drafty room at the end of the barracks with a dumpy frowzy lady who served him good food and plenty of it. That's where he went now, walked right in and surprised her in the kitchen. She yelled at him for surprising her, yelled at him for being filthy and tracking all over her floor, and let him get a slice of apple before she yelled at him for snitching before supper.

He went around and changed light bulbs in five rooms before supper. The families there were all crammed into two rooms each at the most, and most of them had to share kitchens and eat in shifts. Some of the rooms were nasty places, family warfare held off only as long as it took him to change the light, and sometimes even that truce wasn't observed.

Others were doing fine, the place was small but they liked each other. Deaver was pretty sure his family must have been one of the nice ones, because if there'd been any yelling he would have remembered.

Rain and Deaver ate and then turned off all the lights while she played the old record player Deaver had wangled away from Lehi. They really weren't supposed to have it, but they figured as long as they didn't burn any lights it wasn't wasting electricity, and they'd turn it in as soon as anybody asked for it.

In the meantime, Rain had some of the old records from when she was a girl. The songs had strong rhythms, and tonight, like she sometimes did, Rain got up and moved to the music, strange little dances that Deaver didn't understand unless he imagined her as a lithe young girl, pictured her body as it must have been then. It wasn't hard to imagine; it was there in her eyes and her smile all the time, and her movements gave away secrets that years of starchy eating and lack of exercise had disguised.

Then, as always, his thoughts went off to some of the girls he saw from his truck window, driving by the fields where they bent over, hard at work, until they heard the truck and then they stood and waved. Everybody waved at the salvage truck, sometimes it was the only thing with a motor that ever came by, their only contact with the old machines. All the tractors, all the electricity were reserved for the New Soil Lands; the old places were dying. And they turned and waved at the last memories. It made Deaver sad and he hated to be sad, all these people clinging to a past that never existed.

"It never existed," he said aloud.

"Yes it did," Rain whispered. *"Girls just wanna have fu-un,"* she murmured along with the record. "I hated this song when I was a girl. Or maybe it was my mama who hated it:'

"You live here then?"

"Indiana," she said. "One of the states, way east?"

"Were you a refugee, too?"

"No. We moved here when I was sixteen, seventeen, can't remember. Whenever things got scary in the world, a lot of Mormons moved home. This was always home, no matter what."

The record ended. She turned it off, turned on the lights.

"Got the boat all gassed up?" asked Deaver.

"You don't want to go there," she said.

"If there's gold down there, I want it."

"If there was gold there, Deaver, they would've taken it out before the water covered it. It's not as if nobody got a warning, you know. The Mormon Sea wasn't a flash flood."

"If it isn't down there, what's all the hush-hush about? How come the Lake Patrol keeps people from going there?"

"I don't know, Deaver. Maybe because a lot of people feel like it's a holy place."

Deaver was used to this. Rain never went to church, but she still talked like a Mormon. Most people did, though, when you scratched them the wrong place. Deaver didn't like it when they got religious. "Angels need police protection, is that it?"

"It used to be real important to the Mormons in the old days, Deaver." She sat down on the floor, leaning against the wall under the window.

"Well it's nothin now. They got their other temples, don't they? And they're building the new one in Zarahemla, right?"

"I don't know, Deaver. The one here, it was always the real one. The center." She bent sideways, leaned on her hand, looked down at the floor. "It still is."

Deaver saw she was getting really somber now, really sad. It happened to a lot of people who remembered the old days. Like a disease that never got cured. But Deaver knew the cure. For Rain, anyway. "Is it true they used to kill people in there?"

It worked. She glared at him and the languor left her body. "Is that what you truckers talk about all day?"

Deaver grinned. "There's stories. Cuttin' people up if they told where the gold was hid."

"You know Mormons all over the place, now, Deaver, do you really think we'd go cuttin' people up for tellin' secrets?"

"I don't know. Depends on the secrets, don't it?" He was sitting on his hands, kind of bouncing a little on the couch.

He could see that she was a little mad for real, but didn't want to be. So she'd pretend to be mad for play. She sat up, reached for a pillow to throw at him. "No! No!" he cried. "Don't cut me up! Don't feed me to the carp!"

The pillow hit him and he pretended elaborately to die.

"Just don't joke about things like that," she said.

"Things like what? You don't believe in the old stuff anymore. Nobody does."

"Maybe not."

"Jesus was supposed to come again, right? There was atom bombs dropped here and there, and he was supposed to come."

"Prophet said we was too wicked. He wouldn't come 'cause we loved the things of the world too much."

"Come on, if he was comin' he would've come, right?"

"Might still," she said.

"Nobody believes that," said Deaver. "Mormons are just the government, that's all. The bishop gets elected judge in every town, right? The president of the elders is always mayor, it's just the government, just politics, nobody believes it now. Zarahemla's the capital, not the holy city."

He couldn't see her because he was lying flat on his back on the couch. When she didn't answer, he got up and looked for her. She was over by the sink, leaning on the counter. He sneaked up behind her to tickle her, but something in her posture changed his mind. When he got close, he saw tears down her cheeks. It was crazy. All these people from the old days got crazy a lot.

"I was just teasin'," he said.

She nodded.

"It's just part of the old days. You know, how I am about that. Maybe if I remembered, it'd be different. Sometimes I wish I remembered." But it was a lie. He never wished he remembered. He didn't like remembering. Most stuff he couldn't remember even if he wanted to. The earliest thing he could bring to mind was riding on the back of a horse, behind some man who sweated a lot, just riding and riding and riding. And then it was all recent stuff, going to school, getting passed around in people's homes, finally getting busy one year and finishing school and getting a job. He didn't get misty-eyed thinking about any of it, any of those places. Just passing through, that's all he was ever doing, never belonged anywhere until maybe now. He belonged here. "I'm sorry," he said.

"It's fine," she said.

"You still gonna take me there?"

"I said I would, didn't I?"

She sounded just annoyed enough that he knew it was OK to tease her again. "You don't think they'll have the Second Coming while we're there, do you? If you think so, I'll wear my tie."

She smiled, then turned to face him and pushed him away. "Deaver, go to bed."

"I'm gettin' up at four-thirty, Rain, and then you're one girl who's gonna have fun."

"I don't think the song was about early-morning boat trips."

She was doing the dishes when he left for his little room.

Lehi was waiting at five-thirty, right on schedule. "I can't believe it," he said. "I thought you'd be late."

"Good thing you were ready on time," said Deaver, "'cause if you didn't come with us you wouldn't get a cut."

"We aren't going to find any gold, Deaver Teague."

"Then why're you comin' with me? Don't give me that stuff, Lehi, you know the future's with Deaver Teague, and you don't want to be left behind. Where's the diving stuff?"

"I didn't bring it *home*, Deaver. You don't think my mom'd ask questions then?"

"She's always askin' questions," said Deaver.

"It's her job," said Rain.

"I don't want anybody askin' about everything I do," said Deaver.

"Nobody has to ask," said Rain. "You always tell us whether we want to hear or not."

"If you don't want to hear, you don't have to," said Deaver.

"Don't get touchy," said Rain.

"You guys are both gettin' wet-headed on me, all of a sudden. Does the temple make you crazy, is that how it works?"

"I don't mind my mom askin' me stuff. It's OK."

The ferries ran from Point to Bingham day and night, so they had to go north a ways before cutting west to Oquirrh Island. The smelter and the foundries put orange-bellied smoke clouds into the night sky, and the coal barges were getting offloaded just like in daytime. The coal-dust cloud that was so grimy and black in the day looked like white fog under the floodlights.

"My dad died right there, about this time of day," said Lehi.

"He loaded coal?"

"Yeah. He used to be a car salesmen. His job kind of disappeared on him?"

"You weren't there, were you?"

"I heard the crash. I was asleep, but it woke me up. And then a lot of shouting and running. We lived on the island back then, always heard stuff from the harbor. He got buried under a ton of coal that fell from fifty feet up."

Deaver didn't know what to say about that.

"You never talk about your folks," said Lehi. "I always remember my dad, but you never talk about your folks."

Deaver shrugged.

"He doesn't remember 'em," Rain said quietly. "They found him out on the plains somewhere. The mobbers got his family, however many there was, he must've hid or something, that's all they can figure."

"Well what was it?" asked Lehi. "Did you hide?"

Deaver didn't feel comfortable talking about it, since he didn't remember anything except what people told him. He knew that other people remembered their childhood, and he didn't like how they always acted so surprised that he didn't. But Lehi was asking, and Deaver knew that you don't keep stuff back from friends. "I guess I did. Or maybe I looked too dumb to kill or somethin'." He laughed. "I must've been a real dumb little kid, I didn't even remember my own name. They figure I was five or six years old, most kids know their names, but not me. So the two guys that found me, their names were Teague and Deaver."

"You gotta remember somethin'."

"Lehi, I didn't even know how to talk. They tell me I didn't even say a word till I was nine years old. We're talkin' about a slow learner here."

"Wow." Lehi was silent for a while. "How come you didn't say anything?"

"Doesn't matter," said Rain. "He makes up for it now, Deaver the talker. Champion talker."

They coasted the island till they got past Magna. Lehi led them to a storage shed that Underwater Salvage had put up at the north end of Oquirrh Island. It was unlocked and full of diving equipment Lehi's friends had filled some tanks with air. They got two diving outfits and underwater flashlights. Rain wasn't going underwater, so she didn't need anything.

They pulled away from the island, out into the regular shipping lane from Wendover. In that direction, at least, people had sense enough not to travel at night, so there wasn't much traffic. After a little while they were out into open water. That was when Rain stopped the little outboard motor Deaver had scrounged for her and Lehi had fixed. "Time to sweat and slave," said Rain.

Deaver sat on the middle bench, settled the oars into the locks, and began to row.

"Not too fast," Rain said. "You'll give yourself blisters."

A boat that might have been Lake Patrol went by once, but otherwise nobody came near them as they crossed the open stretch. Then the skyscrapers rose up and blocked off large sections of the starry night.

"They say there's people who was never rescued still livin' in there," Lehi whispered.

Rain was disdainful. "You think there's anything left in there to keep anybody alive? And the water's still too salty to drink for long?"

"Who says they're alive?" whispered Deaver in his most mysterious voice. A couple of years ago, he could have spooked Lehi and made his eyes go wide. Now Lehi just looked disgusted.

"Come on, Deaver, I'm not a kid."

It was Deaver who got spooked a little. The big holes where pieces of glass and plastic had fallen off looked like mouths, waiting to suck him in and carry him down under the water, into the city of the drowned. He sometimes dreamed about thousands and thousands of people living under water. Still driving their cars around, going about their business, shopping in stores, going to movies. In his dreams they never did anything bad, just went about their business. But he always woke up sweating and frightened. No reason. Just spooked him. "I think they should blow up these things before they fall down and hurt somebody," said Deaver.

"Maybe it's better to leave 'em standing," said Rain. "Maybe there's a lot of folks like to remember how tall we once stood."

"What's to remember? They built tall buildings and then they let 'em take a bath, what's to brag for?"

Deaver was trying to get her not to talk about the old days, but Lehi seemed to like wallowing in it. "You ever here before the water came?"

Rain nodded. "Saw a parade go right down this street. I can't remember if it was Third South or Fourth South. Third I guess. I saw twenty-five horses all riding together. I remember that I thought that was really something. You didn't see many horses in those days."

"I seen too many myself," said Lehi.

"It's the ones I don't see that I hate," said Deaver. "They ought to make 'em wear diapers."

They rounded a building and looked up a north-south passage between towers. Rain was sitting in the stern and saw it first. "There it is. You can see it. Just the tall spires now."

Deaver rowed them up the passage. There were six spires sticking up out of the water, but the four short ones were under so far that only the pointed roofs were dry. The two tall ones had windows in them, not covered at all. Deaver was disappointed. Wide open like that meant that anybody might have come here. It was all so much less dangerous than he had expected. Maybe Rain was right, and there was nothing there.

They tied the boat to the north side and waited for daylight. "If I knew it'd be so easy," said Deaver, "I could've slept another hour."

"Sleep now," said Rain.

"Maybe I will," said Deaver. He slid off his bench and sprawled in the bottom of the boat.

He didn't sleep, though. The open window of the steeple was only a few yards away, a deep black surrounded by the starlit gray of the temple granite. It was down there, waiting for him—the future, a chance to get something better for himself and his two friends. Maybe a plot of ground in the south where it was warmer and the snow didn't pile up five feet deep every winter, where it wasn't rain in the sky and lake everywhere else you looked. A place where he could live for a very long time and look back and remember good times with his friends, that was all waiting down under the water.

Of course they hadn't *told* him about the gold. It was on the road, a little place in Parowan where truckers knew they could stop in because the iron mine kept such crazy shifts that the diners never closed. They even had some coffee there, hot and bitter, because there weren't so many Mormons there and the miners didn't let the bishop push them around. In fact they even called him judge there instead of bishop. The other drivers didn't talk to Deaver, of course, they were talking to each other when the one fellow told the story about how the Mormons back in the gold rush days hoarded up all the gold they could get and hid it in the upper rooms of the temple where nobody but the prophet and the twelve apostles could ever go. At first Deaver didn't believe him, except that Bill Home nodded like he knew it was true, and Cal Silber said you'd never catch him messin' with the Mormon temple; that's a good way to get yourself dead. The way they were talking; scared and quiet, told Deaver that they believed it, that it was true, and he knew something else, too: if anyone was going to get that gold, it was him.

Even if it *was* easy to get here, that didn't mean anything. He knew how Mormons were about the temple. He'd asked around a little, but nobody'd talk about it. And nobody ever went there, either, he asked a lot of people if they ever sailed on out and looked at it, and they all got quiet and shook their heads no or changed the subject. Why should the Lake Patrol guard it, then, if everybody was too scared to go? Everybody but Deaver Teague and his two friends.

"Real pretty," said Rain.

Deaver woke up. The sun was just topping the mountains; it must've been light for some time. He looked where Rain was looking. It was the Moroni tower on top of the mountain above the old capitol, where they'd put the temple statue a few years back. It was bright and shiny, the old guy and his trumpet. But when the Mormons wanted that trumpet to blow, it had just stayed silent and their faith got drowned. Now Deaver knew they only hung on to it for old times' sake. Well, Deaver lived for new times.

Lehi showed him how to use the underwater gear, and they practiced going over the side into the water a couple of times, once without the weight belts and once with. Deaver and Lehi swam like fish, of course—swimming was the main recreation that everybody could do for free. It was different with the mask and the air hose, though.

"Hose tastes like a horse's hoof," Deaver said between dives.

Lehi made sure Deaver's weight belt was on tight. "You're the only guy on Oquirrh Island who knows." Then he tumbled forward off the boat. Deaver went down too straight and the air tank bumped the back of his head a little, but it didn't hurt too much and he didn't drop his light, either.

He swam along the outside of the temple, shining his light on the stones. Lots of underwater plants were rising up the sides of the temple, but it wasn't covered much yet. There was a big metal plaque right in the front of the building, about a third of the way down. THE HOUSE OF THE LOAD it read. Deaver pointed it out to Lehi.

When they got up to the boat again, Deaver asked about it. "It looked kind of goldish," he said.

"Used to be another sign there," said Rain. "It was a little different. That one might have been gold. This one's plastic. They made it so the temple would still have a sign, I guess?"

"You sure about that?"

"I remember when they did it."

Finally Deaver felt confident enough to go down into the temple. They had to take off their flippers to climb into the steeple window; Rain tossed them up after. In the sunlight there was nothing spooking about the window. They sat there on the sill, water lapping at their feet, and put their fins and tanks on.

Halfway through getting dressed, Lehi stopped. Just sat there.

"I can't do it," he said.

"Nothin' to be scared of," said Deaver. "Come on, there's no ghosts or nothin' down there."

"I can't," said Lehi.

"Good for you," called Rain from the boat.

Deaver turned to look at her. "What're you talkin' about?!"

"I don't think you should."

"Then why'd you bring me here?"

"Because you wanted to."

Made no sense.

"It's holy ground, Deaver," said Rain. "Lehi feels it, too. That's why he isn't going down."

Deaver looked at Lehi.

"It just don't feel right," said Lehi.

"It's just stones," said Deaver.

Lehi said nothing. Deaver put on his goggles, took a light, put the breather in his mouth, and jumped.

Turned out the floor was only a foot and a half down. It took him completely by surprise, so he fell over and sat on his butt in eighteen inches of water. Lehi was just as surprised as he was, but then he started laughing, and Deaver laughed, too. Deaver got to his feet and started flapping around, looking for the stairway. He could hardly take a step, his flippers slowed him down so much.

"Walk backward," said Lehi.

"Then how am I supposed to see where I'm going?"

"Stick your face under the water and look, chigger-head?"

Deaver stuck his face in the water. Without the reflection of daylight on the surface, he could see fine. There was the stairway.

He got up, looked toward Lehi. Lehi shook his head. He still wasn't going.

"Suit yourself," said Deaver. He backed through the water to the top step. Then he put in his breathing tube and went down.

It wasn't easy to get down the stairs. *They're fine when you aren't floating,* thought Deaver, *but they're a pain when you keep scraping your tanks on the ceiling.* Finally he figured out he could grab the railing and pull himself down. The stairs wound around and around. When they ended, a whole bunch of garbage had filled up the bottom of the stairwell, partly blocking the doorway. He swam above the garbage, which looked like scrap metal and chips of wood, and came out into a large room.

His light didn't shine very far through the murky water, so he swam the walls, around and around, high and low. Down here the water was cold, and he swam faster to keep warm. There were rows of arched windows on both sides, with rows of circular windows above them, but they had been covered over with wood on the outside; the only light was from Deaver's flashlight. Finally, though, after a couple of times around the room and across the ceiling, he figured it was just one big room. And except for the garbage all over the floor, it was empty.

Already he felt the deep pain of disappointment. He forced himself to ignore it. After all, it wouldn't be right out here in a big room like this, would it? There had to be a secret treasury.

There were a couple of doors. The small one in the middle of the wall at one end was wide open. Once there must have been stairs leading up to it. Deaver swam over there and shone his light in. Just another room, smaller this time. He found a couple more rooms, but they had all been stripped, right down to the stone. Nothing at all.

He tried examining some of the stones to look for secret doors, but he gave up pretty soon—he couldn't see well enough from the flashlight to find a thin crack even if it was there. Now the disappointment was real. As he swam along, he began to wonder if maybe the truckers hadn't known he was listening. Maybe they made it all up just so someday he'd do this. Some joke, where they wouldn't even see him make a fool of himself.

But no, no, that couldn't be it. They believed it, all right. But he knew now what they didn't know. Whatever the Mormons did here in the old days, there wasn't any gold in the upper rooms now. So much for the future. But what the hell, he told himself, I got here, I saw it, and I'll find something else. No reason not to be cheerful about it.

He didn't fool himself, and there was nobody else down here to fool. It was bitter. He'd spent a lot of years thinking about bars of gold or bags of it. He'd always pictured it hidden behind a curtain. He'd pull on the curtain and it would billow out in the water, and here would be the bags of gold, and he'd just take them out and that would be it. But there weren't any curtains, weren't any hideyholes, there was nothing at all, and if he had a future, he'd have to find it somewhere else.

He swam back to the door leading to the stairway. Now he could see the pile of garbage better, and it occurred to him to wonder how it got there. Every other room was completely empty. The garbage couldn't have been carried in by the water, because the only windows that were open were in the steeple, and they were above the water line. He swam close and picked up a piece. It was metal. They were all metal, except a few stones, and it occurred to him that this might be it after all. If you're hiding a treasure, you don't put it in bags or ingots, you leave it around looking like garbage and people leave it alone.

He gathered up as many of the thin metal pieces as he could carry in one hand and swam carefully up the stairwell. Lehi would have to come down now and help him carry it up; they could make bags out of their shirts to carry lots of it at a time.

He splashed out into the air and then walked backward up the last few steps and across the submerged floor. Lehi was still sitting on the sill, and now Rain was there beside him, her bare feet dangling in the water. When he got there he turned around and held out the metal in his hands. He couldn't see their faces well, because the outside of the facemask was blurry with water and kept catching sunlight.

"You scraped your knee," said Rain.

Deaver handed her his flashlight and now that his hand was free, he could pull his mask off and look at them. They were very serious. He held out the metal pieces toward them. "Look what I found down there."

Lehi took a couple of metal pieces from him. Rain never took her eyes from Deaver's face.

"It's old cans, Deaver," Lehi said quietly.

"No it isn't." said Deaver. But he looked at his fistful of metal sheets and realized it was true. They had been cut down the side and pressed flat, but they were sure enough cans.

"There's writing on it." said Lehi. "It says, 'Dear Lord heal my girl Jenny please I pray'."

Deaver set down his handful on the sill. Then he took one, turned it over, found the writing. "'Forgive my adultery I will sin no more'."

Lehi read another. "'Bring my boy safe from the plains, O Lord God'."

Each message was scratched with a nail or a piece of glass, the letters crudely formed.

"They used to say prayers all day in the temple, and people would bring in names and they'd say the temple prayers for them," said Rain. "Nobody prays here now, but they still bring the names. On metal so they'll last."

"We shouldn't read these," said Lehi. "We should put them back."

There were hundreds, maybe thousands of those metal prayers down there. *People must come here all the time,* Deaver realized. *The Mormons must have a regular traffic coming here and leaving these things behind. But nobody told me.*

"Did you know about this?"

Rain nodded.

"You brought them here, didn't you?"

"Some of them. Over the years."

"You knew what was down there."

She didn't answer.

"She told you not to come," said Lehi.

"You knew about this, too?"

"I knew people came, I didn't know what they did."

And suddenly the magnitude of it struck him. Lehi and Rain had both known. All the Mormons knew, then. They all knew, and he had asked again and again, and no one had told him. Not even his friends.

"Why'd you let me come out here?"

"Tried to stop you?" said Rain.

"Why didn't you tell me this?"

She looked him in the eye. "Deaver, you would've thought I was givin' you the runaround. And you would have laughed at this, if I told you. I thought it was better if you saw it. Then maybe you wouldn't go tellin' people how dumb the Mormons are."

"You think I would?" He held up another metal prayer and read it aloud. "'Come quickly, Lord Jesus, before I die'." He shook it at her. "You think I'd laugh at these people?"

"You laugh at everything, Deaver."

Deaver looked at Lehi. This was something Lehi had never said before. Deaver would never laugh at something that was really important. And this was really important to them—to them both.

"This is yours?" Deaver said. "All this stuff is yours."

"I never left a prayer here," said Lehi.

But when he said yours he didn't mean just them, just Lehi and Rain. He meant all of them, all the people of the Mormon Sea, all the ones who had known about it but never told him even though he asked again and again. All the people who belonged here. "I came to find something here for me, and you knew all the time it was only your stuff down there."

Lehi and Rain looked at each other, then back at Deaver.

"It isn't ours," said Rain.

"I never been here before," said Lehi.

"It's your stuff." He sat down in the water and began taking off the underwater gear.

"Don't be mad," said Lehi. "I didn't know."

"You knew more than you told me. All the time I thought we were friends, but it wasn't true. You two had this place in common with all the other people, but not with me. Everybody but me."

Lehi carefully took the metal sheets to the stairway and dropped them. They sank once, to drift down and take their place on the pile of supplications.

Lehi rowed them through the skyscrapers to the east of the old city, and then Rain started the motor and they skimmed along the surface of the lake. The Lake Patrol didn't see them, but Deaver knew now that it didn't matter much if they did. The Lake Patrol was mostly Mormons. They undoubtedly knew about the traffic here, and let it happen as long as it was discreet. Probably the only people they stopped were the people who weren't in on it.

All the way back to Magna to return the underwater gear, Deaver sat in the front of the boat, not talking to the others. Where Deaver sat, the bow of the boat seemed to curve under him. The faster they went, the less the boat seemed to touch the water. Just skimming over the surface, never really touching deep; making a few waves, but the water always smoothed out again.

Those two people in the back of the boat, he felt kind of sorry for them. They still lived in the drowned city, they belonged down there, and the fact they couldn't go there broke their hearts. But not Deaver. His city wasn't even built yet. His city was tomorrow.

He'd driven a salvage truck and lived in a closet long enough. Maybe he'd go south into the New Soil Lands. Maybe qualify on a piece of land. Own something, plant in the soil, maybe he'd come to belong there. As for this place, well, he never had belonged here, just like all the foster homes and schools along the way, just one more stop for a year or two or three, he knew that all along. Never did make any friends here, but that's how he wanted it. Wouldn't be right to make friends, 'cause he'd just move on and disappoint them. Didn't see no good in doing that to people.

By Fools Like Me

Nancy Kress

Hope creeps quietly into my bedroom without knocking, peering around the corner of the rough doorjamb. I'm awake; sleep eludes me so easily now. I know from the awful smell that she has been to the beach.

"Come in, child, I'm not asleep."

"Grandma, where's Mama and Papa?"

"Aren't they in the field?" The rains are late this year and water for the crops must be carried in ancient buckets from the spring in the dell.

"Maybe. I didn't see them. Grandma, I found something."

"What, child?"

She gazes at me and bites her lip. I see that this mysterious find bothers her. Such a sensitive child, though sturdy and healthy enough, God knows how.

"I went to the beach," she confesses in a rush. "Don't tell Mama! I wanted to dig you some trunter roots because you like them so much, but my shovel went clunk on something hard and I . . . I dug it up."

"Hope," I reprimand, because the beach is full of dangerous bits of metal and plastic, washed up through the miles of dead algae on the dead water. And if a soot cloud blows in from the west, it will hit the beach first.

"I'm sorry," she says, clearly lying, "but, Grandma, it was a metal box and the lock was all rusted and there was something inside and I brought it here."

"The box?"

"No, that was too heavy. The . . . just wait!"

No one can recognize most of the bits of rusted metal and twisted plastic from before the Crash. Anything found in a broken metal box should be decayed beyond recognition. I call, "Hope! Don't touch anything slimy—" but she is already out of earshot, running from my tiny bedroom with its narrow cot, which is just blankets and pallet on a rope frame to keep me off the hard floor. It doesn't; the old ropes sag too much, just as the thick clay walls don't keep out the heat. But that's my fault. I close the window shutters only when I absolutely have to. Insects and heat are preferable to dark. But I have a door, made of precious and rotting wood, which is more than Hope or her parents have on their sleeping alcoves off the house's only other room. I was born in this room, and I expect to die here.

Hope returns, carrying a bubble of sleek white plastic that fills her bare arms. The bubble has no seams. No mold sticks to it, no sand. Carefully she lays the thing on my cot.

Despite myself, I say, "Bring me the big knife and be very careful, it's sharp."

She gets the knife, carrying it as gingerly as an offering for the altar. The plastic slits more readily than I expected. I peel it back, and we both gasp.

I am the oldest person on Island by two decades, and I have seen much. Not of the world my father told me about, from before the Crash, but in our world now. I have buried two husbands and five children, survived three great sandstorms and two years where the rains didn't come at all, planted and first-nursed a sacred tree, served six times at the altar. I have seen much, but I have never seen so much preserved sin in one place.

"What . . . Grandma . . . what is that?"

"A book, child. They're all books."

"Books?" Her voice holds titillated horror. "You mean . . . like they made before the Crash? Like they cut down trees to make?"

"Yes."

"Trees? Real trees?"

"Yes." I lift the top one from the white plastic bubble. Firm thick red cover, like . . . dear God, it's made from the skin of some animal. My gorge rises. Hope musn't know that. The edges of the sin are gold. My father told me about books, but not that they could look like this. I open it.

"Oh!" Hope cried. "Oh, Grandma!"

The first slate—no, first *page*, the word floating up from some childhood conversation—is a picture of trees, but nothing like the pictures children draw on their slates. This picture shows dozens of richly colored trees, crowded together, each with hundreds of healthy, beautifully detailed green leaves. The trees shade a path bordered with glorious flowers. Along the path runs a child wearing far too many wraps, following a large white animal dressed in a wrap and hat and carrying a small metal machine. At the top of the picture, words float on golden clouds: *Alice in Wonderland.*

"Grandma! Look at the—Mama's coming!"

Before I can say anything, Hope grabs the book, shoves it into the white bubble, and thrusts the whole thing under my cot. I feel it slide under my bony ass, past the sag that is my body, and hit the wall. Hope is standing up by the time Gloria crowds into my tiny room.

"Hope, have you fed the chickens yet?"

"No, Mama, I—"

Gloria reaches out and slaps her daughter. "Can't I trust you to do anything?"

"Please, Gloria, it's my fault. I sent her to see if there's any more mint growing in the dell."

Gloria scowls. My daughter-in-law is perpetually angry, perpetually exhausted. Before my legs gave out and I could still do a full day's work, I used to fight back. The Island is no more arid, the see-oh-too no higher, for Gloria than for anyone else. She has borne no more stillborn children than have other women, has endured no fewer soot clouds. But now that she and my son must feed my nearly useless body, I try to not anger her too much, to not be a burden. I weave all day. I twist rope, when there are enough vines to spare for rope. I pretend to be healthier than I am.

Gloria says, "We don't need mint, we need fed chickens. Go, Hope." She turns.

"Gloria—"

"What?" Her tone is unbearable. I wonder, for the thousandth time, why Bill married her, and for the thousandth time I answer my own question.

"Nothing," I say. I don't tell her about the sin under the bed. I could have, and ended it right there. But I do not.

God forgive me.

Gloria stands behind the altar, dressed in the tattered green robe we all wear during our year of service. I sit on a chair in front of the standing villagers; no one may miss services, no matter how old or sick or in need of help to hobble to the grove. Bill half carried me here, afraid no doubt of being late and further angering his wife. It's hard to have so little respect for my son.

It is the brief time between the dying of the unholy wind that blows all day and the fall of night. Today the clouds are light gray, not too sooty, but not bearing rain, either.

The altar stands at the bottom of the dell, beside the spring that makes our village possible. A large flat slab of slate, it is supported by boulders painstakingly chiseled with the words of God. It took four generations to carve that tiny writing, and three generations of children have learned to read by copying the sacred texts onto their slates. I was among the first. The altar is shaded by the six trees of the grove and from my uncomfortable seat, I can gaze up at their branches against the pale sky.

How beautiful they are! Ours are the tallest, straightest, healthiest trees of any village on Island. I planted and first-nursed one of them myself, the honor of my life. Even now I feel a thickness in my shriveled chest as I gaze up at the green leaves, each one wiped free of dust every day by those in service. Next year, Hope will be one of them. There is nothing on Earth lovelier than the shifting pattern of trees against the sky. Nothing.

Gloria raises her arms and intones, "'Then God said, 'I give you every plant and every tree on the whole Earth. They will be food for you.'"

"Amen," call out two or three people.

"'Wail, oh pine tree,'" Gloria cries, "'for the cedar has fallen, the stately trees are ruined! Wail, oaks—'"

"Wail! Wail!"

I have never understood why people can't just worship in silence. This lot is sometimes as bad as a flock of starlings.

"'oaks of Bashan, the—'"

Hope whispers, "Who's Bashan?"

Bill whispers back, "A person at the Crash."

"'—dense forest has been cut down! And they were told—told!—not to harm the grass of Earth or any plant or tree.'"

Revelation 9:4, I think automatically, although I never did find out what the words or numbers mean.

"'The vine is dried up!'" Gloria cries, "'the fig tree is withered! The pomegranate and the palm and the apple tree, all the trees of the field, are dried up! Surely the joy of mankind is withered away!'"

"Withered! Oh, amen, withered!"

Joel 1:12.

"'Offer sacrifices and burn incense on the high places, under any spreading tree!'"

Amy Martin, one of the wailers, comes forward with the first sacrifice, an unrecognizable piece of rusted metal dug up from the soil or washed up on the beach. She lays it on the altar. Beside me Hope leans forward, her mouth open and her eyes wide. I can read her young thoughts as easily as if they, too, are chiseled in stone: That metal might have been part of a "car" that threw see-oh-two and soot into the air, might have been part of a "factory" that poisoned the air, might have even been part of a "saw" that cut down the forests! Hope shudders, but I glance away from the intensity on her face. Sometimes she looks too much like Gloria.

Two more sacrifices are offered. Gloria takes an ember from the banked fire under the altar—the only fire allowed in the village—and touches it briefly to the sacrifices. "'Instead of the thornbush will grow the pine tree, and instead of briars the myrtle will grow. This will be for the Lord's glory, for an everlasting sign which—'"

I stop listening. Instead I watch the leaves move against the sky. What is "myrtle"—what did it look like, why was it such a desirable plant? The leaves blur. I have dozed off, but I realize this only when the whole village shouts together, "We will never forget!" and services are over.

Bill carries me back through the quickening darkness without stars or moon. Without the longed-for rain. Without the candles I remember from my childhood on Island, or the dimly remembered (dreamed?) fireless lights from before that. There are no lights after dark on Island, nothing that might release soot into the air.

We will never forget.

It's just too bad that services are so boring.

Alice in Wonderland.

Pride and Prejudice

Birds of India and Asia

Moby Dick

Morning Light

Jane Eyre

The Sun Also Rises

I sit on my cot, slowly sounding out the strange words. Of course the sun rises—what else could it do? It's rising now outside my window, which lets in pale light, insects, and the everlasting hot wind.

"Can I see, Grandma?" asks Hope, naked in the doorway. I didn't hear the door open. She could have been Gloria. And is it right for a child to see this much sin?

But already she's snuggled beside me, smelling of sweat and grime and young life. Even her slight body makes the room hotter. All at once a memory comes to me, a voice from early childhood: *Here, Anna, put ice on that bruise. Listen, that's a—*

What bruise? What was I to listen to? The memory is gone.

"M—m—m—oh—bee—Grandma, what's a 'moby'?"

"I don't know, child."

She picks up a different one. "J—j—aye—n . . . Jane! That's Miss Anderson's name! Is this book about her?"

"No. Another Jane, I think." I open *Moby Dick.* Tiny, dense writing, page and pages of it, whole burned forests of it.

"Read the sin with the picture of trees!" She roots among the books until she finds *Alice in Wonderland* and opens it to that impossible vision of tens, maybe hundreds, of glorious trees. Hope studies the child blessed enough to walk that flower-bordered path.

"What's her name, Grandma?"

"Alice." I don't really know.

"Why is she wearing so many wraps? Isn't she hot? And how many days did her poor mother have to work to weave so many? "

I recognize Gloria's scolding tone. The pages of the book are crisp, bright and clear, as if the white plastic bubble had some magic to keep sin fresh. Turning the page, I begin to read aloud. "'Alice was beginning to get very tired of sitting by her sister on the bank—'"

"She has a sister," Hope breathes. Nearly no one does now; so few children are carried to term and born whole.

"'—and tired of having nothing to do: once—'"

"How could she have nothing to do? Why doesn't she carry water or weed crops or hunt trunter roots or—"

"Hope, are you going to let me read this to you or not?"

"Yes, Grandma. I'm sorry."

I shouldn't be reading to her at all. Trees were cut down to make this book; my father told me so. As a young man, not long after the Crash, he himself was in service as a book sacrificer, proudly. Unlike many of his generation, my father was a moral man.

"'—or twice she had peeped into the book her sister was reading, but it had no pictures or conversation in it, "and what is the use of a book," thought Alice, "without pictures or conversation?" So she was considering—'"

We read while the sun clears the horizon, a burning merciless ball, and our sweat drips onto the gold-edged page. Then Gloria and Bill stir in the next room and Hope is on the floor in a flash, shoving the books under my sagging cot, running out the door to feed the chickens and hunt for their rare, precious eggs.

The rains are very late this year. Every day Gloria, scowling, scans the sky. Every day at sunset she and Bill drag themselves home, bone-weary and smeared with dust, after carrying water from the spring to the crops. The spring is in the dell, and water will not flow uphill. Gloria is also in service this year and must nurse one of the trees, wiping the poisonous dust from her share of the leaves, checking for dangerous insects. More work, more time. Some places on Earth, I was told once, have too much water, too many plants from the see-oh-too. I can't imagine it. Island has heard from no other place since I was a young woman and the last radio failed. Now a radio would be sin.

I sit at the loom, weaving. I'm even clumsier than usual, my fingers stiff and eyes stinging. From too much secret reading, or from a high see-oh-too day? Oh, let it be from the reading!

"Grandma," Hope says, coming in from tending the chickens. "My throat hurts." Her voice is small; she knows.

Dear God, not now, not when the rains are already so late . . . But I look out the window and yes, I can see it on the western horizon, thick and brown.

"Bring in the chickens, Hope. Quick!"

She runs back outside while I hobble to the heavy shutters and wrestle them closed. Hope brings in the first protesting chicken, dumps it in her sleeping alcove, and fastens the rope fence. She races back for the next chicken as Bill and Gloria run over the fields toward the house.

Not now, when everything is so dry . . .

They get the chickens in, the food covered, as much water inside as can be carried. At the last moment Bill swings closed the final shutter, and we're plunged into darkness and even greater heat. We huddle against the west wall. The dust storm hits.

Despite the shutters, the holy protection of wood, dust drifts through cracks, under the door, maybe even through chinks in the walls. The dust clogs our throats, noses, eyes. The wind rages: *oooeeeeeeeooooeeeee.* Shrinking beside me, Hope gasps, "It's trying to get in!"

Gloria snaps, "Don't talk!" and slaps Hope. Gloria is right, of course; the soot carries poisons that Island can't name and doesn't remember. Only I remember my father saying, "Methane and bio-weapons . . ."

Here, Anna, put ice on that bruise. Listen, that's a—

A what? What was that memory?

Then Gloria, despite her slap, begins to talk. She has no choice; it's her service year and she must pray aloud. "'Wail, oh pine tree, for the cedar has fallen, the stately trees are ruined! Wail, oaks of Bashan, the dense forest has been cut down!'"

I want Gloria to recite a different scripture. I want, God forgive me, Gloria to shut up. Her anger burns worse than the dust, worse than the heat.

"'The vine is dried up and the fig is withered; the pomegranate—'"

I stop listening.

Listen, that's a—

Hope trembles beside me, a sweaty mass of fear.

The dust storm proves mercifully brief, but the see-oh-too cloud pulled behind it lasts for days. Everyone's breathing grows harsh. Gloria and Bill, carrying water, get fierce headaches. Gloria makes Hope stay inside, telling her to sit still. I see in Gloria's eyes the concern for her only living child, a concern that Hope is too young to see. Hope sees only her mother's anger.

Left alone, Hope and I sin.

All the long day, while her parents work frantically to keep us alive, we sit by the light of a cracked shutter and follow Alice down the rabbit hole, through the pool of tears, inside the White Rabbit's house, to the Duchess's peppery kitchen. Hope stops asking questions, since I know none of the answers. What is pepper, a crocodile, a caucus race, marmalade? We just read steadily on, wishing there were more pictures, until the book is done and Alice has woken. We begin *Jane Eyre*: "'There was no possibility of taking a walk that day . . .'"

Birds of India and Asia has gorgeous pictures, but the writing is so small and difficult that I can't read most of it. Nonetheless, this is the book I turn to when Hope is asleep. So many birds! And so many colors on wings and backs and breasts and rising from the tops of heads like fantastic feathered trees. I wish I knew if these birds were ever real, or if they are as imaginary as Alice, as the White Rabbit, as marmalade. I wish—

"Grandma!" Hope cries, suddenly awake. "It's raining outside!"

Joy, laughter, dancing. The whole village gathers at the altar under the trees. Bill carries me there, half running, and I smell his strong male sweat mingled with the sweet rain. Hope dances in her drenched wrap like some wild thing and chases after the other children.

Then Gloria strides into the grove, grabs Hope, and throws her onto the altar. "You've sinned! My own daughter!"

Immediately everyone falls silent. The village, shocked, looks from Gloria to Hope, back to Gloria. Gloria's face is twisted with fury. From a fold of her wrap she pulls out *Alice in Wonderland.*

"This was in the chicken coop! This! A sin, trees destroyed . . . you had this in our very house!" Gloria's voice rises to a shriek.

Hope shrinks against the wide flat stone and she puts her hands over her face. Rain streams down on her, flattening her hair against her small skull. The book in Gloria's hand sheds droplets off its skin cover. Gloria tears out pages and throws them to the ground, where they go sodden and pulpy as maggots.

"Because of you, God might not have sent any rains at all this year! We're just lucky that in His infinite mercy—you risked—you—"

Gloria drops the mutilated book, pulls back her arm, and with all her force strikes Hope on the shoulder. Hope screams and draws into a ball, covering her head and neck. Gloria lashes out again, a sickening thud of hand on tender flesh. I cry, "Stop! No, Gloria, stop—Bill—let me go!"

He doesn't. No one else moves to help Hope, either. I can feel Bill's anguish, but he chokes out, "It's right, Mama." And then, invoking the most sacred scripture of all, he whispers, "We will never forget."

I cry out again, but nothing can keep Hope from justice, not even when I scream that it is my fault, my book, my sin. They know I couldn't have found this pre-Crash sin alone. They know that, but no one except me knows when Gloria passes beyond beating Hope for justice, for Godly retribution, into beating her from Gloria's own fury, her withered fig tree, her sin. No one sees but me. And I, an old woman, can do nothing.

Hope lies on her cot, moaning. I crouch beside her in her alcove, its small window unshuttered to the rain. Bill bound her broken arm with the unfinished cloth off my loom, then went into the storm in search of his wife.

"Hope . . . dear heart . . ."

She moans again.

If I could, I would kill Gloria with my own hands.

A sudden lone crack of lightning brightens the alcove. Already the skin on Hope's wet arms and swollen face has started to darken. One eye swells.

Here, Anna, put ice on that bruise. Listen, that's a—

"Grandma . . ."

"Don't talk, Hope."

"Water," Hope gasps and I hold the glass for her. Another flash of lightning and for a moment Gloria stands framed in the window. We stare at each other. With a kind of horror I feel my lips slide back, baring my teeth. Gloria sees, and cold slides down my spine.

Then the lightning is gone, and I lay my hand on Hope's battered body.

The rain lasts no more than a few hours. It's replaced by day after day of black clouds that thunder and roil but shed no water. Day after day. Gloria and Bill let half the field die in their attempt to save the other half. The rest of the village does much the same.

Hope heals quickly; the young are resilient. I sit beside her, weaving, until she can work again. Her bruises turn all the colors of the angry earth: black and dun and dead-algae green. Gloria never looks at or speaks to her daughter. My son smiles weakly at us all, and brings Hope her meal, and follows Gloria out the door to the fields.

"Grandma, we sinned."

Did we? I don't know any more. To cut down trees in order to make a book . . . my gorge rises at just the thought. Yes, that's wrong, as wrong as anything could ever be. Trees are the life of the Earth, are God's gift to us. Even my father's generation, still so selfish and sinful, said so. Trees absorb the see-oh-too, clean the air, hold the soil, cool the world. Yes.

But, against that, the look of rapture on Hope's face as Alice chased the White Rabbit, the pictures of *Birds of India and Asia,* Jane Eyre battling Mrs. Reed . . . Hope and I destroyed nothing ourselves. Is it so wrong, then, to enjoy another's sin?

"We sinned," Hope repeats, mourning, and it is her tone that hardens my heart.

"No, child. We didn't."

"We didn't?" Her eyes, one still swollen, grow wide.

"We didn't make the books. They already were. We just read them. Reading isn't sinful."

"Nooooo," she says reluctantly. "Not reading the altar scriptures. But Alice is—"

Gloria enters the house. She says to me, "Services tonight."

I say, "I'm not going."

Gloria stops dead halfway to the wash bucket, her field hat suspended in her hand. For the briefest moment I see something like panic on her face, before it vanishes into her usual anger. "Not going? To services?"

"No."

Hope, frightened, looks from her mother to me. Bill comes in.

Gloria snaps, with distinct emphasis, "Your mother says she's not going to services tonight."

Bill says, "Mama?"

"No," I say, and watch his face go from puzzlement to the dread of a weak man who will do anything to avoid argument. I hobble to my alcove and close the door. Later, from my window, I watch them leave for the grove, Hope holding her father's hand.

Gloria must have given him silent permission to do that.

My son.

Painfully I lower myself to the floor, reach under my cot, and pull out the white plastic bubble. For a while I gaze at the pictures of the gorgeous birds of India and Asia. Then I read *Jane Eyre.* When my family returns at dusk, I keep reading as long as the light holds, not bothering to hide any of the books, knowing that no one will come in.

One heavy afternoon, when the clouds steadily darken and I can no longer see enough to make out words, a huge bolt of lightning shrieks through the sky—*crack*! For a long moment my head vibrates. Then silence, followed by a shout: "Fire!"

I haul myself to my knees and grasp the bottom of the window. The lightning hit one of the trees in the grove. As I watch, numb, the fire leaps on the ceaseless wind to a second tree.

People scream and run, throwing buckets of muddy water from the spring. I can see that it will do no good—too much dry timber, too much wind. A third tree catches, a fourth, and then the grass too is on fire. Smoke and ash rise into the sky.

I sink back onto my cot. I planted one of those trees, nursed it as I'd once nursed Bill. But there is nothing I can do. Nothing.

By the light of the terrible flames I pick up *Jane Eyre* and, desperately, I read.

And then Hope bursts in, smeared with ash, sweat, and tears on her face.

"Hope—no! Don't!"

"Give it to me!"

"No!"

We struggle, but she is stronger. Hope yanks *Jane Eyre* out of my hands and hurls it to the floor. She drops on top of it and crawls under my cot. Frantically I try to press down the sagging ropes so that she can't get past them, but I don't weigh enough. Hope backs out with the other books in their plastic bubble. She scrambles to her feet.

"We did this! You and me! Our sin made God burn the trees!"

"No! Hope—"

"Yes! We did this, just like the people before the Crash!"

We will never forget.

I reach for her, for the books, for everything I've lost or am about to lose. But Hope is already gone. From my window I see her silhouetted against the flames, running toward the grass. The village beats the grass with water-soaked cloths. I let go of the sill and fall back onto the cot before I can see Hope throw the books onto the fire.

Gloria beats Hope again, harder and longer this time. She and Bill might have put me out of the house, except that I have no place to go. So they settle for keeping me away from Hope, so that I cannot lead her further into sin.

Bill speaks to me only once about what happened. Bringing me my meal—meager, so meager—he averts his eyes from my face and says haltingly, "Mama . . . I . . ."

"Don't," I say.

"I have to . . . you . . . Gloria . . ." All at once he finds words. "A little bit of sin is just as bad a big sin. That's what you taught me. What all those people thought before the Crash—that their cars and machines and books each only destroyed a little air so it didn't matter. And look what happened! The Crash was—"

"Do you really think you're telling me something I don't know? Telling *me?*"

Bill turns away. But as he closes the door behind him, he mumbles over his shoulder, "A little bit of sin is as bad as a big sin."

I sit in my room, alone.

Bill is not right. Nor is Gloria, who told him what to say. Nor is Hope, who is after all a child, with a child's uncompromising, black-and-white faith. They are all wrong, but I can't find the arguments to tell them so. I'm too ignorant. The arguments must exist, they must—but I can't find them. And my family wouldn't listen anyway.

Listen, Anna, that's a—

A nightingale.

The whole memory flashes like lightening in my head: my father, bending over me in a walled garden, laughing, trying to distract me from some childish fall. Here, Anna, put ice on that bruise. Listen, that's a nightingale! A cube of frozen water pulled with strong fingers from his amber drink. Flowers everywhere, flowers of scarcely believable colors, crimson and gold and blue and emerald. And a burst of glorious unseen music, high and sweet. A bird, maybe one from *Birds of India and Asia.*

But I don't know, can't remember, what a nightingale looks like. And now I never will.

DARK, DISTANT FUTURES

The Store of the Worlds

Robert Sheckley

Mr. Wayne came to the end of the long, shoulder-high mound of gray rubble, and there was the Store of the Worlds. It was exactly as his friends had described: a small shack constructed of bits of lumber, parts of cars, a piece of galvanized iron, and a few rows of crumbling bricks, all daubed over with a watery blue paint.

He glanced back down the long lane of rubble to make sure he hadn't been followed. He tucked his parcel more firmly under his arm; then, with a little shiver at his own audacity, he opened the door and slipped inside.

"Good morning," the proprietor said.

He, too, was exactly as described: a tall, crafty-looking old fellow with narrow eyes and downcast mouth. His name was Tompkins. He sat in an old rocking chair, and perched on the back of it was a blue-and-green parrot. There was one other chair in the store, and a table. On the table was a rusted hypodermic.

"I've heard about your store from friends," Mr. Wayne said.

"Then you know my price," Tompkins said. "Have you brought it?"

"Yes," said Mr. Wayne, holding up his parcel. "All my worldly goods. But I want to ask first—"

"They always want to ask," Tompkins said to the parrot, who blinked. "Go ahead, ask."

"I want to know what really happens."

Tompkins sighed. "What happens is that: I give you an injection which knocks you out. Then, with the aid of certain gadgets which I have in the back of the store, I liberate your mind."

Tompkins smiled as he said that, and his silent parrot seemed to smile, too.

"What happens then?" Mr. Wayne asked.

"Your mind, liberated from its body, is able to choose from the countless probability worlds which the earth casts off in every second of its existence."

Grinning now, Tompkins sat up in his rocking chair and began to show signs of enthusiasm.

"Yes, my friend, though you might not have suspected it, from the moment this battered earth was born out of the sun's fiery womb, it cast off its alternate-probability worlds. Worlds without end, emanating from events large and small; every Alexander and every amoeba creating worlds, just as ripples will spread in a pond no matter how big or how small the stone you throw. Doesn't every object cast a shadow? Well, my friend, the Earth itself is four-dimensional; therefore it casts three-dimensional shadows, solid reflections of itself, through every moment of its being. Millions, billions of Earths! An infinity of Earths! And your mind, liberated by me, will be able to select any of these worlds and live upon it for a while."

Mr. Wayne was uncomfortably aware that Tompkins sounded like a circus barker, proclaiming marvels that simply couldn't exist. But, Mr. Wayne reminded himself, things had happened within his own lifetime which he would never have believed possible. Never! So perhaps the wonders that Tompkins spoke of were possible, too.

Mr. Wayne said, "My friends also told me—"

"That I was an out-and-out fraud?" Tompkins asked.

"Some of them *implied* that," Mr. Wayne said cautiously. "But I try to keep an open mind. They also said—"

"I know what your dirty-minded friends said. They told you about the fulfillment of desire. Is that what you want to hear about?"

"Yes," said Mr. Wayne. "They told me that whatever I wished for, whatever I wanted—"

"Exactly," Tompkins said. "The thing could work in no other way. There are the infinite worlds to choose among. Your mind chooses and is guided only by desire. Your deepest desire is the only thing that counts. If you have been harboring a secret dream of murder—"

"Oh, hardly, hardly!" cried Mr. Wayne.

"—then you will go to a world where you *can* murder, where you can roll in blood, where you can outdo de Sade or Nero or whoever your idol may be. Suppose it's power you want? Then you'll choose a world where you are a god, literally and actually. A bloodthirsty Juggernaut, perhaps, or an all-wise Buddha."

"I doubt very much if I—"

"There are other desires, too," Tompkins said. "All heavens and all hells will be open to you. Unbridled sexuality. Gluttony, drunkenness, love, fame—anything you want."

"Amazing!" said Mr. Wayne.

"Yes," Tompkins agreed. "Of course, my little list doesn't exhaust all the possibilities, all the combinations and permutations of desire. For all I know, you might want a simple, placid, pastoral existence on a South Sea island among idealized natives."

"That sounds more like me," Mr. Wayne said with a shy laugh.

"But who knows?" Tompkins asked. "Even *you* might not know what your true desires are. They might involve your own death."

"Does that happen often?" Mr. Wayne asked anxiously.

"Occasionally."

"I wouldn't want to die," Mr. Wayne said.

"It hardly ever happens," Tompkins said, looking at the parcel in Mr. Wayne's hands.

"If you say so. . . . But how do I know all this is real? Your fee is extremely high; it'll take everything I own. And for all I know, you'll give me a drug and I'll just *dream!* Everything I own just for a—shot of heroin and a lot of fancy words!"

Tompkins smiled reassuringly. "The experience has no druglike quality about it. And no sensation of a dream, either."

"If it's *true*," Mr. Wayne said a little petulantly, "why can't I stay in the world of my desire for good?"

"I'm working on that," Tompkins said. "That's why I charge so high a fee—to get materials, to experiment. I'm trying to find a way of making the transition permanent. So far I haven't been able to loosen the cord that binds a man to his own Earth—and pulls him back to it. Not even the great mystics could cut that cord, except with death. But I still have my hopes."

"It would be a great thing if you succeeded," Mr. Wayne said politely.

"Yes, it would!" Tompkins cried with a surprising burst of passion. "For then I'd turn my wretched shop into an escape hatch! My process would be free then, free for everyone! Everyone could go to the earth of his desires, the earth that really suited him and leave *this* damned place to the rats and worms—"

Tompkins cut himself off in midsentence and became icy calm. "But I fear my prejudices are showing. I can't offer a permanent escape from this world yet, not one that doesn't involve death. Perhaps I never will be able to. For now, all I can offer you is a vacation, a change, a taste of another world and a look at your own desires. You know my fee. I'll refund if it the experience isn't satisfactory."

"That's good of you," Mr. Wayne said quite earnestly. "But there's that other matter my friends told me about. The ten years off my life."

"That can't be helped," Tompkins said, "and can't be refunded. My process is a tremendous strain on the nervous system, and life expectancy is shortened accordingly. That's one of the reasons why our so-called government has declared my process illegal."

"But they don't enforce the ban very firmly," Mr. Wayne said.

"No. Officially the process is banned as a harmful fraud. But officials are men, too. They'd like to leave this earth, just like everyone else."

"The cost," Mr. Wayne mused, gripping his parcel tightly. "And ten years off my life! For the fulfillment of my secret desires. . . . Really, I must give this some thought."

"Think away," Tompkins said indifferently.

All the way home Mr. Wayne thought about it. When his train reached Port Washington, Long Island, he was still thinking. And driving his car from the station to his house, he was still thinking about Tompkins's crafty old face, and worlds of probability, and the fulfillment of desire.

But when he stepped inside his home, those thoughts had to stop. Janet, his wife, wanted him to speak sharply to the maid, who had been drinking again. His son, Tommy, wanted help with the sloop, which was to be launched tomorrow. And his baby daughter wanted to tell about her day in kindergarten.

Mr. Wayne spoke pleasantly but firmly to the maid. He helped Tommy put the final coat of copper paint on the sloop's bottom, and he listened to Peggy tell her adventures in the playground.

Later, when the children were in bed and he and Janet were alone in their living room, she asked him if something was wrong.

"Wrong?"

"You seem to be worried about something," Janet said. "Did you have a bad day at the office?"

"Oh, just the usual sort of thing . . ."

He certainly was not going to tell Janet, or anyone else, that he had taken the day off and gone to see Tompkins in his crazy old Store of the Worlds. Nor was he going to speak about the right every man should have, once in his lifetime, to fulfill his most secret desires. Janet, with her good common sense, would never understand that.

The next days at the office were extremely hectic. All of Wall Street was in a mild panic over events in the Middle East and in Asia, and stocks were reacting accordingly. Mr. Wayne settled down to work. He tried not to think of the fulfillment of desire at the cost of everything he possessed, with ten years of his life thrown in for good measure. It was crazy! Old Tompkins must be insane!

On weekends he went sailing with Tommy. The old sloop was behaving very well, taking practically no water through her bottom seams. Tommy wanted a new suit of racing sails, but Mr. Wayne sternly rejected that. Perhaps next year, if the market looked better. For now, the old sails would have to do.

Sometimes at night, after the children were asleep; he and Janet would go sailing. Long Island Sound was quiet then and cool. Their boat glided past the blinking buoys, sailing toward the swollen yellow moon.

"I *know* something's on your mind," Janet said.

"Darling, please!"

"Is there something you're keeping from me?"

"Nothing!"

"Are you sure? Are you absolutely sure?"

"Absolutely sure."

"Then, put your arms around me. That's right . . ."

And the sloop sailed itself for a while.

Desire and fulfillment. . . . But autumn came and the sloop had to be hauled. The stock market regained some stability, but Peggy caught the measles. Tommy wanted to know the difference between ordinary bombs, atom bombs, hydrogen bombs, cobalt bombs, and all the other kinds of bombs that were in the news. Mr. Wayne explained to the best of his ability. And the maid quit unexpectedly.

Secret desires were all very well. Perhaps he *did* want to kill someone or live on a South Sea island. But there were responsibilities to consider. He had two growing children and the best of wives.

Perhaps around Christmastime . . .

But in midwinter there was a fire in the unoccupied guest room due to defective wiring. The firemen put out the blaze without much damage, and no one was hurt. But it put any thought of Tompkins out of his mind for a while. First the bedroom had to be repaired, for Mr. Wayne was very proud of his gracious old house.

Business was still frantic and uncertain due to the international situation. Those Russians, those Arabs, those Greeks, those Chinese. The intercontinental missiles, the atom bombs, the Sputniks. . . . Mr. Wayne spent long days at the office and sometimes evenings, too. Tommy caught the mumps. A part of the roof had to be reshingled. And then already it was time to consider the spring launching of the sloop.

A year had passed, and he'd had very little time to think of secret desires. But perhaps next year. In the meantime . . .

"Well?" said Tompkins. "Are you all right?"

"Yes, quite all right," Mr. Wayne said. He got up from the chair and rubbed his forehead.

"Do you want a refund?" Tompkins asked.

"No. The experience was quite satisfactory."

"They always are," Tompkins said, winking lewdly at the parrot. "Well, what was yours?"

"A world of the recent past," Mr. Wayne said.

"A lot of them are. Did you find out about your secret desire? Was it murder? Or a South Sea island?"

"I'd rather not discuss it," Mr. Wayne said pleasantly but firmly.

"A lot of people won't discuss it with me," Tompkins said sulkily. "I'll be damned if I know why."

"Because—well, I think the world of one's secret desire seems sacred, somehow. No offense. . . . Do you think you'll ever be able to make it permanent? The world of one's choice, I mean?"

The old man shrugged his shoulders. "I'm trying. If I succeed, you'll hear about it. Everyone will."

"Yes, I suppose so." Mr. Wayne undid his parcel and laid its contents on the table. The parcel contained a pair of army boots, a knife, two coils of copper wire, and three small cans of corned beef.

Tompkins's eyes glittered for a moment. "Quite satisfactory," he said. "Thank you."

"Good-bye," said Mr. Wayne. "And thank you."

Mr. Wayne left the shop and hurried down to the end of the lane of gray rubble. Beyond it, as far as he could see, lay flat fields of rubble, brown and gray and black. Those fields, stretching to every horizon, were made of the twisted corpses of buildings, the shattered remnants of trees and the fine white ash that once was human flesh and bone.

"Well," Mr. Wayne said to himself, "at least we gave as good as we got."

His year in the past had cost him everything he owned and ten years of life thrown in for good measure. Had it been a dream? It was still worth it. But now he had to put away all thought of Janet and the children. That was finished, unless Tompkins perfected his process. Now he had to think about his own survival.

He picked his way carefully through the rubble, determined to get back to the shelter before dark, before the rats came out. If he didn't hurry, he'd miss the evening potato ration.

Dark, Dark Were the Tunnels

George R. R. Martin

GREEL WAS AFRAID.

He lay in the warm, rich darkness beyond the place where the tunnel curved, his thin body pressed against the strange metal bar that ran along the floor. His eyes were closed. He strained to remain perfectly still.

He was armed. A short barbed spear was clenched tightly in his right fist. But that did not lessen his fear.

He had come far, far. He had climbed higher and ranged further than any other scout of the. People in long generations. He had fought his way through the Bad Levels, where the worm-things still hunted the People relentlessly. He had stalked and slain the glowing killer mole in the crumbling Middle Tunnels. He had wiggled through dozens of unmapped and unnamed passages that hardly looked big enough for a man to pass.

And now he had penetrated to the Oldest Tunnels, the great tunnels and halls of legend, where the taletellers said the People had come from a million years ago.

He was no coward. He was a scout of the People, who dared to walk in tunnels where men had not trod in centuries.

But he was afraid, and was not ashamed for his fear. A good scout knows when to be afraid. And Greel was a very good scout. So he lay silent in the darkness, and clutched his spear, and thought.

Slowly the fear began to wane. Greel steeled himself, and opened his eyes. Quickly he shut them again.

The tunnel ahead was on fire.

He had never seen fire. But the taletellers had sung of it many times. Hot it was. And bright, so bright it hurt the eyes. Blindness was the lot of those who looked too long.

So Greel kept his eyes shut. A scout needed his eyes. He could not allow the fire ahead to blind him.

Back here, in the darkness beyond the bend of the tunnel, the fire was not so bad. It still hurt the eyes to look at it, as it hung upon the curving tunnel wall. But the pain was one that could be borne.

But earlier, when he had first seen the fire, Greel had been unwise. He had crept forward, squinting, to where the wall curved away. He had touched the fire that hung upon the stone. And then, foolishly, he had peered beyond the curve.

His eyes still ached. He had gotten only one quick glimpse before whirling and scrambling silently back to where he lay. But it was enough. Beyond the bend the fire had been brighter, much brighter, brighter than ever he could have imagined. Even with his eyes closed he could still see it, two dancing, aching spots of horrible intense brightness. They would not go away. The fire had burned part of his eyes, he thought.

But still, when he had touched the fire that hung upon the wall, it had not been like the fire of which the taletellers sing. The stone had felt like all other stone, cool and a little damp. Fire was hot, the taletellers said. But the fire on the stone had not been hot to the touch.

It was not fire, then, Greel decided after thought. What it was, he did not know. But it could not be fire if it was not hot.

He stirred slightly from where he lay. Barely moving, he reached out and touched H'ssig in the darkness.

His mind-brother was several yards distant, near one of the other metal bars. Greel stroked him with his mind, and could feel H'ssig quiver in response. Thoughts and sensations mingled wordlessly.

H'ssig was afraid, too. The great hunting rat had no eyes. But his scent was keener than Greel's, and there was a strange smell in the tunnel.

His ears were better, too. Through them, Greel could pick up more of the odd noises that came from within the fire that was not a fire.

Greel opened his eyes again. Slowly this time, not all at once. Squinting.

The holes the fire had burned in his vision were still there. But they were fading. And the dimmer fire that moved on the curving tunnel wall could be endured, if he did not look directly at it.

Still. He could not go forward. And he must not creep back. He was a scout. He had a duty.

He reached out to H'ssig again. The hunting rat had run with him since birth. He had never failed him. He would not fail him now. The rat had no eyes that could be burned, but his ears and his nose would tell Greel what he must know about the thing beyond the curve.

H'ssig felt the command more than he heard it. He crept forward slowly toward the fire.

"A treasurehouse!"

Ciffonetto's voice was thick with admiration. The layer of protective grease smeared onto his face could hardly hide the grin.

Von der Stadt looked doubtful. Not just his face, but his whole body radiated doubt. Both men were dressed alike, in featureless gray coveralls woven of a heavy metallic cloth. But they could never be mistaken. Von der Stadt was unique in his ability to express doubt while remaining absolutely still.

When he moved, or spoke, he underlined the impression. As he did now. "Some treasurehouse," he said simply.

It was enough to annoy Ciffonetto. He frowned slightly at his larger companion. "No, I mean it," he said. The beam from his heavy flashlight sliced through the thick darkness and played up and down one of the rust-eaten steel pillars that stretched from the platform to the roof. "Look at that," Ciffonetto said.

Von der Stadt looked at it. Doubtfully. "I see it," he said. "So where's the treasure?"

Ciffonetto continued to move his beam up and down. "That's the treasure," he said. "This whole place is a major historical find. I knew this was the place to search. I told them so."

"What's so great about a steel beam, anyway?" Von der Stadt asked, letting his own flash brush against the pillar.

"The state of preservation," Ciffonetto said, moving closer. "Most everything above ground is radioactive slag, even now. But down here we've got some beautiful artifacts. It will give us a much better picture about what the old civilization was like, before the disaster."

"We know what the old civilization was like," Von der Stadt protested. "We've got tapes, books, films, everything. All sorts of things. The war didn't even touch Luna."

"Yes, yes, but this is different," Ciffonetto, said. "This is reality." He ran his gloved hand lovingly along the pillar. "Look here," he said.

Von der Stadt moved closer.

There was writing carved into the metal. Scratched in, rather. It didn't go very deep, but it could still be read, if but faintly.

Ciffonetto was grinning again. Von der Stadt looked doubtful. "Rodney loves Wanda," he said.

He shook his head. "Shit, Cliff," he said, "you can find the same thing in every public john in Luna City."

Ciffonetto rolled his eyes. "Von der Stadt," he said, "if we found the oldest cave painting in the world, you'd probably say it was a lousy picture of a buffalo." He jabbed at the writing with his free hand. "Don't you understand? This is old. It's history. It's the remains of a civilization and a nation and a planet that perished almost half a millennium ago."

Von der Stadt didn't reply, but he still looked doubtful. His flashlight wandered. "There's some more if that's what you're after," he said, holding his beam steady on another pillar a few feet distant.

This time it was Ciffonetto who read the inscription. "Repent or ye are doomed," he said, smiling, after his flash melted into Von der Stadt's.

He chuckled slightly. "The words of the prophets are written on the subway walls," he said softly.

Von der Stadt frowned. "Some prophet," he said. "They must have had one hell of a weird religion."

"Oh, Christ," Ciffonetto groaned. "I didn't mean it literally. I was quoting. A mid-twentieth-century poet named Simon. He wrote that only fifty years or so before the great disaster."

Von der Stadt wasn't interested. He wandered away impatiently, his flash darting here and there amid the pitch-black ruins of the ancient subway station. "It's hot down here," he complained.

"Hotter up there," Ciffonetto said, already lost in a new inscription.

"Not the same kind of hot," Von der Stadt replied.

Ciffonetto didn't bother to answer. "This is the biggest find of the expedition," he said when he looked up at last. "We've got to get pictures. And get the others down here. We're wasting our time on the surface."

"We'll do better down here?" Von der Stadt said. Doubtfully, of course.

Ciffonetto nodded. "That's what I've said all along. The surface was plastered. It's still a radioactive hell up there, even after all these centuries. If anything survived, it was underground. That's where we should look. We should branch out and explore this whole system of tunnels." His hands swept out expansively.

"You and Nagel have been arguing about that the whole trip," Von der Stadt said. "All the way from Luna City. I don't see that it's done you much good."

"Doctor Nagel is a fool," Ciffonetto said carefully.

"I don't think so," Von der Stadt said. "I'm a soldier, not a scientist. But I've heard his side of the argument, and it makes sense. All this stuff down here is great, but it's not what Nagel wants. It's not what the expedition was sent to Earth to look for."

"I know, I know," Ciffonetto said. "Nagel wants life. Human life, especially. So every day he sends the flyers out further and further. And so far all he's come up with is a few species of insects and a handful of mutated birds."

Von der Stadt shrugged.

"If he'd look down here, he'd find what he's after," Ciffonetto continued. "He doesn't realize how deep the cities had dug before the war. There are miles of tunnels under our feet. Level after level. That's where the survivors would be, if there are any survivors."

"How do you figure?" Von der Stadt asked.

"Look, when war hit, the only ones to live through it would be those down in deep shelters. Or in the tunnels beneath the cities. The radioactivity would have prevented them from coming up for years. Hell, the surface still isn't very attractive. They'd be trapped down there. They'd adjust. After a few generations they wouldn't want to come up."

But Von der Stadt's attention had wandered, and he was hardly listening any more. He had walked to the edge of the platform and was staring down onto the tracks.

He stood there silently for a moment, then reached a decision. He stuffed his flashlight into his belt and began to climb down. "Come on," he said. "Let's go look for some of these survivors of yours."

H'ssig stayed close to the metal bar as he edged forward. It helped to hide him, and it kept away the fire, so he moved in a little band of almost darkness. Hugging it as best he could, he crept silently around the curve, and halted.

Through him, Greel watched:—watched with the rat's ears and with his nose. The fire was talking.

There were two scents, alike but not the same. And there were two voices. Just as there had been two fires. The bright things that had burned Greel's eyes were living creatures of some sort.

Greel listened. The sounds H'ssig heard so clearly were words. A language of some sort. Greel was sure of that. He knew the difference between the roars and grunts of animals and the patterns of speech.

But the fire things were talking in a language he did not know. The sounds meant no more to him than to H'ssig who relayed them.

He concentrated on the scent. It was strange, unlike anything he had encountered before. But somehow it felt like a man-scent, though it could not be that.

Greel thought. An almost man-scent. And words. Could it be that the fire things were men? They would be strange men, much unlike the People. But the taletellers sung of men in ancient times that had strange powers and forms. Might not these be such men? Here, in the Oldest Tunnels, where the legends said the Old Ones had created the People—might not such men still dwell here?

Yes.

Greel stirred. He moved slowly from where he lay, raising himself to a crouching position to squint at the curve ahead. A silent snap brought H'ssig back to safety from the fiery tunnel beyond the curve.

There was one way to make sure, Greel thought. Trembling, he reached out cautiously with his mind.

Von der Stadt had adapted to Earth's gravity a lot more successfully than Ciffonetto. He reached the floor of the tunnel quickly, and waited impatiently while his companion climbed down from the platform.

Ciffonetto let himself drop the last foot or so, and landed with a thud. He looked up at the platform apprehensively. "I just hope I can make it back up," he said.

Von der Stadt shrugged. "You were the one who wanted to explore all the tunnels."

"Yes," said Ciffonetto, shifting his gaze from the platform to look around him. "And I still do. Down here, in these tunnels, are the answers we're seeking."

"That's your theory, anyway," Von der Stadt said. He looked in both directions, chose one at random, and moved forward, his flashlight beam spearing out before him. Ciffonetto followed a half-step behind.

The tunnel they entered was long, straight, and empty.

"Tell me," Von der Stadt said in an offhand manner as they walked, "even if your survivors did make it through the war in shelters, wouldn't they have been forced to surface eventually to survive? I mean—how could anyone actually live down here?" He looked around the tunnel with obvious distaste.

"Have you been taking lessons from Nagel or something?" Ciffonetto replied. "I've heard that so often I'm sick of it. I admit it would be difficult. But not impossible. At first, there would be access to large stores of canned goods. A lot of that stuff was kept in basements. You could get to it by tunneling. Later, you could raise food. There are plants that will grow without light. And there would be insects and boring animals too, I imagine."

"A diet of bugs and mushrooms. It doesn't sound too healthy to me." Ciffonetto stopped suddenly, not bothering to reply. "Look there," he said, pointing with his flashlight.

The beam played over a jagged break in the tunnel wall. It looked as though someone had smashed through the stone a long time ago.

Von der Stadt's flash joined Ciffonetto's to light the area better. There was a passage descending from the break. Ciffonetto moved toward it with a start.

"What the hell do you say to this, Von der Stadt?" he asked, grinning. He stuck head and flashlight into the crude tunnel, but re-emerged quickly.

"Not much there," he said. "The passage is caved in after a few feet. But still, it confirms what I've been saying."

Von der Stadt looked vaguely uneasy. His free hand drifted to the holstered pistol at his side. "I don't know," he said.

"No, you don't," said Ciffonetto, triumphantly. "Neither does Nagel. Men have lived down here. They may still live here. We've got to organize a more efficient search of the whole underground system."

He paused, his mind flickering back to Von der Stadt's argument of a few seconds earlier. "As for your bugs and mushrooms, men can learn to live on a lot of things. Men adapt. If men survived the war—and this says they did—then they survived the aftermath, I'll wager."

"Maybe," Von der Stadt said. "I can't see what you are so hot on discovering survivors for anyway, though. I mean, the expedition is important and all that. We've got to re-establish spaceflight, and this is a good test for our new hardware. And I guess you scientists can pick up some good stuff for the museums. But humans? What did Earth ever get us besides the Great Famine?"

Ciffonetto smiled tolerantly. "It's because of the Great Famine that we want to find humans," he said. He paused. "We've got enough to entice even Nagel now. Let's head back."

He started walking back in the direction they had come, and resumed talking. "The Great Famine was an unavoidable result of the war on Earth," he said. "When supplies stopped coming, there was absolutely no way to keep all the people in the lunar colony alive. Ninety percent starved.

"Luna could be made self-sufficient, but only with a very small population. That's what happened. The population adjusted itself. But we recycled our air and our water, grew foods in hydroponic tanks. We struggled, but we survived. And began to rebuild.

"But we lost a lot. Too many people died. Our genetic pool was terribly small, and not too diverse. The colony had never had a lot of racial diversity to begin with.

"That hasn't helped. Population actually declined for a long time after we had the physical resources to support more people. The idea of in-breeding didn't go over. Now population's going up again, but slowly. We're stagnant, Von der Stadt. It's taken us nearly five centuries to get space travel going again, for example. And we still haven't duplicated many of the things they had back on Earth before the disaster."

Von der Stadt frowned. "Stagnant's a strong word," he said. "I think we've done pretty good."

Ciffonetto dismissed the comment with a wave of his flashlight. "Pretty good." he said. "Not good enough. We're not going anywhere. There's so damn few changes, so little in the way of new ideas. We need fresh viewpoints, fresh genetic stock. We need the stimulation of contact with a foreign culture.

"Survivors would give us that. After all Earth's been through, they'd have to have changed in some ways. And they'd be proof that human life can still flourish on Earth. That's crucial if we're going to establish a colony here."

The last point was tacked on almost as an afterthought, but caught Von der Stadt's approval. He nodded gravely.

They had reached the station again. Ciffonetto headed straight for the platform. "C'mon," he said, "let's get back to base. I can't wait to see Nagel's face drop when I tell him what we've found."

They were men.

Greel was almost sure of it. The texture of their minds was curious, but manlike. Greel was a strong mind-mingler. He knew the coarse, dim feel of an animal's mind, the obscene shadows that were the thoughts of the worm-things. And he knew the minds of men.

They were men.

Yet there was a strangeness. Mind-mingling was true communication only with a mind-brother. But always it was a sharing with other men. A dark and murky sharing, full of clouds and flavors and smells and emotions. But a sharing.

Here there was no sharing. Here it was like mind-mingling with a lower animal. Touch, feel, stroke, savor—all that a strong mind-mingler could do with an animal. But never would he feel a response. Men and mind-brothers responded; animals did not.

These men did not respond. These strange fire-men had minds that were silent and crippled.

In the darkness of the tunnel, Greel straightened from his crouch. The fire had faded suddenly from the wall. The men were going away, down the tunnel away from him. The fire went with them.

He edged forward slowly, H'ssig at his side, spear in hand. Distance made mind-mingling difficult. He must keep them in range. He must find out more. He was a scout. He had a duty.

His mind crept out again, to taste the flavor of the other minds. He had to be sure.

Their thoughts moved around him, swirling chaos shot through with streaks of brightness and emotions and dancing, half-seen concepts.

Greel understood little. But here he recognized something. And there something else came to him.

He lingered and tasted fully of their minds, and learned. But still it was like mind-mingling with an animal. He could not make himself felt. He could not get an answer.

Still they moved away, and their thoughts dimmed, and the mind-mingling became harder. Greel advanced. He hesitated when he got to the place where the tunnel curved. But he knew he must go on. He was a scout.

He lowered himself to the floor, squinted, and moved around the curve on hands and knees.

Beyond the curve, he started and gasped. He was in a great hall, an immense cavern with a vaulting roof and giant pillars that held up the sky. And the hall was bright with light, a strange, fiery light that danced over everything.

It was a place of legend. A hall of the Old Ones. It had to be. Never had Greel seen a chamber so vast. And he of all the People had wandered farthest and climbed highest.

The men were not in sight, but their fire danced around the mouth of the tunnel at the other end of the hall. It was intense, but not unbearable. The men had gone around another curve. Greel realized that he looked only at the dim reflection of their fire. So long as he did not see it direct, he was safe.

He moved out into the hall, the scout in him crying to climb the stone wall and explore the upper chamber from which the mighty pillars reared. But no. The fire-men were more important. The hall he could return to.

H'ssig rubbed up against his leg. He reached down and stroked the rat's soft fur reassuringly. His mind-brother could sense the turmoil of his thoughts.

Men, yes, he was sure of that. And more he knew. Their thoughts were not those of the People, but they were man-thoughts, and some he could understand. One of them burned, burned to find other men. They seek the People, Greel thought.

That he knew. He was a scout and a mind-mingler. He did not make mistakes. But what he must do he did not know.

They sought the People. That might be good. When first that concept had touched him, Greel had quivered with joy. These fire-men were like the Old Ones of legend. If they sought the People, he would lead them. There would be rewards, and glory, and the taletellers would sing his name for generations.

More, it was his duty. Things went not well with the People in recent generations. The time of good had ended with the coming of the worm-things, who had driven the People from tunnel after tunnel. Even now, below his feet, the fight went on still in the Bad. Levels and the tunnels of the People.

And Greel knew the People were losing.

It was slow. But certain. The worm-things were new to the People. More than animal, but less, less than men. They needed not the tunnels. They stalked through the earth itself, and nowhere were men safe.

The People fought back. Mind-minglers could sense the worm-things, and spears could slay them, and the great hunting rats could rip them to shreds; But always the worm-things fled back into the earth itself. And there were many worm-things, and few People.

But these new men, these fire-men, they could change the war. Legends said the Old Ones had fought with fire and stranger weapons, and these men lived in fire. They could aid the People. They could give mighty weapons to drive the worm-things back into the darkness from which they came.

But.

But these men were not quite men. Their minds were crippled, and much, much of their thought was alien to Greel. Only glimpses of it could he catch. He could not know them as he could know another of the People when they mingled minds.

He could lead them to the People. He knew the way. Back and down, a turn here, a twist there. Through the Middle Tunnels and the Bad Levels.

But what if he led them, and they were enemy to the People? What if they turned on the People with their fire? He feared for what they might do.

Without him, they would never find the People. Greel was certain of that. Only he, in long generations, had come this far. And only with stealth and mind-mingling and H'ssig alongside him. They would never find the ways he had come, the twisting tunnels that led deep, deep into the earth.

So the People were safe if he did not act. But then the worm-things would win, eventually. It might take many generations. But the People could not hold out. His decision. No mind-mingler could reach a small part of the distance that separated him from the tunnels of the People. He alone must decide.

And he must decide soon. For he realized, with a shock, that the firemen were coming back. Their odd thoughts grew stronger, and the light in the hall grew more and more intense.

He hesitated, then moved slowly backward toward the tunnel from which he had come.

"Wait a minute," Von der Stadt said when Ciffonetto was a quarter of the way up the wall. "Let's try the other directions."

Ciffonetto craned his head around awkwardly to look at his companion, gave it up as a bad job, and dropped back to the tunnel floor. He looked disgruntled. "We should get back," he said. "We've got enough."

Von der Stadt shrugged. "C'mon. You're the one who wanted to explore down here. So we might as well do a thorough job of it. Maybe we're only a few feet away from another one of your big finds."

"All right," said Ciffonetto, pulling his flashlight from his belt where he had stashed it for his intended assault on the platform. "I suppose you have a point. It would be tragic if we got Nagel down here and he tripped over something we had missed."

Von der Stadt nodded assent. Their flashlight beams melted together, and they strode quickly toward the deeper darkness of the tunnel mouth.

They were coming. Fear and indecision tumbled in Greel's thoughts. He hugged the tunnel wall. Back he moved, fast and silent. He must keep away from their fire until he could decide what he must do.

But after the first turn, the tunnel ran long and straight. Greel was fast. But not fast enough. And his eyes were incautiously wide when the fire appeared suddenly in full fury.

His eyes burned. He squealed in sudden pain, and threw himself to the ground. The fire refused to go away, It danced before him even with his eyes closed, shifting colors horribly.

Greel fought for control. Still there was distance between them. Still he was armed. He reached out to H'ssig, nearby in the tunnel. The eyeless rat again would be his eyes.

Eyes still shut, Greel began to crawl back, away from the fire. H'ssig remained.

"What the hell was that?"

Von der Stadt's whispered question hung in the air for an instant. He was frozen where he had rounded the curve. Ciffonetto, by his side, had also stopped dead at the sound.

The scientist looked puzzled "I don't know," he said. "It was—odd. Sounded like some sort of animal in pain. A scream, sort of. But as if the screamer were trying to remain silent, almost."

His flashlight darted this way and that, slicing ribbons of light from the velvet darkness, but revealing little. Von der Stadt's beam pointed straight ahead, unmoving.

"I don't like it," Von der Stadt stated doubtfully. "Maybe there *is* something down here. But that doesn't mean it's friendly." He shifted his flash to his left hand, and drew his pistol. "We'll see," he said.

Ciffonetto frowned, but said nothing. They started forward again.

They were big, and they moved fast. Greel realized with a sick despair that they would catch him. His choice had been made for him.

But perhaps it was right. They were men. Men like the Old Ones. They would help the People against the worm-things. A new age would dawn. The time of fear would pass. The horror would fade. The old glories of which the taletellers sing would return, and once again the People would build great halls and mighty tunnels.

Yes. They had decided for him, but the decision was right. It was the only decision. Man must meet man, and together they would face the worm-things.

He kept his eyes closed. But he stood.

And spoke.

Again they froze in mid-step. This time the sound was no muffled scream. It was soft, almost hissing, but it was too clear to be misunderstood.

Both flash beams swung wildly now, for seconds. Then one froze. The other hesitated, then joined it.

Together they formed a pool of light against a distant part of the tunnel wall. And in the pool stood—what?

"My God," said Von der Stadt. "Cliff, tell me what it is quick, before I shoot it."

"Don't," Ciffonetto replied. "It isn't moving."

"But—what?"

"I don't know." The scientist's voice had a strange, uncertain quiver in it.

The creature in the pool of light was small, barely over four feet. Small and sickening. There was something vaguely manlike about it, but the proportions of the limbs were all wrong, and the hands and feet were grotesquely malformed. And the skin, the skin was a sickly, maggoty white.

But the face was the worst. Large, all out of proportion to the body, yet the mouth and nose could hardly be seen. The head was all eyes. Two great, immense, grotesque eyes, now safely hidden by lids of dead white skin.

Von der Stadt was rock steady, but Ciffonetto shook a bit as he looked at it. Yet he spoke first.

"Look," he said, his voice soft. "In its hand. I think—I think that's a tool." Silence. Long, strained silence. Then Ciffonetto spoke again. His voice was hoarse.

"I think that's a man."

Greel burned.

The fire had caught him. Even shut tight, his eyes ached, and he knew the horror that lurked outside if he opened them. And the fire had caught him. His skin itched strangely, and hurt. Worse and worse it hurt.

Yet he did not stir. He was a scout. He had a duty. He endured, while his mind mingled with those of the others.

And there, in their minds, he saw fear, but checked fear. In a distorted, blurry way he saw himself through their eyes, He tasted the awe and the revulsion that warred in one. And the unmixed revulsion that churned inside the other.

He angered, but he checked his anger. He must reach them. He must take them to the People. They were blind and crippled and could not help their feelings. But if they understood, they would aid. Yes.

He did not move. He waited. His skin burned, but he waited.

"That," said Von der Stadt. "That thing is a man?"

Ciffonetto nodded. "It must be. It carries tools. It spoke." He hesitated. "But—God, I never envisioned anything like this. The tunnels, Von der Stadt. The dark. For long centuries only the dark. I never thought—so much evolution in so little time."

"A man?" Still Von der Stadt doubted. "You're crazy. No man could become something like that."

Ciffonetto scarcely heard him. "I should have realized," he mumbled. "Should have guessed. The radiation, of course. It would speed up mutation. Shorter life spans, probably. You were right, Von der Stadt. Men can't live on bugs and mushrooms. Not men like us. So they adapted. Adapted to the darkness, and the tunnels. It—"

Suddenly he started. "Those eyes," he said. He clicked off his flashlight, and the walls seemed to move closer. "He must be sensitive. We're hurting him. Divert your flash, Von der Stadt."

Von der Stadt gave him a doubtful sidelong glance. "It's dark enough down here already," he said. But he obeyed. His beam swung away.

"History," Ciffonetto said. "A moment that will live in—"

He never finished. Von der Stadt was tense, trigger-edged. As his beam swung away from the figure down the tunnel, he caught another flicker of movement in the darkness. He swung back and forth, found the thing again, pinned it against the tracks with a beam of light.

Almost he had shot before. But he had hesitated, because the manlike figure had been still and unfamiliar.

This new thing was not still. It squealed and scurried. Nor was it unfamiliar. This time Von der Stadt did not hesitate.

There was a roar, a flash. Then a second.

"Got it," said Von der Stadt. "A damn rat."

And Greel screamed.

After the long burning, there had come an instant of relief. But only an instant. Then, suddenly, pain flooded him. Wave after wave after wave. Rolled over him, blotting out the thoughts of the fire-men, blotting out their fear, blotting out his anger.

H'ssig died. His mind-brother died.

The fire-men had killed his mind-brother.

He shrieked in painrage. He darted forward, swung up his spear.

He opened his eyes. There was a flash of vision, then more pain and blindness. But the flash was enough. He struck. And struck again. Wildly, madly, blow after blow, thrust after thrust.

Then, again, the universe turned red with pain, and then again sounded that awful roar that had come when H'ssig died. Something threw him to the tunnel floor, and his eyes opened again, and fire, fire was everywhere.

But only for a while. Only for a while. Then, shortly, it was darkness again for Greel of the People.

The gun still smoked. The hand was still steady. But Von der Stadt's mouth hung open as he looked, unbelieving, from the thing he had blasted across the tunnel, to the blood dripping from his uniform, then back again.

Then the gun dropped, and he clutched at his stomach, clutched at the wounds. His hand came away wet with blood. He stared at it. Then stared at Ciffonetto.

"The rat," he said. There was pain in his voice. "I only shot a rat. It was going for him. Why, Cliff? I—?"

And he fell. Heavily. His flashlight shattered and went dark.

There was a long fumbling in the blackness. Then, at last, Ciffonetto's light winked on, and the ashen scientist knelt beside his companion.

"Von," he said, tugging at the uniform. "Are you all right?" He ripped away the fabric to expose the torn flesh.

Von der Stadt was mumbling. "I didn't even see him coming. I took my light away, like you said, Cliff. Why? I wasn't going to shoot him. Not if he was a man. I only shot a rat. Only a rat. It was going for him, too."

Ciffonetto, who had stood paralyzed through everything, nodded. "It wasn't your fault, Von. But you must have scared him. You need treating, now, though. He hurt you bad. Can you make it back to camp?"

He didn't wait for an answer. He slipped his arm under Von der Stadt's, lifted him to his feet, and began to walk him down the tunnel, praying they could make it back to the platform.

"I only shot a rat," Von der Stadt kept saying, over and over, in a dazed voice.

"Don't worry," said Ciffonetto. "It won't matter. We'll find others. We'll search the whole subway system if we have to. We'll find them."

"Only a rat. Only a rat."

They reached the platform. Ciffonetto lowered Von der Stadt back to the ground. "I can't make the climb carrying you, Von," he said. "I'll have to leave you here. Go for help." He straightened, hung the flash from his belt.

"Only a rat," Von der Stadt said again.

"Don't worry," said Ciffonetto. "Even if we don't find them, nothing will be lost. They were clearly sub-human. Men once, maybe. But no more. Degenerated. There was nothing they could have taught us, anyway."

But Von der Stadt was past listening, past hearing. He just sat against the wall, clutching his stomach and feeling the blood ooze from between his fingers, mumbling the same words over and over.

Ciffonetto turned to the wall. A few short feet to the platform, then the old, rusty escalator, and the basement ruins, and daylight. He had to hurry. Von der Stadt wouldn't last long.

He grabbed the rock, pulled himself up, hung on desperately as his other hand scrambled and found a hold. He pulled up again.

He was almost there, almost at the platform level, when his weak lunar muscles gave out on him. There was a sudden spasm, his hand slipped loose, his other hand couldn't take the weight.

He fell. On the flashlight.

The darkness was like nothing he had ever seen. Too thick, too complete. He fought to keep from screaming.

When he tried to rise again, he did scream. More than the flashlight had broken in the fall.

His scream echoed and re-echoed through the long, black tunnel he could not see. It was a long time dying. When it finally faded, he screamed again. And again.

Finally, hoarse, he stopped. "Von," he said. "Von, can you hear me?" There was no answer. He tried again. Talk, he must talk to hold his sanity. The darkness was all around him, and he could almost hear soft movements a few feet away.

Von der Stadt giggled, sounding infinitely far away.

"It was only a rat," he said. "Only a rat."

Silence. Then, softly, Ciffonetto. "Yes, Von, yes."

"It was only a rat."

"It was only a rat."

"It was only a rat."

"If I Forget Thee, Oh Earth . . ."

Arthur C. Clarke

When Marvin was ten years old, his father took him through the long, echoing corridors that led up through Administration and Power, until at last they came to the uppermost levels of all and were among the swiftly growing vegetation of the Farmlands. Marvin liked it here; it was fun watching the great, slender plants creeping with almost visible eagerness towards the sunlight as it filtered down through the plastic domes to meet them. The smell of life was everywhere, awakening inexpressible longings in his heart. No longer was he breathing the dry, cool air of the residential levels, purged of all smells but the faint tang of ozone. He wished he could stay here for a little while, but Father would not let him. They went onward until they had reached the entrance to the observatory, which he had never visited. But they did not stop, and Marvin knew with a sense of rising excitement that there could be only one goal left. For the first time in his life, he was going outside.

There were a dozen of the surface vehicles, with their wide balloon tires and pressurized cabins, in the great servicing chamber. His father must have been expected, for they were led at once to the little scout car waiting by the huge circular door of the airlock. Tense with expectancy, Marvin settled himself down in the cramped cabin while his father started the motor and checked the controls. The inner door of the lock slid open and then closed behind them—he heard the roar of the great air-pumps fade slowly away as the pressure dropped to zero. Then the VACUUM sign flashed on and, the outer door parted, before Marvin lay the land which that he had never yet entered.

He had seen it in photographs, of course. He had watched it imaged on television screens a hundred times. But now it was lying all around him, burning beneath the fierce sun that crawled so slowly across the jet-black sky. He stared into the west, away from the blinding splendor of the sun—and there were the stars, as he had been told but had never quite believed. He gazed at them for a long time, marveling that anything could be so bright and yet so tiny. They were intense unscintillating points, and suddenly he remembered a rhyme he had once read in one of his father's books:

Twinkle, twinkle, little star,
How I wonder what you are.

Well, he knew what the stars were. Whoever asked that question must have been very stupid. And what did they mean by "twinkle"? You could see at a glance that all the stars shone with the same steady, unwavering light. He abandoned the puzzle and turned his attention to the landscape around him.

They were racing across a level plain at almost a hundred miles an hour, the great balloon tires sending up little spurts of dust behind them. There was no sign of the Colony; in the few minutes while he had been gazing at the stars, its domes and radio towers had fallen below the horizon. Yet there were other indications of man's presence, for about a mile ahead Marvin could see the curiously shaped structures clustering around the head of a mine. Now and then a puff of vapor would emerge from a squat smoke-stack and would instantly disperse.

They were past the mine in a moment. Father was driving with a reckless and exhilarating skill as if—it was a strange thought to come into a child's mind—he were trying to escape from something. In a few minutes they had reached the edge of the plateau on which the Colony had been built. The ground fell sharply away beneath them in a dizzying slope whose lower stretches were lost in the shadow. Ahead, as far as the eye could reach, was a jumbled wasteland of craters, mountain ranges, and ravines. The crests of the mountains, catching the low sun, burned like islands of fire in a sea of darkness—and above them the stars still shone as steadfastly as ever.

There could be no way forward—yet there was. Marvin clenched his fists as the car edged over the slope and started the long descent. Then he saw the barely visible track leading down the mountainside, and relaxed a little. Other men, it seemed, had gone this way before.

Night fell with a shocking abruptness as they crossed the shadow line and the sun dropped below the crest of the plateau. The twin searchlights sprang into life, casting blue-white bands on the rocks ahead, so that there was scarcely need to check their speed. For hours they drove through valleys and past the feet of mountains whose peaks seemed to comb the stars, and sometimes they emerged for a moment into the sunlight as they climbed over higher ground.

And now on the right was a wrinkled, dusty plain, and on the left, its ramparts and terraces rising mile after mile into the sky, was a wall of mountains that marched into the distance until its peaks sank from sight below the rim of the world. There was no sign that men had ever explored this land, but once they passed the skeleton of a crashed rocket, and beside it a stone cairn surmounted by a metal cross.

It seemed to Marvin that the mountains stretched on forever, but at last, many hours later, the range ended in a towering, precipitous headland that rose steeply from a cluster of little hills. They drove down into a shallow valley that curved in a great arc toward the far side of the mountains. And as they did so, Marvin slowly realized that something very strange was happening in the land ahead.

The sun was now low behind the hills on the right: the valley before them should be in total darkness. Yet it was awash with a cold white radiance that came spilling over the crags beneath which they were driving. Then, suddenly, they were out in the open plain, and the source of the light lay before them in all its glory.

It was very quiet in the little cabin now that the motors had stopped. The only sound was the faint whisper of the oxygen feed and an occasional metallic crepitation as the outer walls of the vehicle radiated away their heat. For no warmth at all came from the great silver crescent that floated low above the far horizon and flooded all this land with pearly light. It was so brilliant that minutes passed before Marvin could accept its challenge and look steadfastly into its glare, but at last he could discern the outlines of continents, the hazy border of the atmosphere, and the white islands of cloud. And even at this distance, he could see the glitter of sunlight on the polar ice.

It was beautiful, and it called to his heart across the abyss of space. There in that shining crescent were all the wonders that he had never known—the hues of sunset skies, the moaning of the sea on pebbled shores, the patter of falling rain, the unhurried benison of snow. These and a thousand others should have been his rightful heritage, but he knew them only from the books and ancient records, and the thought filled him with the anguish of exile.

Why could they not return? It seemed so peaceful beneath those lines of marching cloud. Then Marvin, his eyes no longer blinded by the glare, saw that the portion of the disc that should have been in darkness was gleaming faintly with an evil phosphorescence . . . and he remembered. He was looking upon the funeral pyre of a world—upon the radioactive aftermath of Armageddon. Across a quarter of a million miles of space, the glow of dying atoms was still visible, a perennial reminder of the ruined past. It would be centuries yet before that deadly glow died from the rocks and life could return again to fill that silent, empty world.

And now Father began to speak, telling Marvin the story that until this moment had meant no more to him than the fairy-tales he had heard in childhood. There were many things he could not understand, it was impossible for him to picture the glowing, multi-colored pattern of life on the planet he had never seen. Nor could he comprehend the forces that had destroyed it in the end, leaving the Colony, preserved by its isolation, as the sole survivor. Yet he could share the agony of those final days, when the Colony had learned at last that never again would the supply ships come flaming down through the stars with gifts from home. One by one the radio stations had ceased to call: on the shadowed globe the lights of the cities had dimmed and died, and they were alone at last, as no men had ever been alone before, carrying in their hands the future of the race.

Then had followed the years of despair, and the long-drawn battle for survival in their fierce and hostile world. That battle had been won, though barely. This little oasis of life was safe against the worst that Nature could do. But unless there was a goal, a future toward which it could work, the Colony would lose the will to live and neither machines nor skill nor science could save it then.

So, at last, Marvin understood the purpose of this pilgrimage. He would never walk beside the rivers of that lost and legendary world, or listen to the thunder raging above its softly rounded hills. Yet one day—how far ahead?—his children's children would return to claim their heritage. The winds and the rains would scour the poisons from the burning lands and carry them to the sea, and in the depths of the sea they would waste their venom until they could harm no living things. Then the great ships that were still waiting here on the silent, dusty plains could lift once more into space, along the road that led to home.

That was the dream, and one day Marvin knew, with a sudden flash of insight, he would pass it on to his own son, here at this same spot with the mountains behind him and the silver light from the sky streaming into his face.

He did not look back as they began the homeward journey. He could not bear to see the cold glory of the crescent Earth fade from the rocks around him, as he went to rejoin his people in their long exile.

Afterword

John Helfers

The blue, white, and brown planet is quiet now.

It still continues in its orbit, whirling around the G2 star it has orbited for the past 4.6 billion years, the third of nine planets held in that massive, fiery, red-golden orb's inexorable grip. The energy thrown off by this star, that takes the form of light that is essential for all known life, still takes seven minutes to traverse the ninety-three million miles to the planet's surface, always revealing oceans and continents on one half of the world, and leaving the other half shrouded in darkness.

The third planet is still orbited by its own satellite, a round, white rock that is visible due to the star's reflected light off its desolate terrain. Its airless, cratered surface is littered with debris, including a sun-bleached piece of cloth on a stick upon which can still be seen rows of white stars against what might have once been a dark-colored field. Several vehicles also rest motionless there, and a cluster of cold, silvered domes near several holes dug into the surface give evidence that at some point some kind of creatures had walked on its surface, and perhaps delved under its crust for some long-forgotten reason.

Three-hundred eighty-four thousand kilometers away, beneath black space that has been wiped clean of all artificial satellites long ago, clouds still form in the blue planet's atmosphere, growing, swelling, scudding across the bright blue sky, sometimes releasing violent storms that rage across continents and oceans, sometimes fading back into the rain cycle without shedding a single drop of moisture, just as they have for millions of years, and will do for millions more.

Once an innumerable number of species of animals roamed over this planet, from lowly yet almost indestructible insects—cockroaches, blowflies, and their ilk—to higher forms of life, including reptiles, mammals of both the air and the land, and sea creatures tiny and large. Now all of the animal species on the entire planet number in the thousands; mostly insect life, the hardy cockroach, seasonal cicadas, and flies. There always seems to be flies. The oceans are nearly dead, containing only single-celled animal life, carrying on as it has for millennia. It is rare to see warm-blooded mammals anywhere on the northern half of the planet, anything left with fur or feathers is born, lives, and dies near the equator. Looking north, it is obvious why.

As the blue planet rotates, part of it always turning into the bright sunlight, land masses come into view, many of them unchanged for thousands of years. Except one. This irregular mass, pocketed with hundreds of inlets, bays, rivers, and lakes, with a small peninsula jutting from the southeastern corner into an ocean, and a large swath of land bulging from the northwestern corner that seems to reach out with a scattering of broken islands to almost touch the enormous continent nearby, at first seems just like the rest of the land masses around it. But closer examination reveals a different story.

What used to be a broad, high, unbroken chain of mountains that stretched from the ice caps of the frozen sea at the top of the world to the banana-shaped landmass bridging the ocean between this continent and the next one is now shattered into pieces. What had once been hundreds of lofty, snow-capped mountain peaks in the middle of this once-mighty range is now a huge crater, more than one hundred kilometers wide. The crater would be visible from this planet's moon, if there were anyone there to see it.

As the star's light shines more fully on this vast terrain, it reveals that this land is not like the others. Every one of the other continents has pockets of green, small ones, no doubt, but pockets of vegetation. This land, however, has not a speck of green to be seen. Instead, it is swathed in a thick layer of gray-brown ash stretching from the western coast to a cluster of five large, still, dead lakes that lie directly below a huge bay in the northeast quadrant of the continent. It reaches from the frozen tundra in the north to the end of that mountain chain in the south, and covers everything it touches. The huge canyon to the southwest of the mountain range. The dense, once-verdant forests that ranged the entire length of the west coast, now only dead branches caked in a thick, hardened coating of ash. The remains of a long suspension bridge, its girders and foundation now twisted and buckled by a long-ago earthquake, and turned a dull gray as well. And the buildings.

The hundreds of thousands of houses, skyscrapers, farms, churches, businesses, and every other building dotting the planet are all still and quiet. Ornate spires are choked in dark dust. Mirrored windows, those that were still intact, obscured by a coating of gritty soot, hardened by years of rainfall that had turned them into a solid coating. Nothing living moves throughout the breadth of the land.

The planet turns, as it always has, and reveals more of what has been left behind by those that once lived here. Tall clock towers are now stilled, pointed hour and minute hands stilled centuries ago. Here and there natural wildfires have destroyed what was once dozens of communities, incinerating acre after acre of cities, towns, and forests. Several pyramid-shaped structures near a large sea are slowly being both eroded away by the constant desert wind and buried by the ever-drifting sands. A large lump that might once have been a strange, scuplted amalgam of man and crouching animal is now little more than an eroded hill of featureless stone.

On other continents, nature is reclaiming the land that had once belonged to it long ago. Thick jungle advances over tall buildings, disintegrating roads and foundations, and slowly bringing down what were once monuments to the race that once thrived here. Rivers swollen by melting runoff from the mountains overflow their banks and flood tens of thousands of miles of landscape, altering it each time. In other areas, the desert sands inch forward, covering earth and grass and water and buildings. The unstoppable ocean occasionally builds and releases its fury on the coastlines of the world, destroying, reshaping, renewing. Seasons pass, thick, heavy snow drifting down to cover the once-magnificent cities that were the pride of the race that had built them so long ago.

Once, the race that had erected these buildings had teemed on this planet, spreading over the land and water in multitudes. Ever curious, they traversed almost every inch of the world they had inherited, scaling the highest mountain, descending to the bottom of the ocean, and even splitting the very atoms that comprised existence itself. They conquered disease, joined the world together in technology, and almost destroyed themselves more than once. They split the sky with their vehicles, always seeking to go farther, faster, and eventually slipped the surly bonds of Earth to explore the near reaches of space. They even took enough of an interest in the galaxies beyond their own to send out a signal, hoping for a response from another life form somewhere in the universe. But, as with all cycles, their time had to come to an end eventually, leaving only the scattered monuments to their legacy behind.

Now, the remains of the vast transportation system lies in abandoned rows near what were once centers of civilization. The once-vibrant communications system that used light itself to carry information around the globe in the blink of an eye is long gone. The artificial space stations that had orbited this planet have long since streaked across the sky in a fiery blaze as they re-entered the atmosphere. The history of this race, preserved first in clay and stone, then later on paper, in steel and silicon and electrons, is now dormant, the buildings erected to house their legacy stolen by time.

Perhaps someday, hundreds or thousands of years in the future, another race will evolve on this planet that will discover the remains of this civilization, and will wonder at those who came before them. Perhaps it will be visitors from a distant star, who have received a signal broadcast into space centuries before, or who have recovered an ancient probe launched into space before any of them were alive, and who have journeyed across space to locate the source of this strange technology. Perhaps they will unlock the mysteries of this race in the sealed technology hidden inside a mountain, or uncover records that reveal the history of this race, and what eventually happened to it.

Or perhaps, in about nine billion years, the star that this blue, white, and brown planet orbits around will swell into an immense red ball of flaring helium, incinerating the two smaller planets closer to it, and yes, this planet as well. After a few million more years, having exhausted its fuel, it will collapse into a dense core of tightly packed atoms, forming a white ball about the size of the third planet it had destroyed those many years ago.

And in the end, except for those scattered bits of technology that may have survived their endless journey, and centuries of radio and television signals that have been broadcast throughout the universe, it will be as if that race that had briefly held dominion over that third planet all those billions of years ago had never existed at all.

WITNESSES TO THE END OF THE WORLD

When We Went to See the End of the World

Robert Silverberg

NICK AND JANE were glad that they had gone to see the end of the world, because it gave them something special to talk about at Mike and Ruby's party. One always likes to come to a party armed with a little conversation. Mike and Ruby give marvelous parties. Their home is superb, one of the finest in the neighborhood. It is truly a home for all seasons, all moods. Their very special corner of the world. With more space indoors and out . . . more wide-open freedom. The living room with its exposed ceiling beams is a natural focal point for entertaining. Custom-finished, with a conversation pit and fireplace. There's also a family room with beamed ceiling and wood paneling—plus a study. And a magnificent master suite with twelve-foot dressing room and private bath. Solidly impressive exterior design. Sheltered courtyard. Beautifully wooded Vs-acre grounds. Their parties are highlights of any month. Nick and Jane waited until they thought enough people had arrived. Then Jane nudged Nick, and Nick said gaily, "You know what we did last week? Hey, we went to see the end of the world!"

"The end of the world?" Henry asked.

"You went to see it?" said Henry's wife Cynthia.

"How did you manage that?" Paula wanted to know.

"It's been available since March," Stan told her. "I think a division of American Express runs it."

Nick was put out to discover that Stan already knew. Quickly, before Stan could say anything more, Nick said, "Yes, it's just started. Our travel agent found out for us. What they do is they put you in this machine, it looks like a tiny teeny submarine, you know, with dials and levers up front behind a plastic wall to keep you from touching anything, and they send you into the future. You can charge it with any of the regular credit cards."

"It must be very expensive," Marcia said.

"They're bringing the cost down rapidly," Jane said. "Last year only millionaires could afford it. Really, haven't you heard about it before?" "What did you see?" Henry asked.

"For a while, just grayness outside the porthole," said Nick. "And a kind of flickering effect." Everybody was looking at him. He enjoyed the attention. Jane wore a rapt, loving expression. "Then the haze cleared and a voice said over a loudspeaker that we had now reached the very end of time, when life had become impossible on Earth. Of course we were sealed into the submarine thing. Only looking out. On this beach, this empty beach. The water a funny gray color with a pink sheen. And then the sun came up. It was red like it sometimes is at sunrise, only it stayed red as it got to the middle of the sky, and it looked lumpy and sagging at the edges. Like a few of *us*, hah hah. Lumpy and sagging at the edges. A cold wind blowing across the beach."

"If you were sealed in the submarine, how did you know there was a cold wind?" Cynthia asked.

Jane glared at her. Nick said, "We could see the sand blowing around. And it looked cold. The gray ocean. Like in winter."

"Tell them about the crab," said Jane.

"Yes, and the crab. The last life-form on Earth. It wasn't really a crab, of course, it was something about two feet wide and a foot high, with thick shiny green armor and maybe a dozen legs and some curving horns coming up, and it moved slowly from right to left in front of us. It took all day to cross the beach. And toward nightfall it died. Its horns went limp and it stopped moving. The tide came in and carried it away. The sun went down. There wasn't any moon. The stars didn't seem to be in the right places. The loudspeaker told us we had just seen the death of Earth's last living thing."

"How eerie!" cried Paula.

"Were you gone very long?" Ruby asked.

"Three hours," Jane said. "You can spend weeks or days at the end of the world, if you want to pay extra, but they always bring you back to a point three hours after you went. To hold down the babysitter expenses."

Mike offered Nick some pot. "That's really something," he said. "To have gone to the end of the world. Hey, Ruby, maybe we'll talk to the travel agent about it."

Nick took a deep drag and passed the joint to Jane. He felt pleased with himself about the way he had told the story. They had all been very impressed. That swollen red sun, that scuttling crab. The trip had cost more than a month in Japan, but it had been a good investment. He and Jane were the first in the neighborhood who had gone. That was important. Paula was staring at him in awe. Nick knew that she regarded him in a completely different light now. Possibly she would meet him at a motel on Tuesday at lunchtime. Last month she had turned him down but now he had an extra attractiveness for her. Nick winked at her. Cynthia was holding hands with Stan. Henry and Mike both were crouched at Jane's feet. Mike and Ruby's twelve-year-old son came into the room and stood at the edge of the conversation pit. He said, "There was just a bulletin on the news. Mutated amoebas escaped from a government research station and got into Lake Michigan. They're carrying a tissue-dissolving virus and everybody in seven states is supposed to boil their water until further notice."

Mike scowled at the boy and said, "It's after your bedtime, Timmy." The boy went out. The doorbell rang. Ruby answered it and returned with Eddie and Fran.

Paula said, "Nick and Jane went to see to end of the world. They've just been telling us all about it."

"Gee," said Eddie, "we did that too, on Wednesday night."

Nick was crestfallen. Jane bit her lip and asked Cynthia quietly why Fran always wore such flashy dresses. Ruby said, "You saw the whole works, eh? The crab and everything?"

"The crab?" Eddie said. "What crab? We didn't see the crab."

"It must have died the time before," Paula said. "When Nick and Jane were there."

Mike said, "A fresh shipment of Cuernavaca Lightning is in. Here, have a toke."

"How long ago did you do it?" Eddie said to Nick.

"Sunday afternoon. I guess we were about the first."

"Great trip, isn't it?" Eddie said. "A little somber, though. When the last hill crumbles into the sea."

"That's not what we saw," said Jane. "And you didn't see the crab? Maybe we were on different trips."

Mike said, "What was it like for you, Eddie?"

Eddie put his arms around Cynthia from behind. He said. "They put us into this little capsule, with a porthole, you know, and a lot of instruments and—"

"We heard that part," said Paula. "What did you see?"

"The end of the world," Eddie said. "When water covers everything. The sun and the moon were in the sky at the same time—"

"We didn't see the moon at all," Jane remarked. "It just wasn't there."

"It was on one side and the sun was on the other," Eddie went on. "The moon was closer than it should have been. And a funny color, almost like bronze. And the ocean creeping up. We went halfway around the world and all we saw was ocean. Except in one place, there was this chunk of land sticking up, this hill, and the guide told us it was the top of Mount Everest." He waved to Fran. "That was groovy, huh, floating in our tin boat next to the top of Mount Everest. Maybe ten feet of it sticking up. And the water rising all the time. Up, up, up. Up and over the top. Glub. No land left. I have to admit it was a little disappointing, except of course the idea of the thing. That human ingenuity can design a machine that can send people billions of years forward in time and bring them back, wow! But there was just this ocean."

"How strange," said Jane. "We saw an ocean too, but there was a beach, a kind of nasty beach, and the crab-thing walking along it, and the sun—it was all red, was the sun red when you saw it?"

"A kind of pale green," Fred said.

"Are you people talking about the end of the world?" Tom asked. He and Harriet were standing by the door taking off their coats. Mike's son must have let them in. Tom gave his coat to Ruby and said, "Man, what a spectacle!"

"So you did it too?" Jane asked, a little hollowly.

"Two weeks ago," said Tom. "The travel agent called and said, 'Guess what we're offering now, the end of the goddamned world!' With all the extras it didn't really cost so much. So we went right down there to the office, Saturday, I think—was it a Friday?—the day of the big riot, anyway, when they burned St. Louis—"

"That was a Saturday," Cynthia said. "I remember I was coming back from the shopping center when the radio said they were using nuclears—"

"Saturday, yes," Tom said. "And we told them we were ready to go, and off they sent us."

"Did you see a beach with crabs," Stan demanded, "or was it a world full of water?"

"Neither one. It was like a big ice age. Glaciers covered everything. No oceans showing, no mountains. We flew clear around the world and it was all a huge snowball. They had floodlights on the vehicle because the sun had gone out."

"I was sure I could see the sun still hanging up there," Harriet put in. "Like a ball of cinders in the sky. But the guide said no, nobody could see it."

"How come everybody gets to visit a different kind of end of the world?" Henry asked. "You'd think there'd be only one kind of end of the world. I mean, it ends, and this is how it ends, and there can't be more than one way."

"Could it be a fake?" Stan asked. Everybody turned around and looked at him. Nick's face got very red. Fran looked so mean that Eddie let go of Cynthia and started to rub Fran's shoulders. Stan shrugged. "I'm not suggesting it is," he said defensively. "I was just wondering."

"Seemed pretty real to me," said Tom. "The sun burned out. A big ball of ice. The atmosphere, you know, frozen. The end of the goddamned world."

The telephone rang. Ruby went to answer it. Nick asked Paula about lunch on Tuesday. She said yes. "Let's meet at the motel," he said, and she grinned. Eddie was making out with Cynthia again. Henry looked very stoned and was having trouble staying awake. Phil and Isabel arrived. They heard Tom and Fran talking about their trips to the end of the world and Isabel said she and Phil had gone only the day before yesterday. "Goddamn," Tom said, "everybody's doing it! What was your trip like?"

Ruby came back into the room. "That was my sister calling from Fresno to say she's safe. Fresno wasn't hit by the earthquake at all."

"Earthquake?" Paula said.

"In California," Mike told her. "This afternoon. You didn't know? Wiped out most of Los Angeles and ran right up the coast practically to Monterey. hey think it was on account of the underground bomb test in the Mohave Desert."

"California's always having such awful disasters," Marcia said.

"Good thing those amoebas got loose back east," said Nick. "Imagine how complicated it would be if they had them in L.A. now too."

"They will," Tom said. "Two to one they reproduce by airborne spores," Jane said. "Like the typhoid germs last November,"

"That was typhus," Nick corrected.

"Anyway," Phil said, "I was telling Tom and Fran about what we saw at the end of the world. It was the sun going nova. They showed it very cleverly, too. I mean, you can't actually sit around and experience it, on account of the at and the hard radiation and all. But they give it to you in a peripheral way, very elegant in the McLuhanesque sense of the word. First they take you to a point about two hours before the blowup, right? It's I don't know how many jillion years from now, but a long way, anyhow, because the trees are all different. They've got blue scales and ropy branches, and the animals are like things with one leg that jump on pogo sticks—"

"Oh, I don't believe that," Cynthia drawled.

Phil ignored her gracefully. "And we didn't see any sign of human beings, not a house, not a telephone pole, nothing, so I suppose we must have been extinct a long time before. Anyway, they let us look at that for a while. Not getting out of our time machine, naturally, because they said the atmosphere was wrong. Gradually the sun started to puff up. We were nervous—weren't we, Iz?—I mean, suppose they miscalculated things? This whole trip is a very new concept and things might go wrong. The sun was getting bigger and bigger, and then this thing like an arm seemed to pop out of its left side, a fig fiery arm reaching out across space, getting closer and closer. We saw it through smoked glass, like you do an eclipse. They gave us about two minutes of the explosion, and we could feel it getting hot already. Then we jumped a couple of years forward in time. The sun was back to its regular shape, only it was smaller, sort of like a little white sun instead of a big yellow one. And on Earth everything was ashes."

"Ashes," Isabel said, with emphasis.

"It looked like Detroit after the union nuked Ford," Phil said. "Only much, much worse. Whole mountains were melted. The oceans were dried. Everything was ashes." He shuddered and took a joint from Mike. "Isabel was crying."

"The things with one leg," Isabel said. "I mean, they must have all been wiped out." She began to sob. Stan comforted her. "I wonder why it's a different way for everyone who goes," he said. "Freezing. Or the oceans. Or the sun blowing up. Or the thing Nick and Jane saw."

"I'm convinced that each of us had a genuine experience in the far future," said Nick. He felt he had to regain control of the group somehow. It had been so good when he was telling his story, before those others had come. "That is to say, the world suffers a variety of natural calamities, it doesn't just have one end of the world, and they keep mixing things up and sending people to different catastrophes. But never for a moment did I doubt that I was seeing an authentic event."

"We have to do it," Ruby said to Mike. "It's only three hours. What about calling them first thing Monday and making an appointment for Thursday night?"

"Monday's the president's funeral," Tom pointed out. "The travel agency will be closed."

"Have they caught the assassin yet?" Fran asked.

"They didn't mention it on the four o'clock news," said Stan. "I guess he'll get away like the last one."

"Beats me why anybody wants to be president," Phil said.

Mike put on some music. Nick danced with Paula. Eddie danced with Cynthia. Henry was asleep. Dave, Paula's husband, was on crutches because of his mugging, and he asked Isabel to sit and talk with him. Tom danced with Harriet even though he was married to her. She hadn't been out of the hospital more than a few months since the transplant and he treated her extremely tenderly. Mike danced with Fran. Phil danced with Jane. Stan danced with Marcia. Ruby cut in on Eddie and Cynthia. Afterward, Tom danced with Jane and Phil danced with Paula. Mike and Ruby's little girl woke up and came out to say hello. Mike sent her back to bed.

Far away there was the sound of an explosion. Nick danced with Paula again, but he didn't want her to get bored with him before Tuesday, so he excused himself and went to talk with Dave. Dave handled most of Nick's investments. Ruby said to Mike, "The day after the funeral, will you call the travel, agent?" Mike said he would, but Tom said somebody would probably shoot the new president too and there'd be another funeral. These funerals were demolishing the gross national product, Stan observed, on account of how everything had to close all the time. Nick saw Cynthia wake Henry up and ask him sharply if he would take her on the end-of-the-world trip. Henry looked embarrassed. His factory had been blown up at Christmas in a peace demonstration and everybody knew he was in bad shape financially. "You can charge it," Cynthia said, her fierce voice carrying above the chitchat. "And it's so beautiful, Henry. The ice. Or the sun exploding. I want to go."

"Lou and Janet were going to be here tonight too," Ruby said to Paula.

"But their younger boy came back from Texas with that new kind of cholera and they had to cancel."

Phil said, "I understand that one couple saw the moon come apart. It got too close to the Earth and split into chunks and the chunks fell like meteors. Smashing everything up, you know. One big piece nearly hit their time machine."

"I wouldn't have liked that at all," Marcia said.

"Our trip was very lovely," said Jane. "No violent things at all. Just the big red sun and the tide and that crab creeping along the beach. We were both deeply moved."

"It's amazing what science can accomplish nowadays," Fran said.

Mike and Ruby agreed they would try to arrange a trip to the end of the world as soon as the funeral was over. Cynthia drank too much and got sick. Phil, Tom, and Dave discussed the stock market. Harriet told Nick about her operation. Isabel flirted with Mike, tugging her neckline lower. At midnight someone turned on the news. They had some shots of the earthquake and a warning about boiling your water if you lived in the affected states. The president's widow was shown visiting the last president's widow to get some pointers for the funeral. Then there was an interview with an executive of the time-trip company. "Business is phenomenal," he said. "Time-tripping will be the nation's number one growth industry next year." The reporter asked him if his company would soon be offering something beside the end-of-the-world trip. "Later on, we hope to," the executive said. "We plan to apply for congressional approval soon. But meanwhile the demand for our present offering is running very high. You can't imagine. Of course, you have to expect apocalyptic stuff to attain immense popularity in times like these." The reporter said, "What do you mean, times like these?" but as the time-trip man started to reply, he was interrupted by the commercial. Mike shut off the set. Nick discovered that he was extremely depressed. He decided that it was because so many of his friends had made the journey, and he had thought he and Jane were the only ones who had. He found himself standing next to Marcia and tried to describe the way the crab had moved, but Marcia only shrugged. No one was talking about time-trips now. The party had moved beyond that point. Nick and Jane left quite early and went right to sleep, without making love. The next morning the Sunday paper wasn't delivered because of the Bridge Authority strike, and the radio said that the mutant amoebas were proving harder to eradicate than originally anticipated. They were spreading into Lake Superior and everyone in the region would have to boil all drinking water. Nick and Jane discussed where they would go for their next vacation. "What about going to see the end of the world all over again?" Jane suggested, and Nick laughed quite a good deal.

FLIGHT TO FOREVER

Poul Anderson

THAT MORNING IT rained, a fine, summery mist blowing over the hills and hiding the gleam of the river and the village beyond. Martin Saunders stood in the doorway letting the cool, wet air blow in his face and wondered what the weather would be like a hundred years from now.

Eve Lang came up behind him and laid a hand on his arm. He smiled down at her, thinking how lovely she was with the raindrops caught in her dark hair like small pearls. She didn't say anything; there was no need for it, and he felt grateful for silence.

He was the first to speak. "Not long now, Eve." And then, realizing the banality of it, he smiled. "Only why do we have this airport feeling? It's not as if I'll be gone long."

"A hundred years," she said

"Take it easy, darling. The theory is foolproof. I've been on time jaunts before, remember? Twenty years ahead and twenty back. The projector works, it's been proven in practice. This is just a little longer trip, that's all."

"But the automatic machines, that went a hundred years ahead, never came back—"

"Exactly. Some damn fool thing or other went wrong with them. Tubes blew their silly heads off, or some such thing. That's why Sam and

I have to go, to see what went wrong. We can repair our machine. We can compensate for the well-known perversity of vacuum tubes."

"But why the two of you? One would be enough. Sam—"

"Sam is no physicist. He might not be able to find the trouble. On the other hand, as a skilled mechanic he can do things I never could. We supplement each other." Saunders took a deep breath. "Look, darling—"

Sam Hull's bass shout rang out to them. "All set, folks! Any time you want to go, we can ride!"

"Coming." Saunders took his time, bidding Eve a proper farewell, a little in advance. She followed him into the house and down to the capacious underground workshop.

The projector stood in a clutter of apparatus under the white radiance of fluoro-tubes. It was unimpressive from the outside, a metal cylinder some ten feet high and thirty feet long with the unfinished look of all experimental set-ups. The outer shell was simply protection for the battery banks and the massive dimensional projector within. A tiny space in the forward end was left for the two men.

Sam Hull gave them a gay wave. His massive form almost blotted out the gray-smocked little body of MacPherson. "All set for a hundred years ahead!" he exclaimed. "Two thousand seventy-three, here we come!"

MacPherson blinked owlishly at them from behind thick lenses. "It all tests out," he said. "Or so Sam here tells me. Personally, I wouldn't know an oscillograph from a klystron. You have an ample supply of spare parts and tools. There should be no difficulty."

"I'm not looking for any, Doc," said Saunders. "Eve here won't believe we aren't going to be eaten by monsters with stalked eyes and long fangs. I keep telling her all we're going to do is check your automatic machines, if we can find them, and make a few astronomical observations, and come back."

"There'll be people in the future," said Eve.

"Oh, well, if they invite us in for a drink we won't say no," shrugged Hull. "Which reminds me—" He fished a pint out of his capacious coverall pocket. "We ought to drink a toast or something, huh?"

Saunders frowned a little. He didn't want to add to Eve's impression of a voyage into darkness. She was worried enough, poor kid, poor, lovely kid. "Hell," he said, "we've been back to nineteen fifty-three and seen the house standing. We've been ahead to nineteen ninety-three and seen the house standing. Nobody home at either time. These jaunts are too dull to rate a toast."

"Nothing," said Hull, "is too dull to rate a drink." He poured and they touched glasses, a strange little ceremony in the utterly prosaic laboratory. "Bon voyage!"

"Bon voyage." Eve tried to smile, but the hand that lifted the glass to her lips trembled a little.

"Come on," said Hull. "Let's go, Mart. Sooner we set out, the sooner we can get back."

"Sure." With a gesture of decision, Saunders put down his glass and swung toward the machine. "Goodbye, Eve, I'll see you in a couple of hours—after a hundred years or so."

"So long—Martin." She made the name a caress.

MacPherson beamed with avuncular approval.

Saunders squeezed himself into the forward compartment with Hull. He was a big man, long-limbed and wide-shouldered, with blunt, homely features under a shock of brown hair and wide-set gray eyes lined with crow's feet from much squinting into the sun. He wore only the plain blouse and slacks of his work, stained here and there with grease or acid.

The compartment was barely large enough for the two of them, and crowded with instruments—as well as the rifle and pistol they had along entirely to quiet Eve's fears. Saunders swore as the guns got in his way, and closed the door. The clang had in it an odd note of finality.

"Here goes," said Hull unnecessarily.

Saunders nodded and started the projector warming up. Its powerful *thrum* filled the cabin and vibrated in his bones. Needles flickered across gauge faces, approaching stable values.

Through the single porthole he saw Eve waving. He waved back and then, with an angry motion, flung down the main switch.

The machine shimmered, blurred, and was gone. Eve drew a shuddering breath and turned back to MacPherson.

Grayness swirled briefly before them, and the drone of the projectors filled the machine with an enormous song. Saunders watched the gauges and inched back the switch that controlled their rate of time advancement. A hundred years ahead—less the number of days since they'd sent the first automatic, just so that no dunderhead in the future would find it and walk off with it . . .

He slapped down the switch and the noise and vibration came to a ringing halt.

Sunlight streamed in through the porthole. "No house?" asked Hull.

"A century is a long time," said Saunders. "Come on, let's go out and have a look."

They crawled through the door and stood erect. The machine lay in the bottom of a half-filled pit above which grasses waved. A few broken shards of stone projected from the earth. There was a bright blue sky overhead, with fluffy white clouds blowing across it.

"No automatics," said Hull, looking around.

"That's odd. But maybe the ground-level adjustments—let's go topside." Saunders scrambled up the sloping walls of the pit.

It was obviously the half-filled basement of the old house, which must somehow have been destroyed in the eighty years since his last visit. The ground-level machine in the projector automatically materialized it on the exact surface whenever it emerged. There would be no sudden falls or sudden burials under risen earth. Nor would there be disastrous materializations inside something solid; mass-sensitive circuits prevented the machine from halting whenever solid matter occupied its own space. Liquid or gas molecules could get out of the way fast enough.

Saunders stood in tall, wind-rippled grass and looked over the serene landscape of upper New York State. Nothing had changed, the river and the forested hills beyond it were the same, the sun was bright and clouds shone in the heavens.

No—no, before God! Where was the village?

House gone, town gone—what had happened? Had people simply moved away, or . . .

He looked back down to the basement. Only a few minutes ago—a hundred years in the past—he had stood there in a tangle of battered apparatus, and Doc and Eve—and now it was a pit with wild grass covering the raw earth. An odd desolation tugged at him.

Was he still alive today? Was . . . Eve? The gerontology of 1973 made it entirely possible, but one never knew. And he didn't want to find out.

"Must'a give the country back to the Indians," grunted Sam Hull.

The prosaic wisecrack restored a sense of balance. After all, any sensible man knew that things changed with time. There would be good and evil in the future as there had been in the past. "And they lived happily ever after" was pure myth. The important thing was change, an unending flux out of which all could come. And right now there was a job to do.

They scouted around in the grass, but there was no trace of the small automatic projectors. Hull scowled thoughtfully. "You know," he said, "I think they started back and blew out on the way."

You must be right," nodded Saunders. "We can't have arrived more than a few minutes after their return-point." He started back toward the big machine. "Let's take our observation and get out."

They set up their astronomical equipment and took readings on the declining sun. Waiting for night, they cooked a meal on a camp stove and sat while a cricket-chirping dusk deepened around them.

"I like this future," said Hull. "It's peaceful. Think I'll retire here—or now—in my old age."

The thought of transtemporal resorts made Saunders grin. But—who knew? Maybe!

The stars wheeled grandly overhead. Saunders jotted down figures on right ascension, declination, and passage times. From that, they could calculate later, almost to the minute, how far the machine had taken them. They had not moved in space at all, of course, relative to the surface of the Earth. "Absolute space" was an obsolete fiction, and as far as the projector was concerned Earth was the immobile center of the universe.

They waded through dew-wet grass back down to the machine. "We'll try ten-year stops, looking for the automatics," said Saunders. "If we don't find 'em that way, to hell with them. I'm hungry."

2063—it was raining into the pit.

2053—sunlight and emptiness.

2043—the pit was fresher now, and a few rotting timbers lay half buried in the ground.

Saunders scowled at the meters. "She's drawing more power than she should," he said.

2023—the house had obviously burned; charred stumps of wood were in sight. And the projector had roared with a skull-cracking intensity of power; energy drained from the batteries like water from a squeezed sponge; a resistor was beginning to glow.

They checked the circuits, inch by inch, wire by wire. Nothing was out of order.

"Let's go." Hull's face was white.

It was a battle to leap the next ten years. It took half an hour of bawling, thundering, tortured labor for the projector to fight backward. Radiated energy made the cabin unendurably hot.

2013—the fire-blackened basement still stood. On its floor lay two small cylinders, tarnished with some years of weathering.

"The automatics got a little farther back," said Hull. "Then they quit, and just lay here."

Saunders examined them. When he looked up from his instruments, his face was grim with the choking fear that was rising within him. "Drained," he said. "Batteries completely dead. They used up all their energy reserves."

"What in the devil is this?" It was almost a snarl from Hull.

"I—don't—know. There seems to be some kind of resistance that increases the further back we try to go—"

"Come on!"

"But—"

"Come on, God damn it!"

Saunders shrugged hopelessly.

It took two hours to fight back five years. Then Saunders stopped the projector. His voice shook.

"No go, Sam. We've used up three quarters of our stored energy—and the farther back we go, the more we use per year. It seems to be some sort of high-order exponential function."

"So we'd never make it. At this rate, our batteries will be dead before we get back another ten years." Saunders looked ill. "It's some effect the theory didn't allow for, some accelerating increase in power requirements the farther back into the past we go. For twenty-year hops or less, the energy increases roughly as the square of the number of years traversed. But it must actually be something like an exponential curve, which starts building up fast and furious beyond a certain point. We haven't enough power left in the batteries!"

"If we could recharge them—"

"We don't have such equipment with us. But maybe—"

They climbed out of the ruined basement and looked eagerly toward the river. There was no sign of the village. It must have been torn down or otherwise destroyed still further back in the past at a point they'd been through.

"No help there," said Saunders.

"We can look for a place. There must be people somewhere!"

"No doubt." Saunders fought for calm. "But we could spend a long time looking for them, you know. And—" his voice wavered, "Sam, I'm not sure even recharging at intervals would help. It looks very much to me as if the curve of energy consumption is approaching a vertical asymptote."

"Talk English, will you?" Hull's grin was forced.

"I mean that beyond a certain number of years an infinite amount of energy may be required. Like the Einsteinian concept of light as the limiting velocity. As you approach the speed of light, the energy needed to accelerate increases ever more rapidly. You'd need infinite energy to get beyond the speed of light—which is just a fancy way of saying you can't do it. The same thing may apply to time as well as space."

"You mean—we can't ever get back?"

"I don't know." Saunders looked desolately around at the smiling landscape. "I could be wrong. But I'm horribly afraid I'm right."

Hull swore, "What're we going to do about it?"

"We've got two choices," Saunders said. "One, we can hunt for people, recharge our batteries, and keep trying. Two, we can go into the future."

"The future!"

"Uh-huh. Sometime in the future, they ought to know more about such things than we do. They may know a way to get around this effect. Certainly they could give us a powerful enough engine so that, if energy is all that's needed, we can get back. A small atomic generator, for instance."

Hull stood with his head, bent turning the thought over in his mind. There was a meadowlark singing somewhere, maddeningly sweet.

Saunders forced a harsh laugh. "But the very first thing on the agenda," he said, "is breakfast!"

The food was tasteless. They ate in a heavy silence, choking the stuff down. But in the end they looked at each other with a common resolution.

Hull grinned and stuck out a hairy paw. "It's a hell of a roundabout way to get home," he said, "but I'm for it."

Saunders clasped hands with him, wordlessly. They went back to the machine.

"And now where?" asked the mechanic.

"It's two thousand eight," said Saunders. "How about—well—two-thousand five-hundred A.D.?"

"Okay. It's a nice round number. Anchors aweigh!"

The machine thrummed and shook. Saunders was gratified to notice the small power consumption as the years and decades fled by. At that rate, they had energy enough to travel to the end of the world.

Eve, Eve, I'll come back. I'll come back if I have to go ahead to Judgment Day . . .

2500 A.D. The machine blinked into materialization on top of a low hill—the pit had filled in during the intervening centuries. Pale, hurried sunlight flashed through wind-driven rain clouds into the hot interior.

"Come," said Hull. "We haven't got all day."

He picked up the automatic rifle. "What's the idea?" exclaimed Saunders.

"Eve was right the first time," said Hull grimly. "Buckle on that pistol, Mart."

Saunders strapped the heavy weapon to his thigh. The metal was cold under his fingers.

They stepped out and swept the horizon. Hull's voice rose in a shout of glee. "People!"

There was a small town beyond the river, near the site of old Hudson. Beyond it lay fields of ripening grain and clumps of trees. There was no sign of a highway. Maybe surface transportation was obsolete now.

The town looked—odd. It must have been there a long time, the houses were weathered. There were tall peak-roofed buildings, crowding narrow streets. A flashing metal tower reared some five hundred feet into the lowering sky, near the center of town.

Somehow, it didn't look the way Saunders had visualized communities of the future. It had an oddly stunted appearance, despite the high buildings and—sinister? He couldn't say. Maybe it was only his depression.

Something rose from the center of the town, a black ovoid that whipped into the sky and lined out across the river. Reception committee, thought Saunders. His hand fell on his pistol butt.

It was an airjet, he saw as it neared, an egg-shaped machine with stubby wings and a flaring tail. It was flying slowly now, gliding groundward toward them.

"Hallo, there!" bawled Hull. He stood erect with the savage wind tossing his flame-red hair, waving. "Hallo, people!"

The machine dove at them. Something stabbed from its nose, a line of smoke—tracers!

Conditioned reflexes flung Saunders to the ground. The bullets whined over his head, exploding with a vicious crash behind him. He saw Hull blown apart.

The jet rushed overhead and banked for another assault. Saunders got up and ran, crouching low, weaving back and forth. The line of bullets spanged past him again, throwing up gouts of dirt where they hit. He threw himself down again.

Another try . . . Saunders was knocked off his feet by the bursting of a shell. He rolled over and hugged the ground, hoping the grass would hide him. Dimly, he thought that the jet was too fast for strafing a single man; it overshot its mark.

He heard it whine overhead, without daring to look up. It circled vulturelike, seeking him. He had time for a rising tide of bitter hate.

Sam—they'd killed him, shot him without provocation—Sam, red-haired Sam with his laughter and his comradeship. Sam was dead and they had killed him.

He risked turning over. The jet was settling to Earth; they'd hunt him from the ground. He got up and ran again.

A shot wailed past his ear. He spun around, the pistol in his hand, and snapped a return shot. There were men in black uniforms coming out of the jet. It was long range, but his gun was a heavy war model; it carried. He fired again and felt a savage joy at seeing one of the black-clad figures spin on its heels and lurch to the ground.

The time machine lay before him. No time for heroics; he had to get away—fast! Bullets were singing around him.

He burst through the door and slammed it shut. A slug whanged through the metal wall. Thank God the tubes were still warm!

He threw the main switch. As vision wavered, he saw the pursuers almost on him. One of them was aiming something like a bazooka.

They faded into grayness. He lay back, shuddering. Slowly, he grew aware that his clothes were torn and that a metal fragment had scratched his hand.

And Sam was dead. Sam was dead.

He watched the dial creep upward. Let it be 3000 A.D. Five hundred years was not too much to put between himself and the men in black.

He chose night time. A cautious look outside revealed that he was among tall buildings with little if any light. Good!

He spent a few moments bandaging his injury and changing into the extra clothes Eve had insisted on providing—a heavy wool shirt and breeches, boots, and a raincoat that should help make him relatively inconspicuous. The holstered pistol went along, of course, with plenty of extra cartridges. He'd have to leave the machine while he reconnoitered and chance its discovery. At least he could lock the door.

Outside, he found himself standing in a small cobbled courtyard between high houses with shuttered and darkened windows. Overhead was utter night, the stars must be clouded, but he saw a vague red glow to the north, pulsing and flickering. After a moment, he squared his shoulders and started down an alley that was like a cavern of blackness.

Briefly, the incredible situation rose in his mind. In less than an hour he had leaped a thousand years past his own age, had seen his friend murdered, and now stood in an alien city more alone than man had ever been. *And Eve, will I see you again?*

A noiseless shadow, blacker than the night, slipped past him. The dim light shone greenly from its eyes—an alley cat! At least man still had pets. But he could have wished for a more reassuring one.

Noise came from ahead, a bobbing light flashing around at the doors of houses. He dropped a hand through the slit in his coat to grasp the pistol butt.

Black against the narrowed skyline four men came abreast, filling the street. The rhythm of their footfall was military. A guard of some kind. He looked around for shelter; he didn't want to be taken prisoner by unknowns.

No alleys to the side—he sidled backward. The flashlight beam darted ahead, crossed his body, and came back. A voice shouted something, harsh and peremptory.

Saunders turned and ran. The voice cried again behind him. He heard the slam of boots after him. Someone blew a horn, raising echoes that hooted between the high dark walls.

A black form grew out of the night. Fingers like steel wires closed on his arm, yanking him to one side. He opened his mouth, and a hand slipped across it. Before he could recover balance, he was pulled down a flight of stairs in the street.

"In heah." The hissing whisper was taut in his ear. "Quickly." A door slid open just a crack. They burst through, and the other man closed it behind them. An automatic lock clicked shut.

"Ih don'tink dey vised use," said the man grimly. "Dey better not ha'!"

Saunders stared at him. The other man was of medium height, with a lithe, slender build shown by the skin-tight gray clothes under his black cape. There was a gun at one hip, a pouch at the other. His face was sallow, with a yellowish tinge, and the hair was shaven. It was a lean, strong face, with high cheekbones and narrow jaw, straight nose with flaring nostrils, dark, slant eyes under Mephistophelean brows. The mouth, wide and self-indulgent, was drawn into a reckless grin that showed sharp white teeth. Some sort of white-Mongoloid half-breed, Saunders guessed.

"Who are you?" he asked roughly.

The stranger surveyed him shrewdly. "Belgotai of Syrtis," he said at last. "But yuh don' belong heah."

"I'll say I don't." Wry humor rose in Saunders. "Why did you snatch me that way?"

"Yuh didn' wanna fall into de Watch's hands, did yuh?" asked Belgotai. "Don' ask mih why Ih ressued a stranger. Ih happened to come out, see yuh running, figgered anybody running fro de Watch desuhved help, an' pulled yuh back in." He shrugged. "Of course, if yuh don' wanna be helped, go back upstaiahs."

"I'll stay here, of course," Saunder said. "And—thanks for rescuing me."

"De nada," said Belgotai. "Come, le's ha' a drink."

It was a smoky, low-ceilinged room, with a few scarred wooden tables crowded about a small charcoal fire and big barrels in the rear—a tavern of some sort, an underworld hangout. Saunders reflected that he might have done worse. Crooks wouldn't be as finicky about his antecedents as officialdom might be. He could ask his way around, learn.

"I'm afraid I haven't any money," he said. "Unless—" He pulled a handful of coins from his pocket.

Belgotai looked sharply at them and drew a whistling breath between his teeth. Then his face smoothed into blankness. "Ih'll buy," he said genially. "Come Hennaly, gi' us whissey."

Belgotai drew Saunders into a dark corner seat, away from the others in the room. The landlord brought tumblers of rotgut remotely akin to whiskey, and Saunders gulped his with a feeling of need.

"Who' name do yuh go by?" asked Belgotai.

"Saunders. Martin Saunders."

"Glad to see yuh. Now—" Belgotai leaned closer, and his voice dropped to a whisper—"Now, Saunders, when 're yuh from?"

Saunders started. Belgotai smiled thinly "Be frank," he said. "Dese're mih frien's heah. Dey'd think nawting of slitting yuh troat and dumping yuh in de alley. But Ih mean well."

With a sudden great weariness, Saunders relaxed. What the hell, it had to come out sometime. "Nineteen hundred seventy-three," he said.

"Eh? De future?"

"No—the past."

"Oh. Diff'ent chronning, den. How far back?"

"One thousand and twenty-seven years."

Belgotai whistled. "Long ways! But Ih were sure yuh mus' be from de past. Nobody eve' came fro' de future."

Sickly: "You mean—it's impossible?"

"Ih do' know." Belgotai's grin was wolfish. "Who'd visit dis era fro' de future, if dey could? But wha's yuh story?"

Saunders bristled. The whiskey was coursing hot in his veins now. "I'll trade information," he said coldly. "I won't give it."

"Faiah enawff. Blast away, Mahtin Saundahs."

Saunders told his story in a few words. At the end, Belgotai nodded gravely. "Yuh ran into de Fanatics, five hundred yeahs ago," he said. "Dey was deat' on time travelers. Or on most people, for dat matter."

"But what's happened? What sort of world is this, anyway?"

Belgotai's slurring accents were getting easier to follow. Pronunciation had changed a little, vowels sounded different, the "r" had shifted to something like that in twentieth-century French or Danish, other consonants were modified. Foreign words, especially Spanish, had crept in. But it was still intelligible. Saunders listened. Belgotai was not too well versed in history, but his shrewd brain had a grasp of the more important facts.

The time of troubles had begun in the twenty-third century with the revolt of the Martian colonists against the increasingly corrupt and tyrannical Terrestrial Directorate. A century later the folk of Earth were on the move, driven by famine, pestilence, and civil war, a chaos out of which rose the religious enthusiasm of the Armageddonists—the Fanatics, as they were called later. Fifty years after the massacres on Luna, Huntry was the military dictator of Earth, and the rule of the Armageddonists endured for nearly three hundred years. It was a nominal sort of rule, vast territories were always in revolt and the planetary colonists were building up a power which kept the Fanatics out of space, but wherever they did have control they ruled with utter ruthlessness.

Among other things they forbade was time travel. But it had never been popular with anyone since the Time War, when a defeated Directorate army had leaped from the twenty-third to the twenty-fourth century and wrought havoc before their attempt at conquest was smashed. Time travelers were few anyway, the future was too precarious—they were apt to be killed or enslaved in one of the more turbulent periods.

In the late twenty-seventh century, the Planetary League and the African Dissenters had finally ended Fanatic rule. Out of the postwar confusion rose the Pax Africana, and for two hundred years man had enjoyed an era of comparative peace and progress that was wistfully looked back on as a golden age; indeed, modern chronology dated from, the ascension of John Mteza I. Breakdown came through internal decay and the onslaughts of barbarians from the outer planets, the solar system split into a multitude of small states and even independent cities. It was a hard, brawling period, not without a brilliance of its own, but it was drawing to a close now.

"Dis is one of de city-states," said Belgotai. "Liung-Wei, it's named—founded by Sinese invaders about three centuries ago. It's under de dictatorship of Krausmann now, a stubborn old buzzard who'll no surrender dough de armies of de Atlantic Master're at ouah very gates now. Yuh see de red glow? Dat's deir projectors working on our energy screen. When dey break it down, dey'll take de city and punish it for holding out so long. Nobody looks happily to dat day."

He added a few remarks about himself. Belgotai was of a dying age, the past era of small states who employed mercenaries to fight their battles. Born on Mars, Belgotai had hired out over the whole solar system. But the little mercenary companies were helpless before the organized levies of the rising nations, and after annihilation of his band Belgotai had fled to Earth where he dragged out a weary existence as thief and assassin. He had little to look forward to.

"Nobody wants a free comrade now," he said ruefully. "If de Watch don't catch me first, Ih'll hang when de Atlantics take de city."

Saunders nodded with a certain sympathy.

Belgotai leaned close with a gleam in his slant eyes. "But yuh can help me, Mahtin Saundahs," he hissed. "And help yuhself too."

"Eh?" Saunders blinked warily at him.

"Sure, sure. Take me wid yuh, out of dis damned time. Dey can't help yuh here, dey know no more about time travel dan yuh do—most likely dey'll throw yuh in de calabozo and smash yuh machine. Yuh have to go on. Take me!"

Saunders hesitated, warily. What did he really know? How much truth was in Belgotai's story? How far could he trust—

"Set me off in some time when a free comrade can fight again. Meanwhile I'll help. Ih'm a good man wid gun or vibrodagger. Yuh can't go batting alone into de future."

Saunders wondered. But what the hell—it was plain enough that this period was of no use to him. And Belgotai had saved him, even if the Watch wasn't as bad as he claimed. And—well—he needed someone to talk to, if nothing else. Someone to help him forget Sam Hull and the gulf of centuries separating him from Eve.

Decision came. "Okay."

"Wonnaful! Yuh'll no be sorry, Mahtin." Belgotai stood up. "Come, le's be blasting off."

"Now?"

"De sooner de better. Someone may find yuh machine. Den it's too late."

"But—you'll want to make ready—say goodbye—"

Belgotai slapped his pouch. "All Ih own is heah." Bitterness underlay his reckless laugh. "Ih've none to say goodbye to, except mih creditors. Come!"

Half dazed, Saunders followed him out of the tavern. This time-hopping was going too fast for him, he didn't have a chance to adjust.

For instance, if he ever got back to his own time he'd have descendants in this age. At the rate at which lines of descent spread, there would be men in each army who had his own and Eve's blood, warring on each other without thought of the tenderness which had wrought their very beings. But then, he remembered wearily, he had never considered the common ancestors he must have with men he'd shot out of the sky in the war he once had fought.

Men lived in their own times, a brief flash of light ringed with an enormous dark, and it was not in their nature to think beyond that little span of years. He began to realize why time travel had never been common.

"Hist!" Belgotai drew him into the tunnel of an alley. They crouched there while four black-caged men of the Watch strode past. In the wan red light, Saunders had a glimpse of high cheekbones, half-Asian features, the metallic gleam of guns slung over their shoulders.

They made their way to the machine where it lay between lowering houses crouched in a night of fear and waiting. Belgotai laughed again, a soft, joyous ring in the dark. "Freedom!" he whispered.

They crawled into it and Saunders set the controls for a hundred years ahead. Belgotai scowled. "Most like de world'll be very tame and quiet den," he said.

"If I get a way to return," said Saunders, "I'll carry you on whenever you want to go."

"Or yuh could carry me back a hundred years from now," said the warrior. "Blast away, den!"

3100 A.D. A waste of blackened, fused rock. Saunders switched on the Geiger counter and it clattered crazily. Radioactive! Some hellish atomic bomb had wiped Liung-Wei from existence. He leaped another century, shaking.

3200 A.D. The radioactivity was gone, but the desolation remained, a vast vitrified crater under a hot, still sky, dead and lifeless. There was little prospect of walking across it in search of man, nor did Saunders want to get far from the machine. If he should be cut off from it . . .

By 3500, soil had drifted back over the ruined land and a forest was growing. They stood in a drizzling rain and looked around them.

"Big trees," said Saunders. "This forest has stood for a long time without human interference."

"Maybe man went back to de caves?" suggested Belgotai.

"I doubt it. Civilization was just too widespread for a lapse into total savagery. But it may be a long ways to a settlement."

"Let's go ahead, den!" Belgotai's eyes gleamed with interest.

The forest still stood for centuries thereafter. Saunders scowled in worry. He didn't like this business of going farther and farther from his time, he was already too far ahead ever to get back without help. Surely, in all ages of human history—

4100 A.D. They flashed into materialization on a broad grassy sward where low, rounded buildings of something that looked like tinted plastic stood between fountains, statues, and bowers. A small aircraft whispered noiselessly overhead, no sign of motive power on its exterior.

There were humans around, young men and women who wore long colorful capes over light tunics. They crowded forward with a shout. Saunders and Belgotai stepped out, raising hands in a gesture of friendship. But the warrior kept his hands close to his gun.

The language was a flowing, musical tongue with only a baffling hint of familiarity. Had times changed that much?

They were taken to one of the buildings. Within its cool, spacious interior, a grave, bearded man in ornate red robes stood up to greet them. Someone else brought in a small machine reminiscent of an oscilloscope with microphone attachments. The man set it on the table and adjusted its dials.

He spoke again, his own unknown language rippling from his lips. But words came out of the machine—English!

"Welcome, travelers, to this branch of the American College. Please be seated."

Saunders and Belgotai gaped. The man smiled. "I see the psychophone is new to you. It is a receiver of encephalic emissions from the speech centers. When one speaks, the corresponding thoughts are taken by the machine, greatly amplified, and beamed to the brain of the listener, who interprets them in terms of his own language.

"Permit me to introduce myself. I am Hamalon Avard, dean of this branch of the college." He raised bushy gray eyebrows in polite inquiry.

They gave their names, and Avard bowed ceremoniously. A slim girl, whose scanty dress caused Belgotai's eyes to widen, brought a tray of sandwiches and a beverage not unlike tea. Saunders suddenly realized how hungry and tired he was. He collapsed into a seat that molded itself to his contours and looked dully at Avard.

Their story came out, and the dean nodded. "I thought you were time travelers," he said. "But this is a matter of great interest. The archeology departments will want to speak to you, if you will be so kind—"

"Can you help us?" asked Saunders bluntly. "Can you fix our machine so it will reverse?"

"Alas, no. I am afraid our physics holds no hope for you. I can consult the experts, but I am sure there has been no change in spatiotemporal theory since Priogan's reformulation. According to it, the energy needed to travel into the past increases tremendously with the period covered. The deformation of world lines, you see. Beyond a period of about seventy years, infinite energy is required."

Saunders nodded dully. "I thought so. Then there's no hope?"

"Not in this time, I am afraid. But science is advancing rapidly. Contact with alien culture in the galaxy has proved an immense stimulant—"

"Yuh have interstellar travel?" exploded Belgotai. "Yuh can travel to de stars?"

"Yes, of course. The faster-than-light drive was worked out over five hundred years ago on the basis of Priogan's modified relativity theory. It involves warping through higher dimensions—but you have more urgent problems than scientific theories."

"Not Ih!" said Belgotai fiercely. "If Ih can get put among de stars—dere must be wars dere—"

"Alas, yes, the rapid expansion of the frontier has thrown the galaxy into chaos. But I do not think you could get passage on a spaceship. In fact, the Council will probably order your temporal deportation as unintegrated individuals. The sanity of Sol will be in danger otherwise."

"Why, yuh—" Belgotai snarled and reached for his gun. Saunders clapped a hand on the warrior's arm.

"Take it easy, you bloody fool," he said furiously. We can't fight a whole planet. Why should we? There'll be other ages."

Belgotai relaxed, but his eyes were still angry.

They stayed at the college for two days. Avard and his colleagues were courteous, hospitable, eager to hear what the travelers had to tell of their periods. They provided food and living quarters and much-needed rest. They even pleaded Belgotai's case to the Solar Council, via telescreen. But the answer was inexorable: the galaxy already had too many barbarians. The travelers would have to go.

Their batteries were taken out of the machine for them and a small atomic engine with nearly limitless energy reserves installed in its place. Avard gave them a psychophone for communication with whoever they met in the future. Everyone was very nice and considerate. But Saunders found himself reluctantly agreeing with Belgotai. He didn't care much for these over-civilized gentlefolk. He didn't belong in this age.

Avard bade them grave goodbye. "It is strange to see you go," he said. "It is a strange thought that you will still be traveling long after my cremation, that you will see things I cannot dream of." Briefly, something stirred in his face. "In a way I envy you." He turned away quickly, as if afraid of the thought. "Goodbye and good fortune."

4300 A.D. The campus buildings were gone, but small, elaborate summerhouses had replaced them. Youths and girls in scanty rainbow-hued dress crowded around the machine.

"You are time travelers?" asked one of the young men, wide-eyed.

Saunders nodded, feeling too tired for speech.

"Time travelers!" A girl squealed in delight.

"I don't suppose you have any means of traveling into the past these days?" asked Saunders hopelessly.

"Not that I know of. But please come, stay for a while, tell us about your journeys. This is the biggest lark we've had since the ship came from Sirius."

There was no denying the eager insistence. The women, in particular, crowded around, circling them in a ring of soft arms, laughing and shouting and pulling them away from the machine. Belgotai grinned. "Let's stay de night," he suggested.

Saunders didn't feel like arguing the point. *There was time enough,* he thought bitterly. All the time in the world.

It was a night of revelry. Saunders managed to get a few facts. Sol was a galactic backwater these days, stuffed with mercantile wealth and guarded by nonhuman mercenaries against the interstellar raiders and conquerors. This region was one of many playgrounds for the children of the great merchant families, living for generations off inherited riches. They were amiable kids, but there was a mental and physical softness about them, and a deep inward weariness from a meaningless round of increasingly stale pleasure. Decadence.

Saunders finally sat alone under a moon that glittered with the diamond-points of domed cities, beside a softly lapping artificial lake, and watched the constellations wheel overhead—the far suns that man had conquered without mastering himself. He thought of Eve and wanted to cry, but the hollowness in his breast was dry and cold.

Belgotai had a thumping hangover in the morning, which a drink offered by one of the women removed. He argued for a while about staying in this age. Nobody would deny him passage this time; they were eager for fighting men out in the galaxy. But the fact that Sol was rarely visited now, that he might have to wait years, finally decided him on continuing.

"Dis won' go on much longer," he said. "Sol is too tempting a prize, an' mercenaries aren' allays loyal. Sooner or later, dere'll be war on Eart' again."

Saunders nodded dispiritedly. He hated to think of the blasting energies that would devour a peaceful and harmless folk, the looting and murdering and enslaving, but history was that way. It was littered with the graves of pacifists.

The bright scene swirled into grayness. They drove ahead.

4400 A.D. A villa was burning, smoke and flame reaching up into the clouded sky. Behind it stood the looming bulk of a ray-scarred spaceship, and around it boiled a vortex of men, huge bearded men in helmets and cuirasses, laughing as they bore out golden loot and struggling captives. The barbarians had come!

The two travelers leaped back into the machine. Those weapons could fuse it to a glowing mass. Saunders swung the main-drive switch far over.

"We'd better make a longer jump," Saunders said, as the needle crept past the century mark. "Can't look for much scientific progress in a dark age. I'll try for five thousand A.D."

His mind carried the thought on: *Will there ever be progress of the sort we must have? Eve, will I ever see you again?* As if his yearning could carry over the abyss of millennia: *Don't mourn me too long, my dearest. In all the bloody ages of human history, your happiness is all that ultimately matters.*

As the needle approached six centuries, Saunders tried to ease down the switch. Tried!

"What's the matter?" Belgotai leaned over his shoulder.

With a sudden cold sweat along his ribs, Saunders tugged harder.

The switch was immobile—the projector wouldn't stop. "Out of order?" asked Belgotai anxiously.

"No—it's the automatic mass-detector. We'd be annihilated if we emerged in the same space with solid matter. The detector prevents the projector from stopping if it senses such a structure." Saunders grinned savagely. "Some damned idiot must have built a house right where we are!"

The needle passed its limit, and still they droned on through a featureless grayness. Saunders reset the dial and noted the first half millennium. It was nice, though not necessary, to know what year it was when they emerged.

He wasn't worried at first. Man's works were so horribly impermanent; he thought with a sadness of the cities and civilizations he had seen rise and spend their little hour and sink back into the night and chaos of time. But after a thousand years . . .

Two thousand . . .

Three thousand . . .

Belgotai's face was white and tense in the dull glow of the instrument panel. "How long to go?" he whispered.

"I—don't—know."

Within the machine, the long minutes passed while the projector hummed its song of power and two men stared with hypnotized fascination at the creeping record of centuries.

For twenty thousand years that incredible thing stood. In the year 25,296 A.D., the switch suddenly went down under Saunders' steady tug. The machine flashed into reality, tilted, and slid down a few feet before coming to rest. Wildly, they opened the door.

The projector lay on a stone block big as a small house, whose ultimate slipping from its place had freed them. It was halfway up a pyramid.

A monument of gray stone, a tetrahedron a mile to a side and a half a mile high The outer casing had worn away, or been removed, so that the tremendous blocks stood naked to the weather. Soil had drifted up onto it, grass and trees grew on its titanic slopes. Their roots, and wind and rain and frost, were slowly crumbling the artificial hill to earth again, but still it dominated the landscape.

A defaced carving leered out from a tangle of brush. Saunders looked at it and looked away, shuddering. No human being had ever carved that thing.

The countryside around was altered; he couldn't see the old river and there was a lake glimmering in the distance which had not been there before. The hills seemed lower, and forest covered them. It was a wild, primeval scene, but there was a spaceship standing near the base, a monster machine with its nose rearing skyward and a sunburst blazon on its hull. And there were men working nearby.

Saunders' shout rang in the still air. He and Belgotai scrambled down the steep slopes of earth, clawing past trees and vines. Men!

No—not all men. A dozen great shining engines were toiling without supervision at the foot of the pyramid—robots. And of the group that turned to stare at the travelers, two were squat, blue-furred, with snouted faces and six-fingered hands.

Saunders realized with an unexpectedly eerie shock that he was seeing extraterrestrial intelligence. But it was to the men that he faced.

They were all tall, with aristocratically refined features and a calm that seemed inbred. Their clothing was impossible to describe, it was like a rainbow shimmer around them, never the same in its play of color and shape. *So,* thought Saunders, *so must the old gods have looked on high Olympus, beings greater and more beautiful than man.*

But it was a human voice that called to them, a deep, well-modulated tone in a totally foreign language. Saunders remembered exasperatedly that he had forgotten the psychophone, but one of the blue-furred aliens were already fetching a round, knob-studded globe out of which the familiar translating voice seemed to come:

". . . time travelers."

"From the very remote past, obviously," said another man. Damn him, damn them all, they weren't any more excited than at the bird that rose, startled, from the long grass. You'd think time travelers would at least be worth shaking by the hand.

"Listen," snapped Saunders, realizing in the back of his mind that his annoyance was a reaction against the awesomeness of the company, "we're in trouble. Our machine won't carry us back, and we have to find a period of time that knows how to reverse the effect. Can you do it?"

One of the aliens shook his animal head. "No," he said. "There is no way known to physics of getting further back than about seventy years. Beyond that, the required energy approaches infinity and—"

Saunders groaned. "We know it," said Belgotai harshly.

"At least you must rest," said one of the men in a more kindly tone. "It will be interesting to hear your story."

"I've told it to too many people in the last few millennia," rasped Saunders. "Let's hear yours for a change."

Two of the strangers exchanged low-voiced words. Saunders could almost translate them himself: "Barbarians—childish emotional pattern—well, humor them for a while."

"This is an archeological expedition, excavating the pyramid," said one of the men patiently. "We are from the Galactic Institute, Sarlan-sector branch. I am Lord Arsfel of Astracyr, and these are my subordinates. The nonhumans, as you may wish to know, are from the planet Quulhan, whose sun is not visible from Terra."

Despite himself, Saunders' awed gaze turned to the stupendous mass looming over them. "Who built it?" he breathed.

"The Ixchulhi made such structures on planets they conquered, no one knows why. But then, no one knows what they were or where they came from or where they ultimately went. It is hoped that some of the answers may be found in their pyramids."

The atmosphere grew more relaxed. Deftly, the men of the expedition got Saunders's and Belgotai's stories and what information about their almost prehistoric periods they cared for. In exchange, something of history was offered to them.

After the Ixchulhi's ruinous wars, the galaxy had made a surprisingly rapid comeback. New techniques of mathematical psychology made it possible to unite the peoples of a billion worlds and rule them effectively. The Galactic Empire was egalitarian—it had to be, for one of its mainstays was the fantastically old and evolved race of the planet called Vro-Hi by men.

It was peaceful, prosperous, colorful with diversity of races and cultures, expanding in science and the arts. It had already endured for ten thousand years, and there seemed no doubt in Arsfel's calm mind that it could endure forever. The barbarians along the galactic periphery and out in the Magellanic Clouds? Nonsense! The empire would get around to civilizing them in due course; meanwhile they were only a nuisance.

But Sol could almost be called one of the barbarian suns, though it lay within the Imperial boundaries. Civilization was concentrated near the center of the galaxy, and Sol lay in what was actually a remote and thinly starred region of space. A few primitive landsmen still lived on its planets and had infrequent intercourse with the nearer stars, but they hardly counted. The human race had almost forgotten its ancient home.

Somehow the picture was saddening to the American. He thought of old Earth spinning on her lonely way through the emptiness of space, he thought of the great arrogant empire and of all the mighty dominions which had fallen to dust through the millennia. But when he ventured to suggest that this civilization, too, was not immortal, he was immediately snowed under with figures, facts, logic, the curious paramathematical symbolism of modern mass psychology. It could be shown rigorously that the present set-up was inherently stable—and already ten thousand years of history had given no evidence to upset that science . . .

"I give up," said Saunders. "I can't argue with you."

They were shown through the spaceship's immense interior, the luxurious apartments of the expedition, the looming intricate machinery which did its own thinking. Arsfel tried to show them his art, his recorded music, his psychobooks, but it was no use, they didn't have the understanding.

Savages! Could an Australian aborigine have appreciated Rembrandt, Beethoven, Kant, or Einstein? Could he have lived happily in sophisticated New York society?

"We'd best go," muttered Belgotai. "We don't belong heah."

Saunders nodded. Civilization had gone too far for them, they could never be more than frightened pensioners in its hugeness. Best to get on their way again.

"I would advise you to leap ahead for long intervals," said Arsfel. "Galactic civilization won't have spread out this far for many thousands of years, and certainly whatever native culture Sol develops won't be able to help you." He smiled. "It doesn't matter if you overshoot the time when the process you need is invented. The records won't be lost, I assure you. From here on, you are certain of encountering only peace and enlightenment . . . unless, of course, the barbarians of Terra get hostile, but then you can always leave them behind. Sooner or later, there will be true civilization here to help you."

"Tell me honestly," said Saunders. "Do you think the negative time machine will ever be invented?"

One of the beings from Quulhan shook his strange head. "I doubt it," he said gravely. "We would have had visitors from the future."

"They might not have cared to see your time," argued Saunders desperately. "They'd have complete records of it. So they'd go back to investigate more primitive ages, where their appearance might easily pass unnoticed."

"You may be right," said Arsfel. His tone was disconcertingly like that with which an adult comforts a child by a white lie.

"Le's go!" snarled Belgotai.

In 26000 A.D. the forests still stood and the pyramid had become a high hill where trees nodded and rustled in the wind.

In 27000 A.D. a small village of wood and stone houses stood among smiling grain fields.

In 28000 A.D. men were tearing down the pyramid, quarrying it for stone. But its huge bulk was not gone before 30000 A.D., and a small city had been built from it.

Minutes ago, thought Saunders grayly, they had been talking to Lord Arsfel of Astracyr, and now he was five thousand years in his grave.

In 31000, A.D. they materialized on one of the broad lawns that reached between the towers of a high and proud city. Aircraft swarmed overhead and a spaceship, small beside Arsfel's but nonetheless impressive, was standing nearby.

"Looks like de empire's got heah," said Belgotai.

"I don't know," said Saunders. "But it looks peaceful, anyway. Let's go out and talk to people."

They were received by tall, stately women in white robes of classic lines. It seemed that the matriarchy now ruled Sol, and would they please conduct themselves as befitted the inferior sex? No, the empire hadn't ever gotten out here; Sol paid tribute, and there was an Imperial legate at Sirius, but the actual boundaries of Galactic culture hadn't changed for the past three millennia. Solar civilization was strictly home-grown and obviously superior to the alien influence of the Vro-Hi.

No, nothing was known about time theory. Their visit had been welcome and all that, but now would they please go on? They didn't fit in with the neatly regulated culture of Terra.

"I don't like it," said Saunders as they walked back toward the machine. "Arsfel swore the Imperium would keep expanding its actual as well as its nominal sphere of influence. But it's gone static now. Why?"

"Ih tink," said Belgotai, "dat spite of all his fancy mathematics, yuh were right. Nawthing lasts forever."

"But—my God!"

34,000 A.D. The matriarchy was gone. The city was a tumbled heap of fire-blackened rocks. Skeletons lay in the ruins.

"The barbarians are moving again," said Saunders bleakly. "They weren't here so very long ago, these bones are still fresh, and they've got a long ways to go to dead center. An empire like this one will be many thousands of years in dying. But it's doomed already."

"What'll we do?" asked Belgotai.

"Go on," said Saunders tonelessly. "What else can we do?"

35000 A.D. A peasant but stood under huge old trees. Here and there a broken column stuck out of the earth, remnant of the city. A bearded man in coarsely woven garments fled wildly with his woman and brood of children as the machine appeared.

36000 A.D. There was a village again, with a battered old spaceship standing hard by. There were half a dozen different races, including man, moving about, working on the construction of some enigmatic machine. They were dressed in plain, shabby clothes, with guns at their sides and the hard look of warriors in their eyes. But they didn't treat the new arrivals too badly.

Their chief was a young man in the cape and helmet of an officer of the empire. But his outfit was at least a century old, and he was simply head of a small troop which had been hired from among the barbarian hordes to protect this part of Terra. Oddly, he insisted he was a loyal vassal of the emperor.

The empire! It was still a remote glory, out there among the stars. Slowly it waned, slowly the barbarians encroached while corruption and civil war tore it apart from the inside, but it was still the pathetic, futile hope of intelligent beings throughout the galaxy. Some day it would be restored. Some day civilization would return to the darkness of the outer worlds, greater and more splendid than ever. Men dared not believe otherwise.

"But we've got a job right here," shrugged the chief. "Tautho of Sirius will be on Sol's necks soon. I doubt if we can stand him off for long."

"And what'll yuh do den?" challenged Belgotai.

The young-old face twisted in a bitter smile. "Die, of course. What else is there to do—these days?"

They stayed overnight with the troopers. Belgotai had fun swapping lies about warlike exploits, but in the morning he decided to go on with Saunders. The age was violent enough, but its hopelessness daunted even his tough soul.

Saunders looked haggardly at the control panel. "We've got to go a long ways ahead," he said. "A hell of a long ways."

50000 A.D. They flashed out of the time drive and opened the door. A raw wind caught at them, driving thin sheets of snow before it. The sky hung low and gray over a landscape of high rock hills where pine trees stood gloomily between naked crags. There was ice on the river that murmured darkly out of the woods.

Geology didn't work that fast, even fourteen thousand years wasn't a very long time to the slowly changing planets. It must have been the work of intelligent beings, ravaging and scoring the world with senseless wars of unbelievable forces.

A gray stone mass dominated the landscape. It stood enormous a few miles off, its black walls sprawling over incredible acres, its massive crenellated towers reaching gauntly into the sky. And it lay half in ruin, torn and tumbled stone distorted by energies that once made rock run molten, blurred by uncounted millennia of weather—old.

"Dead," Saunders's voice was thin under the hooting wind. "All dead."

"No!" Belgotai's slant eyes squinted against the flying snow. "No, Mahtin, Ih tink Ih see a banner flying."

The wind blew bitterly around them, searing them with its chill. "Shall we go on?" asked Saunders dully.

"Best we go find out wha's happened," said Belgotai. "Dey can do no worse dan kill us, and Ih begin to tink dat's not so bad."

Saunders put on all the clothes he could find and took the psychophone in one chilled hand. Belgotai wrapped his cloak tightly about him. They started toward the gray edifice.

The wind blew and blew. Snow hissed around them, covering the tough gray-green vegetation that hugged the stony ground. Summer on Earth, 50000 A.D.

As they neared the structure, its monster size grew on them. Some of the towers which still stood must be almost half a mile high, thought Saunders dizzily. But it had a grim, barbaric look; no civilized race had ever built such a fortress.

Two small, swift shapes darted into the air from that clifflike wall. "Aircraft," said Belgotai laconically. The wind ripped the word from his mouth.

They were ovoidal, without external controls or windows, apparently running on the gravitic forces which had long ago been tamed. One of them hovered overhead, covering the travelers, while the other dropped to the ground. As it landed, Saunders saw that it was old and worn and scarred. But there was a faded sunburst on its side. Some memory of the empire must still be alive.

Two beings came out of the little vessel and approached the travelers with guns in their hands. One was human, a tall well-built young man with shoulder-length black hair blowing under a tarnished helmet, a patched purple coat streaming from his cuirassed shoulders, a faded leather kit and buskins. The other . . .

He was a little shorter than the man, but immensely broad of chest and limb. Four muscled arms grew from the massive shoulders, and a tufted tail lashed against his clawed feet. His head was big, broad-skulled, with a round half-animal face and catlike whiskers about the fanged mouth and the split-pupiled yellow eyes. He wore no clothes except a leather harness, but soft blue-gray fur covered the whole great body.

The psychophone clattered out the man's hail. "Who comes?"

"Friends," said Saunders. "We wish only shelter and a little information."

"Where are you from?" There was a harsh, peremptory note in the man's voice. His face—straight, thin-boned, the countenance of a highly bred aristocrat—was gaunt with strain. "What do you want? What sort of spaceship is that you've got down there?"

"Easy, Vargor," rumbled the alien's bass. "That's no spaceship, you can see that."

"No," said Saunders. "It's a time projector."

"Time travelers!" Vargor's intense blue eyes widened. "I heard of such things once, but—time travelers!" Suddenly: "When are you from? Can you help us?"

"We're from very long ago," said Saunders pityingly. "And I'm afraid we're alone and helpless."

Vargor's erect carriage sagged a little. He looked away. But the other being stepped forward with an eagerness in him. "How far back?" he asked. "Where are you going?"

"We're going to hell, most likely. But can you get us inside? We're freezing."

"Of course. Come with us. You'll not take it amiss if I send a squad to inspect your machine? We have to be careful, you know."

The four squeezed into the aircraft and it lifted with a groan of ancient engines. Vargor gestured at the fortress ahead and his tone was a little wild. "Welcome to the hold of Brontothor! Welcome to the Galactic Empire!"

"The empire?"

"Aye, this is the empire, or what's left of it. A haunted fortress on a frozen ghost world, last fragment of the old Imperium and still trying to pretend that the galaxy is not dying—that it didn't die millennia ago, that there is something left besides wild beasts howling among the ruins." Vargor's throat caught in a dry sob. "Welcome!"

The alien laid a huge hand on the man's shoulder. "Don't get hysterical, Vargor," he reproved gently. "As long as brave beings hope, the empire is still alive—whatever they say."

He looked over his shoulder at the others. "You really are welcome," he said. "It's a hard and dreary life we lead here. Taury and the Dreamer will both welcome you gladly." He paused. Then, unsurely, "But best you don't say too much about the ancient time, if you've really seen it. We can't bear too sharp a reminder, you know."

The machine slipped down beyond the wall, over a gigantic flagged courtyard to the monster bulk of the . . . the donjon, Saunders supposed one could call it. It rose up in several tiers, with pathetic little gardens on the terraces, toward a dome of clear plastic.

The walls, he saw, were immensely thick, with weapons mounted on them which he could see clearly through the drifting snow. Behind the donjon stood several long, barracklike buildings, and a couple of spaceships which must have been held together by pure faith rested near what looked like an arsenal. There were guards on duty, helmeted men with energy rifles, their cloaks wrapped tightly against the wind, and other folk scurried around under the monstrous walls, men and women and children.

"There's Taury," said the alien, pointing to a small group clustered on one of the terraces. "We may as well land right there." His wide mouth opened in an alarming smile. "And forgive me for not introducing myself before. I'm Hunda of Haamigur, general of the Imperial armies, and this is Vargor Alfri, prince of the empire."

"Yuh crazy?" blurted Belgotai. "What empire?"

Hunda shrugged. "It's a harmless game, isn't it? At that, you know, we are the empire—legally. Taury is a direct descendant of Maurco the Doomer, last emperor to be anointed according to the proper forms. Of course, that was five thousand years ago, and Maurco had only three systems left then, but the law is clear. These hundred or more barbarian pretenders, human and otherwise, haven't the shadow of a real claim to the title."

The vessel grounded and they stepped out. The others waited for them to come up. There were half a dozen old men, their long beards blowing wildly in the gale, there was a being with the face of a long-beaked bird and one that had the shape of a centauroid.

"The court of the Empress Taury," said Hunda.

"Welcome." The answer was low and gracious.

Saunders and Belgotai stared dumbly at her. She was tall, tall as a man, but under her tunic of silver links and her furred cloak she was such a woman as they had dreamed of without ever knowing in life. Her proudly lifted head had something of Vargor's looks, the same clean-lined, high-cheeked face, but it was the countenance of a woman, from the broad clear brow to the wide, wondrously chiseled mouth and the strong chin. The cold had flushed the lovely pale planes of her cheeks. Her heavy bronze-red hair was braided about her helmet, with one rebellious lock tumbling softly toward the level, dark brows. Her eyes, huge and oblique and gray as northern seas, were serene on them.

Saunders found tongue. "Thank you, your majesty," he said in a firm voice. "If it pleases you, I am Martin Saunders of America, some forty-eight thousand years in the past, and my companion is Belgotai, free companion from Syrtis about a thousand years later. We are at your service for what little we may be able to do."

She inclined her stately head, and her sudden smile was warm and human. "It is a rare pleasure," she said. "Come inside, please. And forget the formality. Tonight let us simply be alive."

They sat in what had been a small council chamber. The great hall was too huge and empty, a cavern of darkness and rustling relics of greatness, hollow with too many memories. But the lesser room had been made livable, hung with tapestries and carpeted with skins. Fluorotubes cast a white light over it, and a fire crackled cheerfully in the hearth. Had it not been for the wind against the windows, they might have forgotten where they were.

"—and you can never go back?" Taury's voice was sober. "You can never get home again?"

"I don't think so," said Saunders. "From our story, it doesn't look that way, does it?"

"No," said Hunda. "You'd better settle down in some time and make the best of matters."

"Why not with us?" asked Vargor eagerly.

"We'd welcome you with all our hearts," said Taury, "but I cannot honestly advise you to stay. These are evil times."

It was a harsh language they spoke, a ringing metallic tongue brought in by the barbarians. But from her throat, Saunders thought, it was utter music.

"We'll at least stay a few days," he said impulsively. "It's barely possible we can do something "

"I doubt that," said Hunda practically. "We've retrogressed, yes. For instance, the principle of the time projector was lost long ago. But still, there's a lot of technology left which was far beyond your own times."

"I know," said Saunders defensively. "But—well, frankly—we haven't fitted in any other time as well."

"Will there ever be a decent age again?" asked one of the old courtiers bitterly.

The avian from Klakkahar turned his eyes on Saunders. "It wouldn't be cowardice for you to leave a lost cause which you couldn't possibly aid," he said in his thin, accented tones. "When the Anvardi come, I think we will all die."

"What is de tale of de Dreamer?" asked Belgotai. "You've mentioned some such."

It was like a sudden darkness in the room. There was silence, under the whistling wind, and men sat wrapped in their own cheerless thoughts. Finally Taury spoke.

"He is the last of Vro-Hi, counselors of the empire. That one still lives—the Dreamer. But there can never really be another empire, at least not on the pattern of the old one. No other race is intelligent enough to coordinate it."

Hunda shook his big head, puzzled. "The Dreamer once told me that might be for the best," he said. "But he wouldn't explain."

"How did you happen to come here—to Earth, of all planets?" Saunders asked.

Taury smiled with a certain grim humor. "The last few generations have been one of the Imperium's less fortunate periods," she said. "In short, the most the emperor ever commanded was a small fleet. My father had even that shot away from him He fled with three ships, out toward the Periphery. It occurred to him that Sol was worth trying as a refuge."

The solar system had been cruelly scarred in the dark ages. The great engineering works that had made the other planets habitable were ruined, and Earth herself had been laid waste. There had been a weapon used that consumed atmospheric carbon dioxide. Saunders, remembering the explanation for the Ice Ages offered by geologists of his own time, nodded in dark understanding. Only a few starveling savages lived on the planet now, and indeed the whole Sirius Sector was so desolated that no conqueror thought it worth bothering with.

It had pleased the emperor to make his race's ancient home the capital of the galaxy. He had moved into the ruined fortress of Brontothor, built some seven thousand years ago by the nonhuman Grimmani and blasted out of action a millennium later. Renovation of parts of it, installation of weapons and defensive works, institution of agriculture . . .

"Why, he had suddenly acquired a whole planetary system!" said Taury with a half-sad little smile.

She took them down into the underground levels the next day to see the Dreamer. Vargor went along too, walking close beside her, but Hunda stayed topside; he was busy supervising the construction of additional energy screen generators.

They went through immense vaulted caverns hewed out of the rock, dank tunnels of silence where their footfall echoed weirdly and shadows flitted beyond the dull glow of fluorospheres. Now and then they passed a looming monstrous bulk, the corroded hulk of some old machine. The night and loneliness weighed heavily on them, they huddled together and did not speak for fear of rousing the jeering echoes.

"There were slideways here once," remarked Taury as they started, "but we haven't gotten around to installing new ones. There's too much else to do."

Too much else—a civilization to rebuild, with these few broken remnants. How can they dare even to keep trying in the face of the angry gods? What sort of courage is it they have?

Taury walked ahead with the long, swinging stride of a warrior, a red lioness of a woman in the wavering shadows. Her gray eyes caught the light with a supernatural brilliance. Vargor kept pace, but he lacked her steadiness; his gaze shifted nervously from side to side as they moved down the haunted, booming length of the tunnels. Belgotai went cat-footed, his own restless eyes had merely the habitual wariness of his hard and desperate lifetime.

Again Saunders thought, what a strange company they were: four humans from the dawn and the dusk of human civilization, thrown together at the world's end and walking to greet the last of the gods. His past life, Eve, MacPherson, the world of his time, were dimming in his mind, they were too remote from his present reality. It seemed as if he had never been anything but a follower of the Galactic Empress.

They came at last to a door. Taury knocked softly and swung it open—yes, they were even back to manual doors now.

Saunders had been prepared for almost anything, but nonetheless the appearance of the Dreamer was a shock. He had imagined a grave white-bearded man, or a huge-skulled spider-thing, or a naked brain pulsing in a machine-tended case. But the last of the Vro-Hi was—a monster.

No—not exactly. Not when you discarded human standards, then he even had a weird beauty of his own. The gross bulk of him sheened with iridescence, and his many seven-fingered hands were supple and graceful, and the eyes—the eyes were huge pools of molten gold, lambent and wise, a stare too brilliant to meet directly.

He stood up on his stumpy legs as they entered, barely four feet high though the head-body unit was broad and massive. His hooked beak did not open, and the psychophone remained silent, but as the long delicate feelers pointed toward him Saunders thought he heard words, a deep organ voice rolling soundless through the still air:

"Greeting, your majesty. Greeting, your highness. Greeting, men out of time, and welcome!"

Telepathy—direct telepathy—so that was how it felt!

"Thank you . . . sir." Somehow, the thing rated the title, rated an awed respect to match his own grave formality. "But I thought you were in a trance of concentration till now. How did you know—" Saunders's voice trailed off and he flushed with sudden distaste.

"No, traveler, I did not read your mind as you think. The Vro-Hi always respected privacy and did not read any thoughts save those contained in speech addressed solely to them. But my induction was obvious."

"What were you thinking about in the last trance?" asked Vargor. His voice was sharp with strain. "Did you reach any plan?"

"No, your highness," vibrated the Dreamer. "As long as the factors involved remain constant, we cannot logically do otherwise than we are doing. When new data appear, I will reconsider immediate necessities. No,

I was working further on the philosophical basis which the Second Empire must have."

"What Second Empire?" sneered Vorgar bitterly.

"The one which will come—some day," answered Taury quietly.

The Dreamer's wise eyes rested on Saunders and Belgotai. "With your permission," he thought, "I would like to scan your complete memory patterns, conscious, subconscious, and cellular. We know so little of your age." As they hesitated: "I assure you, sirs, that a nonhuman being half a million years old can keep secrets, and certainly does not pass moral judgments. And the scanning will be necessary anyway if I am to teach you the present language."

Saunders braced himself. "Go ahead," he said distastefully.

For a moment he felt dizzy. A haze passed over his eyes and there was an eerie thrill along every nerve of him. Taury laid an arm about his waist, bracing him.

It passed. Saunders shook his head, puzzled. "Is that all?"

"Aye, sir. A Vro-Hi brain can scan an indefinite number of units simultaneously." With a faint hint of a chuckle: "But did you notice what tongue you just spoke in?"

"I—eh—huh?" Saunders looked wildly at Taury's smiling face. The hard, open-voweled syllables barked from his mouth: "I—by the gods—I can speak Stellarian now!"

"Aye," thought the Dreamer. "The language centers are peculiarly receptive; it is easy to impress a pattern on them. The method of instruction will not work so well for information involving other faculties, but you must admit it is a convenient and efficient way to learn speech."

"Blast off wit me, den," said Belgoti cheerfully. "Ih allays was a dumkoff at languages."

When the Dreamer was through, he thought: "You will not take it amiss if I tell all that I what I saw in both your minds was good—brave and honest, under the little neuroses which all beings at your level of evolution cannot help accumulating. I will he pleased to remove those for you, if you wish."

"No, thanks," said Belgotai. "I like my little neuroses."

"I see that you are debating staying here," went on the Dreamer. "You will be valuable, but you should be fully warned of the desperate position we actually are in. This is not a pleasant age in which to live."

"From what I've seen," answered Saunders slowly, "golden ages are only superficially better. They may be easier on the surface, but there's death in them. To travel hopefully, believe me, is better than to arrive."

"That has been true in all past ages, aye. It was the great mistake of the Vro-Hi. We should have known better, with ten million years of civilization behind us." There was a deep and tragic note in the rolling thought-pulse. "But we thought that since we had achieved a static physical state in which the new frontiers and challenges lay within our own minds, all beings at all levels of evolution could and should have developed in them the same idea.

"With our help, and with the use of scientific psychodynamics and the great cybernetic engines, the coordination of a billion planets became possible. It was perfection, in a way—but perfection is death to imperfect beings, and even the Vro-Hi had many shortcomings. I cannot explain all the philosophy to you; it involves concepts you could not fully grasp, but you have seen the workings of the great laws in the rise and fall of cultures. I have proved rigorously that permanence is a self-contradictory concept. There can be no goal to reach, not ever."

"Then the Second Empire will have no better hope than decay and chaos again?" Saunders grinned humorlessly. "Why the devil do you want one?"

Vargor's harsh laugh shattered the brooding silence. "What indeed does it matter?" he cried. "What use to plan the future of the universe, when we are outlaws on a forgotten planet? The Anvardi are coming!" He sobered, and there was a set to his jaw that Saunders liked. "They're coming, and there's little we can do to stop it," said Vargor. "But we'll give them a fight. We'll give them such a fight as the poor old galaxy never saw before!"

"Oh no—oh no—oh no"

The murmur came unnoticed from Vargor's lips, a broken cry of pain as he stared at the image that flickered and wavered on the great interstellar communiscreen. And there was horror in the eyes of Taury, grimness to the set of Hunda's mighty jaws, a sadness of many hopeless centuries in the golden gaze of the Dreamer.

After weeks of preparation and waiting, Saunders realized matters were at last coming to a head.

"Aye, your majesty," said the man in the screen. He was haggard, exhausted, worn out by strain and struggle and defeat. "Aye, fifty-four shiploads of us, and the Anvardian fleet in pursuit."

"How far behind?" rapped Hunda.

"About half a light year, sir, and coming up slowly. We'll be close to Sol before they can overhaul us."

"Can you fight them?" rapped Hunda.

"No, sir," said the man. "We're loaded with refugees, women and children, and unarmed peasants, hardly a gun on a ship—Can't you help us?" It was a cry, torn by the ripping static that filled the interstellar void. "Can't you help us, your majesty? They'll sell us for slaves!"

"How did it happen?" asked Taury wearily.

"I don't know, your majesty. We heard you were at Sol through your agents, and secretly gathered ships. We don't want to be under the Anvardi, Empress; they tax the life from us and conscript our men and take our women and children . . . We only communicated by ultrawave; it can't be traced, and we only used the code your agents gave us. But as we passed Canopus, they called on us to surrender in the name of their king—and they have a whole war fleet after us!"

"How long before they get here?" asked Hunda.

"At this rate, sir, perhaps a week," answered the captain of the ship. Static snarled through his words.

"Well, keep on coming this way," said Taury wearily. "We'll send ships against them. You may get away during the battle. Don't go to Sol, of course, we'll have to evacuate that. Our men will try to contact you later."

"We aren't worth it, your majesty. Save all your ships."

"We're coming," said Taury flatly, and broke the circuit.

She turned to the others, and her red head was still lifted. "Most of our people can get away," she said. "They can flee into the Arlath cluster; the enemy won't be able to fmd them in that wilderness." She smiled, a tired little smile that tugged at one corner of her mouth. "We all know what to do, we've planned against this day. Munidor, Falz, Mico, start readying for evacuation. Hunda, you and I will have to plan our assault. We'll want to make it as effective as possible, but use a minimum of ships."

"Why sacrifice fighting strength uselessly?" asked Belgotai.

"It won't be useless. We'll delay the Anvardi, and give those refugees a chance to escape."

"If we had weapons," rumbled Hunda. His huge fists clenched. "By the gods, if we had decent weapons!"

The Dreamer stiffened. And before he could vibrate it, the same thought had leaped into Saunders's brain, and they stared at each other, man and Vro-Hian, with a sudden wild hope . . .

Space glittered and flared with a million stars, thronging against the tremendous dark, the Milky Way foamed around the sky in a rush of cold silver, and it was shattering to a human in its utter immensity. Saunders felt the loneliness of it as he had never felt it on the trip to Venus—for Sol was dwindling behind them, they were rushing out into the void between the stars.

There had only been time to install the new weapon on the dreadnought, time and facilities were so cruelly short, there had been no chance even to test it in maneuvers. They might, perhaps, have leaped back into time again and again, gaining weeks, but the shops of Terra could only turn out so much material in the one week they did have.

So it was necessary to risk the whole fleet and the entire fighting strength of Sol on this one desperate gamble. If the old *Vengeance* could do her part, the outnumbered Imperials would have their chance. But if they failed . . .

Saunders stood on the bridge, looking out at the stellar host, trying to discern the Anvardian fleet. The detectors were far over scale, the enemy was close, but you couldn't visually detect something that outran its own image.

Hunda was at the control central, bent over the cracked old dials and spinning the corroded signal wheels, trying to coax another centimeter per second from a ship more ancient than the Pyramids had been in Saunders' day. The Dreamer stood quietly in a corner, staring raptly out at the Galaxy. The others at the court were each in charge of a squadron, Saunders had talked to them over the inter-ship visiscreen—Vargor white-lipped and tense, Belgotai blasphemously cheerful, the rest showing only cool reserve.

"In a few minutes," said Taury quietly. "In just a few minutes, Martin."

She paced back from the viewport, lithe and restless as a tigress. The cold white starlight glittered in her eyes. A red cloak swirled about the strong, deep curves of her body, a Sunburst helmet sat proudly on her bronze-bright hair Saunders thought how beautiful she was—by all the gods, how beautiful!

She smiled at him. "It is your doing, Martin," she said. "You came from the past just to bring us hope. It's enough to make one believe in destiny." She took his hand. "But of course it's not the hope you wanted. This won't get you back home."

"It doesn't matter," he said.

"It does, Martin. But—may I say it? I'm still glad of it. Not only for the sake of the empire, but—"

A voice rattled over the bridge communicator: "Ultrawave to bridge. The enemy is sending us a message, your majesty. Shall I send it up to you?"

"Of course." Taury switched on the bridge screen.

A face leaped into it, strong and proud and ruthless, the Sunburst shining in the green hair. "Greeting, Taury of Sol," said the Anvardian. "I am Ruulthan, Emperor of the Galaxy."

"I know who you are," said Taury thinly, "but I don't recognize your assumed title."

"Our detectors report your approach with a fleet approximately one-tenth the size of ours. You have one Supernova ship, of course, but so do we. Unless you wish to come to terms, it will mean annihilation."

"What are your terms?"

"Surrender, execution of the criminals who led the attacks on Anvardian planets, and your own pledge of allegiance to me as Galactic Emperor." The voice was clipped, steel-hard.

Taury turned away in disgust. Saunders told Ruulthan in explicit language what to do with his terms, and then cut off the screen.

Taury gestured to the newly installed time-drive controls. "Take them, Martin," she said. "They're yours, really." She put her hands in his and looked at him with serious gray eyes. "And if we should fail in this—goodbye, Martin."

"Goodbye," he said thickly.

He wrenched himself over the panel and sat down before its few dials. *Here goes nothing!*

He waved one hand, and Hunda cut off the hyperdrive. At low intrinsic velocity, the *Vengeance* hung in space while the invisible ships of her fleet flushed past toward the oncoming Anvardi.

Slowly then, Saunders brought down the time-drive switch. And the ship roared with power, atomic energy flowed into the mighty circuits which they had built to carry her huge mass through time—the lights dimmed, the giant machine throbbed and pulsed, and a featureless grayness swirled beyond the ports.

He took her back three days. They lay in empty space, the Anvardi were still fantastic distances away. His eyes strayed to the brilliant yellow spark of Sol. Right there, this minute, he was sweating his heart out installing the time projector that had just carried him back.

But no, that was meaningless, simultaneity was arbitrary. And there was a job to do right now.

The chief astrogator's voice came with a torrent of figures. They had to find the exact position in which the Anvardian flagship would be in precisely seventy-two hours. Hunda rang the signals to the robots in the engine room, and slowly, ponderously, the *Vengeance* slid across five million miles of space.

"All set," said Hunda. "Let's go!"

Saunders smiled, a mirthless skinning of teeth, and threw his main switch in reverse. Three days forward in time . . .

To lie alongside the Anvardian dreadnought!

Frantically Hunda threw the hyperdrive back in, matching translight velocities. They could see the ship now; it loomed like a metal mountain against the stars. And every gun in the *Vengeance* cut loose!

Vortex cannon—blasters—atomic shell and torpedoes—gravity snatchers—all the hell which had ever been brewed in the tortured centuries of history vomited against the screens of the Anvardian flagship.

Under that monstrous barrage, filling space with raving energy till it seemed its very structure must boil, the screens went down, a flare of light searing like another nova. And through the solid matter of her hull those weapons bored, cutting, blasting, disintegrating. Steel boiled into vapor, into atoms, into pure devouring energy that turned on the remaining solid material. Through and through the hull that fury raged, a waste of flame that left not every ash in its track.

And now the rest of the Imperial fleet drove against the Anvardi. Assaulted from outside, with a devouring monster in its very midst, the Anvardian fleet lost the offensive, recoiled and broke up into desperately fighting units. War snarled between the silent white stars.

Still the Anvardi fought, hurling themselves against the ranks of the Imperials, wrecking ships and slaughtering men even as they went down. They still had the numbers, if not the organization, and they had the same weapons and the same bitter courage, as their foes.

The bridge of the *Vengeance* shook and roared with the shock of battle. The lights darkened, flickered back, dimmed again. The riven air was sharp with ozone, and the intolerable energies loosed made her interior a furnace. Reports clattered over the communicator: "—Number Three screen down—Compartment Number Five doesn't answer–Vortex turret Five Hundred Thirty Seven out of action—"

Still she fought, still she fought, hurling metal and energy in an unending storm, raging and rampaging among the ships of the Anvardi. Saunders found himself manning a gun, shooting out at vessels he couldn't see, getting his aim by sweat-blinded glances at the instruments—and the hours dragged away in flame and smoke and racking thunder . . ."

"They're fleeing!"

The exuberant shout rang through every remaining compartment of the huge old ship. *Victory, victory, victory*—She had not heard such cheering for five thousand weary years.

Saunders staggered drunkenly back onto the bridge. He could see the scattered units of the Anvardi now that he was behind them, exploding out into the galaxy in wild search of refuge, hounded and harried by the vengeful Imperial fleet.

And now the Dreamer stood up, and suddenly he was not a stump-legged little monster but a living god whose awful thought leaped across space, faster than light, to bound and roar through the skulls of the barbarians. Saunders fell to the floor under the impact of that mighty shout, he lay numbly staring at the impassive stars while the great command rang in his shuddering brain:

"Soldiers of the Anvardi, your false emperor is dead and Taury the Red, Empress of the Galaxy, has the victory. You have seen her power. Do not resist it longer, for it is unstoppable.

"Lay down your arms. Surrender to the mercy of the Imperium. We pledge you amnesty and safe-conduct. And bear this word back to your planets:

"Taury the Red calls on all the chiefs of the Anvardian Confederacy to pledge fealty to her and aid her in restoring the Galactic Empire!"

They stood on a balcony of Brontothor and looked again at old Earth for the first time in almost a year and the last time, perhaps, in their lives.

It was strange to Saunders, this standing again on the planet that had borne him after those months in the many and alien worlds of a galaxy huger than he could really imagine. There was an odd little tug at his heart, for all the bright hope of the future. He was saying goodbye to Eve's world.

But Eve was gone. She was part of a past forty-eight thousand years dead, and he had *seen* those years rise and die; his one year of personal time was filled and stretched by the vision of history until Eve was a remote, lovely dream.

God keep her, wherever her soul had wandered in these millennia—God grant she had had a happy life—but as for him, he had his own life to live, and a mightier task at hand than he had ever conceived.

The last months rose in his mind, a bewilderment of memory. After the surrender of the Anvardian fleet, the Imperials had gone under their escort directly to Canopus and thence through the Anvardian empire. And chief after chief, now that Ruulthan was dead and Taury had shown she could win a greater mystery than his, pledged allegiance to her.

Hunda was still out there with Belgotai, fighting a stubborn Anvardian earl. The Dreamer was in the great Polarian System toiling at readjustment. It would be necessary, of course, for the Imperial capital to move from isolated Sol to central Polaris, and Taury did not think she would ever have time or opportunity visit Earth again.

And so she had crossed a thousand starry light years to the link lonely sun which had been her home. She brought ships, machines, troops. Sol would have a military base sufficient to protect it. Climate engineers would drive the glacial winter of Earth back to its poles and begin the resettlement of the other planets. There would be schools, factories, civilization, Sol would have cause to remember its empress.

Saunders came along because he couldn't quite endure the thought of leaving Earth altogether without farewell. Vargor grown ever more silent and moody, joined them, but otherwise the old comradeship of Brontothor was dissolving in the sudden fury of work and war and complexity which claimed them.

And so they stood again in the old ruined castle, Saunders and Taury, looking out at the night of Earth.

It was late, all others seemed to be asleep. Below the balcony the black walls dropped dizzily to the gulf of night that was the main courtyard. Beyond it, a broken section of outer wall showed snow lying white and mystic under the moon. The stars were huge and frosty, flashing and glittering with cold crystal light above the looming pines, grandeur and arrogance and remoteness wheeling enormously across the silent sky. The moon rode high, its scarred old face the only familiarity from Saunders's age, its argent radiance flooding down on the snow to shatter in a million splinters.

It was quiet, quiet, sound seemed to have frozen to death in the bitter windless cold. Saunders had stood alone, wrapped in furs with his breath shining ghostly from his nostrils, looking out on the silent winter world and thinking his own thoughts. He had heard a soft footfall and turned to see Taury approaching.

"I couldn't sleep," she said.

She came out onto the balcony to stand beside him. The moonlight was white on her face, shimmering faintly from her eyes and hair. She seemed a dim goddess of the night.

"What were you thinking, Martin?" she asked after a while.

"Oh—I don't know," he said. "Just dreaming a little, I suppose. It's a strange thought to me, to have left my own time forever and now to be leaving even my own world."

She nodded gravely. "I know. I feel the same way." Her low voice dropped to a whisper. "I didn't have to come back in person, you know. They need me more at Polaris. But I thought I deserved this last farewell to the days when we fought with our own hands, and fared between the stars, when we were a small band of sworn comrades whose dreams outstripped our strength. It was hard and bitter, yes, but I don't think we'll have time for laughter any more. When you work for a million stars, you don't have a chance to see one peasant's wrinkled face light with a deed of kindness you did, or hear him tell you what you did wrong—the world will all be strangers to us—"

For another moment, silence under the far cold stars, then, "Martin—I am so lonely now."

He took her in his arms. Her lips were cold against his, cold with the cruel silent chill of the night, but she answered him with a fierce yearning.

"I think I love you, Martin," she said after a very long time. Suddenly she laughed, a clear and lovely music echoing from the frosty towers of Brontothor. "Oh, Martin, I shouldn't have been afraid. We'll never be lonely, not ever again—"

The moon had sunk far toward the dark horizon when he took her back to her rooms. He kissed her goodnight and went down the booming corridor toward his own chambers.

His head was awhirl—he was drunk with the sweetness and wonder of it, he felt like singing and laughing aloud and embracing the whole starry universe. Taury, Taury, Taury!

"Martin."

He paused. There was a figure standing before his door, a tall slender form wrapped in a dark cloak. The dull light of a fluoroglobe threw the face into sliding shadow and tormented highlights. Vargor.

"What is it?" he asked.

The prince's hand came up, and Saunders saw the blunt muzzle of a stun pistol gaping at him. Vargor smiled, lopsidedly and sorrowfully. "I'm sorry, Martin," he said.

Saunders stood paralyzed with unbelief. Vargor—why, Vargor had fought beside him; they'd saved each other's lives, laughed and worked and lived together—Vargor!

The gun flashed. There was a crashing in Saunders's head and he tumbled into illimitable darkness.

He awoke very slowly, every nerve tingling with the pain of returning sensation. Something was restraining him. As his vision cleared, he saw that he was lying bound and gagged on the floor of his time projector.

The time machine—he'd all but forgotten it, left it standing in a shed while he went out to the stars, he'd never thought to have another look at it. The time machine!

Vargor stood in the open door, a fluoroglobe in one hand lighting his haggard face. His hair fell in disarray past his tired, handsome features, and his eyes were as wild as the low words that spilled from his mouth.

"I'm sorry, Martin, I am. I like you, and you've done the empire such a service as it can never forget, and this is as low a trick as one man can ever play on another. But I have to. I'll be haunted by the thought of this night all my life, but I have to."

Saunders tried to move, snarling incoherently through his gag. Vargor shook his head. "Oh, no, Martin, I can't risk letting you make an outcry. If I'm to do evil, I'll at least do a competent job of it.

"I love Taury, you see. I've loved her ever since I first met her, when I came from the stars with a fighting fleet to her father's court and saw her standing there with the frost crackling through her hair and those gray eyes shining at me. I love her so it's like a pain in me. I can't be away from her, I'd pull down the cosmos for her sake. And I thought she was slowly coming to love me.

"And tonight I saw you two on the balcony, and knew I'd lost. Only, I can't give up! Our breed has fought the galaxy for a dream. Martin—it's not in us ever to stop fighting while life is in us. Fighting by any means, for whatever is dear and precious—but fighting!"

Vargor made a gesture of deprecation. "I don't want power, Martin, believe me. The consort's job will be hard and unglamorous, galling to a man of spirit—but if that's the only way to have her then so be it. And I do honestly believe, right or wrong, that I'm better for her and for the empire than you. You don't really belong here, you know. You don't have the tradition, the feeling, the training—you don't even have the biological heritage of five thousand years. Taury may care for you now, but think twenty years ahead!"

Vargor smiled wryly. "I'm taking a chance, of course. If you do find a means of negative time travel and come back here, it will be disgrace and exile for me. It would be safer to kill you. But I'm not quite that much of a scoundrel. I'm giving you your chance. At worst, you should escape into the time when the Second Empire is in its glorious bloom, a happier age than this. And if you do find a means to come back—well, remember what I said about your not belonging, and try to reason with clarity and kindness. Kindness to Taury, Martin."

He lifted the fluoroglobe, casting its light over the dim interior of the machine. "So it's goodbye, Martin, and I hope you won't hate me too much. It should take you several thousand years to work free and stop the machine. I've equipped it with weapons, supplies, everything I think you may need for any eventuality. But I'm sure you'll emerge in a greater and more peaceful culture, and be happier there."

His voice was strangely tender, all of a sudden. "Goodbye, Martin my comrade. And—good luck!"

He opened the main-drive switch and stepped out as the projector began to warm up. The door clanged shut behind him.

Saunders writhed on the floor, cursing with a brain that was a black cauldron of bitterness. The great drone of the projector rose, he was on his way—*oh no—stop the machine, God, set me free before it's too late!*

The plastic cords cut his wrists. He was lashed to a stanchion, unable to reach the switch with any part of his body. His groping fingers slid across the surface of a knot, the nails clawing for a hold. The machine roared with full power, driving ahead through the vastness of time.

Vargor had bound him skillfully. It took him a long time to get free. Toward the end he went slowly, not caring, knowing with a dull knowledge that he was already more thousands of irretrievable years into the future than his dials would register.

He climbed to his feet, plucked the gag from his mouth, and looked blankly out at the faceless gray. The century needle was hard against its stop. He estimated vaguely that he was some ten thousand years into the future already.

Ten thousand years!

He yanked down the switch with a raging burst of savagery.

It was dark outside. He stood stupidly for a moment before he saw water seeping into the cabin around the door. Water—he was under water—short circuits! Frantically, he slammed the switch forward again.

He tasted the water on the floor. It was salt. Sometime in that ten thousand years, for reasons natural or artificial, the sea had come in and covered the site of Brontothor.

A thousand years later he was still below its surface. Two thousand, three thousand, ten thousand . . .

Taury, Taury! For twenty thousand years she had been dust on an alien planet. And Belgotai was gone with his wry smile, Hunda's staunchness, even the Dreamer must long ago have descended into darkness. The sea rolled over dead Brontothor, and he was alone.

He bowed his head on his arms and wept.

For three million years the ocean lay over Brontothor's land. And Saunders drove onward.

He stopped at intervals to see if the waters had gone. Each time the frame of the machine groaned with pressure and the sea poured in through the crack of the door. Otherwise he sat dully in the throbbing loneliness, estimating time covered by his own watch and the known rate of the projector, not caring any more about dates or places.

Several times he considered stopping the machine, letting the sea burst in and drown him. There would be peace in its depths, sleep and forgetting. But no, it wasn't in him to quit that easily. Death was his friend, death would always be there waiting for his call.

But Taury was dead.

Time grayed to its end. In the four millionth year, he stopped the machine and discovered that there was dry air around him.

He was in a city. But it was not such a city as he had ever seen or imagined, he couldn't follow the wild geometry of the titanic structures that loomed about him and they were never the same. The place throbbed and pulsed with incredible forces, it wavered and blurred in a strangely unreal light. Great devastating energies flashed and roared around him—lightning come to Earth. The air hissed and stung with their booming passage.

The thought was a shout filling his skull, blazing along his nerves, too mighty a thought for his stunned brain to do more than grope after meaning:

CREATURE FROM OUT OF TIME, LEAVE THIS PLACE AT ONCE OR THE FORCES WE USE WILL DESTROY YOU!

Through and through him that mental vision seared, down to the very molecules of his brain, his life lay open to them in a white flame of incandescence.

"Can you help me?" he cried to the gods. "Can you send me back through time?"

MAN, THERE IS NO WAY TO TRAVEL FAR BACKWARD IN TIME, IT IS INHERENTLY IMPOSSIBLE. YOU MUST GO ON TO THE VERY END OF THE UNIVERSE, AND BEYOND THE END, BECAUSE THAT WAY LIES—

He screamed with the pain of unendurably great thought and concept filling his human brain.

GO ON, MAN, GO ON! BUT YOU CANNOT SURVIVE IN THAT MACHINE AS IT IS. I WILL CHANGE IT FOR YOU . . . GO!

The time projector started again by itself. Saunders fell forward into a darkness that roared and flashed.

Grimly, desperately, like a man driven by demons, Saunders hurtled into the future.

There could be no gainsaying the awful word which had been laid on him. The mere thought of the gods had engraven itself on the very tissue of his brain. Why he should go on to the end of time, he could not imagine, nor did he care. But go on he must!

The machine had been altered. It was airtight now, and experiment showed the window to be utterly unbreakable. Something had been done to the projector so that it hurled him forward at an incredible rate, millions of years passed while a minute or two ticked away within the droning shell.

But what had the gods been?

He would never know. Beings from beyond the galaxy, beyond the very universe—the ultimately evolved descendants of man—something at whose nature he could not even guess—there was no way of telling. This much was plain: whether it had become extinct or had changed into something else, the human race was gone. Earth would never feel human tread again.

I wonder what became of the Second Empire. I hope it had a long and good life. Or—could that have been its unimaginable end product?

The years reeled past, millions, billions mounting on each other while Earth spun around her star and the galaxy aged. Saunders fled onward.

He stopped now and then, unable to resist a glimpse of the world and its tremendous history.

A hundred million years in the future, he looked out on great sheets of flying snow. The gods were gone. Had they too died, or abandoned Earth—perhaps for an altogether different plane of existence? He would never know.

There was a being coming through the storm. The wind flung the snow about him in whirling, hissing clouds. Frost was in his gray fur. He moved with a lithe, unhuman grace, carrying a curved staff at whose tip was a blaze like a tiny sun.

Saunders hailed him through the psychophone, letting his amplified voice shout through the blizzard: "Who are you? What are you doing on Earth?"

The being carried a stone axe in one hand and wore a string of crude beads about his neck. But he stared with bold yellow eyes at the machine and the psychophone brought his harsh scream: "You must be from the far past, one of the earlier cycles."

"They told me to go on, back almost a hundred million years ago. They told me to go to the end of time!"

The psychophone hooted with metallic laughter. "If they told you so—then go!"

The being walked on into the storm.

Saunders flung himself ahead. There was no place on Earth for him anymore, he had no choice but to go on.

A billion years in the future there was a city standing on a plain where grass grew that was blue and glassy and tinkled with a high crystalline chiming as the wind blew through it. But the city had never been built by humans, and it warned him away with a voice he could not disobey.

Then the sea came, and for a long time thereafter he was trapped within a mountain; he had to drive onward till it had eroded back to the ground.

The sun grew hotter and whiter as the hydrogen-helium cycle increased its intensity. Earth spiraled slowly closer to it, the friction of gas and dust clouds in space taking their infinitesimal toll of its energy over billions of years.

How many intelligent races had risen on Earth and had their day and died since the age when man first came out of the jungle? *At least,* he thought tiredly, *we were the first.*

A hundred billion years in the future, the sun had used up its last reserves of nuclear reactions. Saunders looked out on a bare mountain scene, grim as the Moon—but the Moon had long ago fallen back toward its parent world and exploded into a meteoric rain. Earth faced its primary now; its day was as long as its year. Saunders saw part of the sun's huge blood-red disc shining wanly.

So goodbye, Sol, he thought. *Goodbye, and thank you for many million years of warmth and light. Sleep well, old friend.*

Some billions of years beyond, there was nothing but the elemental dark. Entropy had reached a maximum, the energy sources were used up, the universe was dead.

The universe was dead!

He screamed with the graveyard terror of it and flung the machine onward. Had it not been for the gods' command, he might have let it hang there, might have opened the door to airlessness and absolute zero to die. But he had to go on. He had reached the end of all things, but he had to go on. *Beyond the end of time—*

Billions upon billions of years fled. Saunders lay in his machine, sunk into an apathetic coma. Once he roused himself to eat, feeling the sardonic humor of the situation—the last living creature, the last free energy in all the cindered cosmos, fixing a sandwich.

Many billions of years in the future, Saunders paused again. He looked out into blackness. But with a sudden shock he discerned a far faint glow, the vaguest imaginable blur of light out in the heavens.

Trembling, he jumped forward another billion years. The light was stronger now, a great sprawling radiance swirling inchoately in the sky.

The universe was reforming.

It made sense, thought Saunders, fighting for self-control. Space had expanded to some kind of limit, now it was collapsing in on itself to start the cycle anew—the cycle that had been repeated none knew how many times in the past. The universe was mortal, but it was a phoenix that would never really die.

But he was disturbingly mortal, and suddenly he was free of his death wish. At the very least he wanted to see what the next time around looked like. But the universe would, according to the best theories of twentieth-century cosmology, collapse to what was virtually a point-source, a featureless blaze of pure energy out of which the primal atoms would be reformed. If he wasn't to be devoured in that raging furnace, he'd better leap a long ways ahead. A hell of a long ways!

He grinned with sudden reckless determination and plunged the switch forward.

Worry came back. How did he know that a planet would be formed under him? He might come out in open space, or in the heart of a sun . . . Well, he'd have to risk that. The gods must have foreseen and allowed for it.

He came out briefly—and flashed back into time-drive. The planet was still molten!

Some geological ages later, he looked out at a spurning gray rain, washing with senseless power from a hidden sky, covering naked rocks with a raging swirl of white water. He didn't go out; the atmosphere would be unbreathable until plants had liberated enough oxygen.

On and on! Sometimes he was under seas, sometimes on land. He saw strange jungles like overgrown ferns and mosses rise and wither in the cold of a glacial age and rise again in altered life-form.

A thought nagged at him, tugging at the back of his mind as he rode onward. It didn't hit him for several million years, then: *The moon! Oh, my God, the moon!*

His hands trembled too violently for him to stop the machine. Finally, with an effort, he controlled himself enough to pull the switch. He skipped on, looking for a night of full moon.

Luna. The same old face—*Luna!*

The shock was too great to register. Numbly, he resumed his journey. And the world began to look familiar, there were low forested hills and a river shining in the distance . . .

He didn't really believe it till he saw the village. It was the same—Hudson, New York.

He sat for a moment, letting his physicist's brain consider the tremendous fact. In Newtonian terms, it meant that every particle newly formed in the Beginning had exactly the same position and velocity as every corresponding particle formed in the previous cycle. In more acceptable Einsteinian language, the continuum was spherical in all four dimensions. In any case—if you traveled long enough, through space or time, you got back to your starting point.

He could go home!

He ran down the sunlit hill, heedless of his foreign garments, ran till the breath sobbed in raw lungs and his heart seemed about to burst from the ribs. Gasping, he entered the village, went into a bank, and looked at the tear-off calendar and the wall clock.

June 17, 1936, 1:30 PM. From that, he could figure his time of arrival in 1973 to the minute.

He walked slowly back, his legs trembling under him, and started the time machine again. Grayness was outside—for the last time.

1973.

Martin Saunders stepped out of the machine. Its moving in space, at Brontothor, had brought it outside MacPherson's house; it lay halfway up the hill at the top of which the rambling old building stood.

There came a flare of soundless energy. Saunders sprang back in alarm and saw the machine dissolve into molten metal—into gas—into a nothingness that shone briefly and was gone.

The gods must have put some annihilating device into it. They didn't want its devices from the future loose in the twentieth century.

But there was no danger of that, thought Saunders as he walked slowly up the hill through the rain-wet grass. He had seen too much of war and horror ever to give men knowledge they weren't ready for. He and Eve and MacPherson would have to suppress the story of his return around time—for that would offer a means of travel into the past, remove the barrier that would keep man from too much use of the machine for murder and oppression. The Second Empire and the Dreamer's philosophy lay a long time in the future.

He went on. The hill seemed strangely unreal, after all that he had seen from it, the whole enormous tomorrow of the cosmos. He would never quite fit into the little round of days that lay ahead.

Taury—her bright lovely face floated before him, he thought he heard her voice whisper in the cool wet wind that stroked his hair like her strong, gentle hands.

"Goodbye," he whispered into the reaching immensity of time. "Goodbye, my dearest."

He went slowly up the steps and in the front door. There would be Sam to mourn. And then there would be the carefully censored thesis to write, and a life spent in satisfying work with a girl who was sweet and kind and beautiful even if she wasn't Taury. It was enough for a mortal man.

He walked into the living room and smiled at Eve and MacPherson. "Hello," he said. "I guess I must be a little early."

About the Authors

A multiple winner of the Hugo and Nebula awards, Poul Anderson (1926–2001) wrote dozens of novels and hundreds of short stories since his science fiction debut in 1947. His long-running Technic History saga, a multibook chronicle of interstellar exploration and empire building, covers fifty centuries of future history and includes the acclaimed novels *War of the Wing-Men, The Day of Their Return,* and *The Game of Empire.* Anderson has tackled many of science fiction's classic themes, including human evolution in *Brain Wave* (1954), near-light-speed space travel in *Tau Zero* (1970), and the time travel paradox in his series of Time Patrol stories collected as *Guardians of Time.* He is renowned for his interweaving of science fiction and mythology, notably in his alien-contact novel *The High Crusade.* He also has produced distinguished fantasy fiction, including the heroic sagas *Three Hearts and Three Lions* and *The Broken Sword,* and an alternate history according to Shakespeare, *A Midsummer Tempest.* He received the Tolkien Memorial Award in 1978. With his wife, Karen, he wrote the *King of Ys* Celtic Fantasy quartet. With Gordon Dickson, he has authored the popular comic Hoka series. His short story "Call Me Joe" was chosen for inclusion in the Science Fiction Hall of Fame in 1974, and his short fiction has been collected in several volumes, notably *The Queen of Air and Darkness and Other Stories, All One Universe,* and *The Best of Poul Anderson.*

Gregory Benford has published more than twenty books, mostly novels. Nearly all remain in print, some after a quarter of a century. His fiction has won many awards, including the Nebula Award for his novel *Timescape.* A winner of the United Nations Medal for Literature, he is a professor of physics at the University of California, Irvine. He is a Woodrow Wilson Fellow, was

Visiting Fellow at Cambridge University, and in 1995 received the Lord Prize for contributions to science. He won the Japan Seiun Award for Dramatic Presentation with his seven-hour series, A Galactic Odyssey. His 1999 analysis of what endures, *Deep Time: How Humanity Communicates across Millennia*, has been widely read. A fellow of the American Physical Society and a member of the World Academy of Arts and Sciences, he continues his research in both astrophysics and plasma physics. Time allowing, he continues to write both fiction and nonfiction. Recently he began a series on science and society with biologist Michael Rose, published online at Amazon.com Shorts. You can visit this site at www.benford-rose.com

Edward Bryant was reared in the dry ranching country of southern Wyoming until he made his first fiction sale in 1968. Since then he's written primarily short fiction, some of which has been collected in such volumes as *Among the Dead*, *Cinnabar*, and *Particle Theory*. He also wrote *Phoenix Without Ashes*, a novel in collaboration with Harlan Ellison. Over the decades, he's also worked as a reviewer for *Locus* and *Twilight Zone Magazine*, an Internet interviewer for *Omni* magazine, and chaired the 2000 World Horror Convention. Graduate of the Clarion Workshop and founder of the Northern Colorado Writers Workshop, he's frequently lectured at various universities. In Hollywood he's written for CBS and the Disney Channel. Presently he lives in Denver.

Orson Scott Card is the author of the novels *Ender's Game*, *Ender's Shadow*, and *Speaker for the Dead*, which are widely read by adults and younger readers, and are increasingly used in schools. Besides these and other science fiction novels, Card writes contemporary fantasy (*Magic Street*, *Enchantment*, *Lost Boys*); biblical novels (*Stone Tables*, *Rachel and Leah*); the American frontier fantasy series the Tales of Alvin Maker (beginning with *Seventh Son*); poetry (*An Open Book*); and many plays and scripts. He was born in Washington and grew up in California, Arizona, and Utah. He served a mission for the LDS Church in Brazil in the early 1970s. Besides his writing, he teaches occasional classes and workshops and directs plays. He recently began a long-term position as a professor of writing and literature at Southern Virginia University. Card currently lives in Greensboro, North Carolina, with his wife, Kristine Allen Card, and their youngest child, Zina Margaret.

Arthur C. Clarke's (1917–2008) wrote some of the finest science fiction of the twentieth century and manifests in a variety of forms, including the mysterious extraterrestrial overseers guiding human destiny in his best-known story, *2001: A Space Odyssey*, and its sequels *2010: Odyssey Two*; *2061: Odyssey Three*, and *3001: Final Odyssey* represents the culmination of ideas on man's place in the universe introduced in his 1951 story, "The Sentinel," and elaborated more fully in *Childhood's End*, his elegiac novel on humankind's maturation as a species and ascent to a greater purpose in the universal scheme. Clarke grounds the cosmic mystery of these stories in hard science. Degreed in physics and mathematics, he contributed to numerous scientific journals and first proposed the idea for the geosynchronous orbiting communications satellite in 1945. His Hugo and Nebula Award–winning *A Rendezvous with Rama* extrapolated his solid scientific inquiry into provocative new territory, telling of the human discovery of an apparently abandoned alien space ship and human attempts to understand its advanced scientific principles. He wrote *Islands in the Sky* and *Dolphin Island* for young readers, and his short fiction has been collected in *Expedition to Earth, Reach for Tomorrow, Tales from the White Hart, The Wind from the Sun,* and others. His numerous books of nonfiction include his award-winning *The Exploration of Space,* and the autobiographical *Astounding Days.* Clarke was officially knighted by the Queen of England in 2000.

Lester del Rey (1915–1993) sold his first short story to John W. Campbell at *Astounding,* and by the early 1940s had become one of the key contributors to *Astounding*'s great first decade. Del Rey also contributed to Street & Smith's fantasy companion to *Astounding, Unknown Worlds,* and in 1947 sold his first book, a collection of short stories *And Some Were Human,* to Prime Press. After the war, he worked as an editor at the offices of his new literary agent, Scott Meredith, before becoming a full-time freelancer; he also edited *Space Science Fiction,* a short-lived 1950s digest magazine, and with *The Runaway Robot* (1952) inaugurated a series of juvenile science fiction novels for Winston Publishers that were popular and influential. He married Judy-Lynn (neé Benjamin) in 1970 and with her became joint publisher of Ballantine's Del Rey books in 1975. Del Rey Books under their guidance became the most important and successful of all science fiction publishers, bringing bestseller status to many writers such as Anne McCaffrey, Terry Brooks (Lester del Rey's discovery), and Stephen Donaldson. When Judy-Lynn died in 1986, Lester del Rey presided over the company until his retirement in 1991. Awarded the SFWA Grand Master Award that same year, del Rey passed away in 1993.

Worldwide bestselling author Neil Gaiman has long been one of the top writers in modern comics, as well as writing books for readers of all ages. He is listed in the *Dictionary of Literary Biography* as one of the top ten living post-modern writers, and is a prolific creator of works of prose, poetry, film, journalism, comics, song lyrics, and drama. His *New York Times* bestselling 2001 novel for adults, *American Gods*, was awarded the Hugo, Nebula, Bram Stoker, SFX, and Locus awards; was nominated for many other awards, including the World Fantasy Award and the Minnesota Book Award; and appeared on many best-of-year lists. His official Web site, www.neilgaiman.*com*, now has more than one million unique visitors each month, and his online journal is syndicated to thousands of blog readers every day. Born and raised in England, Neil Gaiman now lives near Minneapolis, Minnesota. He has somehow reached his forties and still tends to need a haircut. Recently his children's book *The Graveyard Book* won several awards, including the Newbery Award, the Hugo, and the Locus Award for best children's novel.

Rick Hautala has had more than thirty books published under his own name and the pseudonym A. J. Mathews, including the million-copy, international bestsellers *Nightstone*, and *Bedbugs, Little Brothers, Cold Whisper, Four Octobers, The White Room, Looking Glass, Follow*, and *Unbroken*. More than sixty of his short stories have appeared in a variety of national and international anthologies and magazines. His screenplay *Chills* was recently optioned by Chesapeake Films. Born and raised in Rockport, Massachusetts, he is a graduate of the University of Maine in Orono with an M.A. in English Literature. He lives in southern Maine with author Holly Newstein and Kiera, the Wonder Dog. Visit him at www.rickhautala.com.

John Helfers is a full-time writer and editor living and working in Green Bay, Wisconsin. During his career, he has worked on anthology and novel projects with many bestselling authors. He has written and edited both fiction and nonfiction, including *Tom Clancy's Net Force Explorers: Cloak and Dagger, The Alpha Bravo Delta Guide to the U.S. Navy*, and the forthcoming nonfiction anthology *From the Jaws of Death.* His most recent nonfiction project, *The Vorkosigan Companion,* coedited with Lillian Stewart Carl, was nominated for a Hugo Award in 2009.

Nancy Kress is the author of twenty-six books: three fantasy novels, twelve science fiction novels, three thrillers, four collections of short stories, one you ads novel, and three books on writing fiction. She is perhaps best known for the Sleepless trilogy that began with *Beggars in Spain.* The novel was based on a Nebula- and Hugo-winning novella of the same name. She won her second Hugo in 2009 in Montreal, for the novella "The Erdmann Nexus." Kress has also won three additional Nebulas, a Sturgeon, and the 2003 John W. Campbell Award (for *Probability Space*). Her most recent books are a collection of short stories, *Nano Comes to Clifford Falls and Other Stories* (Golden Gryphon Press, 2008); a bio-thriller, *Dogs* (Tachyon Press, 2008); and science fiction novel, *Steal Across The Sky* (Tor, 2009). Kress's fiction, much of which concerns genetic engineering, has been translated into twenty languages. She often teaches writing at various venues around the country. Kress lives in Rochester, New York, with Cosette, the world's most spoiled toy poodle.

George R. R. Martin's varied output is divided between horror, fantasy, and science fiction, and has earned him multiple Hugo and Nebula Awards as well as a Bram Stoker Award from the Horror Writers' Association. His science fiction novels include *Dying of Light,* and with Lisa Tuttle, *Windhaven.* Martin has written some of the best novella-length science fiction in the past two decades, including the award-winning "Sandkings," and "Nightflyers," which was adapted for the screen in 1987. Much of his best writing is collected in *A Song for Lya and Other Stories, Songs of Stars and Shadows, Sandkings, Songs the Dead Men Sing, Tuf Voyaging,* and *Portraits of His Children.* His horror novels include the period vampire masterpiece *Fevre Dream* and *The Armageddon Rag,* an evocative glimpse at the dark side of the 60s counterculture considered one of the top rock-and-roll novels of all time. Currently he is working on the next volume in his epic Song of Ice and Fire series. Martin has written for a number of television series, including the new Twilight Zone series, and has edited fifteen volumes of the Wild Cards series of shared-world anthologies.

Though William F. Nolan is known for his great science fiction trilogy Logan's Run (coauthored with George Clayton Johnson), *Logan's World,* and *Logan's Search,* he has also distinguished himself in the crime, mystery, and western genres as well—as a glance at his many awards will tell you. He has received the American Library Association citation (1960), Mystery Writers of America award (1970, 1972), the Academy of Science Fiction and Fantasy award for fiction and film (1976), the Maltese Falcon award (1977) and an Honorary Doctorate from American River College in Sacramento, California (1975). He has written major dramas for both television and movies, including *Burnt Offerings,* which starred Karen Black and Bette Davis. He currently lives and works in Vancouver, Washington.

Robert Sheckley (1928–2005) was born in Brooklyn, New York, and raised in New Jersey. He went into the U.S. Army after high school and served in Korea. After discharge he attended NYU, graduating with a degree in English. He began selling stories to all the science-fiction magazines soon after his graduation, producing several hundred over the next several years. His best-known books in the science-fiction field are *Immortality, Inc.*; *Mindswap;* and *Dimension of Miracles.* He produced more than sixty-five books throughout his career, including twenty novels and nine collections of his short stories, as well as his five-volume *Collected Short Stories of Robert Sheckley,* published by Pulphouse. In 1991, he received the Daniel F. Gallun award for contributions to the genre of science-fiction, and in 2001 he was given the Author Emeritus award by the Science Fiction Writers of America.

Lucius Shepard lives in Portland, Oregon. His latest collection of short fiction is *Viator Plus,* and his latest novel, out in 2010, is titled *Beautiful Blood.* Forthcoming is the novella collection, *Five Autobiographies.*

Born in New York City, Robert Silverberg was educated at Columbia University and has been a resident of the San Francisco Bay Area for many years. His first book, *Revolt on Alpha C,* was published in 1955. He is a four-time Hugo Award winner (1956, 1969, 1987, 1990) and a five-time Nebula Award winner (1970, 1972, 1972 again, 1975, 1986) and has received most of the other significant science fiction honors including being named Grand master by the Science Fiction Writers of America in

2004. He served as president of the Science Fiction Writers of America, 1967–68, and was the guest of honor at the 1970 World Science Fiction Convention in Heidelberg, Germany. He is the author of more than a hundred books and an uncounted number of short stories. Among the best known titles—*Dying Inside, The Book of Skulls, Nightwings, Thorns, Up the Line, Tower of Glass, Gilgamesh the King, Lord Valentine's Castle, The Man in the Maze, Downward to the Earth, at Winter's End, Born with the Dead, Nightfall (with Isaac Asimov), Hot Sky at Midnight,* and *The Alien Years.* An accomplished editor, he oversaw the New Dimensions series of anthologies from 1971 to 1980, the first volume of The Science Fiction Hall of Fame series, and *Robert Silverberg's Worlds of Wonder* (reissued as *Science Fiction 101*), an anthology of great science fiction that is also a collection of his essays on the art of writing science fiction. He was the editor of the Legends and Far Horizons anthology series, and with his wife, Karen Haber, edited the Universe series of science fiction anthologies.

Michael Swanwick's first two short stories were published in 1980 and both featured on the Nebula ballot that year. One of the major writers working in the field today, he has been nominated for at least one of the field's major awards in almost every successive year, and has won the Hugo, Nebula, World Fantasy, Theodore Sturgeon Memorial, and the Locus awards. He has published six collections of short fiction, seven novels—*In the Drift, Vacuum Flowers, Stations of the Tide, The Iron Dragon's Daughter, Jack Faust, Bones of the Earth,* and *The Dragons of Babel*—and a Hugo Award–nominated book-length interview with editor Gardner Dozois. His most recent book is major career retrospective collection, *The Best of Michael Swanwick.*

Norman Spinrad is the author of some twenty or so novels, five or six dozen short stories, a classic *Star Trek* epsisode, a couple of flop movies, an album's worth of songs, political columns, film criticism, literary criticicsm, mini-cookbooks, autobiography, and a bunch of assorted other stuff. The latest to be written is a new and literarily revolutionary novel called *Welcome to Your Dreamtime,* in which you, the reader, are the viewpoint character, and sections of which have been published in a weird assortment of magazines as free-standing short stories. The latest to be published is *He Walked Among Us,* a novel so far ahead of itself that it had to wait until it had become something of the fave rave of a radical viral

Internet distribution experiment before any traditional publisher would bring it out in paper.

Influenced by the novels of H. G. Wells, the theme of humans dealing with catastrophe is prominent in the work of John Wyndham (1903–1969). Born in Knowle, Warwickshire, he was the son of a barrister and lived at Edgbaston, Birmingham, until 1911, when his parents separated. Afterward he moved around the country with his mother and younger brother, the writer Vivian Beynon Harris. After school he tried his hand at several jobs including farming, the law, art, and advertising. He began writing science fiction stories, and found a niche for his work in American magazines. In the mid-1930s he had his work published in British magazines and in book form. During World War II he worked as a censor, including active service in France. The novel *Day of the Triffids* is his best-known work dealing with this subject. Alien invasion, telepathy, mutation, and fantastic events occurring in everyday life are also explored in his work, usually as the catalyst for change in the Earth of his novels.

Roger Zelazny (1937–1995) burst onto the science-fiction writing scene as part of the "New Wave" group of writers in the mid-to late 1960s. His novels *This Immortal* and *Lord of Light* met universal praise, the latter winning a Hugo Award for best novel. His work is notable for its lyrical style and innovative use of language both in description and dialogue. His most recognized series is the Amber novels, about a parallel universe which is the one true world, with all others, Earth included, being mere reflections of his created universe. Besides the Hugo, he was also awarded three Nebulas, three more Hugos, and two Locus awards.